GRACE & FAVOUR

Published by Winterbourne Publishing, Western Australia.

ISBN: 978-1-7637115-5-6 (ebook) / 978-1-7637115-6-3 (print)

Grace & Favour

Wendy Palmer

Winterbourne
Publishing

ONE

Mʀ Cᴏʟʟᴇʏ Fᴀʀǫᴜʜᴀʀ Sᴏʟᴏɴɢ ᴡᴀs ᴀ treasure.

No greater evidence existed than that he smiled when he joined Leo's table, and smiled again when he drew the second lowest card and was thus shackled to the worst whist player in Hampton Court Palace. Any other guest at Lady Augusta Paget's card party would have been hard pressed to hide their dismay.

Not, Leo mused, that he was consistently terrible at whist, but he was widely considered erratic at it, as with most games requiring concentration, and he could hardly argue with that judgement.

If left to his own devices, his skill, luck and preoccupation, in increasing order of quantity, would have made him merely a middling player at best—

'Don't waste your king, Miss Cottin has the ace,' Polly advised.

—yet as it was, he had to not only track the cards and strategise with his hand, as any player who very much did not want to disappoint their partner would do, but also try to avoid forcible cheating.

Leo shut his eyes, doing his best to ignore Polly and think it through for himself. Cole had led with the ten of spades, which might mean it was a singleton, and he was setting up for future trumps. *That* would mean the spades were spread across the other three hands, and Leo should play the king to draw out the higher card from Miss Cottin.

Or perhaps he should save the king and see if Miss Cottin had to sacrifice her highest card to take the trick anyway. Miss Blake had played a two, probably as some sort of signal to her partner that Cole might have been able to interpret, but Leo couldn't.

But Cole's ten could mean he held the other honour cards and was trying to winkle out the king early.

Leo had been hesitating over which tactic Cole might be employing, and which tactic he should employ in return, until Polly had decided to inform on Miss Cottin. Now he had to decide if he had been leaning *towards* or *away* from playing his king before her intervention.

'Mr Sweetwater?' Miss Cottin prompted him. 'We must keep pace with the other tables.'

He played the king almost by reflex. Miss Cottin took the trick with her ace and a satisfied nod.

Polly sighed extravagantly. 'Good Lord, pet, just cheat! It's pennies a point, it's nothing to them.'

He couldn't answer, not even at a mumble. Polly *knew* he couldn't, but annoyed at his lack of spirit, she set her hands akimbo on thinly-clad hips with demonstrative ire.

She wore only a long-sleeved chemise, made from Holland linen and decorated with pleats at the neckline. It was perfectly modest, to the point of unflattering, though utterly scandalous for a drawing room.

Luckily, then, only Leo could see her.

Polly was the first and only ghost he knew who was actually drifting about clad in gossamer white.

To truly be sure he was aware of her irritation – he was – she set about repeatedly announcing the contents of the other hands during the continuing round of play, raising her voice to be heard over the chatter from the other side of the room.

To his stubborn efforts at ignoring her, she escalated to terrible indiscretion regarding his fellow players.

Had he noticed Mr Solong and Miss Blake work together to shuffle Colonel Cottin off to another table and how pleased Miss Cottin had looked about that, and about snagging Miss Blake as her partner?

Leo considered that to be, firstly, relief at escaping the misery of partnering with her father, and secondly, relief at evading the different misery of partnering with Leo. He further considered Cole too conventionally respectable for any thoughts of Polly's ilk to cross his mind; more likely, Cole was merely helping Miss Cottin carve a little space to herself, the same reason Lady Augusta must have extended the invitation in the first place.

Would he look at Colonel Cottin, that horrid old goat, trying to be gallant at his unlucky whist partner, recent widow Lady Maclean, young enough to be his daughter? Here, Polly digressed to explain she was referring to any one of the bastard daughters he had fathered during the decade he had visited his lover in Primrose Hill, since Miss Cottin, his youngest legitimate child, was, in fact, older than Lady Maclean.

Leo did not look. He did not want to catch Cottin's eye. He had known him since his youth, running errands for pennies, all over the Palace, back and forth across the toll-bridge to East Molesey, and, once older, over to Hampton or Kingston. The man was indeed horrid, and liable to feel entitled to make some sort of comment if he caught Leo glancing at him. Leo was not looking forward to losing to him once they rotated into each other's orbits.

Did he know that Lady Maclean, despite the current ill luck manifesting in her partner, had been pathetically grateful to be invited tonight despite Lady Augusta's lingering notoriety, mostly due to the slight of not receiving an invitation to the rival gathering? She should have been natural allies with Mrs Otter, the other widow taking up a grace-and-favour warrant the previous spring, who *was* attending the other party. But Mrs Otter had had the good manners to marry off all five daughters in advance, and bring along a son. Lady Maclean had had the shocking gall to bring not one or two but a full *four* eligible daughters, and no sons at all. A rather large bloc of the marriage-minded Palace matrons had taken against her for that.

The third arrival of last April, the Countess of Cavan, yet another widow – they were thick on the ground here – scooped the pot, for she had no daughters and *two* exceedingly eligible sons, one given to the navy, one to the army, and both due to visit her any day now.

The Countess of Cavan had *definitely* received an invitation to the other party.

At the brief cessation occasioned by losing yet another trick, Leo rubbed between his eyes. He wished Lady Reynett's dancing party had been held another night, rather than sharing this Friday evening with Lady Augusta's card party.

Not that he held any illusions that he would have received one of the coveted invitations to Banqueting House, but Lady Augusta might have garnered one or two more tables for cards. Then she would have had to hold her party in the communal Oaken Room downstairs.

Instead, the card tables were crammed into her drawing room. Full of furniture and people, fire roaring, the room was close and uncomfortably warm (except in Polly's vicinity). There were so many candles that tiny flickers were flashing in his eyes whichever direction he looked, niggling him into a nascent headache even if he hadn't had Polly in his ear, her rolling lilt competing with the chiming voices of the other players.

The next rounds of play proceeded, Leo dragging Cole to inevitable losses through trick, hand, and game because he was so busy trying to disregard Polly on multiple fronts that he could spare no attention elsewhere.

'That's our rubber,' Miss Blake said, politely trying not to sound too satisfied.

'Well played, Miss Blake, Miss Cottin,' Leo said, since there was still skill involved in trouncing even a poor player.

He shook hands with them, and then his partner, adding a murmured apology. Cole waved him off, and they separated towards the opposite tables.

'Not to worry, pet,' Polly said bracingly. 'They say Napoleon also played ill and inattentively.'

She was trying to both provoke and amuse him, and achieved the latter. Lacking cards, he hid his smile behind his hand. Polly grinned, bouncing bare toes off a pretence of a floor; she was floating a few inches above the real one.

The vagaries of the cards had seen Lady Henry Gordon split from her husband, joining Leo to oppose the undefeated Lady Isabella and Mr St John. Lord and Lady Henry and their seven children – five daughters, but too young to be competition; the Banqueting House invitation had been unforthcoming for more pressing reasons – were new to the Palace, and did not yet have their own apartment. They had borrowed the absent Mrs Barnes's residence on the attic storey while they awaited their warrant.

Lady Henry was a short but decidedly vivacious woman, and dimpled at Leo engagingly. She must be too new to know his reputation for peculiarity, at whist and in general.

Mr St John dealt, and Leo led, playing another king. He was able to concentrate during the first trick, because Polly had been mollified by his smile into discontinuing her offensive. She did not like to be ignored. No ghost, as far as Leo could ascertain, liked to be ignored, once they knew he could see them.

He was relieved to be spared further gossip, about Lord and Lady Henry – already on the bad side of at least three officials, a slew of maid-servants, and a host of residents for flooding their top-storey apartment and causing a cascade – nor Mrs Ellice – resident at the Palace long enough that a pair of almost-marriageable daughters had not set her on the outers until she'd made the fatal error of inviting, voluntarily, a *very* marriageable niece to stay – nor slightly deaf Lady Brooke-Pechell, quietly defying her sister-in-law by being one of the few blessed invitees to snub the other party.

Leo, to butcher a phrase, was far too overwhelmed by the shabby grandeur and sheer extent of the forest to be overly concerned about the affairs of any one tree. The trees, in their interconnected, squabbling, jostling glory, were Polly's domain. He heard far too much about the trees.

He rubbed at his forehead again.

'I say, Sweetwater, are you signalling your partner?' Mr St John demanded.

'The cheek!' Polly said.

'I rather think we would be taking more tricks than is quite usual if he were doing *that*,' Lady Henry pronounced. She had a hand resting on her belly. She was in the interesting condition, only partly disguised by loosened corsets.

Mr St John glanced swiftly, one might even say guiltily, at Lady Isabella and subsided. Leo probably should have acknowledged the tri-umphantly knowing look Lady Henry sent his way, dimples at the ascendant again, but he was struggling to block out an increasing commotion, especially now he'd moved to the card table set by the cluster of florally-upholstered chairs jammed into the only spare corner.

The younger Pagets – absent the very youngest, Agnes, no doubt sulking in bed – were gathering in their finery and a veritable cloud of excitement, to attend Banqueting House.

By Polly's report, Lady George Seymour had made a rather nasty comment when Lady Augusta had been granted her warrant, along the lines of, 'I'd thought we'd seen the last of the swarm of Pagets since their brother resigned as Lord Chamberlain, we shall be overrun like the Egyptians during the seven plagues.'

Which was rich, Polly added, because a Seymour had been Lord Chamberlain when Lord George got *his* warrant.

Yet both Lady Augusta and her sister-in-law, Mrs Paget, had received invitations to the evening's dancing.

This was purely because, no matter the array of Regency scandals the six dashing Paget boys had tangled themselves in, their reputations in middle age were rehabilitated, their wives or widows welcomed at Court, and their sons not only eligible and handsome, but some of the very few young men possessing both qualities to be found at the Palace.

To corral the sons, one must draw the daughters, and to draw the daughters, one must invite the mothers, even knowing one of the mothers had already arranged a card party.

Thus, Lady Augusta's daughters, Rose and Laura, were currently giggling with their friend, Miss Stapleton, a normally self-possessed young woman currently rather giddy with freedom from her younger sister for the night.

Mrs Paget's daughter, Matilda, at thirty-one, was a decade or more older than her cousins. She'd recently completed her latest turn as Maid of Honour to Queen Victoria, and from this height of maturity and independence was refusing to lower herself to primp and fuss over lace and flowers with the girls, instead paging through the copy of *Punch* her baby brother had left carelessly by, long evening gloves casually laid to hand.

It would have made a fine portrait, if Ross had not already captured her rosy countenance and steady gaze in her official Court miniature, and if Leo had had any talent for portraiture. He was more a landscape man, after Turner.

Said baby brother, Leopold, had his head together with his cousin, Augustus, whispering and laughing. Both were the youngest of puppies, though Augustus had lately taken up a position as clerk at the Foreign Office, the first step towards greater things. He was rather showing off for Leopold, the antics overseen by Mrs Paget's eldest sons, Frederick and Catesby.

The rules for mourning were different for men, looser; Catesby only bore a crepe armband adorning his dress uniform, having lost his wife early in the year. Lady Augusta still chose to wear shades of lavender, and she'd lost Sir Arthur two years ago: her grief had outlasted her mourning. Leo suspected Catesby especially wanted the armband tonight to hold the circling mothers at bay when he and his brother, both handsome in the blue-eyed, dark-haired way of the Pagets, both captains, both at the beginning of their prime, and both unattached, escorted their siblings and cousins over to the other party.

If Miss Stapleton's admiring glances were anything to go by, Captain Catesby Paget exuded the glamour of the previous decade's charismatic military widower, Sir Horace, a hero of Waterloo whose mere presence in the chapel had produced a rash of fainting among the younger female population during the hopeful interlude between first and second marriage. Much had been made of Sir Horace's gallant transport of swooned ladies to the nearest suitable couch.

Leo hadn't even needed Polly's gossip to notice *that* particular cause and effect.

His attention was repeatedly drawn by the merry group, not helped by the fact that sister and cousins and cousins' friend were all periodically calling for Leopold's attention in tones of reproof or entreaty or command, and the baby of the family was, of course, another Leo.

Leo was not, in turn, another Leopold, nor even a Leonard. He'd been blessed or burdened with the name of Percival Leander Sweetwater, a ponderous designation for a washerwoman's son. He was Percy to his family, or at least to his mother, before he'd lost her, and to Polly, when habit tripped her up. He'd never been anything other than Boy to his grandfather, and he had neither notion of nor interest in what his father might have deigned to call him before he'd abandoned his wife and child for better prospects. Leo was his London name, which he'd kept upon his ignominious return, despite having few people to bestow it upon.

He caught himself glancing at the excited group of young people, attracted by their lively chatter and brightness. Without volition, he framed a painting of contrasts, the silky butterfly hues shining on one side of a parlour scene, the other side a study in mourning colours and the staidness that the long-married and the widowed and the unmarried, sadly or otherwise, gradually converged upon.

He would hate if his hostess noticed his artistic interest and misinterpreted it as furtive admiration, a poor payback for the grace (or was it the favour?) of the invitation.

Much of the gentry of Hampton Court Palace would not have allowed him through their front doors. To them, he was the son of a servant, their former errand boy and now a mere shopkeep, if of a specialist sort, and had no place among the true grace-and-favour residents.

Lady Augusta, however, had not known him in his youth. She seemed to consider him, kindly, as a master of both art and science, and his daguerreotypes to be a shining example of the potential of both. What's more, an earl's daughter who had eloped with her lover, and married him not three days after the granting of a rare and scandalous divorce from the philandering husband they'd so publicly fled, had likely become not merely impervious to social mores, but actively inclined to subvert them.

Further, Leo was unprepossessing in both face and fortune – and form, family, courtly favour, and he could go on – making him extremely unlikely to tempt daughters into any foolish endeavour. The contrast might even make approved suitors more acceptable.

He supposed worldly, unflappable Lady Augusta also adjudged him peculiar, though whether that was in the general, or in a very specific sense, he could not guess. It would be even worse if his flickering attentions towards the glittering group were thought directed at the young men instead of the young women.

Across the card tables, Cole's rich laugh, long and low, made the hairs along the back of Leo's neck prickle.

There was certainly no fear that his affections would be directed towards any other man in this room.

Still, even Polly, who disdained puppies like the Paget cousins but could not resist intrigue, had drifted towards the vortex of energy. She was seemingly of an age with the three giggling girls, though light freckles dusted her unpowdered nose and her waist-length strawberry-blond hair was only loosely plaited, making her look even younger than them.

If she'd been wearing a night-coif to cover her head for sleep, she'd lost it some time during the hours or minutes before her death.

Augustus was now dragging a side table closer to lean on while he drew on a scrap of paper, talking animatedly and gesturing in swoops, splattering ink from the steel nib with the gleeful abandon of someone not responsible for cleaning up after himself. The girls squealed admonishment, moving their skirts aside.

Ignoring them with lofty disdain, Augustus expostulated to a rapt Leopold, 'See, you write out the letters – most of the letters, they skip a few – in a diamond, and then you have a line of five magnetic needles in the middle – we'll use toothpicks.' He upturned a little silver case, rescuing five orangewood toothpicks from the spill.

'Auggie, are you giving away Foreign Office secrets?' his eldest cousin asked sternly.

'No, it's just an electric telegraph, the railways are using it already, Freddie, we'll be using it.' He turned back to his youngest cousin as he rapidly laid out the toothpicks. 'Then there's a commutator, I don't know, wires and conductors and whatnot.' He waved a hand and summed it up with a wise, 'Electromagnetism. And that moves the needles and...'

Augustus twitched toothpicks. Leopold nodded, looking entirely mystified. Rosa, skirts minutely examined for splatter and found unblemished, yawned ostentatiously.

'It is exceedingly warm in here, is it not?' Lady Henry murmured, fanning her hand, and her hand, near her face. Her cheeks were flushed.

The St Johns paused in their trick-taking, faces mirroring alarm. Women in interesting conditions might become dangerously light-headed in a stuffy room, Leo supposed; perhaps Captain Paget, either of them, would need to emulate Sir Horace after all.

Polly hovered by his table again, cooling the immediate area to a notable degree.

'Oh, that's better.' Lady Henry gave her tinkling laugh. 'Thank you, Mrs Penn!'

Polly scoffed, close to legitimately annoyed. *She* was the closest being to a Lady in Grey in this Palace, and the legendary Sibell Penn stealing both thunder and credit was a thorn in her slightly translucent side.

Lady Henry's gay cry caused a ripple of laughter. 'Don't let Lady Emily hear you say that,' Mrs Ellice called.

Everyone was carefully not looking at Leo.

Leo had not been good at hiding that he could see ghosts, in the aftermath of the near-death from drowning which had triggered the gift-cum-curse, and the consequent near-death from pneumonia that had cemented it. In a place where the living population seemed to have the same long memory and inclination to gossip as Polly did, the rumour still plagued him.

'It is the draught from when the front door is opened,' Lady Augusta said, the admonishment subtle but firm, turning towards the drawing room door in expectation of a new arrival.

'Perhaps that is Mr Paget,' Mrs Paget said hopefully, as she had said each time a newcomer had arrived in the wake of her own arrival.

'Mama, he has caught cold and taken to his bed,' Matilda said, as the older three siblings had taken turns to say.

'*I* do not think he was all that ill,' Mrs Paget proclaimed. 'I should think, with a posset and a rest, he could certainly collect himself and come play.'

'Stake's too low,' Frederick said briskly. 'Let the good sir have his quiet evening.'

As a twittery Lady Seymour was shown in, Augustus beckoned to Leo. 'Come here, Sweetwater, take a look.'

Others, upstanding, moved to stretch their legs, knowing that this particular Seymour wife, Lady Beauchamp-Seymour, Sir Horace's second, would monopolise Lady Augusta's attention for a good few minutes. Leo obligingly came to look at Augustus's demonstration.

He'd inked an alphabet board of sorts, the letters, all curves and serifs, arranged in eight rows to make a symmetrical diamond, A in the top row, B and D in the second row – Augustus *had* said some letters were missing from the system – and so on. He'd dashed diagonal lines to connect the staggered letters in neighbouring rows, but no horizontal lines to connect any within the same row.

The two central rows, each consisting of four letters, had a bigger gap between them, where Augustus had evenly spaced the five toothpicks to form the widest part of the diamond. The first and third and fifth tooth-picks were set vertically, pointing past or between the letters in the adjacent rows. The second and fourth were set diagonally, the former leaning left, the latter right. Augustus put his finger on the S, the centre of the third row up from the bottom. Leo mentally extended the paths of the two diagonally-positioned toothpicks and saw that they would intersect at the S.

Switching a few of the toothpicks back and forth, he saw that any given pair, angled to either binary, would be able to jointly indicate any letter. He imagined the real system would flick the needles tick-tock at a cracking rate, spelling out messages from afar with impressive speed.

'Electromagnetism,' Augustus repeated, and only now did Leo catch the prank in the smugness of his plummy tones. 'It can cross the aether, can't it? You could have your ghost talk to us.'

Leo froze, still pincering a toothpick. Leopold guffawed. Augustus's sisters laughed too, but uneasily. Miss Stapleton frowned.

His cousin was less circumspect, snapping, 'Careless fat mouth!'

'Just a joke, Tilda,' Augustus said dismissively. 'Everyone knows ghosts turn out to be hoaxes or an ape in a cap or rabbits or similar silliness.'

This was true enough – in the more respectable fiction stories, at least, where ghost tales always resolved to reveal the superstitious, if not outright sacrilegious, foolishness behind the white sheets and chains.

Mrs Ellice raised her brows. 'Young man, we live in the most haunted place in England.'

'I've read Mackay about haunted—' Augustus began in scoffing tones, before realising he was subject to stern looks from not only the Captains Paget but their mother, and his own mother, too entrapped by Lady Seymour for the moment, but expression promising stern words later.

He blushed, ducking his head, and Leo caught Cole giving the boy a cold stare as well. Cole had four years on Leo, and gravitas, and fine arched brows that could, on the rare necessity, be angled into dark severity, as clear in their message as a pair of needles flicking on a telegraph machine. Leopold treacherously shifted away from his disgraced cousin, eyes downcast.

'There's no C *or* U on that board,' Polly said. 'How am I meant to spell out the relevant word?'

She swiped a carelessly contemptuous hand through the alphabet board, accidentally brushing against Leo's hand, the slight touch enough to give her momentary physicality. It twitched the toothpick he was delicately pinching and drove it up under his nail. He winced, which was at least better than laughing at empty air.

Augustus drew back, eyes widening as his gaze flickered from the toothpick to Leo's face to the general vicinity of his shoulder, where there was nothing to be seen, but where the frosty air was concentrated.

Fortunately, another new arrival furnished the draught excuse, the catch-all explanation across the whole Palace. As the party greeted a third Paget sister-in-law, Augustus mumbled, 'My apologies, Mr Sweet-water. Just a joke.'

Leo mustered a thin smile and returned to his table, rubbing at his minor ghost-induced injury. The pain was startlingly disproportionate, but he supposed needles driven under the nails were said to be torture for a reason.

A chastened Polly, meanwhile, floated by Lady Elizabeth Araminta Paget. She was only visiting the Palace; her mother was the grace-and-favour resident. Her mother was also the other woman in the scandalous affair that had seen Lady Augusta Boringdon elope with Lady Elizabeth Araminta's brother-in-law to become Lady Augusta Paget, around about the time Leo was born.

Polly was hovering, literally, in the pining hope of hearing calumny and slander. She had not, she said, had the opportunity for anything quite so exciting here since Lady Jersey was baiting Queen Caroline, or the all-too-brief overlap of catty Lord Hervey and cattier Horace Walpole.

To her immense disappointment, Lady Augusta and the very elderly and ailing Lady Elizabeth Monck had done nothing more than mutually inflict the cut direct upon each other since the former's arrival, and the two sister-in-laws had never allowed the clash of their family's history to come between them or the Paget brothers.

Lady Augusta had no doubt been resigned to settling Lady Seymour by her and having her attention as split as Leo's usually was. Lady Seymour was hesitant to join the card party – Leo would have gladly stepped out for her – because, like Lady Brooke-Pechell, her in-laws would prefer her to *not* visit with the notorious Pagets. But Sir Horace was at his club, and Lady Seymour was being as daring as she dared to be, which was daring the threshold, but not the card table.

Now Lady Elizabeth Araminta stolidly took her in charge, while Lady Augusta took up her hostess mantle and the whist resumed, fresh glasses of sherry punch all round.

'Oh, I forgot my news!' cried Lady Seymour, disrupting several tricks. 'Did you hear the old Duke of York's suite is occupied at last?'

Polly widened her eyes and clasped her hands to her chest, all aflutter. 'My *dear* Mr Bennet, have you heard that Netherfield Park is let at last?'

Leo, about to take his turn, had to raise his cards to hide his smile. He had it from Polly that the wealthy widow had made her inopportune, if widely envied, second match solely due to a weakness for a man in uniform. The comparison to the similarly-weakened Mrs Bennet still felt cruel, because Sir Horace had remarried merely to clear his debts, and, indifferent to his new wife, now spent most of his time in Clubland.

'Oh, yes,' Mrs Ellice said, slapping a card down at the rear table. She was as sociable and full of anecdotes as Polly, and could be counted upon for reliable reportage. 'Lady Harriet Hoste has come today, and she'll have to stay long enough to satisfy the Lord Chamberlain, or she'll lose the right to her warrant. She's brought her youngest son, and her brother's sons. He's Lord Orford, you know.'

There was a pause in which the mothers with eligible daughters, and the eligible daughters themselves, except Matilda, looked southeast as if they had magically acquired the ability to see through multiple walls.

Matilda lazily turned another page in the magazine, entirely uninterested. If it truly were a woman's sole purpose to serve a household, her husband's or parents', or a surrogate's, she served the highest in the land.

'*And* two daughters and two nieces,' Mrs Ellis finished.

Catesby and the pair of puppies remained unmoved, but Frederick looked thoughtful, if still intent on avoiding Mrs Paget's meaningful stare. It was a sad fact for the eligible daughters of Hampton Court Palace that the eligible sons tended to find their brides elsewhere, Catesby being a case in point.

After another few tricks, one to Leo and Lady Henry, two to the St Johns, Lady Isabella ventured, in an unusually circumspect way, 'Mr Sweetwater…'

Leo knew that tone. She was about to ask about the ghost haunting the passage outside her apartment.

'There's a patch of cold by my front door,' she said. Leo had to stop himself from nodding in satisfaction as his prediction came true. 'And Miss Reynett told me that just before Mrs Wright passed over and her apartment's warrant was granted to us, a soldier was murdered right there.'

'That's true!' Lady Seymour contributed, hand pressed to heart. 'Why, that villain was running for *our* door.' She shivered delicately.

'Miss Reynett says the entire passage has been freezing ever since.'

'It's positively perishing!'

Miss Reynett, Lady Isabella, and Lady Seymour were neighbours on the south side of Base Court. Although Lady Emily Ponsonby, another occupant of the southwest corner, was still inclined to attribute odd noises and cold spots to Sibell Penn, the ladies of the apartments by the old orangery were entirely correct about the true source.

Sergeant Hamilton had received his mortal wound in their passage-way four and a half years ago, while trying to arrest a drunk and dis-tressed private for dereliction of duty. Until Hamilton, Leo had believed ghosts only appeared close to their place of death. The sergeant had expired in the hospital, if before the night was out. Yet now, to Leo's mild chagrin upon his return from London, he haunted the place where it could be said his sudden death had ambushed him and his spirit had departed, though his heartbeat had lasted a little longer.

Leo said, 'I'm sorry to hear that, Lady Isabella. Perhaps you might inform Mrs Grundy.'

'I have. But could you not— I have heard that you—'

She seemed to become aware, from the silence of the other guests, that she was tripping on an unspoken Palace taboo. She stopped, cheeks pink.

'Write to the Lord Chamberlain, then, Lady Isabella.' Leo did not need to look over to know it was Cole speaking. His Scots-French upbringing made his rolling, burring vowels into a calling card among the more uniform accents of the rest of the gentry. 'It sounds like maintenance is required if a draught is getting in.'

This triggered the usual cascade of complaint regarding the Lord Chamberlain and the Board of Works, and Leo was able to finish the hand subject only to sneaking looks of curiosity from Lady Isabella. She was a writer, though she had probably received her invitation to the card party because her daughter and Lady Augusta's youngest daughter were fast friends, rather than for her artistic side. Leo hoped she wasn't plotting him into one of her stories.

Second rubber duly lost, Leo congratulated the winners, apologised to Lady Henry, and met the other loser at Colonel Cottin and Lady Maclean's table. Leo wasn't sure if the lady of that pairing was pleased to be thus far undefeated, or dismayed that she was still trapped with Colonel Cottin. She was a widow. Perhaps, unlike Lady Augusta, she sought remarriage. He did think she could do better. Colonel Cottin had likely not realised he could *not*.

'Oh,' he said to the other loser. 'No luck on your side, either?'

'Never mind.' Cole cast a mild look over at his prior table, and at the St Johns. 'Though perhaps people who have lived with each other for several decades should not be allowed to be partners.'

The Charlottes – Mrs Thoroton, long-time widow, and Miss Dawson, long-time companion of Mrs Thoroton – feigned indignation, laughing under the force of Cole's playfully raffish smile. It was all pleasingly good-natured, a momentary breath of unladen air.

Leo did wonder at the comment, however. Cole could be surprisingly innocent; he'd not gone to boarding, where an awful lot of wealthy scions appeared to receive an eye-opening education, and he could hardly guess about the female activity if the male was not commonly within his purview. It would have been unusual to raise such matters in polite mixed company, regardless.

Not that the mixed company was entirely polite. They took their seats to discover Colonel Cottin and Lady Maclean engaged in a teeth-clenched conversation that was rapidly becoming an argument.

'I do believe I am not entirely ignorant of the nuances of the situation, Colonel Cottin,' Lady Maclean was saying, tone suggesting fraying patience. 'My dear husband was a general.'

'In the army, Lady Maclean, in the army! Our soldiers did their duty, certainly, but we are speaking of our fleet.' He turned abruptly to Cole, cutting off a response which might have justly pointed out that his own commission was also from the army. 'What say you, Solong?'

'I am sure I would venture to say a great deal,' Cole said genially, 'if I knew which aspect of the fleet we are considering.'

'The treaty, man!' Colonel Cottin said. 'Nanking.'

'I suppose it to be an enormous travesty, impossible to justify,' Lady Maclean interjected, 'to blockade a friendly nation's port in so high-handed a manner, and then demand such terms as would make a friendly nation consider itself an enemy instead, all over an iniquitous trade!'

'Balderdash!' The colonel thumped the table. 'We were upholding Britain's honour and defending our women and children from atrocity. It's nothing but pernicious hogwash to blame the opium.' In an aside, muttered to no one, he added, 'This is why women are not suited to speaking on politics.'

Lady Maclean bristled. 'I am hardly the only one who says so. Gladstone himself spoke against it.'

'The Duke of Wellington *himself* commended our navy's actions. You side with Napoleon when you extend more respect to semi-civilised barbarians than they showed our ambassador. Kowtow! Pernicious nonsense. Well, Solong? You must have something to say about it all.'

Unlike Leo, Cole might be considered a good match for the younger daughters of impoverished families of quality with fading Court connections and very little else to their name. He held the gentleman's title of Royal Gardener, something of a sinecure personally gifted by Dowager Queen Adelaide, coming glove-in-hand with a fair income and the occupancy of well-favoured Wilderness House. He was the son of a baronet, the grandson of another, and the Townsend Farquhars were patronised by the Wellesleys, one of the greatest and most influential families of England.

He was, moreover, handsome (exceedingly so, in Leo's very considered opinion), most amiable, and had the great good fortune to be rumoured crossed in love by an earl's daughter, which could surely only add to his appeal in the minds of the young ladies of the Palace.

There was only one small impediment standing in the way of an excellent match.

'No, no, Colonel,' Cole said. 'Sir Robert's mistress wasn't Chinese, she was Malay. I'm his *Malay* bastard. So I cannot, in good conscience, offer any insight into the British bombardment of a Chinese port to force them to accept India's smuggled opium.'

The card party went silent. Lady Maclean vanished behind her cards in a distinctly familiar way. As the chatter resumed in starts and stutters, Colonel Cottin spluttered. Cole looked serious and attentive to a gruff speech that was not an apology, though he found a moment to drop a sly wink at Leo that made him shield his face again, this time in case his sudden fluster was too apparent.

'Ho,' Colonel Cotton said, gesturing towards Leo. Leo looked at the spot of blood under his forefinger, where the toothpick had jammed in on the gust of Polly's spectral irritation. Cottin was indulging some irritation of his own, apparently, for he went on, 'That's a bit of Johnny-foreigner torture, bamboo stalks under the nails. Brought something back from George Town, did you?'

'I was raised in Mauritius,' Cole said, still refusing to take the bait. 'By a French stepmother, monsieur. However, if you find my manners poor, I beg you excuse Mamam and lay the blame at my feet.'

Leo, thinnest smile in place, met Polly's eyes as she floated behind Cottin's chair, examining his card hand with some interest.

'Oh, good,' she said. 'Play your seven, pet.'

Some minutes later, Lady Maclean, smiling, and Colonel Cottin, muttering darkly, were departing the table, having lost every trick Polly could possibly engender. Polly, for all her frivolousness, could have moods where she was serious and incisive, and she'd turned all her determination onto the game like she was planning a battle.

What she *hadn't* been was subtle, and Leo hadn't even tried to be so on her behalf.

He rubbed the spot between his eyes. That had probably been foolish.

After a moment, Cole said, 'Well. I suppose no one says you're a *bad* player. They say you're an *unpredictable* player. That has to lead to the opposite result sometimes, just by the odds.'

There was something of a question to it. Leo made an agreeing sort of noise, still with thumb pressed between his eyes. Polly floated closer, wafting blessedly cool air over him. As new opponents, Mr St John and Mrs Thoroton, their original pairings finally defeated, joined the table, Cole excused himself to speak to Lady Augusta.

He returned to gently take Leo's elbow and lever him from his seat. 'Lady Seymour and Lady Elizabeth Araminta will take our places. Let's get you home, Mr Sweetwater.'

Leo tried to protest. He was aware of the honour Lady Augusta had dealt him, and *also* aware the invitation had been at least a little predicated on his sex, he and Cole both adding to a scant male contingent. But Lady Augusta was a consummate hostess and walked him and Cole to the door herself, genteelly decrying his apologies and wishing him speedy recovery from the headache and them both a good evening.

He felt better almost as soon as they stepped out into Base Court.

The immense expanse of the grand courtyard spread before them, the looming Tudor walls far distant, a faint mist rising off the flagstones, the gas lamps at the arches scant bulwark against the gloom. The stars and waning crescent moon shone in dim splendour overhead, and the air was cool.

He couldn't have found a more apposite opposite to the close, hot, bright, noisy drawing room if he'd set out to paint an allegory.

Leo took his first deep breath for some time.

'So,' Cole said.

Away from the other voices, the musical motif of his accent was less obvious, but it still flicked Leo's attention to him like he was one of those needles on Augustus's telegraph machine.

Electromagnetism. Indeed.

Cole's mischievous smile flashed in the dim light. 'Was it the mention of the bastardry, the mistress, or the foreignness that did me in?'

Leo said, 'I see no reason why it could not have been all three.'

'That's better. You've barely strung two words together tonight.'

He'd been overwhelmed, claustrophobic, exhausted. He stood close by Cole in the stillness and agreed, softly, 'This is better.'

Polly wasn't there to remind him his affections were showing, heart splashed across his sleeve. She had stayed behind, both because she drank in the conviviality that drained him, and also so she didn't give Leo away to Sergeant Hamilton.

The patient, dutiful ghost stood eternal guard at the archway on the south side of the court, an indistinct figure at this distance, that nonetheless glimmered to Leo's eyes amid the deeper shadows of the red-brick facade.

Leo half-turned away, the better to hide from both Cole and the ghost.

'I apologise, Mr Sweetwater. I shouldn't have insisted you come.'

They met up for something of a picnic every Friday, in tiny Chapel Court, close to both Leo's lodgings and his daguerreotype studio. It was usually the most pleasant part of Leo's week.

Today, Cole had been intent on persuading his friend to attend the card party, making him cognisant of the grace of the invitation, and also the lack of any enjoyment Cole could possibly wring from it if Leo did not do him the immense favour of keeping him company.

'I was fine.'

Cole's Scottish father and French stepmother had instilled disarming directness, a mild roguish streak, and no fear of physical contact. Without hesitation or self-consciousness, he took Leo's hand, still bare since the walk home was too brief for gloves.

He raised it so he could examine the backs of Leo's fingers, pressing his thumb briefly to the offended nail. 'You literally would have preferred to drive spikes under your nails than stay a moment longer.'

Leo was meant to laugh. Instead he had to bite his tongue so he didn't declare that he'd've attended a score of card parties and driven tooth-picks under the full score of his nails if it meant he could stand here in the starlight with Cole cradling his hand and smiling at him affection-ately for just a few more minutes.

He had to look away; he had to seal his affections back behind their closed door and add more padlocks. He felt frozen. The moment seemed to be stretching and stretching, as if his wish had come true.

Oh. 'The clock's stopped.'

Cole followed his gaze up to the large slate clock looming above the eastern end of the court. It adorned the entrance to Anne Boleyn's Gateway, which went through to Clock Court. Ironically, the astronom-ical clock on the tower's other side, facing Clock Court, had been removed some years ago, in a bid to put less strain on the clockwork mechanisms. Clock Court currently had no clock.

Base Court's clock, never quite up to its task, stopped frequently enough that a certain legend had grown up around the habit, beginning with the passing of Queen Anne of Denmark.

'Death stalks the Palace tonight,' Cole said ominously, and this time Leo did laugh.

He pulled his hand free, pretending his skin wasn't burning. Compan-ionably, they crossed the court, Cole following Leo's habitual swerve without comment, and went through to Master Carpenter's Court.

Leo turned towards his apartment, and Cole towards the alley that would lead him out of the Palace compound and into the grounds. Wil-derness House was, unsurprisingly, hard by the Wilderness, near the Maze, a short walk northwards by moonlight.

'Good night, Sweetwater,' he called softly as he went.

'Good night, Solong,' Leo said, and paused to watch his back until he was swallowed by the night, running his thumb over the fingers of his other hand, where Cole's touch still lingered.

His affections were showing again. He hurried to his apartment, firmly closing the door.

Two

LEO BEGAN HIS SATURDAY EARLY, POLISHING and sensitising a set of Sheffield plates and taking them out in their lightproof cases, along with his new Voigtländer camera, to catch the clear autumn light in the gardens.

Then he set to work in the studio.

Spring and summer made for the Palace's busier half of the year. By now, late October, not only were fewer tourists making the day-trip, but the residents who could were departing for warmer climes. It meant Leo's favourite stretch of time, the cold, quiet months, was beginning.

But Saturday was still a popular day, and the day the fashionable tended to come from London. They mostly strolled about the extensive gardens, listening to the regimental band and disdaining the art-crammed State Apartments, but they'd also be drawn into his studio.

What's more, October was the month of Queen Jane Seymour's death, and today was both the first Saturday since the actual anniversary of her death, and the last Saturday before All Hallow's Eve, when people's thoughts turned towards departed souls.

It would make Leo's most popular product all but fly from the shelves.

Much of his burgeoning success, he was nowhere near proud enough to deny, was due to the enterprising young woman currently opening the boxes from the printer in the showroom, sorting fresh prints onto racks and shelves, and into the pedlar's tray.

Miss Sarah Jane Fitzhenry was sixteen, quiet and serious, but with a steely gumption that had been apparent even when she was twelve and had defected from selling Mr Grundy's *Stranger's Guide*, where she could already see the inroads of competition, to Mr Sweetwater's novel daguerreotypes. Leo's watercolour prints were subject to just as much competition as Mr Grundy's guidebook, but he held exclusive local rights to the new camera technology, licensed from Mr Beard in Regent Street (not without some resentment that Monsieur Daguerre had gifted the invention free to the rest of the world insultingly soon after filing the British patent).

Young Sally proved almost preternaturally percipient when she walked the crowds with her tray, unerringly identifying from dress and manner and accent those customers open only to the more traditional souvenir of a watercolour print of the Great Gatehouse, or Anne Boleyn's Gateway and the clock tower, or the Baroque eastern front or the Great Hall, or views of the Great Fountain Garden, and those, more fashion-forward, who could be directed towards daguerreotype prints of the same sights, mirrored.

She'd also perfected various methods, exquisitely tailored, of implying that the truly discerning connoisseur could only be satisfied with a Sweetwater original, thus luring customers through the doorway of the studio, where Leo hung a good stock of safe watercolour paintings of favoured views, and a few others that he mentally categorised, perhaps unfairly, as for authentic art-lovers.

The main attraction was, however, the display of daguerreotypes, each image protected with pinchbeck and tightly-sealed glass. Many were kept in satin-lined wooden cases, very much like the miniatures Leo had never quite had the knack for, though they would not make miniatures obsolete until they had full colour. Others were carefully sealed into lockets and brooches.

Being a creature of habit and routine, Leo had begun with landscapes, the views of the Palace that sold well as watercolours, plus commissioned scenes. It was Sally who had nudged him, with the same deft touch she showed with prospective customers, into adding portraiture this year, mimicking Goddard's and Claudet's studios in London.

It was Sally, inveigling assistance from both brothers, who had swept and scrubbed and whitewashed, and evicted copious quantities of cardinal spiders, to carve out a larger portion of the great Tudor kitchens than the corner Leo had dared appropriate. The Fitzhenrys had transformed a dusty, cold and neglected space off the alley that had once been the Serving Place into a front showroom, a smaller portrait studio behind, and, rearmost, a well-ventilated space for the chemical processing.

It was Sally who had learned the Isenring technique to painstakingly hand-tint lips and eyes and jewellery with gum arabic and pigment, transforming the little portraits from faddish novelties into striking mementos.

And it was Sally who'd diffidently pointed out that the Haunted Gallery was one of the most popular stops of the State Apartments tour, and the reason was in its name.

Thus, Leo was currently bent over his worktable in the portrait studio, fresh prints of the Great Hall and the Silver-Stick Stairs stacked before him as he stirred a special blend of highly diluted watercolour pigments, mostly blues.

Walcott and Johnson were working on a copying apparatus, to take daguerreotypes of daguerreotypes, and make enlargements, too. Leo anticipated their success by the end of next year. Until then, the daguerreotype printing followed Berres's German *phototyp* process, with a few modifications added to the etching plates to strengthen the impression. They were still rough, their popularity almost entirely contingent on their cheapness compared to the real item.

Or, in this case, what Leo was about to do to the image, with commensurate effect on the asking price.

'I do not look like that,' Polly grumbled from behind him, as she did every time he replenished the stock of ghost cards. 'Ghosts look nothing like that.'

'I know,' he murmured. Ghosts got caught in patterns and loops. He was used to repeating himself. 'I have to make them look like people expect.'

The cards came ready-printed with the ghosts, from doctored plates now secured at the printer's; Leo had done some delicate layering work to achieve that effect. Now his skills as a watercolourist came to the fore.

He'd attempted hand-colours of the usual landscape prints, but cheap card was not right for it. The cost of the more expensive cardstock, thick to withstand washes of colour, plus a fair remuneration for his time and expertise in the colouring, meant supposedly cheap prints rightly became almost as expensive as one of Sally's hand-tinted daguerreotypes. He might as well give himself the pleasure of true watercolours, and wait on advances in the photographic field.

The ghost cards were a different matter.

Leo laid out a print depicting the fleeing Catherine Howard, doomed for several centuries to run screaming along a Palace gallery in a vain effort to reach her husband and defend her honour and life from accusations of adultery. He'd used the Great Hall for her ghost card, since the eponymous Haunted Gallery itself was too dark to lend itself to a decent daguerreotype.

Perhaps Polly in her long white chemise *had* been glimpsed by those few with Leo's talent over the many years she'd wafted about the Palace: he could not possibly be the sole resident or visitor across its lifespan to have briefly died twice in quick succession, and even a single close brush with mortality might awaken sensitivity to what was often described to Leo, in breathless tones, as the other side of the veil.

Such glimpses of an evocative feminine figure would explain why Henry's fifth queen was long-said to be the haunter of the Haunted Gallery, producer of unexplained patches of frigid air and fainting spells, rather than its *actual* spectral inhabitant, of a mere seventy years' tenure.

Catherine might very well haunt the execution block at the Tower, side by side with Anne Boleyn, if ghosts lingered so long. She could not haunt the Palace, for she hadn't met mortality here.

Leo dipped a very fine, pointed brush into his mixture, carefully swiping away excess wet. He was not aiming to add colour, but rather authenticity (an irony in several dimensions). With a practised swoop of his hand, he laid a thin wash over the white figure with the vague likeness to Queen Catherine, giving the printed ghost an echo of the glimmer he saw on the real ghosts of Hampton Court Palace.

He waved the card gently to speed its drying, and then examined the effect. Since printings varied in ink and paperstock, he always tested and adjusted his recipe with each new batch. He often then handed the task over to John, Sally's younger brother, possessed of an unwavering focus, a steady hand, a mathematical brain, and a commitment to quietude that surpassed his sister's and rivalled Leo's. However, Sally had managed him into a scholarship at Mr Walton's school, and was paying for extra tutelage to catch him up to Walton's standards during the Michaelmas term. Leo had been sufficiently concerned that this might have been a scheme that he'd interviewed Mr and Mrs Walton himself, and been reassured. John was therefore over in Hampton this morning.

Satisfied with the result, Leo set the card onto the drying rack and began the meditative work of painting the rest of the stack. Polly, on the other hand, made a grumble of dissatisfaction, though not from any sort of moral objection regarding the fakery.

Her disapproval arose twofold. Firstly, the rumours about him were relentless enough without actively encouraging them by selling ghostly merchandise. Leo tended to agree, but he was also resigned: the rumours were ingrained now, never to go away. As long as the story remained rumour, the cachet of mystery added welcome pennies to the price.

Secondly, she regarded Henry VIII, and the endless public interest in him, with such disdain that one might be fooled into thinking she'd known him personally.

She couldn't possibly have. Ghosts did not persist so long. They faded into incoherence, drifting about with only the barest thread of memory and emotion to hold their spirit in human form, like the ball of rage, once perhaps a knight, centred in the kitchen gardens, the Tudors' tiltyard. Or—

Leo looked instinctively towards Fountain Court, then very deliberately chose not to complete the thought.

He couldn't know for sure how old Polly was; her night-clothes and accent, for the most part, could have been his mother's. But she'd been trailing tourists brandishing their esoteric historical knowledge for enough years, even before the Palace was formally given over to the nation, that she had picked up gossipy titbits about every ruler who'd resided at Hampton Court, from Henry all the way to George II.

She judged the royal occupants almost uniformly harshly, notwithstanding a soft spot for the queens to whom the new queen would invariably be compared, and Charles II, or perhaps Nell Gwyn. She saved her most scathing opinions for the first Charles, but, confusingly, also Cromwell, so that Leo would have had to toss a coin to answer as to whether her sympathies lay with the Royalists or the Parliamentarians.

Though Polly was very much unlike the other Palace ghosts in the direction and extent of her fixations, the depth of feeling there led Leo to suppose she had been a victim of those turbulent times.

It had to stay as supposition. He'd known her since he was eight, and she'd never spoken of the circumstances of her death.

Leo had been oblivious about her unusual reticence as a child, curious as an adolescent, and obnoxious as a young man, but these days he mostly let it lie. She did not want to tell him, or perhaps, since she was, by his shaky reckoning, the oldest sentient ghost in the Palace, she truly had lost those details into the haze that must eventually fully claim her.

At that dismal idea, he glanced up from his peacefully repetitive work. Polly was floating higher than usual, drifting almost aimlessly, like drying linens in a limp breeze, and appeared lost in thought.

This was an uncharacteristic enough occurrence that Leo blurted, 'Did you hear any more interesting news last night?' because if there was one thing that he was certain kept his oldest and closest friend tethered among the living, it was her preoccupation with their goings-on.

'I doubt *you'd* think so,' she said haughtily (he had been obnoxious about more than one thing as a young man), 'but I will say the Hostes made an impression last night at the Reynetts' dance. Or at least, their youngest girl did.'

Having filled the first tier of the drying rack, Leo picked up the second of the card types, this one depicting a white figure on the Silver-Stick Stairs. 'Did she ogle the naked paintings too blatantly?'

'All the girls peek around the doors into the forbidden room,' Polly said, with enormous satisfaction. 'No, an old family friend of her departed father happened to be invited too, and when I say *old*, he is some thirty-five years her senior, *and* married, if separated. They made eyes at each other half the night, and I cannot say which of them was more besotted.'

Leo could sympathise. He'd conceived something of a passion, thankfully short-lived, for an older man himself, the newly-widowed Sir Horace. At least his mother had not been thrilled to dangle him at a wealthy titled prospect and yet simultaneously jealous over the emerging connection, as Polly said Lady Harriet had been. She was now fully engaged in her tale, lively and ardent, and Leo relaxed.

He made suitably scandalised noises as he glimmered up Queen Jane Seymour. The top of the Silver-Stick Stairs, her setting, was overlooked by a row of windows, flooded with light at the best time of the day. He'd persuaded Mrs Grundy, the Palace's Housekeeper and holder of all sorts of keys, into letting him in there on a Friday, when the State Apartments were closed for the grand endeavour of the weekly cleaning.

The third of Henry's wives, Jane was the only one of the six to have died at the Palace. But she, too, did not haunt it, despite being said to mournfully drift up and down the staircase searching for her baby, begging forgiveness from the queen she had supplanted, because merely dying in a place did not cause a haunting.

It had to be a sudden death, with rue and regret burning to the very last flickering thought. Leo did suppose that death in childbirth might come upon a woman with enough suddenness to qualify, and he could not think of many things that had the potential to create an urgent sense of a task left undone than a newborn baby. He had not been in enough bedchambers around the Palace to know just how haunted they might be.

However, Jane had not died in childbirth, but rather of a fever near a fortnight later. Sickness tended to be too slow to leave ghosts; Leo, informally agnostic, presumed that dying with time enough to order one's affairs, mundane and spiritual, smoothed the way to eternal rest. Whatever the reason, he'd been immensely grateful for this quirk of the supernatural when his mother had died in the first blue cholera outbreak ten years previously, and even more grateful when he'd found out about plague pits.

'Could you make one of me?' Polly asked suddenly. 'You could say I'm Sibell, I suppose.' She heaved a sigh. 'I don't mind.'

Leo looked up at her, brush poised. He did not create ghost cards for the third famous ghost of Hampton Court Palace, Sibell Penn. An elderly nurse, faithfully tending the Virgin Queen through smallpox (again, not likely to leave a ghost) before succumbing herself, was not as glamorous as the young, beautiful, tragic noble wives of Henry VIII, and therefore unlikely to make a popular piece of merchandise.

He also had the idea it would be in poor taste, after the ruckus with Lady Emily Ponsonby back in '29.

Cautiously, he said, with the hint of a question to it, 'People didn't start seeing the Grey Lady until Sibell got a good story.'

'Make one up for me, then,' Polly said. 'You're good at lying.'

'I'm not *good* at it!' Leo protested. 'I've merely had a great deal of practice at it.'

He frowned, realising the gaping hole in his logic just as Polly made the obvious rejoinder. 'Which makes you good at it, pet.'

She grinned at him provokingly, and he melted into a fond smile.

In many ways, Polly had been the worst possible first ghost for young Percy Sweetwater to meet, on the chilly December day he'd fallen off Hampton Court Bridge. She'd given him entirely the wrong impression.

Ghosts drifted about the loose anchor of their place of death, fixated on the moments leading to their demise, and faded away, eventually becoming splodges of extreme cold and bursts of emotion, often terror, of the sort he absently swerved around in Base Court. Polly obeyed none of these rules of thumb.

She'd also been the *best* possible ghost to meet the day he almost drowned (by a technical reckoning, he *had* drowned), and not only because when the current tossed him out forcefully enough to eject the water from his lungs and restart his breath, it had been her voice urging him to crawl up the bank before the rushing water could suck him back in, and her presence calming the other ghosts.

When Leo, roused by tolling, looked up again, Polly had vanished. Once the morning was advanced enough, she liked to haunt the Miss Pagets, or the Miss Stapletons, or the other Palace daughters who were her age when she'd died, looking over their shoulders as they leafed through magazines, discussed the latest fashion plates, bickered about borrowed bonnets and ribbons, and giggled over the men who'd caught their collective eye. For all her years of after-life, part of Polly was perennially that innocently frivolous young woman.

The bells of the clock tower were counting out ten. The State Apartments were open.

Sally had never considered passing down her peddling role to John, who, at eleven, was nearly the age at which she'd first picked up her tray. His big sister was determined he'd have the education his brain deserved instead. It made Leo's heart ache sometimes: it never did seem to occur to Sarah Jane Fitzhenry that her own brain was just as good, or if it did, she'd learned long ago not to dwell.

Instead, she had her favoured few among the servants' children to take her old job. She helped today's choice settle the strap securely about his shoulders, and sent him off with the tray of prints and sample daguerreotypes.

Then she helped Leo carry their heavy wooden painted sandwich board across the way into Clock Court.

A sprinkling of tourists meandered across the courtyard towards the entrance to the State Apartments, some carrying guidebooks. More people, tourists and residents alike, were aiming for the gardens, where the regimental band was striking up its first tune. Lady Albinia Cumberland went by in the Push, an old sedan chair mounted on wheels and pulled by the more sprightly of her footmen.

The Palace was very much the residence of women: the widows and spinster daughters of men who'd had connections or given exemplary service to the Crown, and younger daughters and their governesses, and an army of maidservants that doubled the population. Living husbands and sons tended to wash in and out on unpredictable tides, the exigences of parliament or service or boarding school or university, while male servants attracted higher tax, and were thus a luxury for the, as one Lord Chamberlain so kindly put it, 'decaying ladies' of the Palace.

Therefore, whichever regiment happened to be quartered at the Barracks – currently the Eleventh Hussars, Prince Albert's Own – was of some interest to a substantial portion of the population of the Palace, and the regular Saturday performance of the band was a respectable funnel for indulging that interest.

Leo carefully angled the sign under the northern arcade, not so far into Clock Court that Mrs Grundy would have cause to hear complaints.

'Thank you, Miss Fitzhenry,' he said. 'You may go watch the band, if you like.'

He knew she liked to. The reason was innocently sentimental – her father, Private John Fitzhenry, had been a bandsman of the Fourteenth Dragoons before his discharge.

Sally looked away, and he thought he detected annoyance on her face. He had once overheard Lady Albinia proclaim, with queenly certitude, that one knew where one stood with one's peers and one's inferiors, both of which as a class knew its place and its relation to each other, but that the middling classes were abominably *tedious*. He sometimes wondered if Sally would have preferred an employer who had grown up knowing himself the master of servants so she did not have to navigate his uncertainty.

But he had misinterpreted. Sally had turned to wave across the courtyard, expression still complicated. In the same moment, Leo caught Cole's unmistakable cadence, and turned too, without volition. Cole was cutting through Clock Court, accompanied by Sally's long-legged older brother, Joseph, currently one of his under-gardeners, but with a burgeoning reputation for racing, both himself and horses.

The Fitzhenry siblings had lost first their mother, then their father, in shockingly quick succession earlier in the year. It had been Sally's grief that had provoked her flurry of activity in pushing Leo into becoming a worthy and reliable employer. She'd then moved into the unused servant quarters in his apartment, bringing John with her, the child a buffer against rumours impugning either of their reputations.

Before Sally had concocted her plan, Leo was dependent on the Lord Chamberlain's requirement that absent occupants leave servants to air and maintain their apartments, which meant there were always a few about who had substantial free time and wanted extra coppers to enjoy it properly. Sally regularised this ad hoc cooking and cleaning arrangement, becoming in effect his housekeeper as well as his shopgirl, in exchange for decent pay, board and meals for both her and John.

Leo recognised that she had done all this because she did not want to become the servant of the man her parents had served, nor abandon John to the same. He could only admire and respect her determination and intelligence, and rue, on her behalf, that the very same qualities meant Joseph considered his orphaned younger siblings safely settled. He'd found grooming work near Leeds, and would be leaving within days.

As Leo watched, probably wearing a similarly complicated expression as Sally, Cole clapped Joseph on the shoulder, saying something that made the younger man laugh. Leo made himself turn away and carefully bent to adjust the signboard one last time.

An unpleasant snort sounded by his ear, the familiar complacent contempt of Colonel Cottin. Bewigged and black-coated like a menacing shade from the last century, he glared at Cole and Joseph's backs as they disappeared into the wending passages southwards.

'The half-caste types certainly stick together,' he sneered.

All three Fitzhenrys took after their Jamaican father rather than their Irish mother. Straightening, Leo met Sally's eye and saw the flash of injury, and the stiff forbearance of it, in the way she glanced down.

Cottin was the very man Sally had moved heaven and earth, also known as Mr Sweetwater, to avoid, and there could be no way on heaven or earth that she preferred *this* sort of man, who thought himself the master of her *type*.

And Leo was her employer, bound to protect her, and Cottin was being obnoxious out of petty spite over the whist last night, Leo's fault entirely.

Steeling himself for the worst of all possible fates, a *confrontation*, he started to face Cottin. Sally gave him a quick shake of her head, mouth set firm.

She'd swallowed the truth of it sooner than he had: he was her protector, soon to be her sole protector once Joseph departed, but he was in almost as precarious a position, and had no protector himself. If Cottin took offence, as Cottin was wont to do, he could use the ageing connections that had gained him a grace-and-favour warrant meant solely for widows to have the Lord Chamberlain oust Leo from his caretaking warrant, or depose his studio from the Tudor kitchens, or both.

Leo bit down bitterness. He'd worked hard to be more than an errand boy, and Sally was working even harder to be more than a maidservant, and yet they would both forever carry their antecedents no matter how far into the lower ranks of the middling classes they managed to scrabble, because men like Cottin had dukes to call on, and they had no one.

'Do put a sock in it, you disagreeable fellow,' Miss Smart said cheerily, striding past towards her apartment off Fish Lane.

Miss Smart, Eliza when they were alone, had *her* warrant directly from Queen Victoria's predecessor, King William IV, with two competing and mutually exclusive theories as to which favour or grace had earned it for her, relayed to Leo with relish by Polly.

William, once Duke of Clarence, quite famously fathered many natural children, most by Dorothea Jordan, but perhaps one by the buxom wife of the innkeeper of the old Toye Inn, where the duke had spent many happy hours. That might make Eliza the half-sister of Miss Blake, herself all but certainly one of the few natural children by Dora that the duke had chosen not to acknowledge. The two were certainly close.

Or perhaps Eliza herself had briefly been the ageing king's lover twenty years ago.

The argument had raged for at least a decade. Meanwhile, Eliza had confided to Leo that Clarence had liked her mother's marrow soup recipe, which she surrendered to the royal kitchens in exchange for permanent right to her Fish Lane lodgings.

She encouraged the rumours, though, because either allowed her to embrace the confident spinsterish life that seemed to alarm wider society. Leo rather suspected that, of the dozen or so middle-aged spinsters of independent means in the Palace, the ones who were entirely comfortable with failing to fulfil their so-called sole function of wifedom and motherhood outnumbered the ones who still hoped for a husband. Shocking notion – and that was not even considering that Eliza occasionally dressed as Mr Smart and frequented the same back-street pub in Hampton Wick that Leo did (she had, in fact, introduced him to it), and wrote pseudonymically for *The Gentleman's Magazine*, and smoked hand-rolled continental cigarettes in the garden while wearing a frock coat and trousers and a defiantly unfashionable Titus cut, and defied anyone to treat her as superfluous or incomplete…

…and talked to Colonel Cottin as he deserved to be talked to.

She flashed Leo a familiar amused look over her shoulder from narrowed, intensely blue eyes. It was good to be reminded he was not entirely friendless here, and that the traditional means of power were not the only means of happiness.

He was still pretending not to smile at Cottin's spluttering outrage when a large group went by. He discerned, by guesswork, that the imposing lady sweeping magnificently along at its head must be the rarely-present Lady Harriet Hoste. Her grooming and dress were impeccable but, by Polly's reckoning, a touch too youthful to befit the dignity of her mature years.

He knew, too, even more vaguely, the three grown children accompanying her, two unmarried daughters and a younger son around Leopold's age; her eldest, Lieutenant Sir William, was serving aboard the *Southampton*. Leo knew that from Polly, and, from her animated reportage of the night before, could also make a guess at the strangers with the Hostes.

The tall one with the florid face approaching thirty must be Lady Harriet's nephew, Lord Walpole. Leo didn't take to him; there was something cruel in the set of his thin lips. To the disappointment of the matrons at the dancing party last night, he was recently married. In recompense he had presented two brothers, Henry and Frederick, both in their early twenties and not too young to begin to be hooked towards a wedding.

Two Walpole sisters, conveniently too young to be competition, were also tagging along with their Hoste cousins. The elder was pretending to a lofty composure while the younger was openly agog as Miss Hoste exclaimed, 'But, Priscilla, you can't be spoony over *Black Jack,* he's old enough to be our father!' in delightedly shocked tones.

Priscilla Hoste said something too low-voiced for Leo to hear, and the young women all giggled. Lady Harriet cast an impatiently disapproving look over them.

Leo tucked this very minor bit of gossip away to feed to Polly.

One of the younger Walpole brothers lagged behind his laughing sisters and cousins. He paused, glancing at the sign pointing the way to the daguerreotype studio as a prelude to a more lingering examination of Leo.

Leo never did know how to manage such open appraisal, not even in London when he'd been younger and slimmer and more inclined to wrestle the natural unruly wave of his pale yellow hair into fashionable curls, and of perennial interest to the sort of man who took an odd combination of wide-eyed naivety and abstracted aloofness as a thrown gauntlet. He stood by his sign, feeling foolish.

Much of his dismal failure with portraiture arose from the habit of not looking at people's faces, a defensive tactic to prevent unintentionally meeting the eyes of a ghost. It was a habit he was trying to break, now he was back in a place where he knew every ghost and their regimented paths and would hear of any event that created a new one well before he accidentally gave away that he could see it.

He therefore made himself look the young man over with a daguerreotypist's eye. He was well-dressed, a little dandified with frills on his shirt, tight buff trousers, and Albert boots. Dark hair, under a fashionable topper, fashionably oiled and parted and falling sleek to his shoulders. Face bare of the increasingly popular whiskers. Pale, the barest stain of colour on high cheekbones. Strong features, that would expose well – arched brows, thick lashes, straight nose, full lips, jutting chin, with a pronounced cleft.

And pale grey-blue eyes, now meeting Leo's in full knowledge that Leo had been engaging in open appraisal in return.

Leo dropped his gaze, but not before the Earl of Orford's middle son had smirked and tipped his hat.

He strolled off to catch up with his Walpole siblings and Hoste cousins, leaving Leo under the neutrally curious regard of Sally. With the mild feeling of having dodged the jaws of a trap, Leo dismissed her to attend the regimental band.

He retreated to safety in his studio, where his surroundings were tidy and neat and the interactions with a few early customers proceeded as per the usual formula.

Three

Leo's serenity did not survive.

Lady Jane Hildyard marched through his door. It was a heavy, iron-studded oaken monstrosity, which Leo left wedged open each morning so potential customers did not have to fight their way in. At times like this, he regretted it.

Ignoring a young husband and wife perusing the watercolours, Lady Jane declaimed with a dramatic flourish suited to the stage, 'The rapping, Mr Sweetwater!'

Another dismal result of spending years deliberately not making a study of people's faces was that Leo sometimes had to discern which lady of the Palace he might be expressing a polite greeting to by other cues. The more conventionally fashionable they were, the more he had to memorise voices, posture, way of moving, and, if fortunate, a distinguishing feature. Men were not an exception; rather, they could be even more difficult, especially as moustaches became more and more popular in the wake of the Napoleonic wars.

Some people, however, overcame this foible. Cole, obviously: Leo could have painted his portrait – those eyelashes, those cheekbones, that mouth – with his eyes closed. Miss Eliza Smart, for long, long acquaintance and a certain brusque flair. Lady Albinia Cumberland, and the Talbots, and, sadly, Colonel Cottin, thanks to Leo's youthful years of running errands for their households on the eastern attic storey. The newly-arrived Lady Henry Gordon, being short, plump, golden-haired, and dimpled, though her tinkling laugh was a happy additional clue.

And Lady Jane, marquess's daughter, fifty years old, tall and painfully thin, long-faced, beak-nosed, hair a faded auburn, eyes a watery blue, always slightly frazzled, a little more attuned to the presence of ghosts than she deserved to be, and, unfortunately, resident of an apartment overlooking Fountain Court.

'Good morning, Lady Jane,' Leo said.

She knocked her knuckles on the counter in time with her words. 'I. Hear. It. All. Night. Long.'

'Mrs Otter lives—' He'd started to say *even closer to them than you do*, which would have been dreadful. '—below you. Might I enquire if she hears it?'

'Mrs Otter is not sensitive to the aether as we suffer to be.' Lady Jane had her hands on her hips now, somewhat strengthening her resemblance to a stork. 'You *know* when Mr Hildyard and I had to lodge off the Haunted Gallery during our renovations, I had the most abominable time of it because my sensitivities could not abide Queen Catherine's spirit.'

It was actually Thomas Bradshaw, one of the Palace ghosts Leo had managed to avoid coming to the attention of. According to Polly, he'd received preferment by firstly, acting as pander between the Duke of Grafton and courtesan Nancy Parsons, and secondly, spying upon the duchess to obtain divorce-worthy evidence of *her* adultery, not difficult once she became pregnant by her lover. Bradshaw, having won by ducal favour a suite at the Palace of some twenty rooms, went on to claim an entire wing before shooting himself in 1774, supposedly over debt.

Thanks to this rapacious appetite, he could justly be said to haunt not just the Haunted Gallery, but the Berkeley Pagets' apartment, and the Countess of Cavan's, bothering precisely no-one except, apparently, Lady Jane, whose sensitivities would be greatly exercised to know the truth, given Bradshaw's unpleasant character.

The pair by the watercolours had turned to observe the exchange. They'd been browsing so long, they either wanted a depiction of Fountain Court, a fruitless quest here, or they'd been gathering the fortitude to ask about the ghost cards. Sally had been quietly insistent that a song and dance had to be made, and that included keeping the special prints as closely as if they had been of a less salubrious sort – not that *she'd* made that allusion, of course, but it certainly put Leo in mind of visiting Holywell St: not illegal, but with a definite whiff of it-should-be from more respectable people than him.

It was effective. The shyest customers would even bring up other small purchases as cover before they made some sort of oblique reference, often along the lines of feeling faint in the Haunted Gallery. Sally, the usual ruler of the counter, made hay.

Lady Jane had either no regard for an audience, or too much regard for it. 'And now we are home, and my visitant is ever so much more insistent, and the Lord Chamberlain claims it is not within the scope of his department to attend to the infernal knocking and rapping, and the Board of Works is simply *hopeless* about it.'

'I'm sorry to hear that.'

'I do not wish for your condolences,' she said fiercely. 'I wish you to tell it to stop.'

'I don't share your sensitivities, my lady,' Leo lied. For the benefit of the avidly eavesdropping couple, he added the line Sally had drummed into him, albeit in the very flat tones that left her in confusion as to how he'd ever worked in theatre in London (behind the scenes, of course, assisting Charles-Caïus Renoux paint dioramas). 'The camera's eye captures more than a mere mortal's eye.'

'That is nonsense, Mr Sweetwater, and we all know it.' Only now did she lower her voice, pointlessly. Her audience was on tenterhooks. 'It began since you came home. We were at peace, until you came home and *woke it up.*'

Leo pressed his lips together, smothering a familiar annoyance.

Newly resident back in '29, and far too much a fan of the old phant-asmagoria shows, Lady Jane had been a driving force behind the fuss made over the noises in Lady Emily Ponsonby's apartment after Sibell Penn's tomb was damaged or disturbed or desecrated at St Mary's, the parish church in Hampton. That was when the loyal but forgotten old nurse had gained her ghost story. It had spread like the blue cholera until everyone living in the southwest corner claimed to hear the soft and eerie sounds, the humming spinning-wheel, the muttering voice, the rhythmic tapping of treadle or feet.

Some began to say they had seen her, or felt her cold hands lovingly cupping their face. Polly did tend to make her own fun. To be fair, claiming to feel icy fingers on one's cheeks was an exaggeration: she could touch only Leo.

Lady Emily, and others, bolstered by Lady Jane, had approached – accosted – the then twenty-one-year-old Leo, haunted (indeed) since he was eight by the rumour that he could see ghosts.

If young Sally had schooled him in how best to sell a ghost story, Polly had taught him the opposite: that he was to never admit he could see ghosts, not to any person, and not, if he could at all help it, to any ghosts.

In this case, those were simple instructions. He could hear nothing of the noises, and he already knew by then that a ghost that old would not be able to speak, let alone cause other sounds without human help. It would be, rather, like the angry miasm in the erstwhile tiltyard, or like the tumult in the alley near his childhood home in East Molesey that had terrified him when he'd first gained this ability. Nothing of the like lingered in the Palace's southwest corner.

His mother had pushed him to claim he could sense Mrs Penn's spirit anyway. She begged him to do it. She instinctively grasped that the notoriety would bring income, desperately needed as age stole away her strength to haul sopping linens, her eyesight and dexterity to care for delicate lacework.

It was not the first time he failed her.

That had, arguably, been less than three months after his plunge into the cold, fast waters of the Thames, when the story of the way he'd been found on the riverbank – soaking wet, mostly drowned, and hysterically screaming – was still gaining flavour as it spread, when he'd still been flinching from cold spots and cowering from things glimpsed from the corners of his eyes.

Mr Willis died on a frosty February night in 1817.

Leo could feel the weight of him, up on the third storey. Mr Willis had been on the very cusp of journeying back to Senegambia as Governor. He'd died suddenly, task unmet. Of course he was a ghost now, permanently on the verge of departure. Leo felt the cold, heavy emanation every time he ran up the stone backstairs to tap on back doors to collect his errands and pennies. He held his breath, and wouldn't look, and wouldn't tap on that door.

Mrs Willis, in deepest black, had found him and pleaded for a final message, seizing his shoulders so hard that her nails felt like claws digging into shrinking flesh, breath hot and sweet in his face.

Leo's mother had squeezed his shoulders, too, when she'd urged him to give the widow the message she was begging for.

He'd known Mrs Willis all his life. She'd taken over her mother's warrant to the top-storey apartment, right by Lady Albinia's attic suite, part of Leo's errand fiefdom. She'd always been kind. Her husband was haunting her bedchamber.

With his mother in one ear, and Polly in the other, he wavered, then held firm and denied all. It wasn't entirely selfish. The only honest message he could relay was that Mr Willis was fretful that he'd miss his steamship.

So he'd lied, and Mrs Willis must have known it. She still hated him; so did Miss Willis, because Mrs Willis's subsequent poor nerves had trapped her into caring for her mother instead of marrying as her sister had done, as society demanded she do, and as she, according to Polly, deeply wished to do.

His mother had not hated him, had never hated him, but as on other occasions, her bitter disappointment had temporarily overwhelmed her love.

He thought she'd surrendered the idea, until the furore about the so-called Lady in Grey, when he once again refused, this time buttressed by truth. He could sense nothing, because there was nothing to sense.

Supposedly, there had been a secret room discovered, behind a wall. Supposedly, it had held an ancient spinning-wheel.

This dramatic find, or at least the exaggerated story of it, should have put paid, at last, to the notion that the Sweetwater boy could sense the spirit world beyond the veil. Somehow, it did not. Lady Jane's misplaced faith had been part of that. So, ironically, had the undying hatred of Mrs and Miss Willis, which Lady Jane used as evidence, accurately but mercilessly, as to what he could be capable of as a consultor of familiar spirits, if better attuned to the vibrations of the aether.

So Leo was now annoyed by Lady Jane's outlandish, and loud, claim that his return was the cause of the malignancy in Fountain Court.

And he was alarmed by it.

There had not been such a terrifying presence there, before he'd gone to London ten years ago. Lady Jane had not been complaining of incessant tapping back then, either. There'd been *something*, a cold spot, a haze that he'd dodged around, but he hadn't been reluctant to pass along its arcades and stairways. If he had, he'd not have been so capable in running errands for the apartments in the southeast corner.

And yet, when he'd returned to Hampton Court after eking out six years among the abundant ghosts in the capital, a violent attack of the nerves behind him and an exclusive daguerreotype licence firmly in hand, he had very shortly realised that he would never be able to sell images of Fountain Court's pleasingly symmetrical salmon-pink arches because he could not bring himself to set foot in there for so much as a single moment.

That...had not been a welcome realisation.

Neither was the realisation that Polly wouldn't, either, and would not talk about why.

Leo shook his head, resisting the urge to glance southwards. 'The Palace was opened freely to the public then, my lady. We had a substantial increase in footfall through the State Apartments. Its bones are old, they creak, and they creak more under pressure. You are sensitive to the shift of foundations and struts, that's all.'

'You sound like the Board of Works, and I expected better of you, Mr Sweetwater,' she said witheringly.

Despite having nothing whatsoever in common with Mrs Sweetwater in class, dress, accent, manner or life path, this was delivered in a tone so reminiscent of his mother that Leo was left speechless.

The couple gave up and wandered out, passing at the door a young man, who Leo almost immediately recognised as the Walpole brother who'd lingered to look at the sign, and at Leo.

Leo frowned at the new arrival – the son of an earl, a very promising customer indeed – in a way that would have made Sally despair of him.

Lady Jane followed his gaze. 'I suppose Lord Walpole is thinking of portraits while he visits his aunt. That would make a fine set for Lady Orford.' She turned and said imperiously, 'Mr Walpole, might I present Mr Sweetwater, our daguerreotypist, who is being *very stubborn* and a great disappointment.'

Since she was still parroting a remarkably maternal sentiment, Leo took a moment to find the wherewithal to offer a shallow bow. 'Mr Walpole. I trust the day finds you well.'

'Mr Sweetwater, a pleasure,' Henry Walpole drawled in crawling upper-class tones. He examined the daguerreotypes in their cases, arranged on shelves recessed fetchingly within the great Tudor fireplaces lining most of the walls. 'Quite the fascinating art.'

'I shall tell you what constitutes a fascinating art!' Lady Jane said. 'The *phantasmic pneuma*! Aristotle knew, Mr Sweetwater, he knew!'

Well. He supposed that sounded a good deal fancier than 'insensible perspiration' to describe the faint nimbus he seemed to emit, a sign of the physical or metaphysical damage caused by his two semi-deaths, that let him see the spirits, that let the spirits interact, even slightly, with the material world in his immediate vicinity. He preferred to balance the plain and the mystical and call it his 'subtle matter', if he had to call it anything.

Having received the blankest of Leo's repertoire of blank looks in response to her strident statement, Lady Jane huffily bid them good day and stalked out. Walpole pulled a mockingly bemused face in her wake and approached the counter. He picked up one of the small daguerreotype cases displayed there.

Leo relaxed: he could field questions about daguerreotypes half the day and barely had to watch his words at all.

Instead, setting it down again, Walpole commented, 'I do not believe we encountered one another at Lady Reynett's little gathering last night?'

Taken aback, Leo looked about – he was, for all his artistic pretensions, currently keeping shop – and replied, 'I am not often invited to frequent Banqueting House,' almost as a question. 'I was at whist,' he added, after a moment of silence.

'I'm more for all fours,' Walpole said, speaking idly but watching closely.

Leo had the sense, once again, of a trap closing. 'That's a gambler's game.' He forced himself to meet Walpole's pale eyes and speak clearly. 'I'm not much for gambling, Mr Walpole.'

Walpole made a thoughtful noise. His eyes sharpened. Horribly, he looked like an indolent young man who'd just accepted a wager with one of his chums.

However, showing more manners than Leo had braced for, he turned back to discussing Banqueting House. 'I'm sure Sir James must have had you in. He loves to show off the Verrios.'

Leo could discuss art for the other half of the day. 'He had a showing when he finished his renovations. They are *glorious*. It's a shame...'

Walpole had no qualms about completing Leo's censored thought. 'That Lady Reynett covers them with bookcases? The dear lady allowed Sir James to have them moved aside for the night. I must confess to be such a Philistine as to take her point. It is not a room to engender a restful state of mind.'

Leo could take her point, too, and Walpole's. The Painted Room was overwhelming, even for people who did not overwhelm as easily as he did. The Baroque murals were extravagant *trompe l'oeils*, expertly using shadow and gilt and perspective to create the illusion of ornately-framed paintings. The two towering scenes flanking the fireplace and the crowded array on the ceiling dominated the room, but no surface was left unadorned by garlanded smaller pieces, or by heavy mirrors that reflected the riot of lush colours.

What's more, they depicted risque tales of gods and maidens and nymphs from Ovid, which made for expanses of flesh, modesty barely preserved by convenient foliage or draping cloth. A standard Baroque motif, too rich for the growing conservatism of modern sensibilities.

'Couldn't look in any direction without an eyeful of nymph nipples,' Walpole breezily informed him. 'Not to mention one particular pair of cavorting cherubs. They looked for all the world as if they were engaging in the infamous crime.'

He leaned on the counter. Leo carefully shifted a neat stack of prints away from his elbow. 'Nothing of the sort caught my attention.'

Despite his general facility for lying, he made the error of delivering this falsehood with stiff and, judging from the curve of Walpole's lips, ill-advised propriety. *Of course* those cherubs had caught his attention. He didn't think there was a man of his persuasion who would not look twice at the depiction of a naked cherub on his hands and knees with his equally naked and cherubic friend straddling his hips with a hand in his curls, both of them smiling beatifically out at the viewer.

Undeterred, Walpole went on, 'The ceiling was my favourite, though, and, you know, I think Winter may have been my favourite figure up there.'

Decent only by dint of bent knee, the naked Winter was fuller in the body than Verrio's other men, with a head of cream-coloured tousles, round eyes too dark for his complexion, a longer than necessary nose, and a vacantly surprised expression, perhaps a result of finding himself tangled and tied by the star-spangled crimson ribbons garnishing bare calves and rounded stomach.

'I always think he looks a little gormless,' Leo said, still unwilling to play.

Walpole unfurled his full smile. 'Do you, Mr Winter?

'*Sweet*winter,' Leo corrected, before starting and almost yelping, 'Sweet*water*!'

Walpole laughed, almost to himself. It wasn't malicious, and Leo had to thaw in the face of it and his own folly. He ventured to say, only a touch pointedly, 'I'm fond of Notus, myself.'

The ceiling pageantry depicted, along with Minerva and the Arts and Sciences, all Four Seasons and their corresponding Four Winds. Winter had Boreas, naturally, the North Wind. Notus, attending Summer, was represented by a man darker than the rest, handsomely-proportioned form too hidden under a billowing red banner: a man who worked outside, and used his body well. He was not quite right. His loose hair was a nondescript brown, and long, and looked coarse, instead of a soft near-black, and his beard was scraggly instead of scrupulously trimmed short and well-kept. He looked rather too stern, too, though he had the right sort of eyebrows.

Lifting his own brows, Walpole asked, 'And who might Notus be, then?'

'The South Wind,' Leo said, knowing full well that was not the answer Walpole had asked for, and rather pettily pleased about it.

The temperature cooled, the briefest of harbingers before Polly emerged from the thick whitewashed wall in unseemly haste. She stopped short, diverted from her pressing errand.

'Who is this dandy pratt who bethinks himself Bryon, and why, under the heavens, are you smiling at him?' she demanded, aghast.

Leo was provoked into exclaiming, 'I'm not!' aloud, the sort of slip he wished was rarer, and really should be so by now.

Walpole tilted his head, amusement now tinged with puzzlement. Never mind – he'd be hearing about the oddities of Mr Sweetwater soon enough, if he hadn't been regaled with anecdotes last night.

'Pay attention, pet,' Polly said, rising to hover high in the centre of the showroom. 'Mr Berkeley Paget died last night. The household is in disarray. Leopold and Augustus are coming to you now. You know what they'll demand. You know what you must say.'

'Oh, no,' Leo said, only barely resisting the urge to drop his face into his hands.

'What is it, old chap?' Walpole asked with indulgent familiarity.

Then the Paget cousins burst in, wreathed in grief and urgent purpose.

FOUR

Without a polite word to Leo or acknowledging glance at Walpole, the taller of the cousins – Augustus, then – slapped a loose page onto the counter. It was the diagram of the telegraph machine alphabet board he'd drawn the night before.

He dropped five toothpicks atop. 'Mr Sweetwater, my cousin needs to speak to his father.'

Leopold stood silently by Augustus's side, boyish face drawn and grey with shock. His eyes were red-rimmed. Both young men were otherwise composed and properly dressed, Leopold sporting deep mourning. School beat the tears out of boys of their class, if their fathers hadn't already done it. Not to say Leo's own family had been better, in that regard.

'Master Leopold, I am very sorry for your loss, but—'

'No,' Augustus said. 'I saw it.' He lowered his voice. 'I saw the toothpick move last night.'

'The room was draughty, sir.'

'Everyone knows you see ghosts,' Augustus said, sounding throttled, probably because he was now experiencing the stirrings of thwarted rage amid the welter of other emotions.

It was only going to get worse. 'I *am* sorry, I truly am. He was a good man.'

Floating above him, where he would not be tempted to look at her, Polly scoffed. Mr Berkeley Paget had, in fact, married an heiress, spent very many years enjoying other women, and only settled into responsible political and domestic life as his, once her, funds ran low. This did not, however, make for an unusual marriage among the gentry, as Leo was doomed to discover thanks to Polly's eternal interest in goings-on, and he had not treated his wife poorly, within that narrow context. Indeed, Leopold's very existence, coming so very many years after Matilda's, spoke of reconciliation, and they had seemed on good terms with each other and doting of the young man now trembling at the counter.

'I have to say goodbye.' Leopold clenched his hands together, trying to hide their tremor. 'Please. Auggie said you'd help. Please.'

Walpole, who was the son of an earl and could jolly well have spoken man-to-man to the grandsons of one, propped an elbow on the counter and looked fascinated.

'You *can* say goodbye,' Leo said, as gently as he could. 'That is what the funeral rites are for.'

Leopold's face crumpled before he controlled himself. 'I need to know he heard me.'

Death was women's business. The ladies and maids of the Paget household would be busy with those rituals, washing and laying out the body and all the rest of it. The funeral was the men's business, so Leopold's older brothers would have their tasks, too, seeing to the death certificate or writing to their two married sisters; Frederick had probably already taken the carriage to London, grief subsumed into action, and Catesby might be over at St Mary's.

But Leopold would have no particular purpose except to grapple with mourning. Leo well-remembered the speed with which he became superfluous upon his mother's death, as the sickbed nurse, his mother's friends and his grandfather had taken over the practicalities, efficient in the face of the rampaging outbreak of a heretofore unknown disease.

He'd been left at a loss, holding a complicated grief he did not know what to do with, and he'd been five years older than Leopold, prepared for the death, if not prepared for how quickly the new, brutal illness had progressed, *and* he'd had time for a final exchange of words.

He hesitated.

'Don't do it, Percy,' Polly said from above. 'You'll be hounded for the rest of your life.'

Leo knew as well as she did that rumours were manageable as long as they were never proved true. He took a deep breath.

'Sirs,' he said. 'If I give you an answer, you know – you *both* know – what you will be hearing. You said as much last night, and Mackay laid it out. Ghosts are only hoaxes or superstitious misunderstandings: the story about me is the latter, and if I give you a message from your father, I will be perpetrating the former.'

Augustus leaned in. 'I saw the toothpick move, Sweetwater.'

He was trying to loom over Leo. He was tall enough, but also only nineteen. Despite holding a great deal more power than Leo, he remained unaccustomed, for now, to commanding obedience beyond his household's servants.

Leo held firm. 'You saw a draught.'

Augustus slapped the counter in disgust, but before he could say more, Matilda arrived. She, too, was already dressed for mourning, the severe colour and her grief washing the usual vivacity from her face. Though composed, she was flushed, with embarrassment or impropriety.

She and Walpole steadfastly pretended the other was not there. Walpole dropped his pose of languid and amused curiosity and walked over to look into the portrait studio where the camera apparatus aimed its eye at the sitter's chair, back carefully turned to the uncomfortable scene.

'Leopold, Augustus, home, now.' Matilda's voice was a restrained, courtly murmur, but strangled as if she'd wanted to snarl. 'Mr Sweetwater. I apologise for the intrusion. My brother and cousin are somewhat overwrought.'

'Miss Paget, my deepest condolences,' Leo said with a formal bow and the feeling he was botching the formulas. 'Please don't – the boys have been no bother.'

He earned a filthy look from Augustus. He could only hope it was for the crime of labelling him a boy like his cousin rather than the stubborn refusal to admit to ghosts. But perhaps the Pagets would join the Willises in hating him, depending on how closely the grieving Mrs Paget heeded the distress of her precious youngest.

Matilda shooed Augustus out, catching her arm through Leopold's to draw him to her side in sisterly comfort, tone now coaxing as she led him in their cousin's wake. However, on the threshold, she turned back. Her expression suddenly matched Leopold's, bewildered, a child who'd remembered her father was dead, her world changed forever.

'Don't,' Polly said. 'It's not safe.'

Leo had surrendered to a petitioner only three times in the years since he'd begun to see ghosts.

The first was Sir Horace. Leo had been perhaps sixteen, and engrossed in reading a Scott tale in Chapel Court, when he'd felt a large, firm hand clamp tight onto the back of his neck.

By then, he'd learned not to react to apparitions, and the practice spilt over to other surprises. He'd stayed stock-still until his captor leaned in and he realised he was pinioned by the dashing hero of Waterloo.

So close Leo felt the rasp of stubble against his cheek, Sir Horace growled one word. 'Well?'

Leo had known the first Lady Seymour was ill, and he recognised the thickness in Sir Horace's gruff voice. He didn't even think to dissemble. 'She's gone.'

He was guessing – a long, slow illness, with time to settle affairs, he didn't think she would have lingered – but had been too frightened, in the moment, to say otherwise.

Sir Horace let him go and marched away, leaving Leo to shakily rub at his nape and confront an unsettling facet of his own nature.

The second was purely mercenary. Mrs Grundy had recently accepted the new position of Housekeeper, less exalted than the Lady Housekeeper of previous decades, but respectable and well-paid, if at times beleaguered. When he'd been looking about for lodging, she'd offered up the caretaking for Lady Athlone's rundown apartment, if he would provide assurance that her own southwest apartment, specifically the nursery, was not haunted by Sibell or anyone else. Given her deserved reputation for discretion, he did so.

The third was back in May, the only occasion where he'd acted out of finer feeling instead of base instinct. Sally had not so much as given him a significant look, but she'd been achingly stiff and controlled after the Fitzhenrys finished burying their father, barely three months after their mother.

He'd said, 'Miss Fitzhenry, they're at peace,' and she set down her work and marched into the derelict back area of the Tudor kitchens, returning an hour later with a tear-stained face and grand plans.

Matilda was not truly of Leo's acquaintance; her family had come to the Palace only a year or two before Leo went to London, her elder sisters already married, her brothers at school or in service, and she herself serving the new queen by the time he returned. He barely knew her.

Still, she looked at Leo with grief stark behind the bones of her face.

Polly floated downwards, the better to dissuade him from doing something foolish, but he'd already come out from behind the counter.

'You poltroon!' she cried. The temperature plummeted as she made her displeasure known. 'You muttonheaded calf lolly!'

He looked outside, the sun shining bright over the flagstones even as his breath plumed. Augustus, waiting sulkily nearby, tucked his hands under his armpits. The entire alleyway was rimed with ice, though only to Leo's eyes.

Leo ignored it. 'I know it was unexpected, but was it very sudden?'

'Yes,' Leopold said, voice thick.

Matilda said, gently, 'He had been ill.'

Leo flicked a look at Polly. 'A fie upon thee, addle-pate,' she said sullenly. 'I shan't help thy folly.'

'Did he have...' Leo did not know how to phrase it. 'A great work left undone?'

'He had a place on the Excise Board,' Leopold announced.

'I shouldn't think so,' Matilda said. 'He had retired from political life.'

'For one whose affections lie with other men, you are a wretched soft touch for a woman,' Polly fumed.

Leo waited.

Still mutinous, she said, 'He did not linger.'

He nodded. 'Your father is at peace.'

'Thank you, Mr Sweetwater,' Matilda said, all in a rush.

She took her charges away, down the narrow way towards Chapel Court. Leo did not have time to bask in the glow of a good deed, for, turning back, he immediately encountered the ravenous gaze of Henry Walpole. His cheeks were flushed rosy like a boy playing in the snow.

Any hope that he would remain polite enough to have magically not heard were dashed. 'Good God, man! What was all that ballyhoo?'

'Might I say I told you so now?' Polly said.

Leo studiously ignored them both as he carefully folded away Augustus's makeshift alphabet board, but they persisted.

Walpole asked, 'You were dismayed even *before* they arrived. How did you know they were coming?'

Polly stamped an ineffectually gossamer foot. 'Why wilst thou never *listen?*'

'Bit of a rummy old cove, aren't you?'

Luckily, a customer wanting to sit for a daguerreotype came in then, and Leo could busy himself with avoiding answers to either of them.

FIVE

HE TROUBLE WITH BEING AGGRESSIVELY FLIRTED at by a young man of terrifyingly forward manner yet pleasingly Byronic countenance – and, for that matter, of being winked at and softly handled by one's unrequited love – was that it shone a light strong enough to capture the sharpest of daguerreotypes: a portrait of the loneliness suffered by a reserved and cautious man.

Leo persevered through several routine but busy days, before deciding on an excursion to Hampton Wick on Wednesday evening, the end of Allhallowtide.

He went openly enough, along the new riverside Barge Walk, a trifle muddy after a spell of rain, nodding in polite greeting to other evening perambulators. He had a pot at the White Horse while the sun set, before slipping out and through the backstreets to the Bushey and Wick.

The landlord, a stony-faced man of large beard and middle years, was said to be a good friend of a local magistrate, or a *particular* friend of a local magistrate; either way, he minded his own business, took their coins with neither qualm nor distaste, settled disputes with stoic even-handedness, and seemed confident in the matter of raids.

The evening was not quite satisfactory. In the physical sense, Leo did well enough, a few more mugs of beer in the warmth engendered by a roaring fire and the rare and welcome company of like-minded men, before a circumspect retreat to one of the private backrooms in the company of *a* like-minded man.

But their relations were hurried, with no allowance for Leo's true preferences – a bed, and time, and naked bodies entwined, hearts beating together and mouths engaged, nothing he'd had since London, with Jack, and nothing he dared ask for here – and probably not the other man's true preferences, either. But he'd still accompanied Leo even after he'd made it clear buggery would not be afoot. It was loosened trousers, and hands, and even a little kissing.

He had a pleasant enough interlude, and at least the physical need was sated.

When he emerged, late into the night and somewhat foxed, he could smell rain on the air. It was a new moon, but the twinkling stars sailed clear of banking cloud. He thus elected to take Cobbler's Walk, the footway through the Harewarren and Bushey Park, until he intersected with the avenue of horse chestnuts, set over a century and half previously, during Mary and William's aborted attempt to have Wren pave over the Tudor palace with Versailles-like grandeur.

It was dark under the branches of the hoary chestnuts, but they took him near-due south for the Palace, the grey trunks as good as any wayfarer stone to bring him home.

The still night was full of the soft rustle of the last of the autumn leaves, but nothing more sinister. Sometimes he encountered a forlorn presence weaving disconsolately down the avenue, especially during the spring when the nightingales sang. It was *love*lorn, Polly said, so no wonder he drew it to him. Leo did not consider himself lovelorn. He wasn't pining after Cole; pining would imply hope was enclosed behind his firmly shut door barricaded by all those metaphorical padlocks.

Still, it made him grateful for his own disposition, not much given to either ill-temper or melancholy, which temperaments might have attracted the more threatening of the Palace ghosts.

Though what it said about him that the ghost he *did* attract was an inveterate gossipmonger with a lackadaisical attitude to the truth, he did not know.

With Sergeant Hamilton in mind, Leo might have assumed the lovelorn ghost was King William III, ever fond of his lost Mary, receiving the mortal strike when his horse stumbled during a stag-hunt in the royal chase one hundred and forty years previously. However, Polly said it was one Mr Fitzwilliam, Page of Honour, victim of another fall during another stag-hunt, thirty years and several monarchs later. His neck had snapped on the instant, leaving his burning love for someone – Princess Amelia, Polly thought – forever undeclared.

Since Polly knew intimate details of the early Hanoverian Mr Fitzwilliam, yet very little about the shadowy Tudor in the kitchen gardens, except to suggest that he must have been treacherously murdered in the tilts to be that bloody angry about it centuries later, Leo took this as support for his theory that she'd died under the intervening Stuarts, though even he, with only a lacklustre village schooling, knew the era encompassed more than a century, from King James through to Queen Anne, with that awfully tempting civil war in the middle.

Despite the vigour of her impartial hatred of both Cavalier and Roundhead, it felt ghoulish to speculate she'd been caught up in something as era-defining as the Great Rebellion, instead of accepting it had probably been as simple as the accident that did for Fitzwilliam, and Polly, ancient by ghost standards, had let it slip away.

Meandering through these ale-hazed thoughts, but walking a straight road from trunk to trunk, Leo reached the Great Basin, with the magnificent Diana fountain at its centre (Polly said she was Arethusa), surrounded by her cupids and nymphs. Cromwell had originally set the statue, commandeered from some other, lesser, palace, in the Privy Garden for his own edification. Mrs Grundy would have had conniptions about the bared breasts.

He circled the dark pool, and went on to the Lion Gates with their ridiculously overblown piers. Here, he paused.

The chestnut avenue made for a shorter way home than the curving Barge Walk, but it brought him in on the north side, uncomfortably close to the kitchen gardens, once the tiltyard. He cast about for the glimmering presence of an inchoate Tudor spirit, and sensed nothing.

Still, rather than take Old Moat Lane, the straight, open path that ran right by the kitchen gardens and past Wilderness House, he slipped into the Wilderness itself.

The Wilderness…was not. With its tall hornbeam hedges, it was almost a larger iteration of the Maze, very formal and geometrical, but with far fewer places to get lost. The alleys between the hedges, four sides of a diamond, were laid with raked gravel. Beyond the hedges loomed ancient cypresses and elms in regulated formations. Cole called it a *bosquet,* which a straight-faced Polly translated as bosket, and said he'd see better at Versailles.

There was some relief from the straitlaced, hedged-in lanes (this was, Polly said, so courtiers of the Merry Monarch's decadent court could whisk their paramours out of sight), and Leo turned onto one of these paths to cut through the parterre, a mirrored pattern of subtle curves and circles and semi-circles forming paths that sliced the Wilderness into discrete, and discreet, sections.

The stars had finally been swallowed by cloud, eerily lit southwards by faint reflections from the Palace gas lamps. The sky directly overhead was a gulf of black, and it was beginning to sprinkle. It was near-impossible to lose one's way in the Wilderness, however, and Leo, crunching over gravel and trailing a hand along hornbeam walls, easily reached the southern circle. At its heart was an equally circular garden bed containing a single clipped evergreen, its branches angled downwards as the weight of fresh rain added to the droplets from the earlier showers, the dark green leaves glossy and near-black against the all-encompassing background hornbeam. Here, he'd veer onto another subtly curving path, back to the wide, main, diagonal alley, to pop out by the Tudor tennis court and the final traverse to his apartment door.

Directly beyond the gravel circle was a diversion, a short path to a private *cabinet de verdure*, or garden room, a cloverleaf-shaped space trimmed into the surrounding hedges. In the dark, the only sound the faint drip of moisture, Leo thought he discerned movement down there.

Leo was not precisely afraid of ghosts, not even after what had happened in London. However, he did like that he knew where each of the Palace ghosts tended to be. Polly roamed, yes, but he mostly knew where she was at this hour. The two suicides in Mrs Cuthbert's attic suite stayed there, more or less (Lord Graves more, Mr Tickell less). Mr Willis did not venture far from his wife's apartment, Mr Bradshaw's range was only the northeast first storey, and Sergeant Hamilton patrolled the south side of Base Court. Any other ghosts that might still linger within the walls were old and faint, and did not wish to move.

Outside, the workman was contained along the southern facade, the angry Tudor in the northern grounds, a small cluster of the drowned on the riverbank behind Banqueting House, and Mr Fitzwilliam in the parkland beyond the boundary.

Then there was the effluvium in Fountain Court, but Leo didn't like to think about that.

A pale, quick, shape flitted across his vision, almost glowing in the pitch-dark of the night.

Heart thudding, Leo contained his flinch and stood firm, eyes fixed on the pale grey of the gravel.

If a ghost didn't know he could see it, it wouldn't direct its limited attention his way. If it didn't direct its attention his way, it wouldn't sense the faint nimbus of energy, the subtle matter, he emitted. And if it didn't sense his subtle matter – *electromagnetism* skipped nonsensically through his head – it wouldn't try to take it.

At the edges of his furiously fixated vision, the flash of white blinked across the mouth of the alleyway again. Leo heard a faint snuffling. He had time to think *Jowler,* even though he hadn't believed the ghost story about King James's favourite dog even as a child, and then a great white shape raced down the short passage and flung itself straight at him.

Leo shouted and stumbled backwards, arms thrown up to protect his face.

He shortly found himself sitting in a hole, in the mud, in the rain, in a pickle, and in a pile of wet fur.

'Max!' he complained to the last of these problems.

The dog squirmed over his lap and butted a big nose into his cheek, trapping him even more comprehensively than the root he'd managed to wedge his ankle under, and soaking him to boot. He felt his heart rate settle, his body give an all-over shiver, as relief set in.

Max was a large Italian sheepdog, with deep brown eyes and abundant cream-yellow fur. Cole's brother, Sir Walter Minto Townsend Farquhar, second Baronet of Mauritius, was formerly junior attache to the Vienna embassy, and during his Continental travels became enamoured with the breed, reserved, intelligent and independent, ideally suited to the patient, lonely work of guarding lambs against wolves.

The puppy he'd brought home as a wedding gift to his new wife seven years before had grown into a gentle, loyal, giant dog utterly unsuited to a London townhouse, not least because his instincts were to bark at any threat, and any threat proved to be any noise, and London was a noise factory.

Thus had Max come to Wilderness House a short time after Cole had taken the Royal Gardener position.

Leo wasn't entirely sure why the dog was patrolling the Wilderness tonight. He tried to push him aside while wriggling his ankle free, to little success on either front. The light drizzle was thickening into real rain, while the chill of the mud under his arse was beginning to seep through his coat and into his trousers. He'd trapped himself under the

evergreen at the centre of the gravel circle, which might have offered
shelter, except its branches were now shedding water that runnelled in
startling trickles over his hat brim and beneath his coat collar.

Leo gave up and let a happily panting Max remain on his knees. The
top layer of his fur was soggy, but so would Leo be soon, and their under-
sides were already equally muddy. Absently patting the dog, he concentrated on levering his ankle out from under the root, wincing as it gave a
throb of anticipatory pain. He'd managed to twist it as he fell, he
supposed, and it was going to be a misery to hobble the rest of the way
home, once, or if, he managed to free himself.

Max licked his face, and Leo scruffed the thick fur of his neck. 'At least
you're warm, Mr Fluffy Face.' Sodden, but warm.

'How insulted—'

Leo jolted; he hadn't heard Cole coming up behind him under the
steady beat of the rain, nor noticed the glow of his horn-paned lantern
through the thickly wet air.

'—should I be that you like my dog more than me?' Cole set the
lantern on the gravel and stood at Leo's shoulder, looking down at the
puddle of man and dog with a slight smile, barely visible in the dim light.
'*Bonsoir, mon ami.*'

'So aloof, so independent,' Leo mocked, since this was how Cole had
proudly described the breed to him, before actually meeting Max and
discovering he was nothing of the sort. 'I think you should be insulted *he*
likes *me* more than you.'

'Perhaps you just have a lickable face,' Cole said, eyes glinting.

And there went any relief Leo had obtained from his visit to the
Bushey and Wick.

Cole nudged Max's shoulder with a jerk of his head; the dog adoringly
obeyed, abandoning Leo to sit attentively beyond the cast of the
lantern's light, looking out for wolves for his flock.

'Why are you sitting in a hole in the Wilderness?'

'Why are you *digging* holes in the Wilderness?' Leo countered.

'We're not, it's some blasted gowky tomfoolery.' Heedless of the
muddy ground, Cole knelt in the garden bed and peered closer. 'Fair
jammed your boot in there, didn't you?'

He took off his Macintosh and spread the cold, stiff coat over Leo's
shoulders before Leo could protest the chivalry, then lay on his front and
reached both hands down. For a man of his gentlemanly position, he
never did mind getting his hands deep into soil.

'I'll hoist and you pull free; if it doesn't work, you'll have to wait for me to fetch a shovel, and that's no good in this weather.'

The plan was effected successfully, Leo slithering in an undignified fashion out of the mantrap while Cole held the ensnaring root at bay. Leo rubbed at his ankle, unwilling to rise.

'Come on,' Cole said briskly. 'We're both getting wetter by the minute, Leo.'

Leo felt the small thrill he always did when Cole used his name, the vowels liquid in his musical lilt. Meanwhile, Cole tugged him without ceremony to his feet and wrapped the big waterproof coat as a cloak over both of their backs and necks. When Leo wobbled on his twinging ankle, he interposed an arm around his shoulders, tucking them close together under the scant protection.

The warmth of the contact, blazing against the damp chill, lit up Leo's body, from thigh to hip to ribs to shoulder. He stiffened and tried to pull away.

Cole snugged him in even closer, and stooped to retrieve the lantern. 'If you need help walking, you need help walking, don't be English about it.'

'Excuse me, you're also English,' Leo said, endeavouring to not sound like he was in both utter agony and utter bliss. He'd long since managed to subsume his desire for Cole behind his heavily padlocked mental door, but being pressed tight enough to his lean solidity that he could feel the flex of his thigh was quite the challenge. 'You're supposed to be as uncomfortable about this as I am.'

'Excuse *you*, I'm Scottish. And French-ish. The French don't have these strange notions about men touching each other. Men kiss on the Continent, *mon ami*, and I merely wish to lend a helping hand to my good friend who smells like wet dog.'

Leo perforce ignored this. 'Your grandfather served as personal physician to Prinny.'

'Ay, an he wis Scottish while he did thon.'

'Your father was the Member for Hythe.' Leo was still beer-foggy enough to add, 'That is an English town,' as if Cole would not have known that.

'An yet, astonishingly, still a proud Scotchman.'

They traversed the paths amid the teasing, Cole taking Leo's weight without trouble. As they emerged out of the Wilderness, Cole turned them both so he could address Max, who had been at their heels, and was now sitting on the edge of the gravel, watching them alertly. He'd somehow transformed from a giant cuddly ball of chaos into remarkably wolf-like, with some sea bear thrown in.

'Coming along, laddie?' Cole asked him. 'Or still on the job?'

In answer, Max rose, shook himself vigorously enough that Leo felt fresh splatters on his already soaked trouser legs, and disappeared into the darkness of the hedged alleyway.

'See?' Cole raised the hand holding the lantern as if to salute the vanished dog, and the arm slung over Leo's shoulders tightened. 'Aloof. Independent. Not to say there'll be much on the go with the rain in. Awfie dreich auld night.'

'What's the, ah, gowky tomfoolery?' Leo asked, as they resumed their slow progress past the Royal Tennis Courts towards Leo's apartment.

Cole heaved a long-suffering sigh. 'Treasure hunters. Mr Jesse is having fits.'

'Treasure hunters?' Leo echoed. He didn't know his history as well as he should, for someone residing where he did, with a personal tutor in his ear, but he knew there couldn't be loose treasure lying about.

'Cardinal Wolsey's plate.'

'A plate?' Leo said, in what he now considered justifiable confusion. 'Solid gold?'

'Gold and silver plates, bowls, platters, ewers, cups, cutlery, candle-sticks. Worth a quarter of a million ducats back then, a fair bob now. The whole lot, claimed for the Crown.'

Ah. Wolsey's attempt to appease Henry VIII. 'Along with the Palace…'

''Twas but a gift, Mr Sweetwater,' Cole said loftily. 'To, ah, what was it? Oh, yes. "To show how noble a palace a subject may offer to his sovereign".' He offered a courtly half-bow to empty air, drawing Leo with him. 'Silver-tongued, old Wolsey. Didna save him.'

'Someone thinks his plate is buried in the Wilderness? Well, the Royal Orchard, then, wasn't it?'

'You've been paying attention to my rambling,' Cole said warmly, giving him another squeeze around the shoulders. 'Not all the plate, it'd've been too heavy, but there's a story that a servant filled a trunk with as much as he could carry and fled northwards, realised it was *more* than he could carry, and buried it under an apple tree. None of it's true. They took inventory.'

'Even if it were,' Leo said, 'however would a modern treasure-hunter locate it under all the hornbeam? They can only dig up the paths and garden rooms. They must be quite desperate.'

'Exactly, which explains why you're falling in holes on your way home.' Cole bumped Leo's hip with his. 'Least ye didna run intae a man wi a stolen shovel an daftie ideas o whit tae dae wi it.'

'That would have been alarming,' Leo agreed.

Cole grinned at his steadfast refusal to engage. 'Mr Jesse asked me – asked is a strong word, you know how he is – to keep an eye out. I'll head back with my own shovel, save others a tumble.'

'I imagine others will avoid the pitfall a little more readily than my clumsy self.'

They'd navigated all the way to Leo's door now. Leo proved his point by fumbling to let them in.

'Jist gie it a wee shoogle, loon,' Cole advised.

Leo started laughing, mostly from the sheer jitters of having his oblivious friend heavily leaning into him while he had his egregious fun. The Macintosh slipped from his shoulders. Cole let him go to rescue the coat, and he shivered.

Holding the coat folded over his hands, Cole said quietly, 'I don't understand why you'd walk all the way to Kingston to drink alone, and won't cross the bridge to have a pot with me at the Bell.'

Leo stopped with his hand on the latch, trapped by the subtle note of injury in Cole's soft lilt. He could hardly explain that East Molesey was so small that everyone knew about Margaret Sweetwater's boy, and that was all well and good so long as he kept his business to himself, but Mr Pitcher at the Bell Inn was as civic-minded a landlord as an upstanding citizen could ask for and a partaker in unnatural vice could hope to avoid.

That it was far better that Cole bruise his feelings because his friend wouldn't take a drink with him in public than bruise his reputation because of assumptions about the so-called adhesiveness of the friendship, spread by Pitcher and his cronies on the Local Board if he witnessed them drinking together.

Not to say the population of the Palace, half again the size of East Molesey's, wouldn't speculate about the bachelorhood of the Sweetwater boy, but they hadn't had his grandfather openly denouncing him. Besides, he found both the gentry and their servants mostly unconcerned about discreet bedroom activity, likely because the one class was too busy engaging in more forms of vice than he could dream of and the other was too busy cleaning up after it. Discussion of whether or not his friendship with Cole was a particular one was more a prurient middling concern, if not one that would cross Mrs Grundy's upright mind. Ironically, Leo and Eliza Smart were near enough the only other middling grace-and-favour residents. Even jolly, earthy Mr Talbot was now, belatedly, an Honourable since his widowed mother was created Baroness Talbot of Malahide in the Irish peerage.

Still, Leo kept discretion as his watchword, even with the convenience of an *entire* barracks of Hussars who filled their uniforms remarkably well. That was why, when London friends (Jack) promised to visit, and didn't, he'd been both genuinely hurt, and guiltily relieved.

'Hampton Wick,' he said, laggardly. 'The White Horse.'

He stopped there; Polly, in gifting him her aptitude for lying, had advised that volunteering too many unasked-for details was a technique for amateurs. Instead, he clarified, slowly, 'I don't cross the bridge to Kingston, either. I don't like to cross bridges.'

'Ta, dinna gie me thon buljik, you said you traipsed back and forth across Hampton Court Bridge so often, the tollman gave you a daily rate.'

'Since London.' Leo finished.

He'd been arrested on New London Bridge, for disorderly conduct rather than any more salubrious charge. After a long night locked up in the Borough Compter, huddled into a ball and shivering uncontrollably, the Southwark justice had taken one look at him – a newspaper reported him as appearing pale-faced (fair) and half-starved (gross libel) – and dismissed the charge with a severe lecture on temperance.

He left London within days, having used his connection with Daguerre, the inventor, whom he'd worked for at Regent Park's Diorama, to obtain a daguerreotype licence from Beard, the patent-holder. Beard had been clear, however: if he ever again stood before a magistrate, his licence would be rescinded.

The story preceded him home, thanks ever so much to the newspapers and their interest in the brand-new daguerreotypes, and to the widows and spinsters of the Palace with so very little else to occupy their time except to pore over the driest of reporting. In case the tale grew in the telling until no one would cross his threshold, he'd told Eliza, with overt instructions to spread it, that the disturbance on the bridge had been a belated attack of the nerves brought on by falling off Hampton Court Bridge all those years before.

In a way, it had been. He shuddered.

'Sorry, mait, forgot,' Cole said easily. 'Get the door open, let's warm ye up.'

Leo shoved the door and they stumbled in together, and across the small hall into what Leo supposed Lady Athlone would once have called her drawing room, but which he called the parlour. The apartment at least had a rudimentary lavatory at the very rear, but no kitchen. Leo quite liked that, as it meant the rooms weren't dominated by stale cooking smells, but rectifying the lack would be a focus of the eventual renovations. He kept a filled kettle and a tea caddy by the hearth – to Sally's mild disapproval, but he was never going to roust her late to send her off to make tea in the shared kitchens.

Cole tried to tip him into an armchair by the fire before he baulked. 'I'll stain it, and it's not my furniture.' He looked at the rug with some guilt; they'd both tracked in mud.

'That explains why you possess the aesthetics of an eighteenth-century Dutch countess,' Cole said, looking about. 'I have wondered.'

'Lady Athlone's heirs haven't dealt with her effects yet.'

Admittedly, they'd been busy dying of things like water on the brain and apoplexy. Once the current earl, her grandson, finally turned his attention to it, and Mr Jesse finally finished overseeing the major renovations to the Palace, he, the Lord Chamberlain, the Superintendent, and the Board of Works would come to the long-awaited refit, and the Athlone warrant would be rescinded at last.

Setting the lantern down, Cole turned the Macintosh clean-side out, and had Leo sit on it. He turned up the lamp and poked up the banked fire.

'Cold in here,' he remarked as he hung the brimming kettle on the hook over the low flames.

On cue, Polly floated through the front wall. Leo had promised her a few chapters of Bulwer-Lytton's latest, *Zanoni*, to appease her displeasure regarding the cheek of making alternative evening plans.

'Why are you covered in mud?' she demanded. 'Both of you. My word, you'd think it was the Restoration.'

'I don't really notice the cold,' Leo mumbled.

'Must be why you're not shivering,' Cole said, brows hoisted at his most sardonic angle; slow tremors were rolling through Leo. 'Shall I help you upstairs to your blankets?'

Polly pantomimed wide eyes at Leo. 'You harlot, did you manage to seduce the gardener?'

'No,' Leo said, severe tone perfectly suited to both questions. He squirmed out of his wet coat, and sat in his shirtsleeves, no warmer.

'So aloof, so independent,' Cole teased, taking the coat to hang over the hearth screen with his own, and their sodden hats. The smell of wet wool competed with that of burning coal. 'That'll need a good brush. Boots, now, and roll up your cuff.'

'They say James liked Buckingham's calves, too,' Polly contributed.

'To look at my sore ankle?' Leo said, gritting his teeth while Polly smiled at him: she loved this game. 'No, it will be fine with rest.'

It was throbbing worse now he'd sat, in the manner of these things, but he thought it was merely wrenched, not sprained.

Without fuss, Cole propped Leo's foot onto a cushioned footstool. Eyeing it, he said, 'I can send over a poultice tomorrow morning, at least. Mrs Clarke will have a good recipe.'

'*I* have a good recipe,' Polly said, abruptly abandoning the false coquetry for a dose of possessiveness. 'Flowre of Oyntments, passed down by my mother in her receipt book. I don't hold with any modern patent nonsense.'

'I can ask my own housekeeper for a poultice,' Leo said.

Cole, in the middle of tea-making, made a face. '*J'aime aider mes amis, pourquoi ne me laissez-vous pas faire?*'

'He says stop complaining and take the help.'

Leo ducked his head to stop himself from outright glaring at apparently empty air.

Teapot brewing, Cole refilled the kettle from the ewer and put it back over the fire. 'Let me at least settle ye wi a wee dram tae warm ye up afore ye toss me oot intae the rain, laddie.'

Finally surrendering to Cole's sly sense of humour, and with the sinking feeling he might be using it to hide genuine hurt, Leo said, 'Will ye stop, laddie?'

'A canna richtly ken,' Cole pronounced, flashing his mischievous grin, which broadened as Leo dissolved into a relieved smile of his own.

The rain was very heavy now, the drumming on the flagstones of the alley outside loud enough to penetrate the thick walls. 'It's soaking out there,' Polly confirmed, as disgruntled as if the wet affected her.

Leo supposed it did: she was here to read with him because there was likely not another thing of interest happening anywhere in the Palace, thanks to the quelling effect of a cold, rainy night.

'I suppose *I* am being tossed out into the rain? Your oldest friend, abandoned for a pretty face.'

'I'm not going to throw you out into the rain,' Leo said.

He did feel guilty for leaving her alone for a selfish evening on his own, but that was an echo of his bigger guilt. He'd gone to London with barely a thought for the woman who had been by his side since he was eight, surrogate aunt turning to surrogate sister over the years, and returned to find her wasting into a shade (yes, quite) of herself.

He hadn't known, until then, how much his company, and perhaps his subtle matter, was keeping her vital.

Cole picked up the ceramic bottle by the teacups and sloshed its contents in evaluation. 'You've not touched this since I was last visiting.'

Since Leo kept painfully-taxed malt whisky on hand solely for Cole's occasional visits, he did not find this news surprising. 'I don't often drink alone.'

'But you were drinking alone toni— Ah. Not drinking alone.'

Cole would assume he'd been with a woman. The worst thing he could do was let himself seem flustered by something so entirely unre-markable. 'Don't worry, I wasn't seeing other friends behind your back.'

Cole laughed quietly, and Leo relaxed. His friend doled generous dollops of whisky into the teacups before handing Leo's over and perching on the edge of the other armchair. Only his front was muddy, so he wasn't endangering the upholstery.

'I've always supposed you and Miss Smart had an arrangement,' he said casually.

Leo almost spluttered. 'Miss Smart would be offended!'

'I mean no judgement,' Cole hastened to assure him. 'People might do as they like with their own bodies, to my mind. No harm in it so long as everyone's enjoying themselves.'

Strange how quickly that liberal attitude vanished when the bodies were of the wrong sex, Leo thought cynically, but explained, 'We both have particular tastes, and hers do not condescend to tolerating a wet blanket like me.'

'Don't denigrate yourself, Leo.' Cole's brown eyes were lighter than Leo's, a warm terracotta that now regarded him with great sincerity. 'You're a quiet man, there's nothing wrong with that.'

Leo took a hasty sip, swallowing the hot liquid in an ill-advised gulp.

Polly said, 'Maybe you *should* try to seduce the gardener.'

Leo muttered, 'Stop it,' into his cup.

Satisfied, she floated out, though the room became only slightly warmer; Leo wouldn't have been surprised if she were lingering close by to eavesdrop in lieu of any other entertainment. He didn't mind. Hers must be a long and lonely existence, and he and Cole would discuss nothing untoward.

In fact, he and Cole had settled into a comfortable silence, though Leo supposed Cole didn't find it as comfortable as he did, and he should say something before Cole caught him staring at his perfect lips and finally realised how unsalvageably weird his friend was.

He cleared his throat. 'I had a letter from Goodman. He's the man licensed for daguerreotype in Australia. He was talking about how to make best use of the light, once he's settled in Sydney.'

'Don't imagine he'll have a problem with enough light, in Australia.'

Cole spoke with some authority. His older half-brother, also a Walter, like Sir Walter, and also a natural son, like Cole, had emigrated, long enough ago that Australia had still been New Holland on some maps, and was a regular, if not frequent, correspondent.

'They must have grey skies *sometimes*,' Leo said. 'He said he'll make his studio from blue glass. It does something to the light to make the exposure time less.'

'It mimics daylight,' Cole suggested.

Leo would have to take that on faith. He did not have Cole's head for theory, he'd just memorised the practice and experimented with the variables. 'So even on a cloudy day, the sitter hardly has to hold still for longer than ten seconds.'

'You're thinking of using blue glass?'

'My current set-up is not ideal,' Leo admitted. He felt disloyal. Sally would be asleep in the little box of a servants' quarters on the second storey, the apartment's top floor. She couldn't overhear, but he still lowered his voice. 'Other daguerreotypists have studios with roofs entirely of glass, to maximise the light. If blue glass can help me approximate that...'

'I don't think Mr Jesse will let you replace the glass in your windows. He's quite strict about period details.'

Which was to say, there had been arguments about how the private gardens were being kept during Cole's tenure as Royal Gardener, verses how they had once been kept as part of the now-public grounds several hundred years ago.

'I was wondering about a tinted film or screen, to put in front of the existing glass, easily removed later.'

Cole thought it over, sipping, then said, 'I'll write to Paxton. He's doing innovative work with glass houses, he'll have some ideas.'

Farmer's son Joseph Paxton, coming up under the patronage of the Duke of Devonshire at Chatsworth, and Cole, apprenticing under the Aiton brothers at Kew Gardens, had bonded as two modern young men in the sea of greybeards at the Horticultural Society. They'd been on good terms since they'd met as teens, around the time young Percy Sweetwater was falling off a bridge.

Leo made a non-committal noise, which apparently sounded too ambivalent to be mistaken for the appropriate amount of gratitude.

'Are you jealous?' Cole asked. Before Leo could become too aghast at his own transparency, he went on, 'I'm also allowed to have other friends, *mon très cher ami.*'

Leo smiled, again mostly from relief, and partly because he was quietly pleased to have Cole pick up his light jest and toss it back to him. 'English, Scots, and French. Do you speak Malay as well?'

'*Bahasa Melayu*,' Cole said. 'No. My ayah was Malay, but she'd have been forbidden to speak anything but English with me. She did use to whisper Malayan fairy tales to me when I couldn't sleep, though I don't remember any of the words. She died when I was five, after we'd been in England a few years. We all caught the measles, and her case was severe. Shortly after that, we gained Mamam and a French nanny. *Nounou.*'

'I'm sorry,' Leo said, appalled at bringing up a subject that made Cole's perennial smile fade. He should have known his Malay heritage would be deemed valueless, his only contact with his mother's people relegated to servants.

Cole tilted his head, acknowledging the sympathy without entirely accepting it. 'My name comes from her, though. From Ayah Farquhar, I mean. She called me *Solong*. Something like that, anyway. I don't know what it means.'

He took a long swallow of his tea, then looked over at Leo and said, 'I think she was my mother.'

Leo could tell from his gravity that he didn't mean, *I thought of her as my mother*. 'That's why your father gave you her name, like Walt is Walter Farquhar Fullerton?'

'It wasn't her family name, I don't think, just something my father heard her call me.'

'You don't...' Leo faltered. 'You don't think? You don't know her name?'

'Of course I do,' Cole said, with a tip of his cup and a twist of his lips that was not a smile. 'It was Ayah Farquhar.'

'God, sorry, that's deplorable.'

'I don't see why.' Cole stared up at the ceiling. The rain was quieter now. 'Sir Robert might easily have discharged her the moment we reached London, or even stranded her on the docks. He's positively a saint to keep his mistress around to raise his bastards for him.'

He twitched and smiled as if to apologise for the bitter undercurrent infecting the sarcasm. In brisker tones, he said, 'There's probably nothing to it. She was employed to act like our mother, it's not remarkable my memories of her as a little boy try to put her in that role. Lots of English children over in India probably make that mistake, until someone sets them straight.'

'But not so many of them, ah...'

Cole waved a hand at his face. 'Look like their ayahs, right.'

Leo set down his cup and scooted forwards in his seat, but didn't quite dare lay a comforting hand on his arm. 'You never asked Sir Robert about it?'

'I didn't really start wondering until it was too late,' Cole said. 'His health was failing by then, and he was embroiled in arguments over whether he did a good enough job in Penang and Mauritius, I didn't want to add to his troubles by hashing up ancient history.'

'It wasn't ancient history to you,' Leo said heatedly.

'It is now. He died before I got the guts to ask. I'm certainly not going to bother Mamam over whether her first husband ever mentioned tupping the ayah, and Sir Walter wasn't even born when she died.'

'What about Walt? He's, what, three years older than you? He might remember more.'

'Maybe. If the man would answer a letter in any timely fashion.' He squeezed Leo's half-offered hand. 'There's an Ayahs' Home, that's where I hired Mrs Clarke. She was Ayah Clarke, of course, and won't hear of being called anything else. But the Home's more concerned with abandoned girls, not one who was treated quite decently, all things considered.'

Leo finished the last of his laced tea in a gulp at the unthinking sop thrown to a family that damn well deserved a slap. *All things considered,* what rot. Even if the woman who'd cared for Cole for five years hadn't been his mother, she'd deserved more than silence upon her death, and the fact that he'd been left wondering either way was a damnable indictment on Sir Robert.

'You could...' He hesitated, then, encouraged by Cole's interested expression, continued, 'visit the lascars next time you're in London? I lived by Shadwell, I'm sure there were sailors from Malaya among the Indians. I suppose you already thought of that.'

'I hadn't, actually. That's a good idea.'

'They could at least tell you what *solong* means.'

'And if it means "my darling son", mystery solved.' The refilled kettle had begun to steam, and Cole hooked it off. 'There you are, hot water for washing the mud off.'

'Thanks, Mam.' Cole grinned so Leo added, 'More tea?'

'I best get back now the rain's eased off, see if Max has bailed up our treasure-hunting trespasser.'

'And licked him into submission.'

'Ay, the old boy has a bark on him, but not much bite,' Cole said agreeably. He laid his hand over Leo's propped ankle, sending a shiver up his spine. 'I can't take you up those stairs before I go?'

If only he would. 'I'll manage, you fusspot.'

'My aloof and independent laddie.' Cole smiled down at him, and Leo thought, *Wants an awful lot of pats and strokes all over, any time of the day.*

'Thanks for listening,' Cole went on blithely. 'I didn't mean to turn mawkish on you.'

'Any time. Let me know how you get on.' Leo started to lever upwards.

'Dinna fesh yersel, A'll lat masel oot.' Looking highly pleased with himself to have left Leo both smiling and comfortable in his chair, he singsonged, 'Goodnight, Sweetwater,' from the doorway.

'Goodnight, Solong,' Leo said, and it didn't sound wistful at all.

SIX

The ghost of Sergeant Hamilton was beginning to wander.

Leo stepped out, gingerly, early on Friday morning and was immediately snared by the light of a day dawning shiveringly clear. He should have continued on to his studio, to collect plates and apparatus and foray outside for daguerreotyping. Instead, he went back inside for his watercolour box.

He was complacent, and too entranced with watching the colours change in Clock Court in the brightening silver-edged light. He didn't notice the pacing figure in the shadows of Anne Boleyn's Gateway until he was far too close to about-turn and go around the other way. Only his long-standing habit of not looking directly at people's faces saved him from making eye contact with the ghost. As it was, his step hitched, making his healing ankle give a throb of warning.

As far as Leo knew, Hamilton and another sergeant had pursued Private Rickey from the barrack yard, in through the Great Gateway, across Base Court, and through the archway at the southeast corner. Yet here he was, marching back and forth across Leo's path, spine straight and shoulders squared. The light cavalry had worn blue coats at Waterloo, and wore blue coats again now, but Hamilton had died during the decade they wore red, and the scarlet made a violent splash of colour inside the grey stone gateway.

'He ought not have those pistols,' he muttered. 'Curse it, Chittleburgh, there are ladies down there and he's waving pistols about, the drunken fool.'

It would be like London, Leo told himself, forcing himself to walk on. He'd managed constrained ways, like the bridges, until he hadn't, and he'd managed them by militantly refusing to react to the ghosts as he passed within handspan of them.

Suicides or accidents weren't the main problem on bridges. People did not always die the moment they hit the water, especially when the river was high, the distance to fall less. They drowned instead. Their ghosts, over time, tended to drift along the current and cluster where the bodies did, some way downstream, as he'd discovered firsthand as a child.

No, the problem, at least in London, was the murdered.

Not to say that murder was quite as common as the penny dreadfuls would have their readers believe, but the city had had its dangers and its vices for eighteen hundred years. Layers accreted.

He could bypass the worst of the alleyways and slums. But the more lateral-thinking of the nefarious came to realise that hauling a cold body riverside was a mug's game when one could march a warm body to a disposal point and slit its throat right there. Even with little more than a century's worth of true ghosts to contend with, it made the bridges a gruesome kind of obstacle course for a man with Leo's perception.

He'd picked his crossings carefully. He didn't mind Southwark Bridge; it was the least trafficked, because it had a toll, and London and Blackfriars Bridges did not. But New London Bridge had only opened a few years before, which made it relatively clean of ghosts, and entirely free of the cold spots that had once been ghosts. In a way, those were the worst, because until he learned where they were, he was constantly ambushed by them. London had been dreadful for it.

Leo hadn't known, yet, that all the drowned from further upstream washed up under London Bridge.

'Steady, lad, steady,' Hamilton said soothingly, adding, over his shoulder, 'Go back, Chitty, I know his temper, he'll come along quiet as a lamb for me.'

Gaze straight ahead, Leo passed into the gateway, tracking the trajectory of Hamilton's pacing from the corner of his eye. He could neither allow himself to brush against the spectral soldier, or swerve too violently to avoid doing so; either action would catch the ghost's attention, perhaps for long enough that he'd recognise something different about Leo, something as warm and enticing as blood to Bryon's, or perhaps Polidori's, vampyre.

He and Hamilton were going to collide, ghostly shoulder into solid shoulder. Hamilton would pass through Leo, like he would any living person, but not before he encountered a slight, telltale, resistance, the nimbus of Leo's subtle matter making itself known for the briefest of moments.

Leo stumbled as if his weakened ankle had panged, so that the strap of the bulky box-easel slipped from his shoulder. He paused to recover it, head down, then walked on, slipping successfully behind Hamilton.

He was safely past.

'Rickey, stop!' Hamilton bellowed at a sergeant's battlefield volume.

Through years of practice, Leo managed to not whip about or even check in his stride, but he couldn't help a flinch.

Behind him came silence, and then, 'Can you hear me?'

He shut his eyes briefly, not altering his gait or direction.

'Sir, can you hear me?'

The early morning chill gained an extra bite. Leo's breath puffed white in front of him. He maintained his slow pace, skin at his nape crawling. *Steady, lad, steady.*

'Please, sir?' It was a broken whisper.

Hamilton wasn't following, though. Leo effected his escape across Base Court and reached the Pond Garden, where he set down the easel and put his head in his hands, which were shaking.

His capacity to quell most of his reactions until afterwards had indubitably saved him on London Bridge. Today, the mild aftershock of fear was made worse by guilt.

Hamilton was next, he told himself. First was the workman.

Killed by a falling wall during Wren's renovations, the workman had gradually drifted westwards over the one-hundred-and-fifty-odd years since his death, from the corner of the Baroque half and into the Tudor half of the Palace's south frontage.

This meant that when Leo set up to paint a view of the Pond Garden, he had echoic muttering at his left shoulder.

'Harrison last year,' the workman murmured. 'Maggie got forty shillings. Look at the cracking, Patty. We'll be next. Think they'll be paying forty shillings for us?'

They *had* been next, the workman and his friend, or possibly brother. A dozen men had been injured, but only those two had died, and only the nameless workman had had an urgent final concern, worry for his fellow labourers.

Putting aside Polly (and the cluster of drowning victims haunting the riverbank by Banqueting House), the workman was the first Palace ghost young Percy Sweetwater had met, and promptly given himself away to via the medium of abject terror. With hindsight, this muttering man so concerned for his mates was not at all threatening, which was why Leo felt comfortable with a gloomy spectral presence looming very closely behind him as he took off his coat and clipped back his shirtsleeves.

He also felt comfortable talking to the gloomy spectral presence; he was so early that not even Cole's under-gardeners were about. 'Good morning, sir.'

'It's getting worse.' The ghost poked a finger into empty air. 'My finger goes in up to the knuckle, Patty.'

The adolescent Leo, coming to terms with certain aspects of himself, had been rather immature about the workman's obsession with inserting fingers into cracks. It lost its amusement value when he'd grown old enough to recognise the pathos of a century and a half spent fretting over one's duty in an ever tighter loop.

'It's all crackt,' the workman said mournfully. 'We should tell someone.'

'There's twenty-four piers,' Leo recited. The enquiry had been held in the Oaken Room. Polly had eavesdropped. The piers, as far as he could work out, were the columns of brickwork between the windows along Wren's facade. 'And only four cracks.'

'Every pier is crackt,' the workman insisted, on cue.

'The cracks are stopt up,' Leo said, 'and crampt with iron. Everyone is safe now.'

'A whole finger.' A fretful whisper. ''Tis hollow inside the crack, Patty.'

'No more walls will fall, sir. Everyone is safe.'

'Harrison last year,' the ghost said.

Leo unfolded his easel. It was a new type, ideal for painting *en plein air*. The box atop the telescoping legs opened to reveal an array of pigment cakes, a small glass bottle of water and pipettes, and various brushes and sponges. The lid opened at a tilt, to act as the support, and Leo had already clipped wove paper there, stretched onto a panel. He dampened greys and blues and greens on the palette and set to work trying to capture the light with successive washes and wipes of paint, wet-on-wet.

The Pond Garden…was not. It had indeed previously featured ponds, to supply fish to the Tudor Court, and then had held glass-cases, for Queen Mary II's exotics. It was now a series of sunken enclosures, this section in particular making a pretty container for a vista down to Banqueting House. More importantly, its regimented dark lines stood in stark contrast to the light, so clear and still it was like a pane of purest ice over the scene, ready to shiver away at the slightest touch.

With most of his focus sublimed, Leo kept only a sliver of attention on the conversation, if it could even be called such. He and the workman would run through the recitation several more times, Leo reassuring the workman each time in varying ways around a singular story: most of the injured had survived, Patty had gone to his eternal rest, burial funded from royal coffers, and no more walls had collapsed at the Palace.

Eventually, he hoped, the fading ghost would follow Patty onwards. Leo just had to shepherd him there.

He'd been very reluctant, after Polly's dire warnings had proved true in London, to involve himself with any more of the Palace ghosts.

But Mr Willis still haunted his wife and daughter's apartment, and they hated Leo, and he could not, after losing his mother, blame them for that. He had been eight when Mrs Willis had accosted him; he was a grown man now, and she had been kind to him, before he'd let her down, and deserved better.

Polly was eventually persuaded into an advisory role. She'd decided he should practise first, not least because approaching Mr Willis was going to be difficult when he was behind an apartment door.

She vetoed Leo revealing himself to any of the three suicides, and obviously the tumultuous remnant in the kitchen gardens could not be approached. Fitzwilliam, though merely forlorn instead of angry, was far enough away from sustained living company to be almost amorphous already, as were the handful of ghosts on the riverbank. She was cautious about Hamilton, who seemed benign but who had been murdered, however inadvertently, and was fresh and strong.

They did not discuss Fountain Court.

Polly had actually judged the workman almost as far gone as Fitzwilliam. They'd begun instead with the chorister at the head of Tennis Court Lane. He'd been a very young man, similarly killed during the Wren renovations, this time by a runaway cart as he hurried to choir practice. His had been a simple case. Over the course of about six months, Leo had persuaded him down the lane, a little further each time, until at last he brought him within earshot (however that worked for a ghost) of the chapel.

The chorister, running late on the day of his death, was deeply concerned that the choir would sound incomplete without his tenor and rare ability to reach countertenor. When he heard the voices raised in evensong, not a note out of place, he had frozen, face lifted to the sky, smiled, and faded without ceremony into nothingness.

This had rather given Leo a false sense of his own efficacy.

He'd been talking to the workman, once a week or so, for eighteen months, and had not loosened the ghost's grip on his deathbed. If anything, the workman was ever more intent on the cracks.

'Patty sleeps etern'l.' This was rather papist phrasing, but he thought the pair had been, mostly because the workman sounded Irish, much like Sally did when she wasn't concentrating. 'He's safe. You can rest, too.'

He shut his mouth, then, because he'd been painting long enough that residents were about their morning walks. He could see Lady Albinia Cumberland slowly making her way around the edge of the sunken parterre, in company with a small, trim woman he didn't think he knew. Lady Albinia, though she got about the Palace mostly in the Push these days, had taken her morning constitutional in the southern gardens every morning for as long as Leo could remember, a cane her only concession to bad knees.

Leo quite liked Lady Albinia. He knew where he stood with her: right at the bottom of the grace-and-favour social ladder. He didn't know where she herself stood in the formal peerage rankings, though Cole, with his memory for minutia, or Polly, with her penchant for people, could have told him. He did know that the scions of dukes and marquesses must outrank the daughter of a mere earl, but Lady Albinia had been Lady of the Bedchamber to princesses and Maid of Honour to a queen, and, more importantly, had lived in the Palace since 1794, making her the senior-most resident by a margin that would be very wide indeed if only Colonel Cottin would resign his warrant like a proper gentleman and sod off to Primrose Hill.

For nearly five decades and more than half her life, then, Lady Albinia had rung the changes as successive waves of residents transformed the Palace population from the widows of upper society to the current crop of mostly military-adjacent awardees. She'd been one of the ladies who sat with Lady Mornington in Purr Corner, the nickname for the sunny nook along the eastern front where they'd liked to gather for gossip.

The nickname had been bestowed by Lady Mornington's son, the
– *the* – Duke of Wellington, so it was not going to fade, not even more
than a decade after her passing.

All this was to say that Lady Albinia was indifferent to the fleeting
politics of the other residents. Lady George Seymour might have taken
against the Pagets, thus effectively dividing the Palace into two loose
camps, but Lady Albinia cared not a whit for any of it. Not only had she
outlasted bigger battleships than Lady George, she *was* a bigger battle-
ship than Lady George, scant five foot of height notwithstanding.

Leo therefore found her quite restful.

She greeted him imperiously, just as the workman suddenly said,
loudly and clearly, 'I can fit a whole fist in the crack now, Percy.'

He whipped about. 'What did you say?'

'It's getting worse,' the ghost said serenely. 'It's all crackt. You should
tell Mary Lee.'

'One would hardly think a man of your age needed a hearing trumpet,
if a woman of my age does not,' Lady Albinia declaimed, patting at her
hair under her bonnet. 'I am *trying* to bring you to the notice of Lady Sale.'

Leo, still discombobulated, offered a confused bow which earned a
snort and an 'Awkward creature,' from Lady Albinia.

True, and it was even worse when he finally placed Lady Sale's name:
the wife of General Sale, she'd only recently been freed from nine
months as one of the hostages of Wazir Akbar Khan after the British
retreat from Cabul and subsequent massacre. She'd dug a musket ball
from her own arm, nursed her son-in-law as he died, and, given the
sudden announcement of a new grandchild in the newspapers, steered
her widowed daughter through childbirth in captivity. That was not to
mention the forced marches to every corner of Affghanistan, earth-
quakes, freezing conditions, and fevers, all of which seemed par for the
course for an army wife.

'Since the Boyles have decamped to Devon' – Lady Albinia looked
pleased by the military allusion – 'Lady Sale is borrowing their
apartment to have peace and quiet from a house full of grandchildren
while she prepares her diary for publication. She is your upstairs
neighbour for the interim. Lady Sale, I present our daguerreotypist, Mr
Sweetwater.' She sniffed disdainfully. 'Newfangled nonsense, if you ask
me, but you may wish to partake.'

Lady Sale, a plain and practical-looking woman, as one might expect,
and quite wiry and tanned for a lady, murmured a quiet greeting.

Leo was thrown by the social exigencies. Did he ignore her travail, much as she seemed inclined to, or acknowledge her courage during it? Did he take the cue from Lady Albinia's mention of the diaries and admit he'd read every scrap in the newspaper? He'd been as engrossed as Polly; the two of them were certain to be among the first readers when the full, edited, version was published.

He was saved from having to choose between condolences for the trying times or congratulations for the impressively stiff upper lip by the arrival of Lady Jane in a state.

She greeted the other women in a most perfunctory manner before turning to Leo and launching into full declamation. '*Two* sullen shades, half-seen, advance!'

'Pardon?' Leo said.

'On me, a blasting look they cast—'

'Why are you assaulting Mr Sweetwater with a ridiculous Gothic poem from before either of you were born?' Lady Albinia wore her severest mien.

'Because it's not a singular presence in Fountain Court,' Lady Jane declared triumphantly. 'There's two, I can sense them.'

'Harrison last year,' mumbled the ghost. 'You'll be next.'

Leo twitched.

'I knew it!' Lady Jane cried. 'Two men, rapping, rapping, rapping. Who are they, Mr Sweetwater? I demand you tell me this instant.'

Lady Albinia folded her hands together under the drape of her shawl. 'Two workmen were killed here last century, were they not? Perhaps you hear *them* tap, tap, tapping on the walls as they eternally labour on the Fountain Court facade for Wren.'

She offered Leo the tiniest of smiles as Lady Jane drew herself up into dramatic outrage. 'My sensitivities are not subject to being accosted by common labourers, Lady Albinia.' She set her hands on her hips, at her most stork-like. 'I believe they are Cavaliers.'

'*I* believe you need a cup of tea and a sit-down, Lady Jane,' Lady Albinia announced. 'Let us leave young Percy to his business.'

And with that, she swept the other two ladies away, brooking no argument whatsoever.

Leo wished he had the knack.

$\mathcal{S}$EVEN

$\mathcal{L}$EO SAT IN THE SUNSHINE IN Chapel Court, where he'd once read books aloud to a ghost.

He still did. He spent many evenings reading to Polly, sitting close by the fire to counteract the insidious creep of her chill. While they were currently on a tear with Bulwer-Lytton's works, they'd lately read Catherine Crowe's *The Adventures of Susan Hopley; or, Circumstantial Evidence* and Sara Coleridge's *Phantasmion,* and Charles Dickens's *Oliver Twist,* though Polly had strongly taken against the lattermost upon the revelation of Nancy's fate and was refusing his more recent works.

They read older books, too, like Horace Walpole's *The Castle of Otranto,* that Polly had only had in disconnected patches before, reading over shoulders or haunting parlours where families took chapters in turn on cold, dull evenings.

But back when he'd first reconciled himself to his new ability, and Polly had finally managed to make a friend of a child hovering somewhere between skittish and terrified, he'd had nowhere private to read to her, so he'd come here, to Chapel Court. It had become, more than any other location on the grounds, his own place.

In the days before the Palace was officially opened to the public, it had been a quiet, neglected, sprawling complex, gradually mouldering towards ruin. No monarch since George II a full century before had resided there; George III had instigated the grace-and-favour accommodation grants. The most passing of visits from luminaries such as the King of Prussia were cause for great excitement. The Lady Housekeeper and her maids accepted gratuities to show visitors around the State Apartments, but otherwise the residents were left to gently decline – as were the gardens. The Great Vine, the Pond Garden, the Privy Garden, the Great Fountain Garden, the Wilderness, the Maze, the acres of kitchen gardens, all were under the care of one head gardener and an inadequate staff, and were consequently maintained just enough to attract the mild disdain of residents and tourists alike.

Chapel Court's garden beds, once a Tudor knot, were overgrown and ignored enough for young Leo to feel safe to rest there, between delivering packages of clean laundry for his mother and running errands up and down the staircases and passageways, to read to his new dead friend.

Chapel Court contained no other ghosts. Mr Bradshaw, he knew now, might have overlooked him from the west or north, but did not. The concept of looking out a window did not seem to occur to ghosts.

Polly had played a long game. He could barely read, then, and his earnings went to his mother regardless, so his first faltering attempts used moralistic, simplistic texts borrowed from the parish church school, magazines like *The Youth's Instructor and Guardian*. She must have hated them, but she hovered beside him, patiently helping him sound out words and work out meanings.

He remembered being confused, even offended. Polly could read, even when she complained about the spelling, but she sounded just like him and his mother, and local women of their class couldn't read. It had taken years to understand that Londoners, even wealthy and well-educated ones, had simply sounded more rural in her day. Her day had been a very long time before.

Some of the residents began to notice the boy in the garden, diligently persevering through some very long words. Perhaps if he had not recently almost drowned, he would have been shooed away, but he was already a decided object of interest, and what appeared an enterprising endeavour to improve himself was greeted with approval and patronage. Three countesses – Mornington, Erne and Athlone – of the northeast corner engaged in a minor competition as to which of them could provide him with the most improving works. One of them even ordered the bench he was currently sitting on, where once he'd sit cross-legged on the ground.

He remembered the feeling of weighty tomes on his lap, the slow care with which he turned each heavy, creamy page so he wouldn't accidentally tear an edge. He became a fluent, thoughtful reader, or seemed it. He overheard talk of a scholarship, but, since he could not reproduce his apparent feat of precociousness without Polly in his ear, neither his schoolmaster nor his mother would support it.

At last, Polly's patience with the dreary material was rewarded. Mrs Talbot, less lofty in her tastes, lent him Edgeworth and Scott, and even the *Ladies Monthly Magazine*, apparently on the notion that articles safe for women to read were safe for children. The Sheridans, newly arrived and with children only a few years older than him, began to loan books of greater interest, too. He devoured both *Robinson Crusoe* and *The Family Robinson Crusoe* with its dramatic frontispiece, the family clutching each other and the mast as the storm wrecked their ship, and *German Popular Stories*.

Miss Smart, then an elegant, intimidating young woman who had recently moved into her apartment from the decrepit Toye Inn, began passing him Bryon's works. He'd had the Assyrian one drummed into him in the schoolroom, of course, but she slipped him the rest, and her issues of the new *Ackerman's Repository*, full of not only needlework patterns and fashion plates but short stories and poems, some of which, he knew now, she'd written. Polly unreasonably adored the ghost tales.

The '20s were also the time of the great Regency courtesan memoirs, but the adolescent Leo refused to even turn the pages of those for Polly. He did not want to read or hear about Colonel Cottin's exploits with Mrs Julia Johnstone, even long after she'd thrown him over.

Mrs Cottin came to paint in Chapel Court. Leo learnt his watercolour techniques from her, when she'd taken pity on the strange Sweetwater lad who watched her work so avidly. She'd seemed sad and washed-out, even to the naive boy he'd been, but she was a fine watercolourist; her paintings glowed with feeling. He liked to think his younger self was a pleasant distraction in those days, when all her children except Miss Cottin had married and gone away and Colonel Cottin was making a spectacle of himself, trailing Mrs Johnstone's skirts across London in a futile bid to win her back.

Leo had been in Chapel Court when Sir Horace's wife had died, and Sir Horace had come to put that big hand around his nape and growl, '*Well?*'.

He'd retreated there, instinctively, after his mother had died, and sat shivering on the old bench, asea. He'd felt bereft when Mrs Cottin had died a few years before, but that had been a simple grief for a woman who'd been grandmotherly towards him.

This feeling was far more complex. He could not put words, only shame, to something that felt like relief.

Sir Horace had noticed him then, too, and his distress. He'd put a firm hand on his back and said, 'Come along, Sweetwater,' but Miss Smart had happened by and briskly summoned him away, either ruining a lovely, comforting afternoon, or rescuing him. He'd never entirely been sure which, not even once he'd seen how vulnerable Sally's grief made her: he'd been older, and willing enough.

It was Eliza who had taken him to London to introduce him around, now he had no more family who cared to know him in East Molesey. For, she said, he would never be free of the stories that trailed him within this smallest of worlds, and he was like her, and needed to find his people, as she had done, not spend the rest of his life socialising solely with elderly widows.

Polly had hated her for that, for giving Leo a reason to leave and an argument she could not counter, except to harp on the dangers of it so vehemently that he had ended up assuming she was lying. She had refused to speak to him in the days before he left, and refused, for three days, to speak to him when he returned.

That had been fine. That had been good. He had not come home in a state of mind amenable to ghosts.

Polly hadn't been lying.

She hadn't been sulking, either. It had taken those three days before his presence had drawn her back from her alarming attenuation.

Chapel Court had been his place before he left. Upon return, he held the warrant for the Countess of Athlone's old apartment, perpetually due renovation, and a tiny corner of the disused Tudor kitchens for his prints and daguerreotypes. Even so, the bench in Chapel Court remained his refuge, and he retreated there in the middle of each day to sit in the sun with his hat on his lap and his gloves peeled off.

He understood then, finally, why Polly curled up about familiar, safe stories, a century of them and more. He had only a fraction of her years and it was still enough to cradle him. He'd learned to read here, he'd learned to paint here, he'd made friends here. He came here to soak in every drop of warmth that he could, because he still felt the glacial cold that had invaded his core on his last good day in London.

He'd been sitting in the sunlight with his eyes closed and his face uptilted towards the warmth like a sunflower when he'd first heard the melodious voice of the new Royal Gardener.

His eyes had snapped open, and he'd looked Mr Colley Farquhar Solong full in the face, and if he'd turned out to be a ghost, Leo wouldn't have cared one whit.

Somehow, that first meeting – Cole apologising for disturbing the gentleman, but his men were here to rehabilitate the garden beds, they would try not to bother him – had turned into meeting there every Friday for a picnic.

And here came Cole now, carrying a basket and a book, accompanied by his warm smile and a large dog at his heels.

While the State Apartments closed on Fridays, the gardens never did, and Cole's under-gardeners earned tips for showing off the Great Vine. Cole took over the supervisory role on Fridays from his foreman, in acknowledgement that he was not often about on the weekends. Indeed, though he habitually dressed much like his men, flat cap and jacket, he was more formally dressed now, and very well-scrubbed. He'd be onwards to London, then, with the outflow of tourists.

Max broke from his heel to gallop towards Leo, before stopping abruptly and sitting. He advanced a foot, a dainty tap of one great fluffy paw. Leo waited. Max advanced the other paw.

As per the rules of the game they'd played since Max had arrived at Hampton Court Palace as a half-grown pup, Leo issued the invitation: he patted his knee. Max gambolled to him.

'Hello, Maximilian,' Leo crooned, rubbing him behind the ears. 'Good afternoon, Mr Fluffy Face.'

Cole set down his encumbrances and spread wide his arms. 'Wounded to the quick,' he announced. 'An *iota* of the same enthusiasm, please.'

Leo obligingly said, 'Good afternoon, Mr Fluffy Face,' and congratulated himself on exactly matching it to the way he'd spoken to the dog.

'Better,' Cole said, though Leo noted with amusement that he rubbed his fingers across his impeccably trimmed beard as he took his seat.

Leo's hand twitched in sympathy. He clenched it in his lap. Not even Cole's French sensibilities would countenance Leo running a hand over his cheek, not even accompanied by a tease about fluffiness.

As Max flopped to lie across Leo's feet and lay his head on Cole's boot, Cole waved to Leo's paraphernalia propped at the end of the bench. 'Painting this morning? Can I see?'

'The light was wonderful.' Leo turned the painted panel to display his attempt. 'I was trying to capture its clarity. A little bit like Claude's work, where the sunlight is part of the landscape, it makes it very gentle and mellow.' He glanced up to see Cole gazing at him with the slightest of smiles. 'Sorry, you don't need me going on about the light.'

'I don't see why not, you listen to me bang on about the weather often enough.'

'Still too warm for your bulbs?'

'Too warm. It'll be late tulips this year, if we get them at all.'

Leo considered asking Polly to linger over the trays of bulbs to properly chill them, a technique he now knew was called forcing, and laughed at the image this conjured, a gigantic irritated chicken squatting over dry brown eggs.

Cole tilted the panel, focus absolute. 'Lovely work.'

'I'm no Turner, I know.'

'I'm no Capability Brown, but that doesn't mean I'm Bloody Stupid Johnson.'

'I'm sensing controversy at the Horticultural Society.'

Cole grinned. 'You don't have to be Turner, I mean. Turner's Turner. Sweetwater's Sweetwater. You know Mamam loves your art, too. She doesn't have a Turner on her walls, but she's got Sweetwaters.'

The former Lady Farquhar, now Mrs Maria Hamilton, was intensely charming, energetic and voluble, and her visits were always whirlwinds. She dragged Captain Hamilton, a bluffly genial soldier-turned-writer, and another Scotsman (her sons joked she was personally maintaining the Auld Alliance), from canvas to canvas in Leo's studio, exclaiming rapturously in an endearing mix of French and Scots. Leo, thoroughly overwhelmed, preferred to assume she was being polite in a disconcertingly extroverted way, the works she purchased gifted elsewhere.

He retrieved the watercolour, trying not to blush too obviously, and set it aside in favour of Cole's new book. It was one of Gould's monographs, this one about macropods – kangaroos. Leo paged through, examining the illustrations, in colour but uniformly brown-toned. Some of the smaller ones looked quite rat-like, but the larger specimens were curious, standing up on the big back legs that explained their Latin name, small forearms curled before them, thick, stiff tails ballasting from behind.

'How do they move?' he asked. 'They can't walk on feet that long, surely?'

'They *hop*, the odd creatures,' Cole said, with a corresponding bounce of his hand and quietly satisfied delight. He leaned to look at the page, and their shoulders brushed. The bench was short, for two grown men. 'Walter sent it over.'

'Is that the Walter in Australia, or the Walter in London?'

Leo already knew: the family called the older half-brother Walt. It was the sole legitimate son, the current baronet, who received both the full moniker and the sort of income that let him order in monographs.

'Sir Walter Minto,' Cole said, flashing his grin.

'Or could it be your Uncle Walter, or Sir Walter your grandfather?' Leo went on in wondering tones, though he couldn't quite restrain his smile. 'Are you sure you aren't also a Walter, Mr Solong? Everybody else in the Farquhar family seems to be.'

Cole snorted, then said, 'Pardon me, Mr Percival Leander Sweetwater, are you making fun of my name?'

'Are you implying I'm some sort of hypocrite to do so? *I* have a perfectly normal name, that I do not have to share with a single other person in my family, or, indeed, anyone in the entirety of East Molesey.' Leo pressed his hands together. 'God bless my mother for her forethought and her fondness for Arthurian tales.'

Smiling, Cole bumped his shoulder again, more deliberately this time. 'I brought some new apples from Wilderness House's garden, for Mr and Mrs Talbot.'

Elderly and ailing, the Talbots did not come downstairs from the attic storey often these days. They'd been one of the households Leo ran errands for, and, after his dunking in the Thames, one of the households who had summoned him from back door to drawing room out of curiosity, and then extended their patronage. He couldn't call himself their friend, precisely, that would have been impertinent, but he was a welcome visitor.

'They will appreciate that,' he said. 'Thank you. I'll run them up this afternoon. Well.' He gestured towards his ankle. 'Walk them up slowly.'

If he timed it right, Mrs and Miss Willis would be out for their social rounds, and he'd be able to softly rap on their apartment wall and say a few words to Mr Willis. Polly had recommended he not speak to Mr Willis at all, but if he must, to tell him he had not yet missed his steamboat, and should hurry away to embark.

But Leo, in this one aspect of his life, chose honesty. He always agreed with Mr Willis when he muttered about missing the boat, and reminded him that he was important enough that his people would make alternative arrangements.

Cole nudged his boot gently into Leo's. 'It's not giving you too much trouble?'

'Just a twinge now and again.'

From the basket, Cole withdrew a velvety purple and globular fruit, oozing syrup. 'Picked the last figs of the season.'

Leo hesitated.

'Leo,' Cole said, and Leo felt that flutter in his stomach. 'Queen Vic is not going to jump out of the shrubbery and castigate you for eating her fruit. Apart from anything else, the produce from the kitchen gardens goes to Covent Markets now, remember, not the royal table.'

'Except the grapes from the Vinehouse.'

'I'm not offering you her grapes, am I?' He took out a small paring knife. 'Look, it's bruised on this side. Not good enough for the queen's plate, anyway.' He sliced off the offending part, exposing deep pink flesh.

'But good enough for me?'

'A little bruising doesn't make it less worthy of love.' Cole cut the fig in half and offered it on the flat of his fingers, cocking his head at Leo, inviting, almost daring, him to take it.

Under Cole's warm, direct gaze, Leo felt a mad impulse to dip his head and lick the pieces up. He could draw his fingertips into his mouth and suck the sticky juice from them. He imagined the roughness of callouses against his lips, the stretch of work-thickened fingers. He imagined Cole's eyes widening.

With disgust and alarm.

This is too much, he told himself. *You have to stop this.*

Mentally adding a good dozen more padlocks to the closed door in his head, Leo cleared his throat. He plucked a piece, popping it quickly into his mouth, barely chewing before swallowing with what he hoped was an appreciative-enough murmur of approval.

Cole didn't seem to have noticed Leo's mortification. He merely looked pleased, as he always did when he managed to persuade Leo to eat what Leo could not help but consider royal property, which he successfully did almost every Friday.

Never let it be said Leo Sweetwater couldn't be tempted into a misdemeanour or two by a handsome man with devilry in his warm eyes.

It was true, though, that the Palace's produce no longer graced Windsor. A recent, rather harsh, review had taken away responsibility for the kitchen gardens from the Palace gardeners, leasing them instead to a professional market gardener. Cole, the Royal Gardener, now had the southern, private, gardens under his dominion, while Mr Jesse's head gardener (Johnson, but not, presumably, Bloody Stupid Johnson) had the public areas – the acreage of the Great Fountain Garden on the east front and the Wilderness on the north. For some odd reason, possibly to do with royal prerogative, the hornbeam Maze within the Wilderness remained Cole's.

Leo made a vague gesture encompassing Cole's personage. 'You're dressed for London?'

'I'm escorting Miss Chester to a memorial for the marquess,' Cole said. 'We'll travel with Lady Anne and Reverend Wellesley to London.'

The Marquess Wellesley had died one month ago; the funeral itself had already taken place, but he had been an important man and the Mornington scions were still working through a long list of honours in lieu of the state funeral he no doubt would have resented not receiving. Lady Anne Culling Smith was his sister, the Palace chaplain his brother, while the elderly Miss Chester, the last of five successive Chester sisters to hold the same apartment's warrant through several decades, was some sort of cousin, in that nebulous way half the gentry were cousins.

Meanwhile, the Townsend Farquhar family had benefited extensively from the marquess's patronage over the years – it was not a coincidence that Cole's name harked back to Richard Colley, the first Baron Mornington – so it wasn't surprising Sir Walter would call on his half-brother to escort Miss Chester.

'Sir Walter will assume the chivalrous mantle from there,' Cole went on lightly. 'I'll stay with Lady Erica and the boys while he's away.'

Leo would have suspected that Lady Erica did not like being left alone with her four rambunctious sons, the buffer of nursemaids notwithstanding, except he'd gathered from some oblique comments from Cole that she was carrying her fifth child, and having a difficult time of it. With doting *mémé* Maria currently visiting Italy with her captain, reliable Uncle Cole was always willing to step in.

He tried not to let his expression of pleasant interest change. He'd noticed this pattern before. Cole, and presumably Walt, before he emigrated to try his hand at colonial farming, was often delegated such tasks for the baronet's household.

Maria had shown Leo a miniature of a young Walt, tow-headed and rosy-cheeked, the literal picture of a young English gentleman, bastard born in Calcutta or no (she'd also shown him a young Cole; Leo hadn't been able to suppress a croon of delight at the sight, and Maria had regarded him with far too much knowing sympathy before snapping her four-paned locket shut and whirling off to examine his watercolours). Whoever Walt Fullerton's mother was, she had either contributed little to her son's looks, or had ancestors of an acceptable sort.

But Cole owed a great deal to his Malay heritage in appearance. Not his height or lean strength, Leo supposed, which spoke more to good diet and outdoor activity, but in the dark glossiness of his hair, and the shape of his eyes, and his smooth brown skin.

Cole hadn't accompanied his half-brother to the marquess's funeral. He wasn't invited to the memorial this weekend, though Sir Walter would attend, to try his hand at earning the patronage of the Duke of Wellington, the marquess's even more accomplished younger brother.

He did an awful lot for his brother's family in the background, and yet never seemed to be seen by his side in public.

'I think I'll take them to Madame Tussaud's.' Cole paused. 'Do you think... Would you like to come? Lady E. won't mind an extra guest. She'd be quite pleased to meet you, I think.'

Lady Erica was the daughter of an earl. Leo didn't think for a second she'd be pleased to meet her bastard brother-in-law's odd friend.

'Bridges,' he said.

'We'll take a carriage across the bridges. You can close your eyes. I'll hold your hand.' Cole made each offer in response to a stubborn shake of Leo's head. He grinned at the very certain refusal of the last bid; Leo would absolutely not let himself imagine holding Cole's hand, not after he'd been so transported by the fig. 'I won't nag, then, but don't you want to see the new Chamber of Horrors?'

Before he could stop himself, Leo turned to look southwards as if he could see through the chapel walls to Fountain Court.

'They've put in the daftie bampots who tried to assassinate the queen...' Cole shifted, following his gaze. Very softly, he said, 'What is it, Leo?'

Leo started and made himself turn away. Max had raised his head from Cole's boot to stare intently in a blessedly different direction. 'Oh, look. One of the Walpoles.'

It was, in fact, the Honourable Mr Henry Walpole, unaccompanied, coming down from the direction of Leo's studio. 'Sweetwater,' he said. 'I've been looking for you.'

'Mr Walpole, Mr Solong,' Leo mumbled. He hated introductions; the rules were arcane.

Walpole gave Cole a cool nod and the shadow of a bow, then turned his pale eyes back to Leo. 'I'm wanting a daguerreotype made.'

'The studio's closed on Fridays,' Leo said. The earl's son stared at him. 'Same as the State Apartments?' Now even the baronet's bastard was looking at him in something approaching astonishment. 'Fridays are for the gardens.'

'Open for me,' Walpole said. 'Come on, Sweetwater, I'm back to London tomorrow, this is my last chance.'

Leo met his gleaming eyes and understood he did not, in any way, mean his last chance for a daguerreotype.

He looked up, hoping for a cloud so he had a legitimate excuse to beg off. The sky remained treacherously clear. It was bloody *November*, what did the weather think it was doing?

Stubbornly, he insisted, 'I'm otherwise engaged at the moment, Mr Walpole.'

'Go on, Sweetwater,' Cole said. 'It's just a wee sit with me, nothing special.'

Leo sat motionless, feeling quite spectacularly betrayed.

'Very well,' he managed at last. He untucked his feet from under Max, and collected his watercolour equipment.

Walpole was waiting a polite distance away, but Cole lowered his voice anyway. 'He's an earl's son, Leo. Makes a decent patron, if he shows off your work in London.'

Leo supposed a son of Sir Robert Townsend Farquhar, who had attached himself early to an earl's son and done remarkably well out of it, would be able to spot patronage a mile off.

'Yes,' he said. 'Thank you, Mr Solong. Safe travels.'

'See you next Friday.' Cole sounded puzzled.

'Yes,' Leo said again, still not looking at him. 'This way, Mr Walpole.'

EIGHT

'You've done the very silly thing, haven't you?' Walpole said, breaking their silence as they reached the studio. 'Tell me the conventionally-minded gardener's not your Notus.'

Leo winced – he hated to be obvious – but made no answer.

He'd thought Sally might ask for the key this morning; she'd been burying herself in extra work since Joseph had departed. But she'd held to her usual Friday habit, and walked with John to Hampton for her day out. The shutters of the big front windows, once serving hatches, were closed, but enough light fell through the copious clerestory windows to save him from the intimacy of a dim room.

Leo put his easel and colour box down on the counter, debated, then shoved the heavy door closed. Visitors came every day for the gardens and he didn't want customers wandering in during this interview.

'Now, I don't mind a taciturn man,' Walpole said from behind him, 'but you are going to have to say something eventually.'

Leo turned. Walpole was standing too close. Leo put a hand on his chest and steadily pushed until he took one step backwards.

'Unfortunately for you,' he said, 'I am going to say something you neither wish to hear nor are accustomed to hearing. *No*, Mr Walpole.'

Walpole looped a hand around Leo's wrist and reclaimed the step he'd ceded, and more besides. Leo found himself pressed against the door.

He was confused, not alarmed; Walpole outweighed him, in that broad-shouldered, well-fed, aristocratic sportsman's way, but he was more importuning than predatory. But Leo did not understand why the importuning was being directed at him, unless Walpole was one of those men who couldn't hear a refusal without taking it as a challenge.

'No?' Walpole repeated, eyes alight with amusement. 'But why? Why not take the opportunity for pleasure, Sweetwater? Why not grab it with both hands?' His own hands demonstrated the concept as he spoke, seizing and squeezing Leo's hips.

Leo set his hands over Walpole's, but didn't quite wrest them free. 'How old are you?'

'Twenty-four. Don't raise your eyebrows. If you took a bride my age, people would assume you'd taken pity on an old maid.'

'When I was your age, *a full decade ago*, I went to London—'

'By Jove, the Covent Garden mollies must have eaten you alive.'

Leo smiled thinly. '—where it quickly became apparent to anyone with half a brain that labourers and soldiers risked hanging or transportation for the sorts of crimes that rich men barely got arrested for, and if they did, their good mates would stand character witness and they'd walk away, charges dismissed and reputations unscathed. And that's to say, Mr Walpole, son of one earl, brother of the next, it's a more fraught activity for some than for others.'

'Look at your monstrosity of a door.' Walpole took the iron key from Leo's hand, and turned it in the lock, the tumblers clunking resonantly. 'We're not going to get caught in here.'

There were other doors into the labyrinthine Tudor kitchen complex, but they were latched and locked, the path to them blocked by the forgotten detritus of the grace-and-favour residents, that Sally's brothers had carefully stacked out of her way.

Thus, Leo could not fault Walpole's accuracy when he said, 'We're safe, we're private. We can only report each other, and neither of us is foolish enough to embroil ourselves in that.'

'If you are bored and require diversion,' Leo said, adopting schoolmasterish tones, 'there are Hussars over at the barracks perfectly willing to risk a walk with you in the Wilderness.'

'I dare say they are, but straitlaced men like you go like Vesuvius in bed.'

'I *beg* your p—' and that was as much of the exclamation as escaped his mouth before Walpole kissed him.

Leo didn't kiss him back, but he didn't push him away, either. Walpole was holding him bodily against the door, palms glued to his hips, fingers stretched to cup his arse, chest and shoulders pressed firm to his, mouth moving forcefully over his.

He couldn't deny that the warmth and contact and flattering evidence of strong desire felt good, especially after that *nothing special* remark from Cole.

At this thought, his lips parted and he may have made a very small sound of very slight encouragement. Walpole moaned in agreement and flicked the tip of Leo's tongue with his own. Leo tentatively grasped Walpole's upper arms. They felt well-muscled, through his coat. He dug his fingers in, and Walpole responded, flattening him even harder into the door, its black iron studs biting into his spine.

'*Do* you go like Vesuvius in bed, Leo?' Polly asked from behind them.

With Walpole and his body heat so distractingly close, he hadn't noticed the chill that usually warned him of her arrival. He gasped into Walpole's mouth, his body wholesale jerking against him. Walpole took the reaction as further approval, dropping his head to nibble under Leo's ear while grinding a sturdy thigh between his legs.

Polly was floating, cross-legged, slightly above the wide sill of the closer of the two shuttered windows that let out onto the old Serving Place. As soon as she had his attention, from over Walpole's bowed shoulders, she wafted to the centre of the showroom.

'Do you violently erupt in hot torrents at unpredictable intervals?' she said, hands clasped under her chin in a parody of innocent enquiry. 'I'm very interested to know.'

Leo smothered a laugh into Walpole's shoulder. The blithe quip was the dash of cold water he'd needed. He shoved his assailant off. 'I told you I don't gamble, Mr Walpole.'

Walpole did not look at all annoyed to have been disrupted. 'Harry.' He smiled. 'I let my lovers call me that.'

'Is that so, Mr Walpole? We need to take your daguerreotype before we lose the light.'

He slithered out from between Walpole and the door and crossed to the archway into the portrait studio, swerving around Polly. Walpole followed him, but not the cue to veer, and Polly refused to move, so Leo heard him give a startled shivering grunt as he encountered the frigid effect of walking through a ghost. Served him right, and perhaps it would have a quelling effect.

The portrait studio was dominated by the raised platform where the sitters posed, the height lifting them into the sunlight for more of the day. Wooden steps led up there, a single chair waiting to be angled into the best light. Enormous fireplaces lined the walls, as in the front showroom, some used for storage, but one carefully bricked down into a smaller hearth, lit on their open days to warm the entire space. Sunshine poured in from the clerestory windows high overhead. It was later in the day than he'd usually attempt a daguerreotype in this season.

Walpole had not been quelled. He let his chest brush Leo's back in the archway, where he'd paused to assess the lighting. One hand skated across Leo's hip but he'd somewhat taken the hint, and didn't grab him again.

'Where's the harm, old man? You've given your heart to your Notus, but he as good as said you're nothing special.'

'He didn't say—'

'And I couldn't ask for better than a man with an engaged heart and pent-up need.'

'I don't have—'

He slipped his arms around Leo. 'Come, my darling, sweet Winter,' he murmured in his ear. 'Off with that girdle, unpin that spangled breast-plate, unlace yourself.'

It had a certain cadence, as if he were quoting. Indeed, Polly, sounding both amused and contemptuous, recited, 'Licence my roving hands,' over Walpole's attempt, and drowned out his next words with, 'Donne, to his mistress. Already a seducers' cliché in my time and the man was barely in his grave.'

It must be a day for old poetry. Leo once again unpeeled himself from Walpole, if with more self-induced difficulty this time, and closed the curtain that gave sitters privacy from the showroom.

'Take a comfortable pose,' he said, indicating the chair on the platform. 'I need to prepare a plate.'

He went behind the partition wall to begin the first and most laborious step of the process: polishing the plate. He crimped its edges and fastened it to a plate-holder, then dusted its silver face with rotten stone. He added a few drops of diluted alcohol and, taking his time, began to briskly rub the resulting paste across the surface in overlapping circles with a wad of cotton flannel.

Once done, he removed the plate to a second plate-holder at a station some distance from the dust of the polishing station, careful not to let his fingers touch the lustre. He had a buffing wheel for when he and Sally or John were preparing a batch, but for a single plate, he used hand-buffs of increasing fineness, repeatedly brushing the surface in light, even sweeps, perfecting the mirror-sheen.

The long minutes of polishing and buffing were foundational to a good daguerreotype; Leo found the need for meticulous care meditative. All he could hear from the other side of the partition was the occasional faint rustle. He was surprised Walpole was holding his tongue for so long.

Polly drifted to his side as he removed the plate from the second holder and warmed it over a spirit lamp.

As with her mention of her mother's receipt book the other day, her reference to Donne was one of those unwitting slips his younger self would have made much of. If the Charlottes, Mrs Thoroton and Miss Dawson, had not already made their seasonal departure for warmer climes, he'd have used his teatime visit to their small and longstanding Llangollen on the second storey to consult with the latter, once a governess and still fond of the literary. The result might very well bolster his theory of when Polly's time had been; it might scupper it.

But he really did try not to be obnoxious these days. Therefore, he pretended not to notice her for a different reason. He might have been able to keep a composed countenance for Walpole, but she knew him too well.

Indeed, she announced, 'I don't trust him, Leo.'

Leo shrugged. He went into the cavernous fireplace, long and broad enough to lie outstretched in any direction and tall enough to stand upright, where he kept his chemicals and developing equipment inside a light-tight cabinet.

'Cold air affects the plates,' he reminded her.

She did not take the hint to remove herself. 'He seems like a Wickham to me.'

'He's a Bingley, at worst,' Leo murmured, setting the plate into its recess within the coating-box cover and sliding it face down over the first compartment, filled with iodine. He began to count to twenty in his head.

'Incessantly handsome,' Polly said darkly, since that was how she had misheard the description of Bingley the first time Leo had read the book to her.

He slid the plate, now tinted gold, over to the bromine compartment for just enough time, a few seconds, for the plate to turn the right shade of rose. 'He's going back to London tomorrow.'

'Is that what he told you?'

Leo whisked shut the cabinet's thick curtain, plunging himself into darkness. By feel, he slid the plate back over the iodine to finish the sensitisation process. 'I think he will go away once he's had what he wants.'

'I think you're thinking with your plums,' Polly said from the other side of the curtain, 'which means you're not thinking at all.'

She sounded very sulky. Leo said, 'I'm lonely, Polly.'

But when he opened the curtain, the plate snug in its lightproof case, she wasn't there. He heard her start to laugh over the partition, low and chagrined. 'Henry Walpole, you cheeky harlot.'

Leo came around with a deep sense of trepidation and stopped. 'You might have warned me!'

He received only, 'Where's the fun in that?' in both contralto and alto tones, neither voice holding any remorse whatsoever.

Henry Walpole had indeed made himself comfortable on the chair atop the platform. He was perched there entirely naked.

Polly hovered right beside him, watching with prurient interest as she raised goosebumps across his bare skin. Walpole shivered, but not without pleasure.

'I cannot entirely blame you, I suppose,' she said, if reluctantly. 'He's comely enough. Quite agile, too.'

'I didn't think you could get those dandy styles off without a valet,' Leo said, having recovered his composure on the way to his camera apparatus.

'They remove readily enough, as you see,' Walpole said with a smirk. 'Getting back into them might require assistance.'

He lazily stroked his prick. Leo had to bite his tongue to prevent expostulating that there was a lady present. It was nothing Polly hadn't seen before, anyway; ghosts did not seem to hold on to human inhibitions and Polly, in particular, possessed a frank and non-judgemental curiosity. When he'd confessed his confused and confusing longings to her, in the wake of Sir Horace and his hand about the nape of his neck, she'd given him a laundry list of all the famed men of history who had held similar preferences, or at least indulged the same desires, here at the Palace.

Her cheerful recitation had gone a long way towards diverting any notions of disgust from himself and over towards the rampant hypocrisy of the men who made the laws, where it belonged.

'If there is truly no dissuading you,' Polly said, 'I shall leave you to it until the "I told you so".'

She wafted off through the wall.

Leo, testing his weak ankle on each step, gingerly ascended a low step-ladder to access the camera, sitting on a high shelf so its eye sat even with the posing chair. Unlike when he took the portable apparatus out into the gardens, the distance to the subject was almost static, and needed only the slightest of adjustments for the composition.

Arranging the sitter was a large part of the daguerreotype as an art form, angling their face and the rest of their body such that their true likeness was captured without introducing distortion or artificiality. Leo had had no talent as a miniaturist, but something about the double security of the viewing glass and lens between him and his subjects made him passable as a daguerreotypist. He'd been told he had a favourable eye.

Of course, today's portrait was somewhat different to the usual run of things. Peering through the viewing glass, Leo gave instructions coolly, telling Walpole how to sit, where to direct his gaze, how to spread his legs, where to position his hands, finding him a most willing and eager subject.

Once he was happy with the focus and framing, he replaced the lens cap, then removed the viewing glass and slotted the encased plate in its place. He pulled up the sliding panel of the lightproof case so that, inside the dark of the camera, the sensitised silver plate was revealed.

'Do not move,' he ordered Walpole, taking up his pocket watch.

He waited until the seconds hand, set in a small dial on the watch face, reached its zenith, then uncapped the lens, at last allowing light to fall onto the plate.

The exposure time was at his discretion, and a matter of experience with the variables of light and sensitisation, and the reflectivity of his subject. He had not, naturally, ever taken a daguerreotype of a naked person before; his interest in the experimental effect of that much pale skin instead of dark clothing on the exposure was half the reason he'd chosen to continue on.

Well. Perhaps a touch less than half.

In the most well-lit of studios, on the brightest of days, he'd need, at most, ten seconds, perhaps less. In his studio, at this time of day and year, and accounting for the all-over paleness of his subject, he decided on forty-five seconds.

As the seconds hand swept around, he indulged himself and stared openly at Walpole, letting him see it. Long, muscular limbs, broad shoulders, flat stomach, dark hair trailing down his navel. Jutting hips. Jutting prick, a drop of liquid quivering at its tip.

Walpole's prick stiffened further under Leo's unblinking gaze, and was now reddened and leaking. He groaned through his teeth, a hint of imprecation beginning.

'Don't move,' Leo said again. He smiled, mostly to himself.

At last the seconds hand reached due west, and Leo capped the lens. He pushed down the dark-panel to enclose the plate into its lightproof case again. With a stern *wait* gesture to Walpole, he carried the case through to the back, where he tipped a little mercury into the fuming box, set directly below the ancient chimney, and positioned the spirit lamp underneath to gently heat it.

He went no further. The next step, the developing bath, took only a few minutes, and he'd need longer than that.

Probably not *much* longer, by now.

He returned to tend to Walpole, who he might as well call Harry after all. He went up the short flight of stairs onto the platform and stood between spread thighs, still maintaining a pose of austere indifference. Harry tipped his head back, wearing his lazy smile as well as he wore nudity.

Leo went to his knees.

'Well, then,' Harry murmured. 'Graze on my lips, and if those hills be dry, stray lower, where the pleasant fountains lie.'

Even Leo could recognise the rhythms of a Shakespearean sonnet, thanks to his weekly teas with the Charlottes. Harry was certainly very learned with his conquests.

He'd barely closed his lips around the leaking head when Harry had gripped his scalp, fingers locking into his hair. Leo sat back.

'Don't move,' he instructed for the third time. 'Hands to yourself.'

Harry pulled a mockingly chastened face and ostentatiously set his hands to grip the sides of the chair. Leo bobbed down again, taking the head of Harry's prick back into his mouth and swirling his tongue about. Harry's hips jerked, and Leo accommodated it, opening his mouth wide and taking him deeper, tightening his lips and sliding them rapidly up and down until he ascertained, from Harry's increasingly urgent noises and hip pumps, that he was close. Then he plunged all the way to the root and half-sucked, half-swallowed, making his throat ripple about Harry's pulsing member. Harry shouted and shot with three great thrusts, forgetting himself and clutching at Leo's head as he spent.

Harry collapsed against the chair back with one last heartfelt groan. Leo sat back on his heels, caught his avid eye, and deliberately swallowed one last time.

'You must like that method,' Harry said. 'Very tidy.'

'Quick, too,' Leo said, as he rose. He swayed gracefully out of reach of Harry's grinning attempt to grab him. 'Get dressed. I'll develop your daguerreotype.'

He returned to the nicely heated fuming box. Pulling on his working gloves and tying a cloth about his mouth, he removed the plate from the case and quickly placed it within the darkness of the fuming box. The silver salts would react with the mercury fumes to bring out the image.

He waited.

Sometimes (though not, with guilty effort, today), he'd think of his mother during this stage. She, too, had had a dab hand with an arcane art, delicate, precise, skillful work involving patience, specialist knowledge and chemicals, except her scientific art, or artful science, had been the care of lacework for rich women. It did not have the same glamour as daguerreotypes.

After a few minutes, he removed the plate. Holding it by one corner with nippers, he rinsed it with diluted hyposulphite of soda, to wash away the last of the light-sensitising chemicals, and then, copiously, with distilled water.

Normally, he'd gilt it with gold chloride, to enrich and warm the tones and harden the surface. Since he had no intention of allowing this daguerreotype to remain in existence, he skipped to the next step, drying it by bathing its copper back in the low flame of the spirit lamp.

He stripped off gloves and face-cloth, and took the daguerreotype out to the studio, where Harry lolled still entirely naked, and laid it on his worktable.

It had come out well, the edges of Harry's bared body strong and clear, pearly against the darker backdrop. His head was slightly blurred; knowing he'd have to destroy the result anyway, Leo hadn't forced him to clamp into the headstand. His prick rose proudly, a little muddy at the tip where the droplet had spilt under Leo's steady appraisal.

It begged for a rosy hand-tint. Leo laughed aloud at the thought.

Snuggling close behind him, Harry slung an arm around his waist and rested his chin on his shoulder while he, too, inspected the daguerreotype. Leo closed his eyes. The casual affection, from a lover, was overwhelming. He hadn't had this since London. When he'd admitted to

Polly that he was lonely, this was what he'd meant: lonely to the point of fantasising about licking fig juice off his dear friend's fingertips. He felt an absurd wave of gratitude to the importuning young pup.

Harry gave a low whistle. 'I had no idea my prick was quite so magnificent. I did have my suspicions, of course.'

'Parts of the body closer to the camera appear magnified,' Leo explained, and Harry gave a bellow of laughter. 'Oh, all right.'

He would seal it between brass and glass, were it a normal daguerreotype. Instead, he dragged his thumb across the captured likeness. They were fragile; the rough touch immediately blurred Harry's face. Leo might have recovered it, with more chemical baths, but would not.

'I'm still admiring that,' Harry protested. 'No chance of taking it away for private use, then?' He nuzzled into Leo's neck, rubbing a hand over his stomach, and then lower.

'Not with my name stamped on the back of the cases, no,' Leo said drily. Not *ever*; there weren't so many daguerreotype studios that even an anonymous image couldn't be traced back to him.

Harry ran his hand down the front of Leo's trousers, over his stand, and made a questioning noise into his neck. Leo gave a slight nod. That was all the encouragement Harry needed to tackle his fastenings and push down his trousers. Leo tried to step free (he found trousers around ankles undignified) but it was Harry's turn to take charge. He shoved Leo forwards, only just on the right side of too forceful.

Leo hadn't had relations over a table since his early days in London, and had never found it particularly comfortable, hard edges and surfaces tending to rub against jutting hipbones and elbows or tailbone and shoulder blades. He was better padded now, of course, and couldn't deny he enjoyed the way Harry's hairy muscular thighs pressed his hard into the table edge, the way his arm tightened to hold Leo's back firmly sealed to his chest, the way his other hand tightened too, around Leo's prick.

Harry worked him with consummate skill, murmuring, 'Whatever your hand finds to do, do it with all your might,' which was Ecclesiastes, which meant Leo was helplessly laughing as Harry tangled a hand into his hair and pulled his head back to kiss him, messy and sweet.

He spent like that, his mouth locked to Harry's, spilling seed over Harry's fist, and the table, and the daguerreotype.

He'd quite forgotten the ardour of the highest bloom of youth. Harry was hard again, rocking his hips so his prick rubbed insistently against the cleft of Leo's arse. Leo sucked in a breath, but Harry said, 'Just Oxford, darling,' and slid his prick between his thighs.

Leo squeezed them together, bracing himself on his forearms. Harry leaned over him, pleasantly weighty on his back, interspersing appreciative gasps with muttered praise as he thrust with great enthusiasm, adding splashes of white mess to the disarrayed tabletop in short order.

'Good God,' Harry said, running a hand through his hair. He shifted away, allowing Leo to begin to bring himself back to respectability. 'Thoroughly despoiled.'

When Leo gave him a rather severe look over his shoulder, he added, with a puppyish grin, 'The daguerreotype, darling. I can't see *you* not being snapped up for despoiling the moment some lucky devil spotted you.'

Leo started to protest, thought of Sir Horace, and said nothing.

He helped Harry dress, preening him until he did not look like a man who had stripped to his bare skin. 'When someone asks to see your daguerreotype' – he had no fear that no one had noticed Lord Walpole's brother attending his studio – 'tell them I tried, but the light wasn't right for it today.'

Turning the key, he paused to press one more kiss to Harry's smiling lips. 'Thank you for the pleasant afternoon, Harry.'

'Goodbye, sweet Winter,' Harry said fondly, and slipped out.

Leo tidied up the studio, and then, in a minor fit of what would be paranoia if they lived in freer times, attacked the surface of the ruined daguerreotype like a cat at a scratching post and buried it under other detritus in the waste bucket.

NINE

Naturally, Harry Walpole did not go back to London the next day.

'I intended to,' he protested, when Leo took him to task during a snatched private moment in the studio. 'I've got a little tin owing. Father in his infinite wisdom decreed that if cousin William could be a lieutenant by my age, the least I can do is manage my own vowels.'

The Palace, being royal ground, was out of bounds to bailiffs pursuing civil grievances like writs for debt, a quirk of history more than one past resident had taken advantage of. It was logical for Harry to linger here while he gathered his funds. Leo scoffed disapprovingly anyway, before hurrying off to buff a set of plates.

Lord Walpole had taken it into his head to have daguerreotypes made of the five Walpole siblings, in poses both solitary and combined and in duplicate, leading his aunt to order the same for his Hoste cousins, and then for herself (Leo could already tell she would be exceedingly fussy). Leo supposed he had Harry to thank for the booming business, so could not be too ungracious, but he was rueful. He had certainly enjoyed their brief exchange of mutual gratification, but he'd also been counting on waving the impetuous puppy farewell at the end of it.

He was reminded of the reason when Harry followed him behind the partition to the private developing area, claiming he wanted to see how it was done, and then kissed him urgently, hands squeezing his arse to pull him in tight and hard. Leo had barely shoved him away before his younger brother had called out, wanting to observe the process too.

Leo decided right then that Harry, exactly as his first instincts had warned him, was far too dangerous. He would mark the days until he actually did depart.

The interest also brought in the last few residents who had not already graced his doorway for a sitting, including Lord and Lady George (and now he had a new benchmark for fussiness), as well as customers from among the tourists, drawn by curiosity and the reflected glamour of the Ladies Harriet and George, to queue up for their own portraits.

His week, the weather holding perfectly clear and light-filled, was thus an industrious one.

He did try, in between the bustle, to tell Polly about the workman's strange words the previous Friday. He got as far as, 'Polly, the workman talked about the cracks getting worse.'

Polly said, 'Of course he did, that's what he does,' and whisked off before he could insist on a less flippant answer.

Fair enough. If he could've escaped awkward conversations by ghosting away, he absolutely would have.

He let himself find her nonchalance reassuring.

Pleasantly worn out by the busy week, he was not prepared to be jolted awake in the smallest hours of Friday morning.

He sat up with the breath dragging cold as blades in his lungs and said, 'Polly?' on a shocked gust of white air.

But she wasn't in the room, nor were any other, more alarming, ghosts. Even so, the wallpaper appeared frosted with gossamer chains of ice. He stayed still, gradually becoming aware that he was weighted down by a violently oppressive dread.

The moment he recognised it, he had to move. It was a struggle to push back the bed covers, a struggle to drag on trousers and an overcoat over his nightshirt and shove his feet into shoes. As he near-staggered down the hallway, he had just enough wherewithal to avoid the creakiest of the floorboards. He would have struggled to move his tongue to explain his behaviour if Sally had come downstairs to invest-igate the noise.

He had to lean against the front door, steadying his breath, before he could bring himself to open it.

The alleyway was very dark and still and chilly, probably naturally. He pulled his overcoat tight and set off as if into a thick mist, not bothering with a lantern. Between the moon and the gas lamps and his years of residence, he could manage his path well enough not to stumble.

He hastened through Anne Boleyn's Gateway, barely noticing as he bumped into the pacing Sergeant Hamilton, knocking into his shoulder before passing right through like a normal person.

'What?' Hamilton's ghostly fingers clutched at Leo's arm. 'Sir, can you hear me?'

'Not now!' Leo said, shaking him off without a thought and hurrying across Base Court.

Only as he passed between the orangery and the Great Vine did he realise his trajectory, as instinctual and necessary as a migratory bird's, was towards Banqueting House.

He pulled up short in the wedge-shaped garden across the path from the square, squat house and its long garden walls. Angles of hedges separated this leftover part of the southern gardens from the Pond Garden. A single evergreen tree loomed amid manicured shrubbery. Polly occasionally called it Mount Garden, though Leo thought that was a very old name.

He huddled into his coat. Not even the brisk walk had imparted warmth into his core, and the weighty sense of dread creeping fog-like over the Palace was strongest here. Leo's voice barely managed to rise above a whisper as he called for Polly.

Unlike most ghosts, she did not haunt anywhere specific, unless Leo counted himself. However, she tended to this vicinity in idle hours. It was where she'd been the day a mostly-drowned boy had washed up on the bank by the overgrown barge path behind Banqueting House, after all.

The habit had never meant much to Leo, partly because she did not do it during the daylight hours while he was resident, and partly because Banqueting House had been William III's pet project during the Wren renovation of one hundred and fifty years before, and Polly must predate that, if only because she sometimes slipped and called Base Court and Clock Court by their original names, Green Court and Fountain Court.

However, Banqueting House had been built from reclaimed bricks from other, older, Palace buildings, atop Tudor mill foundations. Perhaps the very act of demolishing the site of Polly's death was what had freed her to wander among the living, their vitality her new anchor and lifeline.

He called her name again, louder this time.

She manifested in front of him.

Once again, Leo's years of not reacting to ghosts stood him in good stead; he managed to not recoil. She was his familiar beloved friend, and not. She somehow seemed more solid, but she also looked right through him, her focus fiercely intent on something he could not see. Her expression bore the same determined set as when she'd decided he should thrash an unpleasant old man at whist.

It was in the nature of ghosts that they did not change, so it took Leo a moment to realise she wore a lace cap atop her strawberry-blonde hair.

'Lucy,' she whispered. 'Lucy, quickly, this way.'

'Polly, it's Leo.' He shook his head. 'It's Percy.'

'Yes, I know, but I know a way out, come with me.'

Her gaze remained fixed past him. 'Can you hear me?' he asked, as lost and disconsolate as Sergeant Hamilton.

'Here, go down that way, you'll find a little door, slip through and you'll be in the gardens. I'll lead them along the Water Gallery. I'll delay them.'

'I don't think you should do that,' Leo miserably told the girl who had died in her nightdress over a century ago.

'No, I'll be fine, they won't hurt a woman.'

The heavy sick dread whirled all about them and crawled down Leo's throat and into his stomach. 'Oh, God, Polly, I think they do.'

'Go! Don't look back. Run, my love, run. Be safe. I want you to be safe.' Almost to herself now, Polly said, 'I will keep you safe. I will keep you safe. I will keep you safe—'

She jerked and began to choke. Her head flew back, her cap tumbled away into a void, and her whole body shook.

It was awful and the air throbbed, no longer with the weight of dread but with shards of terror and rage, and he knew, he *knew*, the worst was yet to come. His superficial calm shattered like rime on a pond.

Seizing her by the shoulders, he shouted, 'Polly, come back!'

The last of his warmth drained from him as her ghostly matter instantly began to drink down his subtle matter. But as his shivering increased, her convulsions eased and then stilled.

She blinked at him. 'Percy?'

He hugged her. He'd been touching her, feeding her, long enough that she seemed almost substantial in his arms, though it had something of the feel of holding a chunk of ice and something of the taste of fog.

'Oh, be careful, pet,' she said, almost fluttery.

'What—' he began, and then noticed that soft lamplight was shining through the shutters of the north-facing windows of Banqueting House.

His loud, frightened shout, shattering the serenity of the night, must have woken the Reynetts.

He did not need Sir James to discover him standing in the garden in his nightclothes in front of the house where his wife and two young daughters slept. That went far beyond the forgivable eccentricity of a so-called artistic temperament.

'Come on.' He hurried over to the Privy Garden, Polly floating in his wake. Once his whispers were unlikely to carry to any living ears, he said, 'What happened?'

'You tell me,' Polly said. 'Why are you out at this time of night?'

She sounded genuine, though there was a slow, heavy note to her voice that suggested her confusion ran deeper than mere puzzlement over his unusual nocturnal wander.

'Who's Lucy?' he asked her.

'Lucy,' she whispered, and Leo feared he'd plunged her back into her personal nightmare. He grabbed her hand.

She covered her eyes with her other hand. They stayed like that long enough for Leo's teeth to begin to chatter, and then Polly gently freed herself.

'I loved her,' she said simply, 'and she did not love me back in any way that mattered.'

Chafing his hands together, Leo said, 'But you died to protect her,' before he could think better of it.

Her glance towards him was acute before she wiped her expression. Drifting away into the chill fingers of the real mist rising off the river, she said, 'You see how I might have become cynical about romance since.'

He could hear from her lofty tone that she was already recovering herself, and would shortly begin to turn away his attempts to pry, as was her habit. 'What happened?'

'It is merely an echo that occurs every year at this time,' she said indifferently. 'It is nought to worry yourself over, Leo, it is near enough to two centuries' worth of over and done with.'

'I've never woken up for it before.'

'Why would you?'

'Why did I, this year?' he countered.

Her mouth tightened. She drifted even further from him, until her edges blurred into the thickening mist, and he thought he'd lost her.

But then she wafted back, face set and strained. 'Fountain Court. Stay away. Stay well away from it. The crack is getting wider.'

'The workman said that,' Leo said stupidly.

'He devotes his existence to keeping it closed. That's why he lingers.'

Leo started to ask one question, before a far more urgent one interrupted it. 'If the workman's keeping us safe from Fountain Court, why would you tell me to help him move on?'

'I knew he wouldn't, with his work left undone,' Polly said with a shrug. 'But it'd keep you occupied, so you wouldn't start talking to any of the others, or worse, get any ideas about me. I'm perfectly happy as I am, thank you.'

Leo's mouth had unflatteringly dropped open. 'That's very...'

'Cunning?' she said. 'Yes, I know.'

'Deceptive!'

She folded her arms. 'I will keep you safe, however I have to do it.'

He stared, shocked. *I will keep you safe.* How had he never realised before that *that* was Polly's urgent deathbed need? It quite quelled his desire to argue, even if she hadn't had a rather more unpleasant time of it tonight than he had, mere echo or no.

But he still hadn't worked around to asking what had happened after Lucy had run and Polly had stood her ground. He touched two fingers to his throat, the reverberation of her awful choking shivering in his ears.

It hit him, then, with somewhat of the force of a frying pan to the skull, that her reluctance to speak of what had killed her might have as much to do with keeping a loved one safe than it did her own benefit.

'I'm not eight any more, Polly,' he said. 'You don't have to protect me.'

She floated before him, silent. Around them, the mist rose thicker, till he could taste mud on his tongue.

Polly said, 'My name was Mary Lee. My family were in wool. My father thought London too dangerous, so he sent me to Hampton Court with my brother, who proved a lax guardian. I had a very pleasant time. Then I met Lucy.'

She paused, gaze abstracted. Leo rubbed his hands together in the chill, damp air, holding his tongue.

'I loved her entirely, and she indulged me until she didn't. But she was still my friend, and when things changed that summer and my brother went home, I remained in her entourage, just another of her many devoted friends. Then she passed on an important letter to someone at the Palace, and her enemies barged down her apartment door in the middle of the night to demand its contents. We fled in fear of our lives, down the backstairs. I helped her escape.'

Her facsimile of breathing quickened. Leo wanted to surrender, to tell her she didn't need to go on.

'They were angry. They wanted to know the contents of the letter. They… One grabbed me. He began to choke me. He said, "Tell me, tell me". But I was trained to never tell, never.'

Though her voice remained detached, Leo felt again the dread that had suffused the Palace, saw again the echo of her body convulsing as the life was choked from her. He shut his eyes.

'See?' Polly said. 'You do not want to hear it.'

'No, I don't,' he said, eyes still closed. 'But finish it.'

'There's someone coming.'

Leo opened his eyes to see a glow, diffused into a pale gold aura through the wet droplets of the river mist. Polly flickered, receding pale into the curtain of mist as the light bobbed closer.

'Lady Jane,' she called.

Leo had been worried it'd be Sir James, and hopeful (if he were going to be unusually honest) it'd be Cole.

Polly's report, however, was immediately unsurprising, nor did Lady Jane appear at all surprised to come across him in her turn.

She set the little house-lamp at her slipper-shod feet. Her cheeks were pink enough that he might have suspected hectic fever if his own face wasn't still flushed with psychic cold as well. She wore only a thick housecoat over her nightdress, and her faded auburn hair was loose under a cap. Something had driven her from her bed, the way something had driven him from his, and, many years ago, Polly from hers.

'It was like being crushed,' Lady Jane told him. She sounded perfectly calm, though it might have been as ice-thin as his own. 'And then it was like being stabbed. Mr Hildyard is in the city, and I couldn't stay in the apartment a moment longer.'

He felt the impulse to return her a blank look, and had to deliberately set it aside. It was unfair, if she had felt even a fraction of what he had. 'Something happened at Banqueting House tonight, a long time ago.'

That wasn't right, though. Polly had told Lucy she'd lead their pursuers along the Water Gallery, which had since been demolished. The old gallery must have been one of the buildings whose materials had been repurposed during the Baroque renovations, shifting and loosening Polly's anchor.

'They found bones there, you know, in the cellars.'

Or perhaps not.

Lady Jane shivered all over. 'When Sir James was renovating, his workmen uncovered an entire human skeleton in a Tudor fireplace down there.'

'Such flummery, it was a few animal bones!' Polly exclaimed, which did not explain why this was the first he was hearing of the exact sort of story she delighted in telling him.

On the other hand, if they weren't just animal bones, *someone* in this gossipy little royal village would surely have mentioned it to the resident ghost-haunted oddity. Mrs Ellice would have taken just as much delight in the story as Polly normally would have.

'But it is most peculiar,' Lady Jane said. 'I've lived at the Palace for years now, and have never experienced such as this. And the infernal tapping is definitely in Fountain Court. Isn't it?'

Leo, again on the cusp of a habitual denial, paused. Polly tutted in disgust but made no other comment, which was basically permission. He still hesitated. Beyond his rare reassurances to the bereft or superstitious, he did not speak of ghosts to people. It was like he had to turn a faucet in his mind, which had rusted shut from years and years of secrets.

On the other hand, Lady Jane had years and years of being a marquess's daughter. She tapped her foot. 'I did say it was getting worse since you came home.'

'I'm not causing it,' Leo protested. 'There's a crack.'

Lady Jane gasped and clasped her hands together over her heart with only the barest touch of theatrics. 'At last!' she cried. 'Two restless spirits, yes?'

'That's one way to put it,' Polly said darkly.

Malign was another. 'Yes.'

'Not labourers, either!'

'I don't think so.' He started to explain about the workman, and stopped, force of habit stilling his tongue.

'Cavaliers, I'd stake on it. Are their very bodies under the fountain even now?' she demanded.

The maleficent dual presence was centred on the doorstep leading to Lady Jane's staircase. He had no idea as to whether their bodies were there, too; spectral and physical remnants were mostly unrelated past the moment of death, in his limited experience. But he supposed the presence of remains might very well make a ghost stronger. It might partly explain why the Fountain Court pair seemed so potent.

He wished he knew what had happened to the bones Sir James's men had found.

He didn't dare look at Polly.

'Is there aught to be done? On a more mundane level, I mean? Should we pray, perhaps?'

Polly said, 'You should both stay away from Fountain Court and stop interfering.'

Since Lady Jane could only avoid the stairs to her own front door by taking the servants' back ways, to which she would never stoop, Leo did not find this a particularly helpful answer.

Once again, Lady Jane was too impatient to tolerate his pause. 'I shall try it, regardless.'

Leo collected the lantern and offered her his arm. 'I should walk you home before we're spotted and Mr Hildyard hears rumours you're having liaisons in the Privy Garden.'

'We haven't had a good duel here since the Restoration,' Polly chimed in, which was more reassuring than alarming, because she sounded, if faintly, like her usual self.

Lady Jane snorted in a most hearty fashion. 'I cannot think of a more harmless man with whom to be caught in the gardens, even in a mutual state of undress.'

This dismissive comment struck Leo rather hard, since he had just been feeling very glad, and slightly guilty, that Lady Jane lived on the east side, and therefore he did not have to cross the expanse of Base Court under the reproachful glare or pleading questions of Sergeant Hamilton.

Polly was going to be very annoyed when she found out he'd walked into, and partially through, the poor man.

'Not as harmless as you act, of course,' Lady Jane said, making him start. 'I must say, Mr Sweetwater, it has been excessively unkind of you to pretend I'm the only one who senses the Fountain Court presence. Lady George has been going about telling all the other ladies I'm at the awkward time of life.'

'I don't know what that means,' Leo said.

'And never you mind, either! Though I do receive invitations for plentiful tea and teacakes now, so it is not *entirely* dreadful.'

She looked somewhere between puzzled and pleased by the kindness of her fellow residents, which was close enough to Leo's usual reaction that he felt quite the spirit of camaraderie, until she added, 'And it was no kinder to perform your stone wall act at Mrs Willis, either.'

'I was eight, my lady,' Leo said, defensive only because he knew she was right.

It wasn't that he didn't want to apologise. It was that apologising had never blunted his mother's constant background hum of disapproval, so he possessed, simultaneously, a reflexive habit of deploying it and yet a dim view of its effectiveness. He *was* gradually working his way towards helping Mr Willis, at least.

They'd come all the way up the Privy Garden and reached the residents' ingress on the south front, which Leo, servant's son, probably wouldn't have felt comfortable using even if it hadn't led on to Fountain Court's southern cloister. Lady Jane had left one of the gates ajar when she'd slipped out, pushed by the invisible smog of dread.

She released his arm. They both knew this was as far as Leo would accompany her; he'd go home the long, northern, way, avoiding both Fountain and Base Courts. At this distance from the river and the rising mist, the air felt very clear and crisp, yet thick and murky on the other side of the gateway – though not, Leo could only hope, to Lady Jane and her lesser sensitivity.

'You are not eight any more, Mr Sweetwater,' Lady Jane said, by way of farewell. 'Perhaps it is time to stop pretending your problems, like your ghosts, do not exist, yes?'

Polly said 'Hah!'

He really did not think it fair to have his moment of brave maturity come back on him so swiftly.

To cap off Leo's long week, even Chapel Court seemed busier than usual that Friday.

As Leo yawned and fretted and shivered in the thin sunshine, Mr Edward Jesse, Deputy Itinerant Surveyor in the Office of Woods, Forests and Land Revenues, cut through the court.

Since Polly wasn't here, this made for a rare opportunity to buttonhole a very busy man, responsible not only for the care of the public gardens and parks, but for the maintenance of the Palace buildings, and, in particular and ongoing, the restoration of the Great Hall.

'Good afternoon, Mr Jesse. Might I enquire…'

It was apparently surprising enough for Leo Sweetwater to volunteer to speak that he managed to stop Mr Jesse mid-bustle. 'I'm off to Brighton shortly, Sweetwater,' he said querulously. 'My constitution, it needs the cold seaside bathing before winter truly bites, but I have yet to deal with this dreadful vandalism in the Wilderness. You know what I say, "the public is expected to protect what is intended for the public enjoyment", and some incorrigible blighter is singularly failing at it! I don't have time for other grievances.'

He had, Leo knew from Cole's mild disgruntlement, a nervous temperament. 'I'm not making a complaint,' he said quickly. 'I thought you'd be the man to ask a history question, given your very interesting guidebook.'

Jesse had published *A Summer's Day at Hampton Court* a few years ago. His senior position meant he had the advantage of Mr Grundy and his earlier guidebook – but Felix Summerly's new handbook was now beating out both of them.

This meant Leo's flattery was welcome, and Mr Jesse's harried expression settled. His thin chest puffed up. 'I will certainly endeavour to provide an accurate answer.'

'Is today the anniversary of something?' Leo asked. 'Did something happen at Hampton Court Palace in the small hours of the eleventh of November, many years ago?'

'Why, yes, of course,' Mr Jesse said. 'On this day in 1647, Charles the First escaped his imprisonment.'

Leo sat back, frowning.

'Not in the early morning, though. It was that evening.'

Surprised, Leo demanded, 'Are you sure?' with an unwise lack of diplomacy.

Mr Jesse looked down his nose, layering on extra officiousness. 'The king claimed he was writing letters to catch the foreign post and was not to be disturbed. By the time Colonel Whalley overcame his squeamish reluctance to break royal protocol and enter his chamber, the king had long since vanished down the Privy Stairs and through the Privy Garden to a waiting boat on the Thames.' He tapped the side of his nose. 'Just as Oliver Cromwell wanted it, when he sent on a letter warning assassination was imminent.'

Leo thanked him and bid him good day, somewhat abstractedly.

Next, Eliza strolled in to pass him the *Graham's Magazine* issue that contained the Poe story, *Murders in the Rue Morgue*. She was trailed by Polly, who appeared entirely her usual self, including pulling a face at him when he stared at her too long. Taken with Mrs Crowe's *Susan Hopley* and hearing talk of Dupin, she'd demanded he ask for the loan. She hovered behind the bench, and, the moment Eliza set the magazine down atop the stack of literature Leo had brought along, she began to badger him to excuse himself and read it to her immediately.

Her incessant bedevilment relieved his mind no end, but it meant he was quite distracted from properly greeting Cole when he joined them. Max snuffled at Polly's bare feet – 'Impudent cur,' she said, though fondly – before heaving himself over Leo's booted ones. The big fluffy body against his shins went some way to keeping the ghostly chill at his back at bay.

Mr Grundy, Palace Superintendent, came by while Leo, Cole, and Eliza were still chatting about the story – 'Do *not* let her spoil it for us!' – and Cole's recent trip to London, though his self-important stride became more of a scurry when he noticed them.

This appeared justified when Cole called, 'Mr Grundy!' in censorious tones.

Polly said, 'Ooh,' and left off harassing Leo so she could watch the unfolding drama. It had to be said that both Leo and Eliza sat back and watched with their own interest.

'Big dogs belong in the Royal Mews, Mr Solong.' Mr Grundy sounded quite harassed himself, and was plainly deploying attack as the best form of defence.

'The dog is doing his job, Mr Grundy.'

They all four (five) stared at Max, laid comfortably across Leo's feet. The dog lazily thumped his tail, eyes slitted half-closed in pleasure at the attention.

'Does his job entail keeping Mr Sweetwater warm?' Mr Grundy demanded.

'Of course,' Cole said, very gravely. 'It is his primary duty.'

Mr Grundy huffed. 'In that case, Mrs Grundy is also merely doing her duty!'

With this obscure pronouncement, he made his escape through to Fountain Court.

Eliza took her own farewell, taking a pile of penny dreadfuls in exchange for the magazine, not without a shake of her head at Leo's appalling taste. It was in the spirit of the sensational stories to blame a ghost for it, but he refrained.

Once they were alone, Cole sat on the bench by Leo and tucked his feet under the great lump of dog as well. 'I'm wondering if you could help me out with something, Leo.'

'You are busy tonight,' Polly interjected fiercely. 'You're staying indoors with me tonight.'

Recognising the only way to make it through the rest of the day without constant badgering, Leo obligingly said, 'Not tonight.'

'No, next week. It'll be a full moon and Mrs Grundy will be visiting her sister.'

Leo was about to protest that he wouldn't cross Mrs Grundy when Cole added, eyes glinting, 'We're going to raid her erotica room.'

Leo started helplessly laughing.

Mrs Grundy, notoriously, was sternly convinced that certain sights were not appropriate for the eyes of women and children. She kept a locked room full of priceless national artwork, all depicting naked people, often mid-cavort.

'What did she confiscate this time?' Leo managed to ask eventually, recovering both from his laughing fit and the way Cole was grinning at him in unfettered delight.

'A statue, right out of the garden. I can't ask any of my men to help me carry it back down, it's not fair to embroil them in a fight amongst the senior staff.'

'But it's all very well for me to risk annoying her?'

'Oh, I rather think you might be good for a lark or two under that quiet exterior, Leo,' Cole said, and Leo's stomach performed a lazy twirl in alarm and pleasure and spasming need.

'Your affections are showing,' Polly whispered, wafting cool air his way.

He hastily leaned to scratch Max's ears, fingers burrowing into sun-warmed fur. He reminded himself that Cole didn't think their Friday meetings were anything special, and that was as it should be. He reminded himself Cole had chuckled warmly at several quips from Eliza, after casually ascertaining that Leo had no arrangement with her.

Leo hadn't wanted to notice that, but he had.

Cole shifted his weight. In more serious tones, he said, 'Stayed in London longer than I planned, this week.'

'I know,' Leo said, before clearing his throat. He hadn't meant to sound so certain, as if he felt Cole's comings and goings like a needle responding to electromagnetic pulses to spell out a secret. 'How are the boys?'

Cole's face immediately softened at the mention of his four nephews, none as yet christened Walter, though one bore the Minto homage.

'Scamps,' he said, with a tender smile to belie the incriminating word. 'Running their mother ragged. But I didn't see much of them, after Tussaud's. I was about my own errand.'

Cole, in Leo's opinion, spent a good deal too much of his spare time about errands for the Townsend Farquhar family, so he was pleased to hear this evidence of selfishness. 'Oh?'

'I went to Shadwell, like you suggested.'

'Did you?' Leo said, pleased. 'And did you find what you needed?'

'I met some lascars from George Town, in fact, where I was born. It's a real mix there, they – we – are descended from Arabs and Chinese and

Indians and other peoples from the local region. They were having a sort of…' Cole frowned. 'An annual fast, called Ramadan.'

'Like Lent?' Leo said, though he was about as passing familiar with that as with this other observance.

'Maybe. No food or drink may pass their lips between sunup and sundown for the month – their month, not ours. They very generously invited me to their evening fast-breaking meal.'

'That must have been an experience.'

'Yes,' Cole said. 'An odd feeling, to be surrounded by faces much like I see in the mirror, but not understand a word they were saying, and generally be quite hulking.' He shrugged. 'I don't usually feel like a large man.'

'You're not a small man,' Leo said, provoking Polly into gusting cold air over the back of his neck.

'I felt like a giant,' Cole said. 'Poor underfed devils. Not to say they didn't lay on a good meal for me, with an awful lot of very hot spice.'

He smiled as he said it. Leo said, 'They hadn't reckoned with Mrs Clarke's influence on your menus?'

'Would you believe it was a different kind of heat than Indian food? I all but choked from the burn of it.' He laughed. 'So that amused everyone well enough, broke the ice. I also learned a lovely little word: *stengah*.' He lifted his brows at Leo, his smile becoming wry. 'From *sa tengah*, meaning one-half. It's for ordering a mixed drink.'

Leo had already begun to wince as Cole finished, 'Or referring to a half-caste.'

'That doesn't sound like a pleasant evening at all.'

'No, it was,' Cole said. 'If all I have to complain of is a spicy meal and a word thrown back at me that was thrown at them first, I have little cause, right?'

'Were you at least able to ask about your name?'

'Oh yes, they had plenty of English between them. They had two ideas for Solong. One is that it's from *sayang*, which is a word for love, for families. Not romantic love.'

'It might have made for an interesting time, otherwise,' Leo said, before he could think better of it.

Cole looked blank. 'Oh, no, it was all unmarried men, they segregate from women.'

Leo knew that, from his time in London. He gave a short nod, smiling to himself while simultaneously ignoring the amused snort from Polly.

'The other idea,' Cole went on, a fraught note entering his voice, subtle but still enough to catch Leo's notice, 'was that it's a bastard-isation of *anak sulung*.' He looked down at his hands, resting placidly in his lap. 'That one means eldest child.'

Leo's heart gave a painful thump at those calm words. 'And you're not your *father's* eldest child.'

'Exactly. But he gave me that name because that's how he heard my ayah referring to me. My mother. She was my mother.'

'I'm sorry,' Leo said quietly.

Cole gave a minute shake and said, hearty, 'A'll stop ma mumpin, it's no sae baud.'

'No—' Leo checked himself. He delved under Eliza's magazine, pulling out a volume that had arrived from London the day before. 'This is for you.'

He'd been in two minds about this gift, but now he all but thrust it into Cole's hands. Cole read the title, and the ever-informative subtitle, aloud. '*Malayan Literature: Comprising Romantic Tales, Epic Poetry and Royal Chronicles Translated Into English for the First Time.*' He looked up, eyes shining. 'Leo. I don't know what to say.'

'Percy, thou utter calf lolly!' Polly cried. 'He will know how you feel about him.'

'It's nothing,' Leo said quickly. 'I just thought... You said she used to tell you stories, and maybe you'll read these ones and they'll sound familiar somehow... I know it's not...'

'It's not nothing,' Cole said. He traced slow fingers over the black and gold decorations stamped onto the maroon cloth binding. 'This is terribly thoughtful. I think it might be the most thoughtful thing anyone has ever done for me.'

This was, as far as Leo was concerned, yet another damning indict-ment on the entire Townsend Farquhar family.

Cole was now gazing at him with such intensity that he had to look away. It had been a stupid, sentimental act, and Polly was right, he'd be lucky if Cole didn't start to wonder at a man taking a single throwaway comment so much to heart that he'd written to book-adjacent acquaint-ances in London to ask after Malayan titles.

Indeed, when he dared glance back, Leo saw that there was something askance in Cole's expression, a nascent frown, like a scurrilous suspicion was dawning on him, about just how much he must have been inhabit-ing Leo's thoughts, to produce such a magnitude of thoughtfulness.

Leo flushed and turned away again, desperate for a distraction. His gaze caught on a figure wandering into Chapel Court: Harry, in a reprise of the previous week.

Not an exact reprise. Max lifted his head again, and this time his whole aspect altered. His body tensed against Leo's shins, and his soft brown eyes turned narrow and hard, the livestock guardian spotting a threat to his flock.

Still clutching the book, Cole dropped his free hand onto the dog's head, thick fingers spread soothingly over the broad expanse of soft fur. 'Haud yer wheesht, laddie.'

Harry held back, eyeing dog and gardener with equal suspicion, before all his attention came to Leo. 'Wouldn't mind another try at a daguerreotype, what do you say, Sweetwater? One more go round?'

Leo's stomach gave another slow swoop, this one a less complicated frisson of lustful anticipation.

But, no. He had decided he wasn't risking Harry again. He had very firmly decided that.

Harry smiled at Leo with intent, and it was the last thumb on the scales of his shivering unbalance. He laid aside his firm decision and all his good sense and seized the opportunity to escape Cole's regard with both hands.

Anyway, he was still cold from the incident in the small hours. He needed body heat to truly warm up.

Cole looked taken aback, almost to the point of put out, when Leo whipped his feet out from under Max and rose. With a mean-spirited, self-defensive pang, Leo thought, *See how* you *like it when time spent with* you *isn't anything special.*

He was, however, immediately contrite. Cole could hardly be blamed for treating Leo as a friend, when that was all Leo could ever be to him. He couldn't be blamed that his friend had betrayed his partiality in seeking out an obscure book just for him. He could certainly not be blamed for treading the well-laid path towards matrimony, especially when he was so obviously besotted with his nephews and must want sons of his own. Eliza wasn't the woman for that job, but he'd find someone else soon enough, if his mind had turned that way.

And that was as it should be, and Leo had no call to be cattish about any of it, especially not his own sentimentality.

'Apologies, Mr Solong,' he said, 'we'll manage next week without interruption. And yes, I will help you with that errand.'

'See you, then,' Cole said. He half-lifted the book. 'And thank you again.'

'Goodbye,' Leo said, though this probably sounded strangely loud and definite, because it was aimed more at Polly than Cole. 'Mr Solong.'

'Good afternoon, Mr Sweetwater. Mr Walpole.'

Polly floated along with him and Harry anyway. 'He outright lied about leaving last week,' she reminded him. 'He kissed you with his brother just around the other side of the partition wall. He's careless, and a liar, and you are being foolish for the sake of a pretty face and prettier thighs.'

He let Harry, and his face and his thighs, into the shut-up studio. Harry had him against the door the moment he turned the key behind them, working busily at the fastenings in his way, freeing Leo from layers of clothing with a proficiency remarkable in that he managed to rain kisses upon him the entire time.

'Batter my heart, three-person'd God, for you,' he murmured in Leo's ear, with the cant of more poetry to it, as his hands slid over his shoulders and down his ribs.

Polly bobbed. 'Donne again, how dull. I do have to give due for using one of the holy sonnets, though, admirably bold as a precursor to vice.'

Leo opened his eyes and glared until she sighed. 'I just want you to be safe, Leo.'

His breath hitched, the reminder of that morning too stark.

She huffed at his silence. Departing, she called over her shoulder, 'I am very much looking forward to the "I told you so", muttonhead.'

Harry, apparently sensing Leo's focus was not wholly on him, caught his chin and kissed him with some demand to it. 'As yet but knock, breathe, shine, and seek to mend; That I may rise and stand, o'erthrow me, and bend' – he was accompanying each verb with a soft kiss to newly bared skin, moving inexorably downwards – 'Your force to break, blow, burn and make me new.'

Leo came to his senses just in time, pulling Harry, and his tellingly light-coloured trousers, back up. 'Your knees will mark on this floor.'

'I'll wear your stains with pride, old man.'

'Not walking out of my studio, you won't!'

Harry turned spiteful as Leo pushed him away. 'You are bordering on tiresome, Sweetwater.'

'And you are well across the border into brazen,' Leo said flatly.

He'd known it, he'd known it the moment he'd seen him. Polly had been correct, he'd been led by his long plum, as she ever so delightfully called it, and his own silly embarrassment and fluster, and was now only failing to belatedly regain his usual equilibrium because he was too busy kicking himself.

With a sulky fold of his arms that served to remind Leo how young he was, Harry said, 'Gossip doesn't drag one before the magistrate.'

'You risk nothing but idle talk; my entire livelihood here rests on my discretion.' Leo reached for the key sticking from the big iron lock. 'We'll say you changed your mind.'

'Hold there,' Harry protested, closing his hand around Leo's. 'I haven't.'

'I have.' Leo remembered he couldn't open the door until he'd made himself decent. He collected his undershirt.

'No, no.' Harry became all charming smiles and coaxing tones again. 'I repent, my dear, I repent! I'm too used to London, I forget what a gossipy little village we're in.'

Leo, having miraculously recovered his common sense, wanted to cling onto it like a shipwrecked sailor to a raft, but Harry's hands were warm, and Leo's core was still cold.

Harry's lips were warmer yet, and they traced pleasure and spoke poetry.

Leo drank the attention down. It had been so long, too long, since London, since being held by someone who knew him and was fond of him and wanted him in the way Harry wanted him, and who didn't look at him with a frown forming between fine, dark eyebrows because he'd been too tender in his sensibilities.

Eventually, they were both naked on blankets on the floor of the backroom, Harry moaning with his mouth around Leo's prick and his large hands spread over Leo's ribs, fingertips digging in, pinning him down in the firm way he liked, sending waves of shivering heat through him.

He spent quietly; too quietly for Harry.

'You haven't erupted yet,' he complained, smiling.

'I just erupted in your mouth,' Leo pointed out. 'I'm not sure what more you want.'

Harry, lying atop him now, laughed into his neck, and Leo smiled at the ceiling, enjoying the weight and warmth. He stroked his back. 'I think you have the wrong idea, Harry. I'm quiet, out of bed and in it. I'm bound to disappoint, if you expect otherwise.'

Scoffing, Harry slid his hands down between them. 'I have oil.'

Leo hesitated, then made a small noise as one of Harry's hands probed.

'That's it,' Harry murmured. 'I came, I saw, I view'd, I slipped in.'

'I don't, ah...'

'I'll make it good.'

Men said that. Men seemed to think their pricks were magic wands. 'I don't,' Leo said, firmer.

Harry sighed, but desisted obligingly enough. His stand pressed against Leo's thigh. If Leo had trusted him, he might have rolled onto his stomach and let him rub off against the cleft of his arse. But he thought that temptation would be too much. He closed his thighs tight over the hard length of Harry's insistent prick and dragged him down for a kiss.

This would be, he thought, the last time.

ELEVEN

THE HOSTE HOST LINGERED, THROWING A sop to the Lord Chamberlain, whose remit to Mrs Grundy had her recording how many nights each resident was actually resident, another reason the poor woman copped the brunt of Palace ire. He became decidedly peevish when he perceived ingratitude regarding receiving royal favour for winning royal grace.

Lady Harriet's guests, the Walpoles, departed at last.

Harry did not depart. He was still dodging the attentions of bailiffs, Leo supposed, but he did also seem unfathomably intent on a third liaison.

Since Harry had proved, in the end, obliging, Leo was not adverse in principle, with the awareness that he would have to be the one who took the precautions. He could not allow another meeting in the studio, because Harry's off-hours visits did not go unnoticed, and there were only so many daguerreotypes of himself one man could reasonably want.

Someone of Leo's station couldn't go through Lady Harriet's front door, which, anyway, was on the ground floor directly off Fountain Court. Conversely, a man like Henry Walpole had no clear cause to be calling on a man like Leo Sweetwater. Either event would raise eyebrows from one side of Hampton Court to the other; Palace society would talk of little else. Skulking over late at night or knocking on back doors was an invitation to be talked of even more.

Nor could they repair to one of the little nooks or crannies Leo knew well from his days as errand boy. The need to avoid servants and ghosts, both his concern rather than Harry's, put paid to that notion.

The Palace was such a tiny, tiny village.

'Julia Johnstone had the same problem when she was carrying on with Colonel Cottin,' Polly informed him. If the teasing was any indication, she had suffered no lingering ill effects from the incident the previous week, though she was also quick to vanish if he tried to bring it up. 'She wrote about it in her memoir, claimed they barely managed three times in four months. Or was it four times in three months? Enough to get herself into a situation, anyway.'

'I truly do not want to hear about Colonel Cottin's exploits,' he said, before offering up an innocent smile. 'Three or four times?'

'She said he hid under her bed and waited for the household to go to sleep.'

'That seems...'

'Ridiculous and entirely made up for salacity?' Polly said. 'She also said he first seduced her on a stone staircase.'

'Putting aside how quick they would've had to be to fit it in — that is very immature, Polly — between servants' comings and goings, it sounds decidedly uncomfortable.'

'And this was when dresses were very simple, so there wouldn't have even been any padding under her derriere.'

'The edge of the step would have dug right into the lower back,' Leo agreed. 'Ah, which staircase?'

'I am not helping you, sheep-for-brains!' she said, smiling. Then she said, 'I've never seen you come this close to reckless. Are you infatuated with the dandy, pet?'

Leo shook his head. He knew where his heart lay, and it wasn't with Harry. 'I'm fond of him.' It sounded weak and Polly's expression told him so. 'He's immature and impulsive, I suppose, but it's quite pleasant to feel a little swept away for once in my life.'

'Also he's very good with his mouth?'

'Also that,' Leo said. 'By which *I* mean the poetry, and I have no concept of what *you're* referring to.'

'I like that he puts you in fine humour,' Polly conceded. 'I reserve my right to the "I told you so".'

'He'll be gone soon enough, with his aunt.'

'Good,' Polly muttered. 'They're hither and thither across Fountain Court far too often.'

Finally, Leo suggested to Harry that they walk across to the Bushey and Wick. The loan of a backroom would make for another hasty coupling, but it would be private, with the all-important lock on the all-important door, as well as removing their activities from the immediate environs of the Palace. Leo had not gone entirely muttonheaded: he knew discretion was the primary means of keeping the goodwill of the gentry despite any rumours Harry was complacent enough to let fly.

Harry was not a man who wore boots suitable for a cross-country stroll, yet he assented to the plan with alacrity. They set out on Thursday evening. It was still quite early, but the sun had gone down two hours before, the nights drawing in as November advanced. Mr Abnett, the lamplighter, had been about his duties, however, and the moon was full in an unseasonably clear sky. The trek down the chestnut avenue would practically be a romantic moonlit stroll.

Leo would have been content, in company, to walk up Old Moat Lane directly to the Lion Gates, but Harry wanted to meander through the Wilderness.

'I don't trust that,' Polly said darkly, floating along behind them, not adding noticeably to the chill evening air for Leo, though Harry shivered and drew his overcoat closer. 'I've seen too many courtiers luring innocents into those byways.'

She had been looking forward to the final chapters of *Zanoni* tonight, after their satisfying Dupin digression. Leo, on the other hand, was looking forward to sex, so he had sympathy for her, but very little willingness to heed another round of dire warnings, especially now he knew his safety was a deathbed fixation, likely imposed from the first moment they met. It was cold; Harry would want the warmth and ease of the pub, not a brief and uncomfortable clinch in a hedge.

Leo shortly stood corrected when he turned down the first bypass off the main path and Harry tugged him the other way.

'Don't let him,' Polly said sharply.

'This is the long way round.' Leo tried to plant his feet against Harry's insistence, but stumbled on a patch of roughened ground, the remnant of a hasty repair. 'And watch out for holes in the path.'

'Oh, I know about those,' Harry said, waving a casual hand.

'Wandering the Wilderness often, are we?' Leo said drily.

'You were quite right about the willingness of the Hussars,' Harry said with a wink. Leo felt a flare of something quite like jealousy, a little like hurt. But he couldn't be surprised: he'd been reluctant, and Harry was not patient. 'But it's not just that.'

They'd come to the side path to another *cabinet de verdur*, and Harry pulled Leo down it, his familiarity with the winding paths and secret corners now explicable. He finally let go, and delved into the thick hornbeam, producing, of all astonishing things, a shovel.

He flourished it. 'I've been *digging* the holes.' He laughed at Leo's expression; he must have been agape. 'Darling, I did tell you I owe rather a lot of brass to some rather unpleasant people.'

He hadn't, quite. 'And a treasure hunt is your solution?'

'The only one within my reach, while the old man plays silly buggers with his purse strings.'

Polly wrinkled her nose. 'What the dickens is this foppish lout blathering on about?'

Leo said, 'You'd rather chase a wild story about Wolsey's stolen plate than follow your cousin into a fruitful profession and please your father?'

'Wolsey's plate? I never heard such nonsense!'

'Tosh, not Wolsey.' Shoving the shovel back into its hiding place, Harry confidently reclaimed Leo's hand and drew him further down the path. 'Bacon.'

'Bacon,' Leo repeated.

'He has lost the little sense he had.'

'Francis Bacon wrote about it.' This *cabinet de verdur* was a small circle. There were two even smaller garden rooms, to the east and west, and Harry laughingly dragged Leo into the eastern one. 'Near the end of Queen Elizabeth's reign. Thieves broke into a guest chamber in one of the tiltyard towers. Absconded with a purse worth four hundred pounds in jewels and coins. It'd be worth a lot more now, nearly two hundred and fifty years later.'

It was worth a lot as it was. 'But—'

'One of the thieves claimed they dumped it right about here when they heard the hue and cry. He hanged anyway, alongside his friends, and they never found the loot. It's still buried under our feet.' He looked around, rueful. 'Somewhere in this southeast quadrant, anyway.'

'Does this utter poltroon not know it was an orchard until the Orange pair?' Polly demanded.

Leo repeated the question, somewhat more diplomatically, adding, 'There's no point digging up the paths when it could be anywhere under the greenery.'

'If it's even still here, or was ever here.' Polly swooped about the tight confines of the hornbeam. 'Nothing has ever been said of it in my hearing, not by the living, not by the dead.'

'Yes, I realise that *now*,' Harry said with a roll of his eyes, all affable good humour. 'Perhaps I am being presumptuous' – Polly snorted – 'but your ghost must know where it is.'

Both Leo and Polly froze. Then Polly began to slowly rise in the very centre of the tiny garden room, the temperature dropping in concert.

Leo concentrated very hard on not looking at her and her ice-cold outrage. 'You know that's just a foolish story about me, don't you?'

'My dear, sweet Winter,' Harry said, smile turning sardonic. He huffed a breath, and they both watched it whiten. 'You do bring the cold.'

'It's November.'

'How did you know the Paget boys were coming to your shop that morning?'

'I didn't,' Leo said flatly, quailing internally.

'You were alarmed well before they burst in.'

'Coincidence.'

Harry smirked. He looked like he was enjoying himself. 'Who do you talk to, when you talk to yourself?'

'You answered your own question.'

'Who do you smile at, when you smile at empty air?'

'Empty air.' He effected disdain. 'It's a *story*. It sells ghost cards.'

Catching his chin between finger and thumb, Harry tilted his head up and told him, rather fondly, 'Little liar.'

'Brazen-faced lubberwort!' Polly shouted.

Leo shook him off, stepping back. A true gentleman would be violently outraged to be accused of lying, regardless of the truth of the accusation. He mustered an icy, 'Good evening to you, sir,' and made a valiant attempt to stalk away.

Harry seized his arm and pulled him back. Leo bristled; the edge of coercion was much less pleasant when he hadn't chosen to indulge it.

'Come now, Sweetwater, calm down, tell your ghost to calm down, it's freezing in here.'

'Don't tell me to calm down, you great dandy pratt,' Polly seethed. 'Get your hands off him!'

Leo's nerve broke. He looked up at Polly floating above them, arms folded, freckled face thunderous. She'd risen above the hornbeam hedges enclosing them, and their tops were silvering with frost.

'There it is,' Harry said, following Leo's gaze to the aforementioned empty air. He didn't seem alarmed by swathes of leaves turning frosty-white, so Leo supposed it one of those ghostly sights for his eyes only.

'Tell him to let you go at once, or I shall lay hands upon him and he shall be very sorry indeed!'

Leo unpeeled Harry's fingers. He couldn't relay the threat without acceding to the accusation, and it was an empty threat anyway. Polly couldn't touch anyone but him. She'd just make Harry slightly colder than he already was, not even the sort of bone-deep chill that took Leo when touched.

Polly dropped, then, to float beside him, brushing close enough for his subtle matter to imbue her. The leaves of the hornbeam began to rustle, a frantic whispering in the quiet night. He felt a thread of ice run through his core.

'Let it be,' he said to both of them, shivering.

Polly subsided. She knew he didn't like it when she used him like that, however accidental and well-meaning. But Harry, who'd apparently noticed nothing more threatening than a swirl of wind, pushed him bodily against the quietened hornbeam.

'I like you in high dudgeon,' he murmured. 'Puts colour in your cheeks.'

Leo fended off a kiss. 'Not here.'

Polly hissed but, rather than impose on Leo again, channelled her feelings into a snarled, 'Thou presumptuous dollop of runny excrement, fie to thee!'

Leo was inclined to agree. He corrected himself. 'Not *anywhere*, Walpole.'

Harry sighed theatrically, holding up his palms in appeasement. 'Fine, fine. I apologise, darling. I'll speak not one more word about it to you.'

He didn't resist when Leo wriggled from his hold, though his eyes were alight with lazy amusement as Leo huffily dusted himself down and straightened his clothes.

'I am sorry,' Harry said then, taking a stab at sounding sincere. 'We were going to have a lovely evening together, and I've quite spoiled it.'

Another statement Leo was inclined to agree with. He gave a small shrug.

'Don't be like that.' Harry chafed his gloved hands between his own. 'Let's take a walk over to your little molly pub, you'll be in good humour again by then, and if not, an ale or three will do it.'

'Do not let him cozen you, Percy!'

'I'm not going to,' Leo said.

'You're being tiresome, darling.' Harry still seemed amused, but Leo could hear the note of sulky impatience beginning to tinge his voice. 'You've said as much twice before, you've given in twice before.'

'Not this time.'

Harry snorted, reaching for Leo. Leo flinched, and, in the same instant, so did Harry. His gaze was directed over Leo's shoulder, at the entrance to the garden room.

Leo, alarmed, turned to look, but there was nothing to see.

By the time he turned back, Harry had recovered his composure. 'Do I need a little poetry to grease my way? Let's see.' He set a finger against his chin, mockingly thoughtful. 'We're in the Hampton Court gardens, so let's try this one.' His voice assumed its tone of smooth recitation. 'Dull and insensible, couldst see—'

'Suckling!' That wasn't an insult Leo had heard from Polly before.

'—A thing so near a deity—'

'Lucy.' All the fierceness had stripped from her voice; she sounded near tears. 'So lost a thing—'

The extra bite in the air was gone. Leo looked up: Polly was gone.

He was in no danger. Harry had cottoned on to Leo's penchant for firm treatment, but he wasn't the type to use true force. Leo was still surprised to be abandoned, but it was mingled with pity.

'—Move up and down,' Harry pressed closer, rubbing his thigh against Leo's groin, 'and feel no change?' He smiled. 'Well, now. I think I'm feeling a change.'

Leo's body had responded to the familiar scent and warmth, Harry's weight leaning on him, the insistent friction. He was still in no mood to indulge the impudence.

Nuzzling him, Harry recited, 'And upon that discovery, Searched after parts that are more dear' – sliding his hands under Leo's coat, he tangled fingers into Leo's waistband – 'As fancy seldom stops so near.'

Leo pushed him back with both hands, not roughly, but with great certainty.

Something about his expression must have conveyed his resolve, for Harry pulled a rueful face and turned placatory again. 'But I'm off to

London tomorrow, darling. Truly, this time.' When Leo remained unmoved, he looked away, and in different tones, said, 'A goodbye kiss, at least?'

Despite his assurance to Polly that he wouldn't be cozened, Leo thawed, softening in accord with the sudden softness of Harry's manner.

He had been a generous lover, and given Leo something he'd needed, and their acquaintance did not need to end on such a sour note. Leo had no intention of resuming the walk to Hampton Wick but he could unbend enough to grant the more modest request, in the privacy of a moonlit garden room where no one wandered at this time of night. He nodded.

'Dear, sweet Winter.' Harry gripped his face and lifted it so he could take his kiss, long and possessive.

Leo, magnanimous enough to already feel nostalgically fond, played along, even sliding one hand to the nape of Harry's neck by way of silent thanks, without begrudgery.

Harry was smiling smugly when he finally let him go. 'I suppose a goodbye suck is out of the question?'

'You're welcome to get on your knees, if the mood's struck you,' Leo said in return, confident Harry was merely messing about, and willing to keep their final leave-taking pleasant.

Harry's smile became downright triumphant. He took Leo by the shoulders and turned him about to reveal, standing at the entrance, the one person in the entirety of Hampton Court Palace who might be wandering the moonlit garden rooms at this time of night.

Cole.

TWELVE

THE SHOCK ON COLE'S FACE WAS stark in the low light of his lantern. Leo met his eyes for a blank moment of equal shock before Cole started, lowered his gaze and quickly hurried away.

Harry laughed, though he stopped abruptly when Max, white fur ghostly in the moonlight, padded down the path. The dog sat precisely where Cole had been, in the decisive way that meant he was not intending to move. He stared at them calmly.

Enlightenment dawned. Max was why Harry had flinched a few moments ago: he'd seen the dog patrol past. He must have therefore suspected Cole was nearby, hunting the Wilderness vandal.

All further thought foundered. 'You knew he was there!'

'Who cares, he scurried off quickly enough.'

He was insufferably pleased with the trick. Leo spoke through gritted teeth, the skin of his face tight. 'He could go straight to the magistrate.'

'He won't, he's too fond of you.'

'He *was*,' Leo said, which was the truer fear: that horrible past tense. But he didn't entirely discount the threat of Cole calling on the law; people did worse to exposed sods they'd once held in higher regard than Cole held him. 'He could inform on both of us.'

'What of it? I'm Lord Orford's son, he's a jumped-up gardener,' Harry said comfortably.

'He's the Royal Gardener,' Leo said, now somewhat confused as to the direction of his outrage. 'He came up under the Aiton brothers at Kew.'

Harry straightened, face abruptly rigid with cold scorn. 'The man's a half-caste coolie.'

Shocked again, Leo drew back. 'Beyond the pale, Walpole.'

A shamed expression crossed Harry's face before he turned sulkily, defiantly spiteful. 'He's never going to want you, you know.'

'What has that to do with anything?' Leo exclaimed heatedly.

'Pining over him, leaping to defend him. He will never want you like you want him, never.'

'That's my business, you had no right to make it yours.'

'It's pathetic,' Harry said, voice creeping with unseemly sullenness. 'You're hiding away in this cramped little village, squandering yourself on a man who might let you suck his prick if you get him drunk enough, but won't ever return your regard.'

Leo checked at the vulgarity, and then checked again. 'Are you *jealous*?'

Harry gave a hard bark of contemptuous amusement. His generous mouth was suddenly thin and cruel, just like his older brother's. 'Think much of yourself?'

Leo rubbed between his eyes. His anger had ebbed; he was mostly just confused now, shading to hurt. More for his own comfort than to Harry, he said, 'I suppose nothing will come of it, with you away to London.'

Harry was correct in one sense, the local magistrate wouldn't chase a lord's son with any great enthusiasm, and he'd want Leo's sin overlooked as well, so he wasn't obliged to. Leo didn't truly fear the law. He feared what Cole could do to his reputation.

He didn't need to fear the shattering of their friendship, merely regret, bitterly, that it had already happened, the instant Cole had finally recognised what he was.

The quiet anticipation of fond memories was extinguished. He would have done anything to take back the moments spent with Harry. He couldn't even manage a cold farewell; he turned away in silence.

Harry grimaced. 'Leo, darling, I didn't mean—'

Max gave a single bark as Harry tried to grab Leo's arm, and he jerked back, glancing warily between the dog and Leo. Leo took that as his cue to make good his departure, not wasting a look back.

Max padded at his heel all the way to his apartment, and sat on his stoop. Leo gave him a rub around the ears and a final, 'Good boy.'

He wasn't sure Cole would ever let him pat Max again.

He spent a horridly fretful night, and was so listless over tea and toast in the morning that Sally was hesitant to accompany John to Hampton for her usual Friday out, unnecessarily asking permission to go as if she hoped he would deny her.

Once he'd waved them off, Leo resisted crawling back under his blankets, which translated to sitting in the parlour instead, staring blankly into space while he stewed, cursing himself for allowing that kiss without a locked door between them and the world, excoriating himself for an utter fool for letting Harry turn his head in the first place, dreading his next encounter with Cole, who had to be disgusted, and would probably also be furious that Leo had let him tar himself with close association with a sod.

Eventually he realised he was waiting to see if the local constabulary would come knocking, and this was enough to force him outside.

He considered marching over to Wilderness House, or walking the grounds until he found Cole, but not seriously. Lady Jane had precisely put her finger on it: he'd never met a problem he wouldn't rather pretend didn't exist, and just identifying a poor habit did not make the poor habit go away. It had served him well enough with ghosts, until it didn't.

Speaking of…

It wasn't unusual for Polly to be absent, since his mornings were routine and large families' mornings were interestingly varied. But, despite his personal calamity, he couldn't forget the heartbroken way she'd whispered Lucy's name last night.

He started by Banqueting House, looking for Polly in the little wedge of garden.

She wasn't there. Given he now had to skirt both Fountain Court and Chapel Court, much of the eastern end of the Palace was out-of-bounds, but he walked a slow circuit of the southern gardens, and then Clock and Base Courts.

Sergeant Hamilton trailed him piteously across the latter, which he had also been avoiding for the last week. Today he could spare no attention for any ghost but his missing friend, and ignored every plaintive call, even as the timbre of them began to slide from plaintive to frustrated.

He found no sign of her, nor came across any fresh gossip which might indicate she was haunting one of the residents' apartments to eavesdrop, though he did have the muted satisfaction of hearing that the Hostes and Henry Walpole had departed.

He was returning home in defeat when Eliza caught up with him, coming from her own apartment off Fish Lane.

'Are you on your way to Chapel Court?' she asked, falling into step. 'I'll come along too, Mr Solong lent me an auld Rabbie Burns collection.' She flourished the book of poetry. 'Don't worry, I shan't linger about sticking an extra oar in your boat this week.'

'Not today.'

Since this was terse even for him, Eliza frowned. 'You go to Chapel Court every Friday.'

Leo rubbed at his temple. 'Headache.'

'What's wrong, Leo?'

'Headache,' Leo said, stubbornly.

'Did you have an argument with Solong?'

'No.' *I'm avoiding an argument with Solong.*

Narrow-eyed, Eliza said, 'I shall pass along the message, but do not be surprised when he comes knocking to make sure your *headache* is not a more serious ailment.'

Leo thought it unlikely in the extreme, but said, 'Tell him not to bother himself, then,' and bid her good day at his door, leaving her confused and slightly offended.

Cole wouldn't say anything to Eliza. She was Miss Smart to him and therefore would not make a suitable audience for any conversation he might be itching to have. As confidently brash as Eliza was, Leo didn't think she'd demand answers of Cole, either. If she did, and he answered, she'd almost certainly start an argument of her own.

Sally was still out at Hampton, and Leo breathed a quiet sigh for the pleasure of solitude before remembering he actually wanted his spirit familiar at the moment. He checked the parlour, without hope. She didn't venture upstairs, one of her sops to his scant privacy.

At a loose end, and inclined towards fretfulness, he laid down an oilcloth square under his north-facing window and set to losing his thoughts in painting.

Polly interrupted him. 'You must have been in a fine mulligrubs today.'

Leo, as accustomed as he was to ghostly manifestations, started violently from a deep, and judging by the light, long rumination. He followed her gaze and beheld his own painting.

'Well, that's not good,' he said.

'I'm no art critic, but I'd say it's *very* good,' Polly said.

This was terribly disingenuous. He'd finally painted Fountain Court.

The court, intended as a vista for royal eyes, was one of the prettiest locations of Hampton Court Palace, its symmetrical arches and stacked rectangular, circular and square windows a fine example of Baroque elegance. Any decent watercolour of it should have been beautiful, if conventionally so.

Leo, in his trance-like state, had imparted a deep sense of menace, a hint of screaming mouths to the arches, an open gullet to the salmon-pink bricks, gleaming eyes to the windows. The fountain at the centre was murky, its surface rippling as if a denizen under the dark water had just lazily flashed a fin.

He was having trouble tearing his gaze from the canvas. His body – hair prickling, heart racing, breath catching – was trying to tell him something would leap out at him if he did. The room was freezing.

Still, he had practice staving off this sort of reaction. He made himself turn to his friend. 'Are you well? I'm sorry you were upset last night.'

'I wasn't expecting to hear that vile poem, that's all,' she said. 'Men were disgusting about her back then.' She wrinkled her nose. 'I am sorry I left you. Tell me you sent Walpole off with a flea in the ear.'

'I did,' Leo said. She caught the hesitant note, but before she could chastise him, or pry, he waved his hand at the painting, watching it from the corner of his eye like it was a ghost. 'Isn't this a problem?'

'The workman will control them,' she said firmly. 'This time of year is difficult, and all the extra people walking over the court don't help. But the workman has been set on fixing cracks for well over a century, Leo. He knows his business.'

Leo set down his brush and took a few slow steps back from the easel. '*Are* there bodies buried under Fountain Court, then?'

'I don't know,' she said. 'I wasn't any different to other ghosts at first. I was anchored to the vicinity of the Water Gallery, playing out my last moments, over and over. Perhaps they dragged the bodies away, for a hasty burial in Cloyster Green Courte, as it was then. Perhaps I'm there, too. Perhaps I *was* those bones they found in Sir James's cellar. I don't know.'

He rubbed a hand over his roiling stomach. He'd felt a general pity for the Palace ghosts; it was why he'd wanted to help them move on, beyond the veil Lady Jane talked about. It was very different, hearing those words and knowing Polly, his vibrant, goodhearted friend, had suffered through the reality of them.

Still, she seemed more willing to answer than usual, and he was unnerved enough to press. 'You didn't finish telling me what happened to you.'

'It was the most tedious thing,' she said airily, though her face, eternally fresh and freckled, seemed drawn, pallid. 'They were trying to force secrets out of me, their enemies charged in – not to rescue me, mind you, they wanted the same information. I was killed because two men didn't notice me while they were busy killing each other. The rest fled.'

'You said you were trained to never tell.'

'Did I?'

'Did you mean trained like I've been inadvertently trained to not risk telling people certain things? Or did you mean in a more formal sense? Was Lucy…using you?'

Polly's translucence flickered. This was usually a precursor to fading away, but she steadied. 'It is hard for me to speak of this, even now. Not' – she held up a hand – 'emotionally, do not concern yourself. It's just an old story now. But I was accustomed to keeping Lucy's secrets and you know as well as I do how hard a habit that is to break.'

'Yes,' he said, layering as much sympathy as he could into the syllable.

'She was what was called an intelligencer. A she-intelligencer. It's an old word. Women made good couriers, in particular, because no one suspected them, at first, and then later, no one dared search them. She took messages to and from the king.'

'During the Great Rebellion,' Leo said. 'She was a Royalist spy?'

'By the time I knew her, she'd turned her coat and gone to work for Pym.' She showed a flair of her usual spirit at his blank look. 'Cromwell's man, muttonhead.'

'Cromwell?' Leo said, surprised. 'But you hate Cromwell.'

'I,' Polly said, 'was staunchly for limiting the power of kings, in fact. And I died for that cause, and then I had to linger and learn that Old Ironsides turned himself into a king in all but name. Brutalised the Irish. Claimed the Palace as his own. Destroyed the stained glass windows, closed the right of way, diverted water from the villages, moved Arethusa at his own whim! Raised taxes without approval from Parliament, he might as well have been Charles. He named his *son* the next Lord Protector, what is that if not just another king? He and Betty were called "Your Highness", for God's sake!'

She took a deep breath. In more mellow tones, she said, 'So, no, Lucy was not using me. I was working for her on a cause I believed, and still believe, was just. I believed it so righteous that I held by her side even after she stopped tumbling me, even though my heart hurt at every moment to know she didn't love me as I loved her. She carried a letter from Cromwell's hand to Colonel Whalley's, who was in charge of keeping Charles imprisoned at Hampton Court. I didn't know what the letter said, then, though I know now it was enough to scare Charles into escaping not even a day later, lest he become a "dead dog". I don't know if that was Cromwell's intention. I don't know if Lucy changed some words before she handed it over. She was never entirely on one side or the other. All I know is that both factions discovered she'd been the courier, and came to find out the contents. They couldn't harm her, so they harmed me. I wanted it that way. I died wanting it that way.'

'You wanted to keep her safe,' Leo said.

'Yes.' She let out the simulacrum of a breath. 'I wanted to keep her safe.'

Leo did not have enough facility with words to know what to say, nor did her manner suggest she desired consolation. Instead, she let him take her hand, just for a moment, not even long enough for the cold to sink its teeth in.

'It's just a story, Leo,' she said, pulling free. 'Too long ago to worry about. Now throw a cloth over that thing, and let's go read.'

She hovered close by him while he finished the last chapters of *Zanoni*, in between eating soup provided by a still-worried Sally, who, tired from her day out, went upstairs to her little room early. John stayed the night in Mrs Walton's household, spending both Friday evening and Saturday morning under Mr Walton's tutelage before coming home on the coal cart at midday.

They reached the final page and Leo closed the book. Polly tutted. 'Well. You wouldn't catch *me* giving up eternal life for love.'

The obvious comment about learning her lesson the first time hung in the air a moment, before Leo rallied enough to match her tone and say, 'But, Polly, you're already dead.'

She feigned a gasp. 'You can't go about telling ladies they're dead, Percy, it's not the done thing!'

He mostly smiled because she did, and she did because he did, a pleasantly reciprocal comfort. Then she said, hopefully, 'The Reynetts are having another party tonight.'

She wanted to go, of course. She fairly well might *need* to go, after all their recent upsets and revelations, for the warmth and noise and light. 'Are they? My invitation must have gone astray, *such* a shame.'

This weak attempt at a joke was enough to convince Polly he was only withdrawn, not distressed. She wafted away for her restorative convivial evening, leaving him to his quiet evening alone, for his own form of recuperation.

It did not stay quiet for long before a confident knock on his front door ruined it.

Sally would hasten to throw clothing on and rush down the stairs to answer it herself, if Leo tried to ignore it.

He opened the door to Cole.

Thirteen

Cole was wearing his gardening coat, thick gloves tucked into a pocket, no cap. On the heels of Leo's mumbled greeting to his boots, he said, 'You didn't come to Chapel Court today.'

Leo gave an extremely intelligent and eloquent response, to wit: 'Ah?'

'We're stealing the statue from Mrs Grundy's locked room tonight, remember?'

'You...' Leo flicked a glance at his face, and away. He couldn't bring himself to speak in more than a mutter. 'You still want my help with that?'

An ember of hope flared in his chest. Perhaps they would adhere to cultural tradition and simply pretend the whole sordid episode had never—

Cole said, 'Does indecent behaviour make your arms drop off, Leo?'

Startled, Leo finally looked at him properly, and was met with Cole's cheerful smile. 'Not...' He twitched, and said, stronger, 'Not as a rule, no.'

'Then, yes, I still want your help. Fetch your coat.'

Leo fetched his coat.

Mrs Grundy's storeroom was on the second storey, deliberately difficult to reach via the State Apartments tour route. Leo knew the servants' routes to reach it without needing keys, which he'd presumed was the real reason Cole had tapped him for assistance. Cole handed him a small lantern, and he led the way, in a silence that began to feel heavy enough to weight his lungs.

At last, on the final flight of narrow stone stairs, he said, 'You truly don't mind?' and winced. Stupid, stupid question. Of course Cole *minded*.

'Didna I say, scant days ago, that people might do with their bodies as they liked?' Cole said mildly. 'Do you think me so much the hypocrite?'

'I don't, no,' Leo said, without looking around at him.

'You do!' Cole, on the step below Leo, caught the tails of his coat, jerking him to a stop. 'Why?'

Leo reluctantly turned to face him. 'Leviticus?'

'Non-Conformist,' Cole said, thumping his chest.

'That's not...' He was on shaky ecclesiastical ground now. 'I don't think that's what that means.'

'In the literal sense, then,' Cole said. 'I choose to not conform in this matter.' He smiled up at Leo, then nodded. 'I see you need a great deal of reassurance, *mon ami*.'

'I would prefer,' Leo said, 'to never speak of it again. I would find that *very* reassuring.'

Cole's mouth quirked. 'You brought it up.'

'I know, and I regret it as much as I regret last night, so could we please—'

'Proceed,' Cole said, with a gracious wave of a hand, and the sort of smile that meant he was absolutely *not* going to never speak of it again.

Indeed, once they were making their way along an unlit and window-less corridor and could walk side by side, Cole said, 'Here's how I see it. The Australian marsupials in that monograph Sir Walter sent me.'

'Kangaroos?'

'Long feet on the back legs, thick tail on the counterbalance, silly wee front paws, can't move in any other way than hopping. A benevolent creator isn't going to make them that way, then turn around and tell them they shouldn't hop, is He? If He expects them to walk, or to not move at all, that's not merely unfair, it's outright sadistic.'

While Leo had heard arguments in London around this very concept – shades of Utilitarianism – he was touched that Cole had decided to devote thought to it from what had to amount to a standing start.

He began to hope their friendship might weather the shock.

'Did you lie awake last night coming up with justifications for my vice?' he asked, as they came to the door of the isolated room where Mrs Grundy stashed her confiscated nudes.

'Among other things.' Cole pulled a large brass key from his pocket, confiding, 'I dragged the spare from the Board of Works,' presumably so Leo wouldn't suspect him of purloining from Mrs Grundy's ring of master keys, or even subverting Mr Grundy against his wife.

The door unlocked with a loud thunk. Cole drew on his gloves and, taking the lantern from Leo, pushed it open. Leo followed him inside, head lowered as he pulled on his own gloves in anticipation of the heavy lifting to come.

He'd been so pleased and relieved that he, and evidently Cole, had missed the bigger picture. 'But, Cole, aren't you worried— Oh, that is an overwhelming amount of naked flesh.'

Cole had lifted the lantern so that the golden light reflected off gilt frames and skin of every hue, though mostly pale. Beautiful women adorned the walls in very many bigger pictures indeed, the modesty of gossamer garments and flowing hair only serving to emphasise thighs and calves, breasts and nipples, softly rounded bare arms and bellies, and graceful curving spines and hips and buttocks. The paintings were hung all about, with more stacked and covered. He couldn't see the statue Cole was hunting.

'You can understand why lovers – of art – might go to the trouble of petitioning the Lord Chamberlain for permission to visit,' Cole said. 'I don't think Mrs Grundy anticipated the effect of an *en masse* display, and I certainly don't think these classicists ever saw a pretty girl they didn't want to pose as a naked nymph.'

He set the lantern down on a convenient side table by the door, and cleared his throat. 'Let's play it fair. I'm sure we've got pretty boys here, too. Ooh, Mrs Grundy confiscated Van Dyke's *Cupid and Psyche* right off the King's Stairs, and Cupid's got a top-notch—'

'I'm perfectly capable of appreciating the female form in an artistic sense, thank you!'

Cole smiled, looked away, looked back, jiggled his knee and then said, 'More than capable of appreciating the male form in a physical sense, I believe.' He openly laughed at Leo's expression. 'Not that I approve of your taste. That dandy? You could do better.'

'No, no,' Leo said, holding up a hand. 'You were right to think twice, we are not yet at the point of you teasing me about this.'

'We obviously are, because I am going to tease you mercilessly about it,' Cole informed him cheerfully. He broke out into another smile, this one positively wicked. '*Darling.*'

Leo's cheeks heated, even as he desperately riffled his memory for the last time Harry had called him that in the *cabinet de verdur*. He covered his burning face. 'You observed more than I'd hoped.'

He'd assumed the kiss, which meant the casual invitation for Harry to get on his knees. That was bad enough, that had thoroughly spilt the secret. But the thought of Cole overhearing even a few seconds more of that private, frank conversation, even if it was as innocuous as Harry's plans for London, made the near-constant roil of his stomach worse.

Making a rueful sound, Cole pulled Leo's hands down. '*Mon ami, rien n'a changé. Nous sommes toujours amis. Tu es toujours à moi pour te taquiner.*'

Cole tended to deploy his second mother tongue when he was being earnest or emotional, perhaps as an unconscious signal of sincerity when he was so often playful in English and downright mocking in Scots. Leo, a poor student of other languages, was too used to Polly translating for him, and Cole was speaking too fast.

Cole's hands firmly enclosed his. Leo bowed his head over their clasp. Only now that Cole was touching him in his usual casual Continental way did Leo understand how bereft he'd been at the thought that he never would again.

'Ah,' Cole said, rueful again. '*Il ne fait pas assez froid pour que vous compreniez le français.*'

He stripped off his gloves, dropping them unceremoniously to the ground. Then, Leo wholly paralysed by the firm grip of bare fingers around each wrist in turn, he slowly peeled free Leo's gloves, pinching and tugging at one fingertip after the other.

Leo closed his eyes. Cole must be able to feel his pulse, frenetic under his thumb.

Cole linked their bare hands, sliding his fingers between Leo's for a more intimate hold than ever before. 'Nothing has changed,' he said, running his thumb over the back of Leo's hand. 'We are friends, it doesn't matter to me who you take to bed. Well.' He tipped his head. 'You truly do have poor taste, but I won't think less of you for it.'

'But aren't you worried…'

'About?'

Leo looked down at their entwined fingers. Cole wasn't worried Leo had feelings for him, that was obvious, or he'd be on the far side of the room, not standing so close Leo could feel the warmth radiating off his skin.

'Aren't you worried people will think you're a sod, too?'

Cole's lips parted. He looked enlightened. 'Is this why you won't come for a drink with me across the bridge?'

'My grandfather rather gave the game away in East Molesey,' Leo admitted

'Why would he do that to you?' Cole said, both puzzled and offended, because here was a man who did not think families let you down.

'People can be judgemental, in a small village, if you evict your daughter and her son just because he's touched in the head.' Leo shrugged. 'Easier to let it be known among your cronies that it's actually because he's peculiar in an even more unsavoury way and your daughter won't beat him for it.'

Cole took a breath, held it, then stepped in and hugged Leo in lieu of words.

'Years ago, Cole,' Leo said, rather smothered.

'Losing my mother was years ago, and you still gave me sympathy.'

Leo tried some awkward patting. 'Appropriate English sympathy, not "my stepmother is French and terrifyingly demonstrative" sympathy.'

Cole laughed into his hair. Leo, concerned Cole was about to receive a first-hand example of his capacity for appreciating the male form in a physical sense, stood frozen until he finally deigned to let go.

Leo scooped to collect their gloves, explaining, 'My point was, people would make assumptions, if they saw you with me. Some people might, in the Palace.'

They surely already had, now he let himself admit it. Cole's sympathy would evaporate into anger, once he made that realisation.

'*Je m'en fous.*' Leo knew that one, but Cole provided a polite translation as they regloved. 'Do you think I care?'

'I think,' Leo said carefully, 'you are underestimating how unpleasant the whispers can be.'

'Whispers, name-calling, snubs, the occasional missile,' Cole listed off. 'Leo, look at me. Malay bastard, remember? And fairly well Frenchified, *alors*! If I haven't grown a thick skin by now, I've wasted my education.' He smiled suddenly. 'Which, to be fair, Sir Robert would agree with.'

He lifted the lamp and went on into the Aladdin's cave of fleshly delights. Leo followed, frowning. Cole was such an intelligent man that Leo had always assumed the Kew Gardens apprenticeship was the product of Sir Robert stinting on his bastard's higher learning, yet another example of the way the Townsend Farquhar family did not appreciate Cole enough.

'Is that—' He was abruptly distracted. 'Is that a *Rubens*?'

'You tell me,' Cole said. 'Wasted my education.'

Leo, shaking his head at Cole's grin, approached the large canvas of a sleeping goddess and her nymphs, their fleshy nude curves unsettlingly peered at by a leering satyr, complete with the usual unsubtle visual joke, a thick tree trunk positioned just so.

He ascertained that it was indeed a Rubens, most likely from Queen Anne's tenure. 'It should not be locked away in here.'

'On the other hand, Mr Grundy says visitors keep poking the paintings with their umbrellas and tearing holes.'

Leo almost gasped aloud. 'Horrifying.'

'Quite the notion of what counts as horrifying there. But maybe it's better the ladies are tucked here safely for now.'

'That's another one,' Leo said, of the canvas beside the Rubens, before a closer look. 'No, just styled after Rubens.'

He stared at the painting. Three nude women, each turned to show off a different perspective of their bodies, a standard device, if one Leo found just as leering as the satyr.

'A cheeky one, because the goddess in the middle has Lady Carlisle's face,' Cole said. 'I recognise her from a portrait I saw at a country estate, another Van Dyke actually. She was accounted the beauty of her age, in her time.'

'Lady Carlisle?'

'Lucy Hay, Countess of Carlisle.'

'Lucy,' Leo repeated, still staring at the young woman beside the renowned countess.

The body was typically Rubenesque, all wrong, but the artist had captured the shade of the long, loose tresses precisely. He reached a hand up, close to stroking long-dried oil, pigments blended to create pale red-gold hair, lightly freckled cheeks. Her gaze was directed at Lucy. She'd probably resent how nakedly her longing was depicted.

'Do you know her?' Cole asked, which was odd enough phrasing that Leo snapped into caution.

He turned quickly away, saying, 'We should find your statue.'

Cole took the lamp to the back of the room, saying over his shoulder, 'I doubt it's one of the more prized works, so Mrs Grundy probably has her tucked a— Ah, here we are.'

Leo joined him, and they contemplated the waist-high chunk of marble carved into the curvaceous shape of a naked woman, some modesty preserved by a carved drape about her waist, but well-shaped top half left bare.

'A fair beauty, isn't she?' Cole said fondly. 'If her breasts weren't quite so pert, I'm sure Mrs Grundy would have let her be. I'll take the plinth, you take her head.'

They shortly found it was awkward, both hands full of marble, trying to manage the lantern. After some attempts to juggle, Cole hung the wire loop of the handle over one breast. 'Sacrilegious?'

'Is she a goddess?' Leo said, tone making it obvious she wasn't.

Innocently, Cole asked, 'Aren't they all Diana?'

'No!' Leo said, and explaining about that took them all the way down the stairs and out to Base Court, where they set their lady – a nymph, not a goddess – down for a breather. 'Sorry.'

'Do I apologise when I talk about the properties of perennials, Leo?'

Cole was so obviously determined to treat him as he ever had. Leo took a deep breath in, relief and gratitude intermingled. The cold air made his chest ache.

It had been raining. The full moon had risen to directly overhead, its light glimmering off wet stones.

Sergeant Hamilton drifted towards them from the shadows, pale as moonbeams. 'Sir?'

Leo stared steadfastly past him. 'Where are we taking her?'

'I thought the Maze,' Cole said, and he still sounded entirely casual but he was suddenly scrutinising Leo with unnerving attention. 'Under royal purview, but away from Mrs Grundy's gimlet eye.'

'Please talk to me, please.'

'The Maze is quite popular with children,' Leo said. *And also very close to the angry remnant of a Tudor ghost.*

'I am of the opinion that the human body is not a source of shame,' Cole said. 'I'd hoped I'd already made that clear.'

'Say something. I know you can hear me. Please. Sir, *please.*'

If Polly had been with him, she'd have been ordering him to hold firm. Looking mostly at Cole, he said, 'Sergeant Hamilton.'

Hamilton stopped, and the look of hope suffusing his face made Leo briefly close his eyes.

'Poor old chap,' Cole said reflexively. 'Is...he relevant as to where we place the statue?'

'I was just thinking of him, because he was killed here,' Leo said. 'No one else was hurt that day, because of him. He did his duty, to the utmost degree.'

'I did my duty,' Hamilton echoed. His broad shoulders relaxed, and he stood taller. 'I did my duty.'

'He did,' Cole agreed. 'Though I'm glad Rickey didn't hang for it. I know I'm soft for thinking it, but it wouldn't have been fair. The poor man wasn't in his right mind that night.'

'What?' Hamilton's face, so light a moment ago, was darkening.

Leo had not been planning to follow Polly's advice and outright lie to Hamilton about the outcome of the trial for his wilful murder, but a judicious withholding of the truth had been on the cards. That had been too much honesty, far too soon.

'But he shot me,' Hamilton said. 'He killed me!'

'Transported for life,' he said quickly. 'Some might say that's worse than hanging.'

'He intended to kill Sergeant-Major Murphy,' Hamilton shouted. 'He planned to kill someone that night, it doesn't matter that he got the wrong man, he still intended to kill a man!'

Leo could have pointed out that Rickey might have been cursing Murphy and spewing threats, but he'd been in no state to truly intend anything, let alone plan a murder. His character witnesses had uniformly called him quiet, harmless, inoffensive, as Leo's character witnesses might do, if he ever had to stand trial for his own capital crime.

But an incoherent fury had come over the steadfast, dutiful soldier. He balled his fists, his edges threading into snarls that made him look more spectral than usual. The tangled tendrils wafted towards Leo, as if tasting the air for his scent.

Despite himself, Leo took a step backwards, almost tripping over the statue.

'The Maze, was it?' he said, trying to sound brisk and likely sounding decidedly unnerved. 'Let's get going.'

FOURTEEN

To Leo's dismay, Hamilton, lost in rage and despair, harangued him across Base Court. But he did not continue the pursuit beyond the moment Max padded out of the shadows in Master Carpenter's Court and directed an intensely canine stare his way.

The dog followed at their heels as they took the direct route up Old Moat Lane. He snuffled enthusiastically at the statue whenever they set it down for a rest, which was at Cole's instigation, on Leo's behalf. His arms were shaking.

He might have been shaking in general. The workman's voice ran through his head, looping like a tightening wire. *It's getting worse. It's all crackt.* Polly's blithe reassurances made for scant shelter.

They were halfway to the Maze, the dark acreage of the kitchen gardens stretching to their left. Leo looked that way, jittery. He couldn't think of any decent reason not to go on to the Maze.

Sorry, I'm especially wary of the Tudor ghost tonight because the modern one just shouted at me and that forced me to take the late Stuart one's warning more seriously than the Caroline one wanted me to seemed unconvincing.

Cole broke the silence. 'I didn't intend to bring up unpleasant associations for you.' Leo failed to break his own silence out of sheer puzzlement, so Cole added, 'Talk of hanging and transportation, ye ken?'

When Leo remained nonplussed, he said, 'Isn't it dangerous?' with an edge of frustration to his voice.

'Oh.' Leo answered cautiously; he knew a leading question when he heard one. 'Less so than you're assuming.'

'Bletheration,' Cole protested with some heat. 'Two men hanged for it at Newgate not seven years ago. You must have been *in* London then. Didn't that scare you?'

'Yes,' Leo said, 'two men were hanged for engaging in consensual activities behind a closed door, doing harm to no one at all with their depravity except to the very fabric of our society. I am *aware* it's a hated act, Mr Solong. I'm *also* aware that if they'd been gentry—'

'I'm not defending the bloody law, I'm not turning moralistic on you. You do as you like, but allow me to be worried about the thought of you running that risk.'

Leo's hackles settled. He rolled his shoulders and took a renewed grip, nodding to Cole. They lifted together, and went on up the lane. The looming bulk of Wilderness House, single lamp burning to guide Cole home, was up ahead. They turned down the path to the Maze entrance, losing Max's attendance when he loped deeper into the Wilderness.

As they crunched over the gravel, the beam of light from the lantern swinging in arcs around them, Leo said, 'It would set your mind at ease, I think, to know how many *don't* get caught. It's rarer than death by lightning strike, with the same degree of bad luck to it. Those men were terribly, terribly unlucky, every step of the way to the noose.'

From his silence and expression, Cole remained unconvinced. Out of respect for the well-meaning concern he knew lay behind it, Leo asked, 'How much do you know about the actual…'

'Do I know how sodomy works?' Cole asked, eyebrows raised. 'I think I can work it out from first principles.'

Leo, remarkably, felt himself smile. 'The law about it? Ah. Do you know for it to be a capital crime, there has to be…'

He found himself incapable of announcing *penetration and emission* into the open air.

'Spit it out,' Cole said, and then laughed. 'Did I answer the question?'

Leo snorted and muttered, 'Good Lord,' but Polly wasn't about to appreciate it. 'There's misdemeanours, and there's the felony. You understand what the felony is, yes?'

Cole looked at him down the length of the statue, eyes glinting. 'No, darling, explain it to me. Use small words.'

'Is "sod off" small enough for you?' Leo said, helpless not to smile again at Cole's self-satisfied amusement. 'Suffice to say, I am not at risk of being found guilty of the felony. All right?' Despite himself, he was blushing. He couldn't match Cole's cheery matter-of-factness. 'I don't do the felony, only the misdemeanours. That's still two years in the House of Correction, and I'd lose my daguerreotype licence, and there's the public shame and the—'

He made himself stop. It was best not to dwell. 'But it's not hanging and it's not transportation.'

Cole opened his mouth, then paused, thinking twice. That usually resulted in him saying what was on his mind anyway, so Leo went first. 'You want to ask *so badly* why I don't engage in buggery, don't you?'

'I only want to say,' Cole said, with great dignity, 'if that's you taking precautions, on the one hand, it relieves my mind, but on the other, that means their repulsive law worked to stop you doing something you might otherwise enjoy, and I'm cross about it.'

'I *do* take precautions, but that's not one of them, that's just prefer-ence. The things that get you caught are raids, provocateurs, and witnesses, and I have the means to avoid those. I can afford to be careful where I go, who I let approach me, who might see me.'

Looking down as he minutely adjusted his hold, Cole said, 'I feel like you might have broken all those rules with Walpole.'

'I was lonely.'

Leo concentrated on his grip, his gloved fingers aching as he held on tight. The statue felt like it was growing heavier by the second. They were at the mouth of the Maze. Leo's cheeks were glowing from the exertion, despite the cold, and even Cole wore a healthy flush. Cole paused, setting down his half of the burden.

Leo followed suit, but kept his gaze down. 'Not asking for pity, not excusing my folly. But I was lonely.'

'That's why you go to Hampton Wick, ay? You don't drink with me in East Molesey because you're protecting me. But you don't invite me to drink with you in Hampton Wick because you're...'

Leo, with the same unhealthy fascination of picking at a scab, waited to see how Cole would finish the sentence.

'Having relations with men,' Cole said, remaining impressively neutral. 'Or a man, in particular?'

'The former,' Leo said. He picked the scab. 'Strangers, vouchsafed by the barkeep. That makes it safer.'

'And you like it?'

'I thought we'd established that.'

'No. You like anonymous sex with men you won't see again?'

'It's what there is.' He shrugged, meeting Cole's eyes with something of a challenge. 'It's not without its merits.'

He'd liked it more in London, when it hadn't been the only option and so choosing it carried an erotic charge, unsmothered by dull necessity.

Carefully, Cole said, 'Not meaning to be presumptuous, but I'd have thought you'd prefer to find a friend who shares your tastes?'

That's who Jack had been. That's who Harry might have become, because at least he was proven willing to visit from London – if he hadn't also proven willing to be reckless.

He admitted, 'I thought I had, for a moment there.'

'Walpole rather let you down.' Amid light censure aimed at the absent Honourable sat the sympathy, more than Leo expected or even deserved: just deserts would be Polly's *I told you so*.

Another admission, then. 'I allowed him to push me into more than I would've normally risked. I was lonely, and he was interested.'

Cole crooked a smile. 'And he's handsome, isn't he? Got a little of the look of Tennyson about him.'

Taken utterly by surprise by this sharp turn in the winding road of their conversation, Leo said, 'Oh, he's not a patch on y—' before he bit his tongue on the very first breath of that telltale Y.

Cole frowned, expression in the lamplight transparently calculating. Leo watched, with growing horror, as he quite plainly worked his way down a list of men of their mutual acquaintance for a suitable name.

He didn't know if he was hoping he'd come up blank, because then he might arrive at the realisation that Leo had been about to say *you*, or if it would be worse if he actually uncovered a name—

'Yates?' Cole raised an eloquent brow. 'Prefer older men, do we?'

Which was fair, because Mr Yates was Cole's cartman, and had to be seventy if he was a day.

Cole stopped smiling. 'Oh, well, you don't.' It was the first time he'd sounded disapproving this entire interview. 'That's obvious enough.'

'I don't prefer *young* men,' Leo said, stung but with no recourse to shout *I prefer* you, *you great daftie poltroon!* 'Fine, he's handsome. He's pretty-mannered. He was sweet to me. He said I was like Winter on the Banqueting House ceiling.'

'Hah! You are *not* Baroque.'

This pronouncement was so immediate and assured that Leo had little choice but to feel somewhat wounded.

He brushed at his coat, frowning. 'Mostly he said nice things and recited poetry at me.'

'He seduced you flat like a virgin milkmaid fresh to the city,' Cole translated.

'I think you're trying to imply I have low standards.'

'My God, *you do*, darling.'

Leo put his hands on his hips with conspicuous indignation, which just made Cole laugh. Shaking his head, but also smiling, Leo signalled he was ready to start off, and they hoisted their marble lady and entered the Maze.

'This is unfair,' Leo said as they laboured along. 'I can't tease you in return about your tastes.'

'It's not my problem I'm far better at keeping secrets than you are,' Cole said smugly.

'That's not true,' said Leo, with some vigour (he was *made* of secrets). 'You think you're courting Miss Smart.'

'No, *you* think I'm courting Miss Smart, for some ungodly reason,' Cole returned. 'Neither she nor I think that.'

He was stymied, but only for a moment. 'Then you must have someone in London.'

'Must I?'

Leo was provoked into saying, 'Everyone says you were thwarted in love by an earl's daughter.'

Cole shrugged, jostling his end of their shared burden. 'Everyone says you see ghosts.'

This was not quite the rebuttal Cole thought it was, of course, but it did force Leo to rethink dancing so close to a line he could not ever cross. He fell silent. They tromped along through the Maze, barely paying attention to the familiar turns towards the centre.

'Shall we compromise?' Cole asked. Leo looked up, puzzled. 'Put her in one of the stops, not right in the centre? Her nipples won't be seen by quite so many people.'

Leo thought that Cole's familiarity with the Maze made him optimistic there, but he concurred. They thus failed to take the next correct turn, continuing on around a switchback towards one of the four stops, or dead ends. Here Cole's expertise came to the fore; Leo knew the right path, Cole every wrong one.

'Can we keep teasing you about your taste in men now?' Cole said conversationally as he led Leo around another unfamiliar u-turn. 'It rather passes the time.'

He was puffing, but obviously unwilling to rest again as they closed in on their destination. Indeed, one last turn took them into a cosy nook, hornbeam tight on three sides. If Leo's sense of direction was holding, they were a few hedges south of the true centre.

'Mostly he was good company and made me laugh,' he said, somewhat defensively. 'It's attractive.'

Cole scoffed lightly as he lowered the plinth into position, Leo keeping firm hold of the head to give him leverage. '*I'm* good company and make you laugh and you're not attracted to—'

Leo dropped his half of the statue.

'Whoops!' he said, so brightly it cracked in the cold air.

And Cole said, '*Oh.*'

Leo didn't dare look at him. He bent to raise the half-naked nymph from her prone position, keeping his head down. Cole leaned in to help, saying not a word.

They settled her, nestling her into the gravel at the very end of the stop. Leo gave her a last pat. If he didn't look at Cole, then maybe—

'You,' Cole said. '"Not a patch on *you*". Me.'

He sounded more enlightened than disgusted. Leo risked it.

Cole looked as shocked as he had upon spying Leo and Harry kissing. Leo, face burning, took a shuffling step away.

Cole raised a hand. 'Leo…'

'Don't! Oh, God, *don't*,' Leo blurted on a wave of humiliation, and, oddly and unfairly, anger. He stalked back down the short alley, hot and bristling all over.

Cole called after him urgently. 'You didn't give me time to respond.'

'How else can I expect you to respond except to be grateful you don't hit me.'

'I would never do that! If anything, I'm flattered.'

'Don't patronise me,' Leo snapped. He rounded the corner into the next lane…

…and the temperature plummeted.

Only then did Leo realise it wasn't his own anger he was feeling.

He stopped dead.

He stared down the hedgerow, the leaves black in the moonlight, all still in the clear, cold night, except the shadows. They danced wildly as

Cole came up behind him with the lantern heedlessly swinging from one hand.

'Leo?'

The breath shuddered from him, misty white in the chilling air. He waited, frozen, for the Tudor remnant to come around the corner at the end of the lane, nothing but rage.

It came through the hedge, mere feet away.

Leo's years of practice in ignoring ghosts failed him. His mind blanked. All he could think of were the penny-dreadful stories of Spring-Heeled Jack, the hideous spectre stalking London, leaping about with his cold and clammy breath and his cackling squawk of a laugh.

In a moment it would turn, it would turn and he would see its faceless face and it would *know him*.

It took every inch of self-possession to turn his back, each tiny scrape of his feet as loud as the toll of a graveyard bell.

Don't see me. Don't see me.

Cole had stopped when he had, and now watched him with a silent question writ loud on his face. Leo knew he was wide-eyed and shaking, and had no right, no right whatsoever, to fix his gaze to his in mute appeal.

'I feel a fair eedjit,' Cole said, 'but, Leo…is there a presence here with us?'

Leo nodded, the merest dip of his chin.

'But not your usual friendly ghost?'

Leo shook his head once, not without a minor mental note.

'What do you need me to do?' Cole asked.

Leo shook his head again.

Cole set the lantern down, the clink of its metal base against the gravel making Leo twitch.

Then he marched forwards and engulfed Leo in his arms. 'Can it hear us?' he murmured into Leo's hair.

'I don't know,' Leo whispered.

'We can't run, can we, or you would have?'

'It's blocking the path.' Leo bullied himself into showing a trace of a spine. 'You can go. You don't need to run. It'll feel a little cold when you walk through it, that's all. It can't hurt you.'

'But it can hurt you.'

Dozens of ghosts, swarming him on New London Bridge. Spectral hands, clinging to him, siphoning his subtle matter, sending icicles across his skin. Metaphysical frostbite, spreading through his entire body, splinters of ice in his lungs and lodging in his veins.

He'd crawled out from under the tempest, the bodiless brawl over who would have him, before those jagged splinters had reached his heart, or who knew what might have happened then.

'It just feels a little cold,' he repeated, but his body betrayed him, shuddering and cringing into the shelter of Cole's lean strength.

Cole's hold tightened. He had both arms wrapped around Leo's back, hauling him in as close as he could. 'I'm not leaving you. Tell me what you need.'

The temperature dropped again; the leaves were silvering on either side of them, to Leo's eyes at least. It was coming closer. His scalp prickled, with the chill, with terror. Any moment now, he would feel its fingers on the nape of his neck.

He buried his head into Cole's chest and said, 'I need it not to see me,' as if the sentence were a single word.

Cole swung him around, putting his own back to the threat, a courageous move if he could have sensed so much as a smidgen of the cloud of anger and betrayal and fear.

Leo felt a vertiginous envy crack through his frozen insides. Not for him that easy luxury. What would it be like to walk through the Palace without having to swerve around painstakingly memorised cold spots and avoid the regular haunts? What would it be like to travel anywhere one liked in England, the world, without a constant watch for fresh apparitions? What would it be like to wander the Wilderness at night, fearing nothing at all?

His fingers closed on the rough serge of Cole's coat. Another thought, wistful but pointless, occurred to him. What would it be like to step into the arms of the one you loved and not have to worry about the eyes of the judgemental, the fists of the violently opposed, the heavy hand of the constabulary?

Cole began to shuffle Leo backwards, towards the dead end. Even knowing he was already trapped, Leo baulked.

With Cole his bulwark, he was managing more rational, if irrelevant, thought, but he still couldn't shake the memory of the bridge, all those ghostly fixations coming to bear on him.

If he had no other option, he'd have to run through the miasm. Forever after, it would know him. And right now, it might chase him, like Sergeant Hamilton had chased him across Base Court until Max had shepherded him away. He didn't want to disadvantage himself in a race for the exit by going any further into the Maze, not when he had to run around the hedgerows and the Tudor could float through them.

Cole, still intent on persuading him back around the corner like a recalcitrant horse, soothed him with strokes down his spine, making hushing noises that would have been patronising if they weren't so comforting.

And that was it, Leo realised. He'd been upset, and he'd attracted the ghost which was now merely an echo of the roil of dark emotions in which its existence had begun. It wasn't any more dangerous than any of the other Palace ghosts. He and it were merely feeding off each other.

He should be grateful this wasn't Fountain Court.

'I have to calm myself down,' he whispered to Cole. 'It's attracted to my distress, I think.'

'So, I should tell you I am *genuinely* flattered?'

Leo huffed. 'Do you think that is still top of my mind, Cole?'

'Likely not,' Cole conceded genially. 'But just so you know. Flattered. Very.'

Decidedly disbelieving, but appreciating the attempt to distract him, Leo said, 'If you find the attentions of sods so pleasant, I'll tell you which street to dawdle down next time you're in London.'

'I'm off tomorrow, actually.'

He didn't need to lift his head from Cole's chest to know his eyes would sparkle with that mischievous gleam. Definitely an attempt to distract him, because Cole Solong was a treasure of a man.

He took a deeper breath. Was his imagination deceiving him, or was the air already losing its deathly chill?

He managed, 'Are you calling my bluff, or...'

Cole laughed. 'The captain's fallen ill, so Walter leaves for Pisa tomorrow, to help Mamam. I'll keep Lady Erica company for a spell, until her sister arrives.'

It must be bad, for Sir Walter to rush to his mother's side, and Cole wasn't saying so, because Cole was trying to calm him down. 'I'm sorry, I do hope Captain Hamilton makes a good recovery.'

'I do, too,' Cole said.

He'd not ceased stroking his palm down Leo's back. Between his thick gloves and the layers of clothing between them, Leo should have felt it only as a muffled pressure. It shouldn't feel like a ripple of sunlight along his spine, growing warmer at every stroke.

And that was probably a good indication that the inscrutable remnant of an ancient ghost truly was moving away, now it had lost his radiating distemper as a beacon. Pressing a hand to Cole's chest, Leo made himself straighten out of his huddle so he could peek over Cole's shoulder, eyes carefully lowered.

The miasm no longer lingered just behind their embrace. Slowly, Leo lifted his gaze until he had taken in the entire dim lane.

He sighed, sagging. 'Gone.'

'Guid mon.'

Cole sounded a little stifled, and when Leo turned his head, his expression seemed both strange and strangely familiar. He had a very good view of it, because he was pressed so tight against him, his face was mere inches away.

It occurred to him Cole might think he'd made the whole ghost story up just for the excuse to rub up against him, the exact sort of crafty trick a molly might try to subvert upright men.

Cole was strangely reluctant to let him go, if so.

Leo said, 'Much obliged, Mr Solong,' as a less-than-subtle hint, and Cole blinked and released him. He rubbed at his mouth awkwardly before collecting the lantern and turning to lead Leo out.

They were halfway to the entrance when Max galloped in from one of the other paths, the flash of white making Leo start before he recognised the dog, who must have squeezed his bulk under a hedge. He nuzzled their hands, and sniffed around at their feet, and then stalked along with them in his most alert pose, head high with watchful purpose.

'Does Max see the ghosts?' Cole asked. 'I should've whistled him up.'

'I think he senses them, yes,' Leo said. 'I used to see dogs barking at them, in London. Lady Henry's little dog yips at...' The bizarre nature of the conversation caught up with him. 'I've hardly ever talked to anyone about the ghosts before.' He folded his arms over his chest, shivers running through him.

Cole eyed him. 'You need a stiff drink and a warm bed.'

They emerged from the Maze; without a word, Leo took the path through the Wilderness rather than head anywhere in the vicinity of Old Moat Lane and the kitchen gardens. With Cole close by his side and Max close on his heels, he was escorted like the very queen down Tennis Court Lane.

He'd have felt both amused and comforted, if he hadn't begun to feel very odd indeed.

At his apartment door, Max lay down across the threshold, head raised and ears alert, and Cole followed Leo inside to the parlour, where he immediately stirred the coals to life and put the kettle on.

Leo perched silently on the overstuffed armchair. He was trying to find words to thank Cole, to send him away. He couldn't stop shivering, and the shivers kept shaking the thoughts out of his head. His stomach roiled in sour protest.

Cole pushed a cup into his hand. Leo put it down to pull his gloves off, and cradled it back into his bare palms, relishing the heat sinking into his skin. He almost gagged on his first sip. Hot tea, with the syrup of sugar and the smoke of whisky. He pressed the cup to his closed eyelids, his cheeks, his lips. He was freezing, but Polly wasn't here.

'Oh, I see,' he said. 'I'm having an attack of the nerves.'

'You're shaken, and need to rest,' Cole said soothingly. He swooped a blanket around Leo's shoulders. 'Drink up, and I'll tuck you into bed.'

Leo held the blanket pinned with one hand, and pressed the cup against his mouth, the heat a balm. His eyes managed to focus on Cole, who had squatted before him, hands resting lightly on his knees. He'd taken off his gloves to make the tea.

Leo lowered the cup. 'This seems unnecessary,' he informed his over-reactive body. 'It wasn't nearly as bad as last time.'

'What happened last time?'

'London Bridge,' Leo said. 'Quite…a lot of ghosts, actually. All at once. Quite a lot. I don't want to talk about it anymore, Cole.'

'Drink up, then, so I can't make you,' Cole said, patting his knee, and Leo took an obliging second sip.

Too sweet, too peaty, but the heat travelled down his throat and glowed in his stomach. Leo slumped back into the armchair, eyes closed, and drank his tea in increments to the accompaniment of soft French murmuring. If he wasn't curled securely into the armchair, he thought Cole would have drawn him into his arms by now.

Cole used his body to comfort. Leo would very much have liked to use his body for comfort.

The reaction was leaving his own body, the shivering settling, the embarrassment growing.

'Sorry,' he said at last.

'*Aucun problème, mon ami*,' Cole said.

He still had his hands resting on Leo's knees, crouched before the armchair looking up at him with sympathetic concern. Again, the layers of fabric separating bare skin from bare skin should have made the touch feel like nothing. Instead, Leo felt the weight and warmth tingling up his thighs.

'The stories are true, then. You've been haunted by spirits since you fell off the bridge as a child?'

'You know stories are exaggerated,' Leo said, ever reflexively defensive after too many years of protecting too many secrets from too many prying questions. 'Did *you* truly lose an affair of the heart with an earl's daughter?'

Cole smiled at him. 'Lady E.'

Leo had a moment of complete blankness before exclaiming, '*Your sister-in-law?*'

'Lady Erica and her mother are Kew patrons,' Cole said. 'We met there, and connected over a mutual love of gardens and growing up the bastard offspring of Scottish gentry.' He flashed his mischievous grin, evidently revelling in Leo's expression. 'We're *friends*. I introduced her to Sir Walter with the purest of intentions. So, yes, I *do* know how stories are exaggerated, Leo. Is yours?'

It seemed only fair, now, to give something back. Slowly, Leo said, 'I was watching the lock.'

'Upstream of the bridge?'

'Yes. I watched them build it, and once it was operational, I liked to watch it open and close when the boats came. Lots of boys liked to. I was watching it, so I didn't see a cart split its wheel and go careening. It knocked me off the side.'

'Must have been terrifying.'

'I don't remember much of the actual drowning part,' Leo said. 'I was lucky, I think, the river was running fast, and I was quickly thrown up on the bank behind Banqueting House.' He raised his eyes to meet Cole's. 'All the drowning victims off the succession of bridges built in that location fetch up along there, eventually.'

Cole opened his mouth, started to speak, stopped, then said, 'Ah.'

'Yes. I woke up vomiting water and hearing voices urging me to crawl up the bank before the river sucked me back into its current, and opened my eyes to find myself in a small crowd.'

The one shouting loudest – *come now, boy, you have to move, follow my voice* – had been Polly. The restless ghosts of the drowned were spread out along the long curve where he'd washed up. They'd all converged, drawn together in a way that Polly assured him was unusual for ghosts, by the disturbance Leo's near-death made in their spectral senses. She'd been protecting him from that very moment.

'I didn't realise at first what they were, and then I saw the bushes and reeds right through their bodies. That's the part where they say I was found screaming hysterically.'

'Right. Lots of people – lots of children – have times when they come close to death, though.'

'Pol—' It was still so hard to speak openly after the years and years of secrecy. He tried again. 'I have been told that it's not uncommon to be left with some sort of sensitivity after such an experience. Lady Jane… Well, she doesn't have children, but that doesn't mean she didn't suffer through a travail that proved too taxing for a baby and almost too taxing for her, if you understand the implications?'

'I do.'

'My advantage' – he smiled grimly – 'was to fall immediately into a fever which almost killed me again. My temporary glimpse of the spirit world whilst death's door was ajar became a permanent window.'

'Since you were eight years old,' Cole said. He squeezed his hands around Leo's knees, sending another dangerous spike of heat through him. '*Mon pauvre petit.*'

In drastic need of escape for a multitude of reasons, Leo said, 'You're right, I need to rest. I'll take myself to bed.'

'I'll help you upstairs.'

Leo demurring, Cole insisting, they both tried to stand in the same instant, and collided, thigh to thigh, chest to chest. Cole caught his arm around Leo's waist to stop them both toppling over the side of the armchair.

Leo took a breath into lungs that felt tight, his lips close enough to Cole's that they might have been sharing the same air, Cole's natural woodsy scent tantalisingly warm.

Cole should be pushing him away. Cole was looking at him with the same odd yet oddly familiar expression as in the Maze.

His gaze flickered, for the barest moment, to Leo's lips.

Leo recognised it, then. He knew what it meant when a man looked at him like that. He just hadn't ever expected Cole to look at him like that.

Cole wanted to kiss him.

As if lost inside the exact daydream he'd had to ruthlessly suppress to act in any regular fashion towards this man, Leo slowly cupped Cole's face and traced the ball of his thumb across his cheekbone. Cole's lips parted, and not all the imaginary padlocks in the world could have prevented Leo from closing the last inch to brush his mouth over his.

He drew back, heat rushing across his skin, from his mouth down his throat and chest.

'Leo…' Cole breathed. He was frowning, those elegant black brows drawn down into his worst scowl.

Leo's stomach plummeted. He'd misread, obviously. He was about to receive another *I'm flattered*, this one with a *but* attached so large it would smash his foolish, hopeful heart to smiddereens, and he could only be grateful it was merely his heart receiving the blow, not his body.

A scuff sounded from the stairs. 'Is that you, Mr Sweetwater?' Sally called.

Cole took three sharp steps backwards, precise as a soldier. Leo sank into the armchair. When Sally entered, candlestick held high, they were at a distance too far apart to be anything but respectable, and yet so far apart as to be awkward.

'Oh, and Mr Solong,' Sally said. She looked between them, and at the expanse of space separating them. 'Good evening, sir.'

'Good evening, Sally.' The relief in Cole's voice was palpable. He and Sally exchanged pleasantries, with Cole asking after John's studies, and the departed Joseph. 'Has he sent a letter yet?'

'Several.' Quiet Sally was enthused by the topic of her brothers, and recounted Joseph's luck in his good position at a Wakefield ostelry, leaving Leo to marinate in guilt, because he'd been too distracted by Harry Walpole to remember to ask after Joseph.

After a time, Cole said gently, 'Sally, Mr Sweetwater is not feeling well. Will you keep an eye on him for me while I'm away in London?'

'Yes, sir, of course.'

'Then I shall say *adieu.*' He solemnly tipped an invisible cap. 'Good night, Sally. Good night, Sweetwater.'

'Good night, Mr Solong,' Leo said numbly.

FIFTEEN

Cole was gone to London the next morning. He'd said he would be; there was no need to assume he was avoiding the friend who had so foolishly made unwanted advances towards him.

There was better cause to assume he was avoiding Leo when he returned a full week later – their Friday Chapel Court appointment conveniently bypassed – with all four Townsend Farquhar offspring in tow. He spent much of the next week, the last days of November, deeply engrossed in herding his nephews, the eldest of whom was a respectable six, the youngest barely two, toddling stoutly after his older brothers with his pudgy fingers clutching the hand of a Wilderness House maid.

To the audible delight of the female residents braving winter at the Palace, the four curly-haired tots trailed their uncle about his duties wearing pantalettes and caps and serious expressions, all in a row like little ducklings, at least until garden oversight lost its gloss and they began to romp about the grounds. They were joined by the three Grundy children and the two Reynett daughters in games of chase, biblocatch (the Farquhar boys warming their grand-mère's heart *in absentia* with their proper pronunciation of *bilboquet*), and hitting cricket balls to Middlesex from the bottom of the Privy Garden while Cole and his men tried to remedy waterlogging down there.

The crisp weather finally gave way to overcast skies and an intermittent dismal drizzle. Leo erased himself in work, using every drop of scant sunlight he was gifted, between grey, wet hours of painting watercolours in the showroom while customers offered commentary over his shoulder.

Polly became restless when he was too absorbed in his own business, and drifted about the residents who hadn't left for the season, reading their letters and listening in on their arguments. She was delighted to catch Lady Henry eating chocolate bonbons and giggling over a smudgy copy of *Fanny Hill*, which she was obliged to shove under a cushion whenever anyone entered her drawing room.

But her delight was muted: she had, after all, caught many respectable ladies reading *Fanny Hill*, and worse, in her long years. To Leo, it almost seemed as if she were playacting as her usual artlessly warm and spirited self. He hoped the winter would be a short one, the residents and tourists returning in droves for her entertainment.

He ventured to ask her if she would like him to find out what had happened to Lady Carlisle. She'd looked at him witheringly.

'I already know,' she said. 'This is half the reason I did not want to tell you, Leo, I'm not the victim you're trying to turn me into, and I haven't spent my afterlife pining over someone who never once gave me a second thought.'

This last was delivered with a pointed look. She could not have failed to notice Cole's lengthy absence and Leo's low mood.

He was relieved not to experience anything like the stupor that had seen him produce the uncanny Fountain Court scene, which he had burnt, skin prickling as the flames licked at the canvas. His nerves were not rubbed-raw agitated, as they had been in the immediate wake of Cole's discovery of his secret nature. Rather, he was struggling with a tired admixture of embarrassment and guilt, and the dull ache of a reawakened longing. He had folded it away, as carefully as his mother folding up clean laundry, and now it had all tumbled out.

It was proving difficult to cram back in and lock away, despite what could only be called an *excess* of regret.

Cole missed the next Friday as well, in returning the boys to the care of the baronet's household. Perhaps Captain Hamilton had recovered and Sir Walter had returned already, though that would have entailed him practically boarding the same train he'd disembarked from. More likely, then, Lady Erica's sister had belatedly arrived to assist.

On that same Friday, Leo received a letter in the penny post, back-stamped from London. It was a couple of lines, dashed off quite carelessly and left unsigned.

I'll make you a deal, sweet Winter, Harry had written. *You have your particular friend assist my particular friend, and I won't tell anyone about our particular friendship. Write back soonest.*

Leo read this cryptic missive several times before accepting he was being extorted.

As when Harry had first pressed himself on him, he was more puzzled than alarmed. For all that the Honourable had dumped him into hot water with that last kiss, his behaviour even then had been impetuously spiteful, but not cruelly malicious. Harry simply did not have the sheer malevolence required to turn Leo over to a magistrate, nor did Leo think his father and brother, Lords Orford and Walpole, would thank him for it. Nor was Harry's guess about the existence of Polly, if that was what the note even referred to, likely to benefit anyone, least of all himself.

So it was, he thought, an empty threat, another impulsive act, one of many irons Harry was helter-skelter setting into the metaphorical fire to raise funds, presumably in service of his debt. Some old university mate would come through, and Harry would forget all about Leo and whatever half-baked scheme he'd precipitously alit upon.

And so Leo tucked the note into the middle of his other correspondence, and ignored it as thoroughly as if it were just another ghost he did not want to come to the notice of.

He realised his mistake towards the end of the following week.

He and John, just in from school, were at the rear of the studio, tidying up after a portraiture session. The bright morning had stayed fine long enough to complete the sitting, but the sky outside was now dark and beginning to spit cold rain against the windows in rattly gusts.

A male voice, familiar enough to make Leo tilt his head like a shaggy-haired dog, floated in from the showroom, where Sally was at the counter. Sally's reply was the merest murmur. It should have been an everyday interaction with a customer, someone ducking in to spend a few rainy moments browsing, but John immediately turned towards the sound of his sister's voice, and, after a moment, so did Leo.

There was a strange note in Sally's voice, discordant in the quiet studio. They were both already starting for the showroom even before the second male voice rang out, hearty and jocular.

Sally was frightened.

And Harry was frightened, too, Leo realised, when he entered the showroom and realised who the first voice belonged to. Leo should have recognised it immediately, but the strain of the situation had altered it.

The situation, short and brawny, was standing next to Harry.

Leo had time for a single burst of instinctual pleasure – the man's accent, flashy dress and cocky stance were purest London, Leo's London rather than Harry's – before the man smiled beatifically with large, white, very even teeth, pristine in a hardened, weathered face.

When people started using the teeth of fallen soldiers from Waterloo to make dentures, Leo had been very grateful ghosts did not follow their body parts about. If they did, this man would have been walking about with a train of dead soldiers in coats of red or blue.

He did not seem like the kind of man who'd have a qualm about that.

'Mr Sweetwater, good afternoon!' Harry exclaimed as Leo halted by the arch, wary. Then, horribly, he widened his eyes and mouthed, 'Sorry.'

John slipped past Leo and went to Sally's side. He was only eleven, and he was trying hard not to cower, repeatedly drawing his shoulders back from their instinctive hunch. Sally put her hand on his back, chin lifting as her own steely mettle rose in the face of her brother's fear.

Leo said, 'Miss Fitzhenry, you and Master Fitzhenry are late to meet Mr Fitzhenry. Best get going, or he'll come here looking for you.'

'You head off, my dusky beauties,' the stranger said genially, magnanimously nodding his permission, eyes bright and hard as buttons. 'Big boy business. We don't want interruptions.'

Sally looked at Leo, but she wasn't foolish enough to protest. She took John's hand and they hurried out, heads down. The stranger put his shoulder to the big oak door and swung it shut behind them.

'Well, well. Introduce me, Harry.'

'Sweetwater, this is Mr Guy,' Harry said. He swallowed. 'He's the…inspector…at the house holding my notes.'

It wasn't the man's real name, of course. The principal man at certain establishments was often called that, after Guy Fawkes.

Leo had been assuming Harry's debt was the usual run of minor obligations accrued by the younger sons of nobility left at loose ends. He thought Lord Orford had washed his hands of endless tailor's bills and other itemised odes to extravagant living, and perhaps a few losses at the private clubs.

He hadn't for a moment considered that Harry owed serious money to serious men, the hellites of the West End gambling-houses, not above subjecting unwary adventurers to hectoring, loaded dice, cozening women, big-talking puffs, and drugged wine.

'Oh, Harry,' he said.

Leaning hard into a heavy parody of his own accent, aitches merrily dropped, Guy said, 'Our mutual friend here got a taste for beggar-my-neighbour as a kiddie, and lo and behold, he's gone and beggared himself at hazard.'

'I won at first,' Harry muttered, and Leo wasn't sure if he wanted to sink his face into his hands in despair, or slap the fool for being the most plucked pigeon he'd ever encountered.

Guy tutted in sympathy. 'But he tells me, Mr Sweetwater, you have an interesting talent that'll help him all the way out of his troubles.'

'I rather think Mr Walpole has the wrong idea about me if he thinks I have the means to settle his debt for him.'

Guy flashed his white, even teeth. 'I rather think,' he mocked, 'he very much got the right idea about you around about the time you were sucking his prick for him, buttercup.'

Leo shot Harry a violently repressed look. Harry flung up his hands, playing helpless, like he hadn't volunteered information he should have kept pinned tight to his chest.

'Now, don't go getting me all wrong,' Guy soothed. 'It makes no difference to me who's planting whose tulip in whose fundament, you boys enjoy yourselves. But if our Harry decides to make a complaint...' He tutted again. 'Far be it from me to speculate, but I can't see that going well for you, Mr Sweetwater.'

He took a short stroll around the studio, ostentatiously admiring the displays of daguerreotypes, before he paused at a shelf. 'In fact, I see your pleasant little life going the way of the Dodo bird.'

Still smiling, he swept the shelf clear with one arm, sending daguerreotype cases crashing to the ground in a great clatter of brass and the higher tinkle of broken glass.

Harry recoiled, but Leo stood frozen, his stomach tight and his chest hollowing out.

He had to clear his throat a few times before he could speak. 'Your time would be better employed applying to Mr Walpole's father. Extort me all you like, I do not have his means.'

If anything, Harry became more wretched. 'He doesn't know about this, he thinks I've overspent my allowance. I asked for an advance, just fifty pounds, and he decided to teach me a lesson.'

'Tell him who you're really in debt to, I doubt very much he wanted the lesson to be quite so...' Leo eyed Guy. 'Instructive.'

Guy smirked. He crunched across the mess he'd made to the next fireplace arch. Leo winced, already anticipating the next crash.

Harry shook his head. 'I can't tell Orford about this, Leo, I just can't.'

Lord Walpole, Orford's heir, had that cruel, tight mouth, the sort of mouth that might spell trouble for his new wife. It had to come from somewhere. Leo didn't want to have to wonder too hard about what could make Harry cringe more in fear of an absent father than a very present 'inspector'.

'I can't help you, Harry,' he said. 'Surely you've got mates who'll stand you shares of fifty pounds.'

Leo couldn't imagine it himself – it was an annual salary in his circles – but Harry ran with the aristocratic crowd. He could pass his fancy topper around.

'It's not fifty,' Harry said to the floor.

'The young buck here owes three hundred pounds,' Guy said, resting his elbow on the shelf. He was toying with a daguerreotype.

Leo choked. Harry was in even deeper than he'd guessed. '*How?*'

Still at a mutter, Harry admitted, 'They let me borrow,' and Leo couldn't restrain a groan. 'The game's not worth the candle, otherwise!'

'I'm sure you see the dilemma, Mr Sweetwater,' Guy said. 'If he owed the clubs, he might be facing ruination, prison, exile. My establishment takes the view we'd rather have his money than his honour. And he can't pay.'

Leo waited.

'Me and Harry have settled on what you might call a compromise.' Guy chewed over the three syllables, com-pro-mise, laying them down one by one in gloating contemplation. 'He'll stump up a third as a show of good faith. I'll personally chance the remaining on his ever-so-sincere promise of what *you* can do.'

He tossed the daguerreotype aside to smash on the floor, and strolled over to Leo. 'Don't fret, buttercup,' he crooned, chucking Leo's chin. 'It's not the prick-sucking. God knows you'd be on your knees a while to earn two hundred pounds.'

'You can ask your ghost,' Harry blurted. 'Ask it where the stolen purse is buried.'

Twitching away from the rough touch of Guy's fingers, Leo said, 'My ghost? Mr Guy, Walpole is *deluded*. There's no such thing as ghosts.'

Naturally, this was exactly when Polly floated through the wall. 'Leo, why did the Fitzhenrys go tearing through the Palace like they set the studio on fire?'

Leo gave not a whisker of acknowledgement, but as her accompanying chill dropped the room temperature, Harry cried, 'See, Guy! It's here.'

'What's Walpole doing back?' Polly dropped lower to stare into Guy's eyes. 'And who is *this* ghastly creature? I don't think I like him.'

Her dismay was only making the room colder. Guy gazed about, and his craggy face was suddenly alight with a disconcertingly open pleasure. The look in his eye was reminiscent of Lady Jane's fervour. This man was a *believer*. Polly wafted further from him, frowning, trailing icy air in her wake.

Leo, in practised tones of utter incredulity, said, 'You want me to ask a ghost where mythical stolen loot was supposedly buried a quarter of a millennia ago? Every step of this plan is fantastical.'

'He's telling his ghost what's been happening,' Harry confided to Guy.

Infuriatingly, he'd adopted his old drawling tones, confidence manifesting the same moment Polly had.

'I can't help you,' Leo said coldly. 'You need to leave.'

'That's right, out, out, out,' Polly seethed. The walls were silvering.

Guy turned, smiling. 'Here's where I'd normally be making my threats and indulging my lads in a spot of batter-fang. But today I don't have to expend the effort. Right, Harry?'

Harry cleared his throat. 'I'll be marching straight to the Hampton magistrate, Sweetwater.'

'How will you like a couple of peelers dragging you off in front of all the gentry?' Guy enquired. 'Give the widows heart palpitations, it will.'

Leo didn't bother to point out that it was a felony to make a false accusation for the purposes of extortion, even when the false accusation was actually true. That newish law protected Harry from Leo, not the other way round, and all of them knew it.

Instead, above Polly's furious outcry, he tried to speak reasonably. 'Harry, if your father would be angry to know the kinds of places you've been frequenting, surely he would be angrier if you made public the kinds of *men* you've been...'

'Frequenting,' Guy finished for him, winking grotesquely.

'All it means is the magistrate will be induced to dispense summary justice for indecent advances rather than commit you to trial,' Harry said softly. 'That's still two years on the tread-mill.'

And his precious daguerreotype licence gone. And his caretaker warrant gone. And the Fitzhenrys left without position with their employer and guardian under correction. Freedom, livelihood, home, all held in the palm of a spoilt and indolent boy who'd rather destroy his ex-lover than face his father.

Tiredly, Leo said, 'Does it absolve your conscience that you're not threatening me with hanging?' and saw from Harry's chagrin he had the right of it.

'Poxy villains!' Polly cried. 'Motherless rogues!' The walls were caked with frost now, of the spectral kind that only Leo could see. It didn't matter: every breath, white in the chill air, was telltale.

'Come now, I am a man of limited time.' Guy looked Leo up and down, lingering offensively. 'You don't look it, but if you're the sort who needs a visit from my lovelies outside to prick you into action, I'll oblige.'

'Hell and devil confound thee, feculent miscreants!' Polly snarled. She whirled through the two men, trying ineffectually to herd them towards the door.

Harry shivered. 'It's angry.'

Guy rubbed his hands together. 'Show us what else you've got, chuckaboo,' he called, like a man heckling at a stage show. 'I'll batter your boy, I surely will, what will you do about it?'

The heavy oak door flew open and thumped into the wall.

SIXTEEN

LEO STARED WITH SOME BESTARTLEMENT AT this unexpected physicality, hands locked into fists with the sheer effort it took to not look at Polly.

'I didn't do that,' she called, even as Guy crowed in unfeigned delight.

Then Cole strode through, coatless, sleeves rolled back to show off the lean muscle of his forearms, cap firmly in place, looking very much the doughty man of toil.

'Afternoon, Sweetwater.' He smiled at Leo, who was too confused to do other than blink at him, before turning to the two men. 'The studio's closing early today.' He gave Guy a cool stare. '*You'll* find the whole Palace is closing early today, mate.'

Guy straightened, bright eyes gone beady, jovial grin becoming a sneer, hand straying towards a pocket.

Behind Cole came two of his more hefty under-gardeners, and, peeking around the door with wide eyes, John. Leo had made up the spurious meeting with their departed brother to get the Fitzhenrys safely away. It hadn't occurred to him they'd fetch help. He wondered, vaguely, how John had managed to convey the message.

Harry muttered, 'Careful, he's got—'

Guy whistled, short but piercing, and the doorway became crowded as a couple of bruisers came up on Cole's men, shoving John aside.

'Bundle'm in here, sharpish,' Guy ordered and his heavies shoved at the gardeners, who, young and on their dander, pushed back. Beyond them, Max's deep bark sounded out.

The melee looked likely to become a proper brawl, knives due any moment, when a ringing voice cut through the incipient chaos and stilled it instantly with the sheer weight of generations of domination. Even Max went quiet.

'Be so kind as to clear the way at once,' Lady Albinia enunciated, bludgeoning them with the vowels. 'I am attempting to proceed through this door, and you are blocking the egress.'

The men fell back, and Lady Albinia sailed in without her cane, only barely preceded by a damp and nervous footman, sweating either because he'd just pulled the Push across the Palace at pace, he'd failed to gain the attention of the tussling men quickly enough for his mistress's stringent liking – or he was worried he *had* gained their attention now, and didn't appreciate the idea.

Sally was hiding behind Lady Albinia in the same way John had hid behind the gardeners. John had run for muscle. Sally had run for authority.

Leo didn't understand why authority had come, but she had.

'Mr Sweetwater, I have arrived for my… Do we call it a sitting?'

'Yes,' Leo said faintly.

Lady Albinia swept every man in the room with cool disdain. 'I believe I specified complete privacy, did I not, girl, for my sitting.'

Sally had followed Lady Albinia in, John close by her side. 'You did, my lady,' she said meekly.

'Awa oot, laddies.' Cole made a shooing gesture at Guy, who returned him such a vicious smile that Leo bit his tongue.

He folded his arms about himself. He was only now beginning to feel the full weight of the fear that had been trying to get his attention since he'd laid eyes on Guy. His sort, activities illegal, became accustomed to rubbing shoulders with Guy's sort, activities also illegal, in the London underbelly. He'd never experienced this level of menace.

'Our business is about done,' Guy said. He bared his preternaturally white and even teeth. 'You'll be sure to think long and hard, won't you, Sweetwater? But don't take *too* long.'

With a last sullen glance at Cole, he jerked his chin at his men and they all strolled out. The under-gardeners followed, and Cole went with them to quieten the newly aroused Max. The footman stood by the wall until a nod from Lady Albinia sent him outside.

Sally threw her arms about John, squeezing him tight, taking in a deep and shaky breath as she rested her cheek atop his head.

Then she straightened her pinny and went and fetched a dustpan and brush from behind the counter.

Leo blankly watched her begin to sweep up the mess Guy had made. 'You don't have to do that, Miss Fitzhenry.'

'I do, sir,' she said, not looking at him.

'I am so sorry,' Harry blurted. 'He made me bring him here.'

'He didn't make you make me responsible for your gambling debt,' Leo snapped, quite forgetting Lady Albinia's presence.

'Gambling,' she said. 'I thought as much. I know that type of old, my parents invited the devils home with them. I cannot say I approve, Mr Walpole, but why on earth have you not applied to Lord Orford to extricate yourself from this mess?'

'He won't hear it,' Harry said sulkily.

'More like you don't want him to hear it,' Cole said flatly from the doorway.

Max, pale fur damp, was at his feet, peering in past the invisible barrier of the threshold he knew he was not allowed to cross. He stared at Harry.

'Mr Solong is quite correct,' Lady Albinia said decidedly. 'You cannot go about making your difficulties into Mr Sweetwater's, Mr Walpole, it is abominable behaviour.'

Apparently considering the matter settled upon the dispensation of her judgement, she walked to the arch into the portrait studio to look over the arrangements.

Harry scowled as if considering whether or not he had the spine to tell Lady Albinia to mind her own business. Instead, he stepped closer to Leo.

'Leo,' he whispered, 'I can't tell my father, I just can't. He'll *punish* me.' His eyes were wide and pleading. 'Please, you understand, don't you?'

'You can get out,' Cole told him. 'Palace is closing early for you, too.'

'You can't give me orders!'

He sounded so childish that Leo blushed on his behalf, and his own, since Cole briefly wore a *you-took-this-puppy-to-bed?* look, entirely the twin to Polly's expression.

His dark brows drew into a thunderous frown. 'Walpole, I will drag you out by your ear.'

'Try it!'

'Yes, do!' cried Polly with unholy glee.

Alarmed, Leo raised his hands, beseeching calm. 'Mr Walpole, please leave. Lady Albinia desires privacy.'

'The light's not right,' Harry said crossly.

Leo turned his back and went to Lady Albinia's side so Harry would know he was not open to cajolery. She jabbed a finger towards the raised platform. 'Well, Sweetwater. Must one clamber up this contraption?'

'It lets us find the light, Lady Albinia,' Leo explained. 'I'll give you my arm. But he's right, it's much too dark this afternoon. You shall have to come back on a sunnier day.'

Lady Albinia arched her brows imperiously. 'I have no interest in posing at the beck and call of some finicky demanding machine.'

'Oh. But...'

'Do you find it so hard to believe I came because your girl told me you needed assistance, Percy?' she asked. She sounded no softer, but her eyes crinkled with a warmth he was not used to seeing in her. 'I've known you all your life. I knew your mother since she was a mere slip not much older than the Fitzhenry girl. You're an odd fellow, I won't deny it, but you're not a friendless one. Mr Solong alone proves otherwise.'

Behind them, Cole snarled, '*Nique ta mere!*'

There came a crunching thump, and a cry. The young gardeners shouted, somewhere between surprise and awe. Both Fitzhenrys gasped. Polly cackled.

Leo spun, followed in a more stately, or perhaps creaky, fashion by Lady Albinia.

Cole was shaking his hand, face scrunched in pain, and Harry was clutching his nose, reeling, also in pain.

'You hit me!' he said, voice thick and muffled, sounding as stunned as Leo felt.

'Run and tell your father why,' Cole said, rubbing his knuckles. 'You like poetry so much? Here's a line for you: wee, sleekit, cow'rin, tim'rous *beastie.*'

Polly laughed again.

'I will! I'll tell him enough, certainly.' Harry took his hand away from his face, discovered blood, and went pale. 'He's an earl, he'll have your job.'

'I'll see your earl and raise you a queen, one notoriously fond of bastards.'

'Language, Mr Solong!'

'In the literal sense, Lady Albinia, she coped with the Clarence dozen admirably.'

'It remains a topic unsuitable for polite discourse,' thundered the relic of a highly notorious era.

Cole pointed out the door, gaze fixed on Harry. 'Shall we walk across the park to Bushey House right now? We can explain to Dowager Queen Adelaide why exactly her personally-appointed Royal Gardener felt the need to punch Lord Orford's son in the face.'

Harry wavered, then said, 'Sweetwater, I'll be in touch.' Still attempting to blot his dripping nose, he walked out.

'Oh, no,' Polly muttered. 'I hope he's not going to the Hoste apartment.' She floated out after him.

'Mr Solong,' said Lady Albinia. 'I cannot say I approve of fisticuffs.'

'My sincerest regrets, my lady,' Cole said, extremely insincerely.

'And your patroness is currently taking the air in more healthful climes.'

'Ay, I was bluffing.'

She sniffed and affected a stern look. 'Mr Sweetwater, I trust that is the end of the matter, and the last I shall hear of any of it. I will not have you bringing the Palace into disrepute with your associations.'

This struck Leo as singularly unfair, but also entirely what he would expect. 'Yes, my lady.'

'Very well. Take this foolish man somewhere to tend to his hand. He evidently failed to learn how to throw a punch at Kew.'

Cole mutinously muttered, 'Walpole didn't learn how to *take* a punch at Eton,' before Leo swiftly guided him out.

SEVENTEEN

THE SUN WAS BREAKING THROUGH TO silver the drizzle, delineating every drop until it looked like snowfall, slow and silent. With the two under-gardeners lingering so Sally and John could keep the studio open through the last of the afternoon without fear, Leo walked Cole over to his apartment.

Still lost in belated reaction to the invasion, he said nothing, only vaguely noticing that Cole was, uncharacteristically, quiet as well. Max walked at their heels, soft and persistent as a ghost, and sat on the threshold.

Leo hung up his coat and their hats. He sat Cole at the big oak table in the underused dining room to examine his knuckles, a better use of his time than shivering by a fire. They were swollen and mottled with bruising. He supposed Polly, were she here, would have all sorts of poultices and herbal creams from her mother's receipt book, but he arrived only at the idea of a damp cloth.

The linens were folded away with lavender sprigs, the scent competing with lemon oil and beeswax polish. He fetched out a napkin, wet it in the kettle water, and returned to lay the cool folds over Cole's injured hand.

This was the closest they'd been since he'd kissed him.

He shifted away. 'Why *did* you feel the need to punch him in the face? It seems unlike you.'

Cole examined stolid oaken carpentry with minute interest. 'Aside from him bringing that ruffian into your studio to threaten you?'

'Yes,' Leo said, after a pause. 'Aside from that.'

'And aside from—'

'Assume aside from every point you're about to make,' Leo said, tetchy. 'You don't hit people, Cole, so why did you hit him?'

Left-handed, Cole traced the grain of the bare tabletop. His abused right hand clenched under the draping, dripping cloth, no doubt stretching tight skin.

'Poetry,' he said. 'He spouted poetry at me.'

'Oh.' Leo folded his arms and sidled another step away, flushing. 'I should be grateful I didn't receive a facer for—' He was a grown man, and he couldn't say *kissing*. '—imposing on you myself, then.'

Cole finally looked up, indignation written across his face. 'I would never hurt you, Leo. It wasn't the fact of the poetry, it was the poem he quoted. You didn't hear him?'

'I was talking to Lady Albinia.'

'John Donne.'

'One of his favourites,' Leo said with a shrug that seemed to ratchet Cole's affront higher.

'*The Flea*. That daftie line.' When Leo shook his head, he quoted, wearing a dire frown, 'It sucked me first, and now sucks thee.'

'I see.' Leo concentrated very hard on keeping his voice steady. 'And now *you* see. You *do* mind being associated with a sod and having to weather those sorts of accusations, I told you—'

'What have I done that you insist on believing the worst of me?' Cole demanded. 'He insulted you. You do see that? He equated you to a plague pest and called you an "it" and I won't have it.'

Catapulted from unjustly wounded to roundly astonished, Leo exclaimed, 'You hit him for *me*?'

'And I'd do it again.'

Leo discovered he did not know what to do with his hands. He edged closer to adjust the damp cloth over Cole's knuckles to give them a purpose in life.

Cole angled his chair towards Leo and set his left hand over his, stilling their fretful motion. 'I didn't mind that you kissed me, either. Quite the opposite.'

'You very much appeared to mind,' Leo said, wincing even as he said it. He sounded as sulky as Harry.

'Awa ye go!' Cole said. 'You'd had a scare, you were in a nervous state, I thought I was imposing on *you*!'

'But you know I'm—' More words to trip his tongue on, *in love with you*. He rallied. '—attracted to you.'

'It doesn't follow that you'd have wanted anything more than chaste comfort if you hadn't just been frightened half out of your wits.'

'But then you didn't talk to me for two weeks.'

'Not on purpose, my family needed me.' Cole sat straighter, squeezing Leo's hand. 'Well, a little on purpose. Partly because Sally walked in on us, and I felt bad I'd almost got you caught out twice in two days. Partly because I needed some time to think.'

Leo nodded, drawing his hand back, but Cole caught and held it. The glint was in his eyes now, the usual mischief mingled with something else. 'I was thinking about seeing Walpole kiss you.'

'Sorry,' Leo said automatically. Though lucky there himself, he'd seen other men beaten for similar transgressions.

'And about how you told him to get on his knees if the mood had struck him.'

Face instantly afire, Leo mumbled, 'I don't... I'm not normally that way.'

'And I was thinking most of all,' Cole said, turning his grin onto Leo like a Congreve rocket, 'Leo, *mon cher*, the mood's struck me.'

Faintly, belatedly, and laggardly, Leo breathed, '...What?'

Cole leaned in, eyebrows raised. 'Are you regretting saying you're not that way now?'

'No, I—' He stopped, because he was, actually, behind a solid wall of surprise.

'You're attracted to me, I'm very curious about, well, about all of it.' He waved a hand demonstratively, apparently encompassing an entire gamut of unnatural acts. 'What do you say? Shall we, *mon ami*?'

Leo opened his mouth, closed it on an exhale of wordless air, and was abruptly in Cole's arms. He didn't know if Cole had pulled him in or if he'd flung himself onto him like a drowning man clutching for the proverbial.

Their mouths met, hard. Cole grunted under the onslaught. Leo *had* been pent-up, after all; he shoved himself even harder against Cole's body and took his mouth with fervent, urgent, wild hunger, and if it left him bruised and rubbed raw from the rasp of his beard, he couldn't care.

He was mostly outside his own head, except a distant thread below the clamour of need: *Too much, don't scare him, don't scare him.* He tried to rein back.

Cole would have none of it. He chased the kiss, just as starved for the taste of it, palms clasped to Leo's cheeks, prayful. Leo's world became the pursuit of Cole's soft lips, the soft prickle of his well-groomed beard, the spice of his earthy fragrance, the slide of his hands.

The lightning pulse of response sparked across Leo's skin, curling in his stomach, stirring him beyond reason. Cole's hand tightened at the nape of his neck, sending shudders of pure molten heat down his spine.

'Your hand?' he managed to ask.

Cole flexed his thighs under Leo and pushed up from the chair, strong hands spread under Leo's thighs, fingertips grazing the curve of his arse.

'I've had worse pruning roses,' he said, not a hitch in his voice to betray any sort of effort.

He tipped Leo flat onto the table with the same smooth confidence. Hooking an ankle around the chair leg to drag it until he could get a knee onto the seat, he was suddenly leveraged over Leo, pressing bodily between his legs as he demanded his mouth again.

He was making small sounds, startled and delighted, each time he made a new discovery: Leo's lips parting with goodwill to his tongue, Leo's stand thrusting back against his own, Leo's spine arching to rub harder, Leo's fingers digging into his ribs.

Cole gasped a single, 'You—' and Leo said, 'Like Vesuvius, yes, I know,' and Cole's lips came down on his again.

Leo groaned into Cole's mouth and wrapped his legs around his hips, locking him in tight, and Cole all but climbed on top of him. They were frigging against each other with wild indecorum, the table shaking with their frantic haste but sturdy enough to take it.

Cole pulled away, muttering, '*Grimper aux rideaux!* I'll have us naked before I spend in my trousers, *mon Dieu.*'

He clawed at Leo's studs between kisses, while Leo failed to catch his breath. He didn't want to catch his breath. He didn't want to think.

He was dragging at Cole's clothes in turn when Polly whisked in.

'Walpole bled all over Fountain C—' she began in some distress, before a high-pitched, 'Good Lord, Percival!'

Leo moaned in agreement, trusting she'd take the hint.

He'd found in London that sex, like many human states of arousal, sometimes drew in ghosts, silent and disinterested observers. Since it couldn't be called voyeurism – it felt like being stared at by a pet – he'd learned to ignore their presence as per usual practice, even under such circumstances.

Of course, he didn't think of those spectral Peeping Toms as somewhere between friend, aunt and sister.

They weren't, as a rule, actively barracking him, either.

'I don't think you should do this,' Polly said, floating by the table.

Leo shut his eyes, shaking his head. Cole, having successfully bared Leo's torso, was now kissing his way down his chest on a foray towards his trousers, hands sliding over Leo's nipples, ribs, hips, the callouses on his fingertips and palms shooting tingles along Leo's nerves.

'He's only touching the womanly parts of you,' Polly observed.

Leo's eyes snapped open. He glared at her. He didn't need reminding that he was no longer the slender youth who might have matched better with Cole's lean muscular figure, he didn't need his attention directed to his rounder, softer parts just as he was baring them to scrutiny, and he didn't need to be told that Polly was right.

'He's pretending you're a girl,' Polly said. 'He'll close his eyes and roll you onto your stomach, you'll see. And what if he comes to his senses once he's taken his pleasure and feels nothing but disgust, Leo? Can you bear it if he looks at you with disgust?'

Cole, all unaware of the literal manifestation of Leo's private worries, ran the flat of his palm over the bulge of Leo's stand, which had remained impervious to Polly's dire litany even as the rest of him quailed. He made the sort of anticipatory grunt a hungry man might make when presented with a laden plate, and pressed his face against the strained fabric.

Getting his other knee up on the seat of the chair, he leaned eagerly over Leo. 'I won't say I'll be much good at this, but I'm giving it a red-hot go, you can't ask for more.'

Leo whispered, 'I can't, no, but I don't think it's a concern.'

Polly's brows went up. She hovered for a moment, watching Cole and his blatant enthusiasm, then said, 'You're right. He's not a man who'll fool himself or turn on you. But, pet, *think*. That's worse. He's nothing but please and thank you now, pretty as can be, and tomorrow he'll clap you on the back and be nothing but your good friend again.'

Leo's gaze flicked to hers. *I'm very curious about all of it*, Cole had said, and he'd been subjected to the curiosities of conventional men before, quite often conspicuously soon before they married.

'Thanks, but no thanks, *mon ami*,' Polly recited. 'Thanks, but I'll try a soldier now. Thanks, but here's the notice for my wedding breakfast.'

Leo flinched.

'It'll tear out your heart, Leo,' Polly said. 'There's almost nothing worse than a lover demoting you back into a friend when you don't want it so. Trust me, pet, I know.' She wrapped her arms around her translucent body, edges fraying.

Fighting himself for every inch of progress, Leo lifted himself onto his elbows. Cole was tackling the fall of Leo's trousers, intent, eyelashes lowered, licking his lips.

Leo cleared his throat several times before he got out, 'I have to stop.' Cole looked up, bemused. 'I'm sorry, I have to stop.'

Busy hands fallen still, Cole stared at Leo with parted lips and eyes so dark with arousal, they looked liquid.

He shivered, an all-body shrug. 'Ay, of course we'll stop.' He hesitated. 'Did I…'

'No, you did nothing wrong,' Leo said. His eyes felt swollen and hot. He wanted to roll off the table and hide under it.

Rising lithely to his feet, Cole chastised himself. 'Ay, you've got more to worry about than indulging me and my curiosity.'

Polly hissed between her teeth to be proven correct.

Running his hands through his hair, Cole added, 'I haven't been that distracted by sex since… Well. Since *ever*.'

He gave a short laugh, a touch strained, quite missing Leo's reach towards him in reflexive reaction to that confession as he collected their discarded clothing.

'Hold firm, Leo, you'll thank me,' Polly said, and Leo accepted the bundle of shirt and waistcoat humbly, sliding to his feet and beginning to dress.

Cole, fastening his shirt, turned to the door, calling back, 'Tea in the drawing room and we'll see what's to be done.'

Eighteen

Cole had the kettle over the coals by the time Leo came into the parlour, trailed by Polly, and greeted him with undimmed smile.

'Sorry,' Leo said again, heart trying to rip in two regardless of his self-protective sacrifice.

'I did say attraction and acting on attraction aren't in lockstep,' Cole said, entirely his usual amiable self. 'It occurs to me you'd just had another scare, too, and I felt bad enough the first time, so I'm glad you stopped me.'

'That wasn't—' Leo bit his tongue. It was a better reason than the truth, though it made him seem a milk-veined, nervy creature.

'The first time?' Polly was lingering in the doorway, letting the room grow toasty warm as Cole poked up the flames. Leo twitched his chin, a tiny shake of negation.

Cole busied himself making the tea. Leo stared out the small-paned parlour window. The rain had set in properly. It was a miserable afternoon. He hoped Max wasn't waiting on his doorstep for Cole to emerge, though the dog, thickly coated, was mostly impervious to rain, and often lay on his back in it like a lesser creature might lie in sunshine.

Cole handed him his teacup and sat in the other armchair, stretching out his legs. 'You ready to tell me why Walpole's inviting miscreants into your studio?'

'Oh, extortion,' Leo said, tipping his cup with false good cheer. 'He's threatening the law if I don't help him pay off his gambling debt.'

Cole nodded, singularly unsurprised, while Polly called Harry a filthy name, furious but also not surprised. Leo could only hope it hadn't been completely obvious to Lady Albinia that the young Walpole and his unpleasant companion had a hold over him.

'If he informs on you, he informs on himself,' Cole pointed out, as if Leo had never once had to weigh his risks.

Patiently, he said, 'I'm sure it'll be rather tiresome for him, explaining to all and sundry how shocking he found my indecent advances.'

'And if you beat him to the magistrate and accuse him first?'

'Oh, he hasn't a notion, has he,' Polly said.

'It's a felony to make an accusation of unspeakable acts for the purposes of personal gain,' Leo explained. 'Parliament saw to that, after Castlereagh.'

'But you've no personal gain,' Cole said.

'He will say I demanded money.'

'He can have no proof of something that didn't happen.'

'It…doesn't quite work like that,' Leo said carefully. 'Given his standing, and mine.'

Cole's mouth tightened, but the son of a baronet, even an illegitimate one, couldn't argue with the entire world of inequity and injustice buried inside that simple statement. For Leo, it was normality, one he'd long ago come to terms with. It was almost amusing, in a frustrating way, to watch Cole wrestle with its edges.

'I don't understand why he'd do this to you, though. Fine, he's too cowardly to front his father, but why not dun one of his…' Cole squeezed his strong fingers about his cup. Leo worked out what he wanted to say just as he came out with the more tactful, 'London friends.'

'He owes that horrid man three hundred pounds,' Leo said bluntly. Cole coughed up his sip of tea, which made Leo feel slightly better about his own reaction; he'd assumed he was being very precarious middling to blink at the amount. 'He'll scrape from mates with deep pockets, certainly, but that won't touch the sides.'

'I know you work hard…'

'I don't have the savings, no. I've been putting it all back into the equipment.' He gave a thin smile. 'It's a fast-evolving field.'

Cole sat back, looking both relieved and satisfied. 'You'll call his bluff, then?'

'I daren't risk it,' Leo said, with a peculiar shiver: fear like a stone in his stomach, but the tightness of his shoulders easing.

It was a rare but familiar feeling, one he'd experienced twice before: first, after his twin temporary deaths, when he'd accepted he'd see ghosts for as long as he lived, and second, after he'd confronted his own nature and known he'd walk a harder road than he'd have wanted, given a choice.

Yes, it was unfair. And yes, he dared not risk it. Even if the magistrate was an honest one and disregarded Harry's status to dismiss the indecency charge for lack of independent testimony (which Leo did not put it past Guy to supply), the accusation alone could very well sink his livelihood.

Plunking his cup down with a sharp clink, Cole said nothing for a moment, his brows angled sternly. Then he said, 'If you truly insist, I can pull some funds together, and Sir Walter—'

'No!' Leo said, alarmed, almost offended, that Cole assumed he could safely waltz in and out of this sordid affair without harm to the Townsend Farquhar reputation. 'No, I won't take money from you for this.'

'I don't see where else you're digging up the needful.'

Polly snorted, while Leo near-yelped a laugh. He covered his mouth with one hand, almost spilling the tea in the other. He placed his teacup carefully on the doily-covered occasional table. Cole looked at him quizzically.

The apartment was too small to have anything like a proper study. Leo's correspondence sat in a secretarie, another of the Countess of Athlone's pieces, prettier than the rest, made from some kind of East Indies wood with ebony inlay. He opened the front and drew out Harry's note from where he'd buried it, and handed it over.

'You have your particular friend assist my particular friend, and I won't tell anyone about *our* particular friendship,' Cole read aloud. He looked up, frowning. 'I have no idea what he thinks he's getting at.'

'He doesn't expect ready money from the likes of me,' Leo translated. 'He was the one digging holes.' In all the turmoil, he'd forgotten to relay that to Cole, who now muttered a curse under his breath. 'He wants me to ask a ghost where the treasure is buried. Not Wolsey's plate. A late Tudor purse, apparently.'

Cole set down the note. 'You told Walpole about your ghost?'

He sounded, bizarrely, hurt, in a way that made Leo bristle at what could be taken as presumption, as if Cole thought his friendship entitled him to Leo's secrets.

'He guessed,' he said tersely. He remembered now: *but not your usual friendly ghost?* As with the culprit of the Wilderness vandalism, it had been quite driven out of his head. 'As did you, even before the Maze.'

'Your French comprehension declines when the room's not draughty, but your whist game markedly improves.' Cole picked up the poker. As he tended the fire, he said, softly, 'Dining room caught a draught, didn't it?'

Leo kept his gaze steadfastly from Polly. She was hovering in the doorway so the parlour wouldn't catch that suspicious draught. If he didn't look, Cole wouldn't know she was there. He hadn't earned any extra entitlement to Leo's secrets by unearthing most of them.

Luckily, Cole knew better than to expect an answer. He abruptly snatched up Harry's note, holding it high in triumph. 'This is proof of the extortion. If he tries to accuse you of one felony, you can show him guilty of the other.'

'Let's see.' Leo weighed the air with one open palm. 'An earl's son.' He weighed the air with the other. 'A washerwoman's son, with a circum-spect, anonymous, easily discredited note. Which of us will be transport-ed to Australia, I wonder? I'll be sure to wave hello to Walt from the chain-gang.'

'But *you* have a witness to support your side.'

It actually took Leo a moment before he understood Cole was talking about himself. 'I certainly do not!' he said. 'You are not getting yourself involved in this, Cole.'

'I'm not leaving you to deal with it alone,' Cole said, a stubborn set to his mouth. 'I'll front the magistrate and tell him I saw Walpole pressuring you into indecency, and you can tell Walpole so.'

Leo was about to insist, even more strenuously, that Cole keep out of business he barely understood the shape of, when Polly said, 'That dreadful brute won't care. Not the way his eyes lit up. He was Lady Jane with a moustache and a knife hidden in his pocket.'

Leo sucked in a breath. She was right. 'It's not about what Harry will or won't do now,' he said slowly, thinking it through as he spoke. 'Even if he let me be and paid up on his own, Guy wouldn't quietly go away with his purseful. He *wants* to talk to...my ghost.'

He and Polly would have to give the man the spectral show he plainly craved, in such a way that he was satisfied with his taste of the supernatural, but wouldn't come back for more. Leo did not know how to strike that balance yet, though he could be comforted that Polly wouldn't, *couldn't*, give up the location of a treasure she didn't even believe existed.

Further, he was lucky that Harry, and therefore Guy, assumed Leo only had a single familiar. He must be careful to maintain the pose that his ability was confined to one ghost at one location. If Guy realised it was more generalised, he might drag him to London and use him to question dead men. Leo shuddered.

'Walpole told him all about you, I suppose, in talking him out of cutting off a finger and posting it to Lord Orford.'

Polly scoffed. 'What has this man been reading?'

Cole sounded disgusted. He also sounded like he'd been reading the penny dreadfuls. The hell-keepers trod carefully when threatening noble scions. The trick was to scare them enough to pay up, but not so much they'd run to Papa or the law. Guy was probably enjoying his hold over a young man greatly opposed to doing either.

Leaning back into the soft cushioning of his armchair, Leo closed his eyes and let the warmth of the fire wash over him. 'It's my own fault,' he murmured. 'I knew he was indiscreet the moment I saw him, and I still—'

'It's *not* your fault,' Cole snapped, unwontedly heated. 'Put it on Walpole, where it belongs. He made a bed he wants *you* to lie in.'

'The nature of unspeakable vice is that the practitioners of it are constrained to be more careful than I chose to be,' Leo said. 'His bed, yes, but I hopped on into it without a second thought. I'm waiting for the "I told you so".'

This last was to Polly. 'It's rather lost its savour,' she said sourly.

'I don't believe I ever threatened it,' Cole said. 'Though, you did claim the risk was as low as that of being hit by lightning.'

'Not when you go outside and dance in the storm.'

A fraught pause, and then Polly outright laughed and Cole snorted and said, 'Numptie,' just as Leo buried his face in his hands and said, 'Horrendous.'

Heaving a mournful sigh, Cole said, 'You're an artist, not a poet, for a reason, I suppose.'

Leo laughed softly, his irritable tension easing. He tried not to look at Cole with too open an expression.

He didn't succeed. Cole brushed his fingers over his. 'This is a fair fankle and no mistake,' he said, voice burring. 'But stop acting like you earned it and let me help you. Walpole's got his connections to protect him, let me call in mine to protect you. We'll send him back to Dade and be sure Guy doesn't dare cross the Palace threshold again.'

Though he knew Cole was sincere and genuinely concerned for him, Leo had to suppress vexation, surging up stronger than before.

He'd been navigating his world, by necessity an underworld, for half his life. He'd learned its needless, pointless, cruel dangers, but such darkness was outshone, always, by simple joys, the expansive feeling of meeting like men, the snatched and vital pleasures they took together, the strength and beauty and independence of a life not tightly bound into the strict confines of convention.

Irrationally, it felt like a betrayal, of who or what he didn't know, to have an ignorant outsider waving off a dire situation with a casual promise to solve it using all those things Leo had never had, money and reputation and status, without anticipating, or even acknowledging, potential consequences.

It brought into sharp relief that every careful risk Leo had ever taken to be with another man, whether a man he loved or a man he'd never met before, had meant absolutely nothing, had been absolutely unnecessary, would not have even existed, if he had been born privileged enough.

Trying not to sound too annoyed, he said, 'And what will you tell your connections, by which I mean, how will you explain to Sir Walter that you're not only associating with a sodomite, but you're prepared to let the Townsend Farquhar name be associated with a squalid legal skirmish with an earl's son?'

Cole said, 'He'll support me,' with such simple faith that Leo clenched his hands, breath stolen by the sheer naivety.

His calm shredded.

'He will not,' he said, because families *didn't*, they hung you out to dry, and that was just another advantage Cole was throwing in his face, too complacent to realise it was a false security. 'He keeps you out of sight of his aristocratic patrons as it is.'

'No, he doesn't.' Cole spoke pleasantly enough, but he withdrew his hand.

'You didn't go to Wellesley's funeral.'

'I didn't want to.' Cole's face creased. 'Making pretty talk with dull, important men? Not for me.'

'Because Sir Robert never expected you to learn,' Leo said, 'because he never expected better for his bastard.'

'Leo?' Polly said slowly. 'Ah, pet?'

'It's not like that.' Cole's arms had gone akimbo; he was tensely upright in the armchair, perched as if he wanted to stand up and loom. 'Father and Mamam never made me or Walt feel lesser for being natural sons, he left us both generous legacies in his will, Walter always treated us both as full brothers.'

The steadfast but misplaced loyalty was infuriating. 'You're their errand boy,' Leo said, unable to control the sneering edge to his voice, 'as much as I ever was for Lady Albinia, and you see how she treats me.'

'Fondly?' The word was very pointed. 'She came to the studio today, for you.'

'Oh, but if I ever step from the lines she draws to keep me precisely in my place, I'll see how far that goes. And you'll see exactly how far the love and support of your family goes, if they find out you've indulged your *curiosity* with perversion.'

He all but snarled the last few words, because, *actually*, how *dare* Cole come in here and assume the local sod would service him at the drop of a kind word just because he wanted the novelty of vice?

Polly said, 'You might be overwrought, pet.'

Cole, frowning, said, 'I know your grandfather was harsh with you, and I'm sorry for it, but my family would never do that to me. They love me, they'd stand by me.'

That stung. Leo's mother had loved him, and stood by him. It hadn't made her constant disapproval easier to bear. 'They love you? Sir Robert let *your mother* die without a word to you!'

Cole held up his hands. 'Haud up. I wish it'd been different, but at least I had her love for the first years of my life. No one in his social circle would have batted an eye if he'd left her on the docks, and he kept her with us and didn't marry until after she died. Fair, he could have done better, but he could have done worse. He certainly did his best by me.'

This judicious, forgiving response, so emblematic of what Leo loved about his goodhearted, reasonable friend, served only to incense him. 'Is that why he didn't send you to Westminster School and on to Oxford like his real son?

'*Real* son?'

'Percy, stop!'

Leo was not listening. 'Is that why he pushed you off into apprenticing with gardeners?'

'Pushed me?' Cole repeated over him, voice sharpening ever further. 'I see. So when Walpole called me a jumped-up gardener and you defended me, you didn't mean a word of it?'

Leo, in the full flight of this most unusual ire, finally faltered. 'You heard that?' He recalled the rest of the conversation. Horror overwhelming anger, he blurted, 'You heard *all* of that?'

'I left when he called me a half-caste coolie. I'd only waited to be sure he wasn't going to try forcing you to more than you wanted.'

Even though Cole wouldn't have heard anything he didn't now know or guess, Leo was still relieved beyond measure.

And, apparently, beyond basic sense. He said, 'No, he wouldn't, he's harmless.'

'Oh, *pet*,' Polly said, hand over her eyes.

Cole's face, already stiff, hardened further. He tapped the extortion letter, once, a very solid punctuation.

'Physically speaking,' Leo clarified, wincing. 'He was unkind about you that night, I know. I'm sorry.'

'Don't apologise, not for *him*! Come awa, is his prick—' Cole broke off with a visible effort.

Leo's hackles had been settling into shamed chagrin, but the rare illtemper immediately flashed up again.

'Oh, no, do ask,' he said coldly, rising. The room chilled, too, as Polly came closer, satisfyingly indignant on his behalf. 'Is his prick what? A fine enough specimen to addle my thinking?'

Cole finally stood as well, and did indeed seem to tower over Leo despite not being so very much taller than him. 'Why are you being nastier about me wanting to help you out of trouble than about that daftie bampot getting you into it?'

Leo rubbed at his eyes, roiling inside. It was a fair point. If Cole was relying on advantages Leo didn't have and never did have, Harry was outright actively deploying them, to Leo's disadvantage.

But Leo didn't love Harry. Leo didn't expect a nebulous better of Harry.

Leo didn't expect Harry to be able to read his mind and work all this out, either.

He was sick to his teeth of himself, and he could find neither the words nor the detachment to try to explain it to Cole, who was already aggravated, and wouldn't want to listen anyway.

'Just leave,' he said wearily, 'before I say something I regret.'

'*Before?*' Cole said. 'I've already discovered you find me contemptible for letting myself be used by the people I love and deigning to only aspire to gardening, dare I wonder what other truths you have for me? Gae me it, then.'

Polly hovered in his way. 'Perhaps not, Percy, I think your nerves are a little overdone and you shouldn't—'

'Then I suggest you tell Sir Walter and Lady Erica you have an urge to suck pricks, and see if you ever see your nephews again.'

As Polly groaned, Cole stepped back, lips pressed into a tight line, eyes averted. 'Good afternoon, then,' he said evenly. 'Mr Sweetwater.'

As the door closed behind him, Leo sat back in his chair and put his face in his hands.

Too late, he was remembering Maria, Cole's stepmother, showing him the miniatures of her family, the two bastards right there beside her own son and husband in the unfolded locket, all equally as treasured in gold.

Too late, he was remembering Cole's cheerful jape about wasting his education, because his father had, in fact, wanted to send him to Westminster and Oxford just like Sir Walter Minto.

The chill spiked. Leo dropped his hands. Before Polly could offer any sort of hypocrisy, he said, still in the grip of blind righteousness, 'Are you happy now? I'll be alone, just like you wanted.'

'That's not what I want.' She was entirely, tediously, affronted. 'I want you not to break your own heart.'

'And how did that work out?'

His bitterness was enough to send her into a two-hundred-year regression. 'I didst not tell thee to vent thy spleen against one attempting only thy succour!'

'He had no right!'

'Thou art ridiculous!' Polly snapped.

'I know!' he shouted back. 'I've been ridiculous my whole life and it's your fault! My God, I live like a shade, hiding from life, just so you can have extra years that must taste like the thinnest of gruel.'

She gasped, horrified and outraged, and the temperature plummeted to arctic. 'I hast ne'r asked for aught from thee, Percy!'

'You knew you didn't have to.'

'How darest thou?' she cried. 'I hast only ev'r tried to keep thee safe.'

'You've tried to keep me for yourself,' he snarled.

She stomped her insubstantial foot, seething in fury and frustration. 'Tempt not too much the hatred of my spirit, for I am sick when I do look on thee!'

She vanished.

'I'm not an idiot, I know that's Shakespeare,' he shouted to empty air.

It might have been Marlowe.

He wondered if the Bard or the Muses' Darling had any decent quotes for when a three-inch fool had made an utter shambles of his own life.

184

Nineteen

THE NEXT MORNING, LEO HID IN his bedroom until Sally and John departed for their Friday routine, and then tripped over the breakfast tray Sally had left outside his door.

Her quietly responsible maturity was taking the fun out of his funk.

He mopped up the tea, ate the crumpets, and began to write a letter.

It was not to either of the two people to whom he'd have liked to be writing a letter – a deeply felt, abjectly apologetic letter – but, rather, to Harry.

He was a good way into a cautiously couched invitation to speak to a ghost, if she ever even spoke to *him* again, when a knock sounded. He peeked from the corner of the parlour window, and discovered Mrs Grundy, the Palace Housekeeper, on his doorstep.

He opened the door with distinct relief, and some surprise. While Mrs Grundy did occasionally conduct a cursory inspection of Lady Athlone's apartment to fulfil the terms of his caretaker warrant, he didn't think she'd schedule that duty on a Friday. That was her busiest day, the day she supervised her army of maids as they thoroughly cleaned the State Apartments.

She was holding a smooth white envelope, and looked rather affronted that he'd answered his own door on his own behalf. She was a great believer in the strict lines drawn by decent society.

Despite her generally severe dress, straitlaced aspect, and formality, Leo had always thought Mrs Grundy rather liked him. About his age, with three young children, she played scapegoat for the animus of the other residents. They issued a constant stream of complaints, from the inarguable (decrying the tourists peering in through private windows and tapping the glass like they thought they were at a zoological exhibit) to the indefensible (resisting contribution to the Poor Relief) and the downright incomprehensible (disputing the conversion of an old game larder in Round Kitchen Court into public conveniences – surely, if the public were not provided with conveniences, they would relieve themselves where it was distinctly *inconvenient*).

Leo, on the other hand, was himself: quiet, tolerant of minor tribulation, and disinclined, in the normal run of things that weren't yesterday afternoon, to express discontent; he really was very far from having an *actual* artistic temperament. He was especially uncomplaining about his warrant, since he recognised the grace and favour of it in a way the Lord Chamberlain might have held up as a shining exemplar to the rest of them, if he had been aware of Leo's existence.

He was proven correct about Mrs Grundy's liking for him when she apologised as she handed him his eviction notice.

Leo tore open the envelope and read the short impersonal note without taking in more than the overall gist, partly from the inked words, partly from Mrs Grundy's sheepish explanation. The apartment had finally come due for its renovation.

'Most unexpected,' she finished, tone turning brisk as she offloaded the bad news. Leo almost asked if this was retaliation for the raid on her erotica room when she added, as a final flourish, 'It came down from on high in the first post this morning.'

On high meant the Lord Chamberlain himself, though the note, when Leo looked at it again, was from an anonymous clerk. The Lord Chamberlain likely *remained* unaware of Leo's existence.

Mrs Grundy tsked; he must have looked as gormless as he ever did. 'My instructions say you need to be out within the fortnight, but I don't believe they'll begin renovations for some weeks yet. I would have liked to give you much more notice, myself.'

It *was* retaliation, Leo realised. Harry had used his Court connections to good effect. He, or Guy, had seen that if they played their ace card, they lost all hold on Leo, because he'd lose his whole hand in one fell swoop. But if they approached it from the other direction – first his home, then his studio, then his licence, and only *then* his freedom – they could ratchet the winch turn by turn. They could, in fact, make the game worth the candle.

They might, he thought, have at least given him until the second post to get his capitulation sent.

'I would have liked to offer you another warrant, too, but there simply is not an unoccupied apartment available, or at least not one where the official warrant-holder has not made a nod to the forms and left a servant in place as caretaker. And, of course, Marchioness Wellesley will have priority when the next warrant comes up. You shall have to find lodgings across the bridge, or in Hampton. It will be a walk for you, but not one you would not soon become accustomed to.'

She was near to prattling. His silence was unnerving her. He cleared his throat. 'Thank you, Mrs Grundy. I shall look for new lodgings immediately. I won't be any trouble.'

'I know you won't be, Mr Sweetwater.' She sounded reproachful. 'You have always been a most sober and obliging resident.' Confidingly, she went on, '*I* think the same madness that infected the whole Palace yesterday afternoon must have wormed into the Lord Chamberlain's office as well. I don't know who he thinks will take care of the apartment as well as you have, and it'll do no good to have it standing empty when the pipes freeze.'

Leo was distracted by thinking about the Fitzhenrys – he'd badly ballsed up Sally's quiet but steely plans – and so almost missed the salient point in Mrs Grundy's abashed chatter.

'Madness yesterday afternoon?' he repeated.

'I am not one to gossip,' Mrs Grundy said, 'so I will merely say that the sooner some of the more fractious residents finally depart for winter, the better. And I do not know what Mr Jesse is going to say about that poor tree when he comes back from Brighton. Mr Solong is going to have his hands full saving it in the meantime, which is very good of him, considering it is in the public garden and he would be well within his rights, as the Royal Gardener, to say that it is beyond his purview.'

Leo watched her march away with lifted chin and straight spine, through the arcade to Clock Court, presumably on to the State Apartments. Normally, he'd have been apprised of Palace contretemps by Polly, so he did not quite know what to make of her oblique intimations.

He closed his door. He felt the urge to climb back into bed and pull the covers over his head and pretend he hadn't driven away his closest friends and let down the orphans who had entrusted themselves to his care.

He returned instead to the parlour, and finished his letter to Harry. He had been agonising over its wording as a form of procrastination, he saw now. He threw away his first attempt and wrote simply, *My particular friend is at your disposal. Name your time and place.* He toyed with specifying that the surrender was for one occasion only, but knew it would be empty bluster. He had to make sure it was one occasion only in the execution.

He folded the letter, and addressed it to the Hoste apartment off Fountain Court; if Harry had returned to London, or lodged himself elsewhere, the servants would know where to send it on.

Having handed the letter and a ha'penny to one of the young errand-runners loitering by the gate, the echo of his childhood self, Leo milit-antly ignored Sergeant Hamilton's insistent attempts to speak with him – the ghost could at least learn that Leo couldn't answer when gossipy errand boys and maids were in earshot – and went around to the Privy Garden.

It was a gloriously sharp morning, the sky high and pale blue, washed clear. The day before had begun like this, before the rain; he'd been out early taking daguerreotypes. Today he'd cowered in his room too long. It was late enough that many of the residents were taking their constitutionals.

He was doing much better at recognising individuals now he had been practising looking at faces properly, though the bevy of widows and spinsters, and the mother and daughter pairs, remained a challenge.

Except Mrs and Miss Willis, of course.

Leo exchanged greetings where he could not avoid it. For the umpteenth time, he almost accidentally acknowledged the ghost of Mr Tickell, who, on the one hand, was attired in the wig, skirted coat, breeches and white stockings of fifty years before, but on the other hand, was therefore attired as if for Court, which was precisely how the rare gentlemen of the Palace were often attired.

Mr Tickell had tumbled from the window of his third-storey apartment and hit the gravel hard enough to leave a visible dent. He'd haunted the apartment in Leo's childhood, but tended to wander the north end of the Privy Garden these days. Polly suggested this was because Lord Graves, married to a Paget as renowned, for good or ill, as her brothers, had cut his own throat in that apartment twelve years ago. Ghosts tended to avoid each other.

No wonder Mrs Cuthbert, Lord Graves's daughter, did not often make use of her grace-and-favour warrant. Even the Lord Chamberlain granted leeway on that.

Pacing under the yews, he met Eliza Smart, smoking her scandalous cigarette like a Frenchwoman. He hadn't realised he was looking for a friend to talk to until he saw her. He'd have preferred the uncritical sympathy of the Charlottes, but a good dose of Eliza's bracing buck-up would do.

She interrupted his greeting with her own, a loud and jolly, 'What ho, Sweetwater? You look wretched. *Don't tell me* you're still tiffing with Mr Solong?'

This was so queerly mannered that he gazed at her in open puzzlement, until Matilda Paget stepped sheepishly out from behind a trunk, dressed in deep mourning and holding her own cigarette low.

'Miss Paget, Miss Smart,' Leo said, offering a small bow and turning to take his leave. He'd not known Eliza had cultivated this particular connection, and was certainly glad she'd headed him off from bursting into his tale of woe.

Both women urged him to stay, insisting he was not intruding. 'I just didn't want Leo, my Leo, to catch me,' Matilda explained. 'He's become very self-righteous lately.' She made a helpless gesture towards her black crepe with the same long-fingered hand holding the cigarette, embarrassed.

'He thinks he's the man of the house now,' Leo surmised.

'Well, Cats and Freddie would have something to say about that, but they're not here anymore, are they?' Matilda shook her ringlet-adorned head, bonnet bobbing dangerously. 'And he is a great comfort to Mama. It shall relieve my mind when I return to Court for my next term.'

'Miss Paget has been regaling me about the copious amount of shawl-holding required as Maid of Honour,' Eliza said.

'I mustn't, I'm being very disagreeable.' She delicately puffed on the cigarette, then, on a sharp exhale of smoke, said, 'At least actual lady's maids earn tips for shawling! Oh, I mustn't be ungrateful, it's better than the alternative.' Her eyes widened. 'I don't intend to offend, Mr Sweetwater' – Leo was nonplussed – 'it's simply that one finds it difficult to imagine being married when some men are so very hard to get along with.'

'I know I often find men hard to get along with,' Eliza agreed. 'I'm sure Leo here finds plenty of men hard to get along with.'

Matilda raised her eyebrows, thankfully because she'd noticed Eliza's intimate use of his name rather than her insinuating smirk. It was Eliza's rough brand of kindness: it pulled rumours the wrong way.

'I am being particularly disagreeable this morning,' Matilda repeated. 'Yesterday's nonsense left a bad taste in my mouth.'

Leo seized his chance. 'What happened yesterday?'

'Lady Henry set fire to an elm in the Great Fountain Garden.' Eliza blew a smoke ring before stubbing her cigarette.

'She didn't intend to,' Matilda hastened to assure Leo as she absently ceded her own cigarette to extinction. 'Well, it was her eldest, Augustus, another foolish Auggie! Yesterday morning was so lovely, they decided on an impromptu picnic, and the rain came on suddenly enough that they were drier huddling under the trees than making a dash for it.'

'I cannot see Lady Henry dashing, in her situation,' Eliza said.

'A sad sort of shelter at this time of year, of course. Augustus had the bright idea of lighting a fire to keep his mother warm, the dear, silly duffer. Next thing they knew, the lower branches had caught. The whole thing started to smoulder, and they had to call out Mr Abnett and the rest of the fire brigade.'

'And then Lady George decided she should lecture Lady Henry,' Eliza said, 'and Lady Augusta came to Lady Henry's defence.'

Pulling her gloves back on, Matilda bemoaned, 'Aunt Augusta was most put out, and she is normally so serene.'

'And then all of a sudden it was not about the fire anymore, and it wasn't between only those ladies anymore, and everyone had something to say about everyone else.'

Matilda shivered. 'It was like the entire Palace was furious at itself. I've never experienced anything like it, and I was at Court during the dreadful Lady Flora debacle.'

Eliza directed Leo's attention outwards, over the rest of the Privy Garden. 'You can see it, when you know it. No one's talking to anyone.'

He did see now what he hadn't taken in before. Lady Albinia and Lady Sale perambulated in companionable serenity along the facade from the direction of the Pond Garden, but the other promenading residents were distinctly avoiding each other.

As usual, the Paget and Maclean and Stapleton daughters engaged in pointed mutual disregard with the Seymour and Montgomery daughters, but the enmity appeared to have spread beyond the two loose camps of Paget verses Seymour.

The Countess of Cavan swept past Lady Emily Ponsonby without a word, the cut direct delivered against a background of soft holly and in scathing disregard for the congratulations near-mandated due to her eldest, Henry, achieving both his majority and a commission just this week.

Miss Copley, the youngest and most hopeful of the spinsters, outright glared at Matilda and Eliza, touching her nose as if the scent of tobacco lingered strongly enough to offend her.

Mrs and Miss Moore, a pair of cheery gossips who lived in the clock tower, did not appear to be in harmony with each other or anyone else, discontent faces turned aside, their usual natter absent.

Lady Reynett marched along with her sister-in-law, Mrs Vesey. Miss Reynett, the other sister-in-law, trailed in their wake, face wan, eyes reddened.

And Cole walked by with his planning sketchbook, shoulders stiff, gaze averted.

'Oh, dear, did you have a falling-out with Mr Solong?' Matilda said.

Max walked at Cole's heel. He looked Leo's way, tail giving three slow wags, before he trotted after Cole around the central fountain.

Slyly, Eliza murmured, 'Was he granted custody of the dog?'

'He's his dog!' Leo hissed back.

The foreman and two under-gardeners followed, along with a larger cluster armed with scythes and shears and struggling to push a Ransome's mechanical lawnmower over the lumpy grass. Cole's smaller party diverted to the bottom of the Privy Garden where the cart waited, Yates on its seat, its trayful of dark loamy material steaming in the cool air.

Cole's duties usually followed the seasons, planning sequential floral displays of annuals and managing the budgets and men for the never-ending cycles of planting and pruning, trimming and tidying, weeding and pest control.

The recent installation of railings between the new Barge Walk and the south side of the Palace grounds had given him new garden beds to play with, as well as a newly triangular and orphaned expanse of water-logged lawn. The residents' desire for privacy was a prime consideration, while their competing but less vital preferences were a challenge. Today, his men were digging up and digging in, preparing the beds for later planting, while he and his foreman measured and recorded the growing conditions, discussing and discarding ideas in between poking the soil and making notes and sketches.

It was a project he'd been looking forward to immensely. Though Leo could only see his back, he did not seem to be savouring it. Leo wished he could assure himself that was because he was already being converged upon by residents with opinions, Lady George chief among them.

'I… have not conducted myself well, recently,' he said slowly. 'I need to apologise.'

'Well, I shouldn't think of doing it now,' Eliza said. 'The poor man's under siege. Who knew we had so many expert gardeners among the residents?'

Lady Henry came past at a meander, condition barely evident under layers and stays but very apparent in her slow pace and flushed face. She dimpled at their small group, pausing to exchange greetings.

'I was intending to apologise to Mr Solong for the tree,' she told them, usual bright cheer moderately checked, 'but he does look rather…'

'Besieged,' Eliza supplied.

'That is the word for it.'

The three women and Leo watched in silence as Cole turned to a fresh page and began to patiently write down the suggestions of the residents surrounding him. This had the immediate effect of forcing them to form a polite queue.

'I might as well join the ranks,' Lady Henry said, smiling at the ridiculous sight. She turned to Leo. 'I don't suppose you would escort me, Mr Sweetwater?'

Leo hesitated. He didn't want to approach Cole in public, but then, Cole might not receive him in private. He could not refuse the lady, anyway. He offered his arm. Taking farewell of Eliza and Matilda, they conducted a stately progression down the central boulevard between the yews and hollies towards the fountain.

He was feeling quietly grateful that Eliza hadn't openly announced that he needed to join the queue for apologies with Lady Henry, when that very lady, one hand hooked around Leo's elbow, patted his arm with the other and said, with enormous earnestness, 'I trust you will make reparations with Mr Solong. I do so hate to see you two at odds.'

Since Leo found not a single word readily available to answer this, he said nothing.

'Not to say you do not have yourself to blame,' she went on blithely. If she was trying to be stern, it was quite lost in her dimples. 'Tarrying with Mr Walpole under Mr Solong's nose like that! I only wonder that he tolerated it for as long as he did.'

Leo stopped dead, almost committing the terrible *faux pas* of wrenching an *enceinte* lady by the shoulder. A wave of cold went over him.

Stiffly, he said, 'I don't know what you mean.'

'What do you think she means?' Polly said from behind him. Leo started violently. 'She was reading *Fanny Hill*, you poltroon, there's a sodomy scene in it. There's a very short step from finding out it exists to wondering who does it.'

Pinned under Lady Henry's frank gaze, pretty blue eyes wide and innocent, Leo said, 'I said awful, awful things with no truth to them. I *do* wish to apologise. I have not yet had the opportunity.'

He couldn't resist adding, when Polly floated into view wearing a half-mollified expression, 'There's no call to be unkind before I do.'

'I was not being unkind, Mr Sweetwater!' Lady Henry said, drawing her shawl tighter about her shoulders. 'I merely wish to express that I have no objection to being your whist partner again.'

Leo became so blank at this that Polly, still annoyed with him or not, was moved to assist. 'Good Lord, Leo, she's not proposing to reenact more scenes from that atrocious book with you, she's trying to tell you she is not as offended by your activities as you assume.' Darkly, she added, 'She likely wants a pat on her head, though who knows if that's for feeling clever or magnanimous.'

He was saved from having to answer either of his challengers by Lady Jane, as ever obliviously barging in, though this time his gratitude was tempered by the awkward presence of her two companions, Mrs and Miss Willis, who he had so disappointed all those years before, and offended ever since by never admitting it.

After greetings all round, Lady Henry graciously ceded to Lady Jane, who demanded, 'Mr Sweetwater, what happened yesterday afternoon?'

'I had an argument?' Leo said, beginning to wonder if *absolutely everyone* in the Palace had noticed Cole wasn't talking to him.

'Everybody had arguments! Did you do something to cause it?'

Leo was so alarmed by this notion that he looked directly at Polly, who scoffed and rolled her eyes. 'It was nothing to do with you, addle-pate. Or, not exactly.' She lowered her voice, for her own benefit. 'Cole punched Walpole, and Walpole was bleeding as he crossed Fountain Court. And you know everyone in the old families are related to everyone else, he dripped blood onto his restless ancestors!'

'Did that make them—' Leo bit his tongue, hard.

'It was the equivalent of rolling over in their sleep.' She glanced north-wards, muttering, disconcertingly, 'I think they went back to sleep.'

All four women had turned to look at the patch of empty air that the man rumoured to see ghosts was staring at with open horror.

Leo blurted, 'Mrs Willis, Miss Willis, I want to say how sorry I am about Mr Willis.'

Diversion and practice, in one happy bundle.

Mrs Willis, a frail, slender woman, immediately began to weep. Her daughter, similar in height, hair and eyes, but more stolid and eminently more practical, gave Leo a frustrated glare as she dutifully fussed over the older woman, pressing a lace-edged handkerchief into her hand.

Practice, Leo told himself, *practice. No more hiding from things that are better off faced.* 'I did see him,' he said. 'But I was a child, and I was frightened, and I didn't know how to tell you.'

'Oh, pet,' Polly said, but resignedly.

Both Willis women had frozen, mother with balled-up handkerchief pressed to watery brown eyes, daughter reaching to wrap her tighter into her voluminous shawl. Lady Jane had joined her hands together and looked positively thrilled. Lady Henry was merely fascinated.

'He was only worried about missing his steamship, you see,' Leo went on. 'He didn't have a final message for you. If he'd had time to think of a final message, he wouldn't have become a ghost.'

Mrs Willis began to sob in earnest, Miss Willis patting her back and staring at Leo accusingly.

'This is why I didn't tell you before,' Leo said helplessly.

Attracted by the emotional turmoil, Mr Tickell drifted by under a line of hollies. Beyond him, Leo was perturbed to see Sergeant Hamilton marching down from the south facade, round face reddened. He must have worked out how to move further from his anchor point – or was angry enough to break free.

Leo watched with dawning dismay as he determinedly advanced all the way down the garden, to finally stop only the barest inch away. 'Stop ignoring me,' he snapped.

Leo couldn't help taking a step back, though he tried not to look directly at the sergeant. He wasn't sure if Mr Tickell would notice—

'I say, can the lad see you?' Mr Tickell said.

Sergeant Hamilton ignored him. Ghosts tended to ignore each other. Polly flitted with agitation, commanding Hamilton to go away in strident tones. He ignored her, too.

He roared, 'Stop ignoring me!' and shoved Leo.

His hands sank deep into Leo, but not before the little telltale hitch as his ghostly matter met Leo's subtle matter.

'My God!' he said, staring at where his hands vanished inside Leo.

Leo, shuddering, recoiled, freeing himself. He pressed his hands to his upper chest. Hamilton was staring, eyes wide as saucers.

'What is it, Mr Sweetwater?' one of the women called. He thought it was Lady Henry.

Mr Tickell, closer, said, 'Can you *touch* him?'

The ghost seized him by the wrist, or attempted it, holding firm long enough to jerk Leo's arm before his fingers sank in and Leo pulled free.

'Is he having some kind of fit?' Miss Willis said, not kindly.

Mr Tickell stared at his hand, the hand that had just passed through Leo's wrist. 'I can *taste* him.'

'*Run*,' Polly said, but it was too late.

When Tickell moved, Hamilton copied. As one, the pair converged on Leo. This time, when their hands touched him, the brief moment of solid contact lasted longer, because both had already taken some of his subtle matter into themselves. By accident, the first time. Not anymore.

Worse, it wasn't just Tickell and Hamilton. Lord Graves had already been drawn, and behind him wafted Bradshaw, the mid-Georgian pander giving the Haunted Gallery its eerie reputation, and Mr Willis, floating right through his own wife and daughter.

Each set hands on Leo's shoulders or back as he tried to retreat and found himself surrounded. The touches were analgesic: painless, but leaving a cold trace pulsing in his veins. For all they were from five different ages, one in uniform, the rest in the gentlemanly fashions of their times, they wore identical expressions: a curious, innocent wonder.

He said quietly, 'Gentlemen, you need to stop.'

No longer caring what the witnesses would think of him, he began to resolutely pull off the spectral hands one by one. He was a little chilled, but, absent the miasma of high emotion that accompanied the Tudor remnant, stubbornly making himself stay calm. Each time he removed a hand, it came down again, firmer.

The ghosts on London Bridge had been so numerous, their attempts to steal his subtle matter had interfered with each other. The ghosts who had touched him found they could touch each other, violently, while later arrivals swooped through and around them and each other, frantic for a taste.

When he'd been driven to the ground, he'd been able to crawl out from under what had devolved into a frenzied spectral brawl, all consciousness or intention lost into chaos, and get off the bridge hidden among the crowds, into the meaty hands of a constable.

He hadn't imagined fewer ghosts would be riskier, but he could already see that he was in great danger. Then, it had helped that the ghosts had become a mindless mass. Here, that would be a deadly outcome, because there were too few of them to distract each other.

'Mr Willis,' he said, over the sound of Polly's increasingly strident imprecations, 'you know me. It's Percy. I used to run errands for you.'

'He's here?' Mrs Willis cried. 'My dear Mr Willis. Darling, can you hear me? Are you warm enough? Are you in turmoil, darling? How can we bring you peace?'

The five ghosts had enclosed him, solid enough now to impede escape. There might have been other shades amassing beyond, the drowned ghosts from the riverbank, the secret ghosts of bedrooms he'd never been into. It may have been spikes of alarm blurring his vision, or the fact that he was staring through a wall of translucent men, pressing every closer, their expressions of wonder hardening into need.

'Ladies,' he said, still plucking ghostly hands off himself – like leeches, just like salting leeches that had been secretly sucking blood – 'it's best you move away.'

The women were chattering to and over each other, a great flurry of confusion. Then Lady Jane cried out. 'Goodness, I see them!'

That was because they were siphoning Leo's subtle matter, gaining substance as they did so. They were beginning to cling to Leo now, clamping on tight to prevent him peeling their hands off, no longer sinking through him at all. The cold was spreading through him fast, far faster than in the chaos of London Bridge.

Leo turned in confused circles as he tried to push out of the shrinking trap, stumbled, lost his hat, began to fall, tried desperately to stay on his feet, and ended on his knees.

Polly said, 'I have to, Leo,' and grabbed for him too, wrapping her hands over his head as if trying to push him underwater.

He gasped, bewildered and betrayed. The air sent icy spikes into his lungs.

Then she spun and slapped Tickell across the face. 'Stop!'

Tickell rocked back, stunned, and then seized her by the arm and threw her aside.

'Stop,' Leo repeated, 'stop, stop.'

He knew they wouldn't. They weren't the echoes of mostly decent people anymore. They were ravenous spectres. He could barely think through the cold.

'Lady Jane,' he heard Polly saying. She was trying to pull Mr Willis, the oldest and smallest of the men, away, but he was resisting strenuously. 'Lady Jane, can you hear me? Jane! Help him!'

'He's being swarmed by spirits,' Lady Jane announced. 'Lady Henry, I should move away if I were you, in your condition.'

'No, help *him*, you skinny crone,' Polly shouted, now clawing uselessly at Bradshaw, who shoved her contemptuously. Leo used his moment of distraction to pull free from him, but the other four were holding firm.

'I can't go, I'm looking after Mama,' Miss Willis informed someone.

'I shall go, I'll fetch Mr Solong,' Lady Henry said breathlessly. 'Hullo there, Lady Albinia, Lady Sale. Poor Mr Sweetwater is quite overcome. I am fetching help.'

'Who is with you amid this great phantasmagoria, Mr Sweetwater?' Lady Jane was, quite courageously, standing in front of Leo now, as he rapidly sank under the predation of the ghosts, already unable to climb back to his feet from his deepening slump. 'Mr Willis, you said? Mrs Willis, tell your husband to behave like a gentleman!'

'Husband?' Mrs Willis said waveringly. 'Willis, darling?'

'Don't hurt him, Papa,' Miss Willis said suddenly, speaking like the young girl she'd been when Mr Willis had died. Even more girlishly, she lilted, 'Daddy? Don't hurt Percy, he fetches me ribbons.'

Mr Willis abruptly released Leo, shaking his head. 'Flora? Emily?' His eye fell on Leo. 'Percy, my boy! I beg your pardon.' He looked about confusedly. 'Gentlemen, Lord Graves, this is no way to behave.'

The other ghosts naturally ignored him, crowding in harder now they had one less competitor. A solid body moved through them: Eliza, coming to crouch beside Leo.

She chaffed his arms through his coat, saying, 'You look freezing.' She dragged a shawl about him, and within moments was layering more over it, as some of the other women rushed to offer the only assistance they could. 'Did you send for help?'

'Lady Henry has gone for Mr Solong,' someone told her.

'A woman in her condition, waddling the entire length of the garden! Send someone who can run!' Eliza's tone of voice appended a *you fools* but she managed not to say it. 'For a doctor! Oh, goodness bloody sake, I'll go.'

This pronouncement was followed by gasps, either due to the language or the fact that Eliza had set off at an inappropriately manly speed.

'Who else, Mr Sweetwater?' urged Lady Jane. 'Come now, Percy, who?'

Polly shouted, 'Hamilton, Hamilton, Hamilton!' in her ear. She shook her head, touching her ear.

'Sergeant Hamilton,' Leo whispered.

A new voice instantly cut through the bedlam, one unfathomably loud. 'Sergeant Hamilton,' it bellowed. 'You are a soldier of the British Empire, you will defend civilians as your honour and your duty dictates!'

It was Lady Sale, stalwart army wife of Fighting Bob, barking like an officer on a parade ground. Hamilton leapt back and snapped off a salute, almost vibrating as he stood to rigid attention.

Shame reddening his face, he coughed, 'Stand down, lads.'

The others ignored him, of course. The sergeant caught Tickell and began to try to haul him away, muttering, 'I do my duty.'

'Thank you, Sergeant,' Leo got out in short gasps as Tickell clung on stubbornly, wrenching him about.

'Who else?' Lady Jane demanded.

'Lord Graves,' Polly shouted. 'Tell them, pet.'

'Graves, it's Graves.'

'No, Percy, don't give up, we shall— Oh, *Lord* Graves! Who— Miss Paget, perfect!'

'Uncle Thomas!' Matilda called loudly. 'My father and his brothers allowed you the privilege of marrying their precious baby sister because they thought you were a man of honour.'

She abruptly grabbed Leo's arm, pulled him aside, and staring in entirely the wrong direction, snapped with immense hauteur, 'Act like it!'

Lord Graves said hoarsely, 'Mary,' and wafted backwards. He and Mr Willis waved their arms at other, fainter, shades trying to press in now that space was opening up around the involuntary supplier of delicious subtle matter.

'Did that work?' Matilda whispered and Leo nodded jerkily. 'He did love Aunt Minnie, though she was terribly eccentric. Who else is here?'

'Who else?' the crowd of women surrounding Leo called, enthusiastically joining the game. 'Who's here, Mr Sweetwater?'

'Tickell,' Leo managed. 'Bradshaw.'

That set the women murmuring urgently amongst themselves, the gossipy Mrs Ellice and Mrs and Miss Moore chief among them. Both ghosts were too old to have family here, nor did anyone know them well enough to discern a prybar for getting them off Leo.

'I always thought Tickell was Sheridan's friend,' Mrs Ellice suggested. 'Shall someone run and fetch Mrs Sheridan?'

Someone protested she wouldn't know a dead friend of her dead husband's, and then someone else made it moot by pointing out she'd gone to one of her daughters for winter. No one knew Bradshaw at all. The crowd was stymied.

It seemed no use. Tickell dug in like a tick as he struggled against both Hamilton and Polly. If anything, with only two ghosts touching Leo now, the drain was exponentially worse, the cold sinking teeth into his very core.

His mind was turning dreamy. He began to instinctively curl into a ball, resistance all but exhausted.

The workman suddenly landed atop him, their matters fully mingling. Leo yelped and convulsed.

Then, knees and elbows spiking like daggers of ice, the workman scrambled all the way over him and tackled Tickell in a full body assault.

He howled, 'You're making the crack wider, you great idjits!'

'Mr Thomas Bradshaw, was it, who shot himself?' Lady Albinia suddenly said. 'That old pander, my mother told me about him, there's no appealing to *his* better nature.'

Bradshaw hauled Leo all the way to his feet, making him shout again and the crowd cry out in fear and amazement. He wrapped his hands, all but solid now, around Leo's throat. Lady Jane screamed.

'By Jove, all mine,' Bradshaw whispered as Leo began to choke.

Max barrelled in.

Barking and snarling, he launched at the ghost and his teeth seemed to find purchase for a vital moment before snapping shut on empty air. Max shook his big head violently, lips curled back like he'd tasted something acrid, but lunged again, his most menacing bark sounding deep from his chest.

Bradshaw retreated, cursing, joining a general exodus of the fainter ghosts, repelled by the dog.

Leo almost dropped to his knees again. A white figure rushed at him. He flailed in a panic he could not control. 'Don't touch me, get away from me!'

'Pet, it's me—'

'Get away from me!'

Polly, shocked, backed away, then turned away, then went away. Leo sagged with a relief he vaguely recognised he would know was unfair later.

He scrubbed cold hands over his face and through his hair. His shivers were growing more emphatic. He was perishingly cold, yes, but reaction was setting in. This was about when he'd been arrested for disorderly conduct, in London.

Most every grace-and-favour resident had joined the crowd, the commotion drawing them as much as it had drawn the ghosts. All were staring at him, a sea of pale, concerned faces that he was abruptly having trouble telling apart again.

Lady Albinia, leaning heavily on her cane, gazed at him, expression stern. *I will not have you bringing the Palace into disrepute.*

'Upon my soul, he's potty,' he could hear among the babbling brook of voices, and, 'Barmy creature!' and 'Well, it's the artistic temperament, isn't it?'

He recognised Colonel Cottin's voice readily enough, from somewhere near the back. 'The rummy fellow's lost his senses at last.'

'He is seeing into the spirit world!' Lady Jane insisted.

'Codswallop! He's throwing fits because the Lord Chamberlain evicted him.'

Ah. That story was already spreading, too. He'd thought better of Mrs Grundy. He slowly shrugged off the shawls and held them out. Someone – Matilda – took them. She had the practice, he supposed.

Wiping at his face again, he said, 'Sorry.' And then, 'I had a funny turn.'

More commentary arose, Colonel Cottin's gruff opinions providing the bass note. Max, circling back from seeing off the spirits, pushed through the legs and came to Leo, who sunk his icy fingers into the thick fur.

Again, he only barely held his feet. He wanted to sink down and wrap his arms around the warm, solid dog.

Instead, he began to walk away, shaky. He would hide behind his closed door, by the fire, he thought, and ask Sally not to answer the door for a week. That would give him a whole second week to find new lodgings for them all.

Max dogged his heels in a most appropriate way. The dog was tall enough, or Leo short enough, that he could keep his cold-stiffened fingers buried into the thick ruff at his neck. He allowed himself that comfort.

A woman appeared at his other side and he flinched, but it wasn't Polly, and it wasn't anyone he might have expected, if he'd been in a shape to expect anyone. When she began to speak, he realised it was Lady Sale.

'Mr Sweetwater, listen to me,' she said, very low. 'My group was held captive for nine months and the diary I am about to publish will show us all coming through it with calm and aplomb, because that is what the English public expects from its heroes.'

Leo nodded, expecting chastisement for failing to show the same stiff upper lip. Well, he was hardly a hero. He scritched trembling fingers through Max's fur.

'And I will tell you now, between us, that not a single one of us survived that experience without having a "funny turn" at one time or the other. The only way through it was to help each other. You see?'

He nodded. 'Yes, thank you, my lady,' he said, voice thready.

'Your friend is here to help you.'

Leo steeled himself. He did not know how he would cope with this last hurdle, Eliza's brusque care, her questions and demands. He needed to be alone.

But Lady Sale stepped aside to reveal Cole, flushed and panting, bent over with hands on knees, looking up under his brows with wild concern. His under-gardeners were only just arriving in his wake.

The entire dreadful ordeal had taken very little longer than a hasty waddle down the garden and an all-out sprint back up the garden.

'I'm fine,' Leo said by rote.

Cole pressed his hand over his heart. 'Ay? A'm fair puckled, masel.'

Scots, not French. Leo nodded. 'Thank you, Mr Solong. I'm sorry for the trouble. Thank you, Lady Sale. Good day.'

He started to walk around his two obstacles, hands shaking, stomach cramping, head pounding.

'No.' Lady Sale spoke with the same quiet intensity. 'You will go with Mr Solong now.'

It wasn't a suggestion. Leo surrendered.

TWENTY

To Leo's immense embarrassment, his shivering became so bad he wasn't capable of walking, even with Max on one side and Cole on the other. He had to be loaded into the back of Yates's emptied cart, the bed hastily brushed off and covered to make a clean seat. The loamy remnants in the cart bed made a sweet and earthy perfume.

Cole put his arm around him to hold him steady, their legs dangling side by side off the back. Leo closed his eyes so he didn't have to bear the undiminished stares of the other residents.

Cole sent one of his men jogging on ahead, so when they arrived at Wilderness House, the fire in the drawing room was already roaring, tea and blankets were to hand, and Mrs Clarke was overseeing the making up of a hot bath and a guest bedroom. A very short and pleasant woman with a lovely smile in a round face, an imperturbable disposition, and unshakeable loyalty to her employer, Mrs Clarke descended to greet them, firmly sending Max outside when he persisted in following Leo.

'Give him a bone, he's done well,' Cole said by way of reparations to the put-upon guardian dog.

While sitting a shaking Leo by the fire and pressing doctored tea into his hands, Cole had a further discussion with his housekeeper. Shortly, the pair determined that one of the Wilderness House maids would attend Leo's apartment to intercept Sally. The moment she crossed into the Palace grounds, she'd be accosted by the story of her employer's attack, but at least she would receive reassurance as quickly as possible.

As soon as Mrs Clarke departed to see to this and a new menu plan, Cole closed the drawing room door. Leo's hands were trembling enough that his tea was in danger of sloshing over the sides of the cup. He set it down, and took off his gloves. He needed its warmth directly against his skin.

Cole caught his sleeve before he could reclaim the cup. 'I've told Mrs Clarke to send the doctor away, when he arrives, is that fair? And any other visitors.'

'Yes,' Leo said through frozen lips. Eliza would be annoyed. 'Thank you.'

'The staff is under strict instructions not to disturb us,' Cole went on, 'so if you want heat on your skin, you're welcome to undress by the fire here. Or I can take you up to the bath, but the girls are still drawing it.'

The idea of sinking into piping hot water was tempting, of waiting to do so intolerable. The fire was here, and burning hot. His fingers danced across his buttons, too shaky to manage the coordination of the task. Cole leaned in to help.

'Sorry,' Leo said, teeth chattering, 'sorry, sorry.'

'Don't, I'm happy I have a way to help you.'

Cole stripped him all the way to his undershirt, and then took that off, too, leaving him bare-chested. Leo was not cognisant enough to be self-conscious, and Cole had a blanket over him in moments anyway. He pulled Leo's chair closer to the fire.

The heat radiated over and through him, flushing his skin. Cole had worked his shoes off, too, and rubbed his feet, thumbs rasping across the wool. 'Bare here, too?'

Leo nodded, and Cole wriggled his socks off, adding them to his pile of garments. 'Good?'

Again, Leo nodded. He drained his cup, near-scalding his throat without care. His chest and stomach and toes were rosy with heat now, but his back felt icy. The blankets weren't enough. With some effort, he tried to shift about, before sliding to the floor.

He turned his back to the flames, letting the blanket slip so he could bathe in the heat. His chest was shortly cold again. He was going to have to turn himself about and about as if on a rotisserie spit.

Cole pushed the chair out of the way, and threw more blankets to the ground. He guided Leo to lie down, Leo unresistant even when Cole made him face the fire. His back hadn't been warm enough yet.

And then it was, because Cole lay down behind him, bare chest pressing warmth into his bare back, bare arms looping over his side and under his head, bare feet tucking around his own bare feet.

Pulling another blanket over them both, he murmured, '*Tu es en sécurité, repose-toi.*'

Leo patted Cole's hand, tried to speak, and closed his eyes without volition.

He didn't exactly fall asleep. It was more that his mind, exceedingly taxed, needed to absent itself. Last time he'd been in a Compter cell. This was at least more comfortable.

When his eyes blinked open again, he was still lying on the floor before the fire, Cole curled bodily around him. It hadn't been long – the flames were still high. He felt steadier, the headache already eased.

Nestled in the warm security of Cole's arms, he experienced a moment of sheer bliss, quickly overwhelmed by regret. He might have had this, lengthy and untainted, if he hadn't sabotaged himself yesterday. What would it have mattered if it had been only once? At least he'd have had it.

Though then they might have been in the midst of relations when the Fountain Court presence stirred and turned the Palace against itself, and who knew what would have happened. He made a small sound, somewhere between a sigh and a whimper.

'Your bath will be ready by now,' Cole murmured, so close to Leo's neck that the words shivered into his skin. 'Still cold?'

'No.' Leo patted Cole's hand again, this time his signal that he was feeling terrifically awkward and wanted to be released.

Cole twisted to close his other hand over Leo's, making a *non* sort of noise into his hair. Tightly clasping Leo's hand in both of his, he asked, 'Was that what happened in London?'

'A little worse,' Leo said, pushing past his reluctance to speak of it. It was easier, facing away.

'And London must have been awfie bad.'

'I was crossing the bridge,' he whispered. 'I didn't see... It was crowded, and I got jostled, and I bumped into one. It knew I was there, it grabbed me. And then the rest came, up over the side of the bridge.' He closed his eyes, remembering the great wave over the parapets. 'The murdered, the drowned.'

'How did you escape then?'

Leo gave a laugh like a ghost in his chest, hollow. 'They swarmed. I dropped to my hands and knees and crawled out from under them.'

'You did well to keep your head.'

'I crawled away,' Leo repeated.

'You kept your head and escaped,' Cole repeated, with a press of his fingers. 'And today was the same?'

'Less of them, but more intense.' A shiver ran though him, and Cole's hold tightened.

'You've lived with the Palace ghosts your whole life. Was it because of whatever's in Fountain Court that they attacked?'

Leo hesitated. 'Have you been listening to Lady Jane?'

'No, *mon ami*, I've been watching you, and you are rather concerned about something in Fountain Court.'

'It's making them erratic.' He thought of Hamilton, the steadfast soldier. 'Angrier. One of them tried to get my attention today, and touched me. That's why I don't want them knowing about me, because it's best they don't touch me. Not even Polly knew a ghost could take a twice-dead human's subtle matter, until the first time she tried to hug…'

He trailed off, astonished to find himself talking so openly.

Cole said, 'Polly? Your friendly ghost?'

'My friendly ghost. My friend, all my life.' He covered his eyes. 'I told her to go away. I told her not to touch me. She was barely speaking to me as it was.'

'I'm sure she'll understand. Let's get you warmed up properly, then we can go find her.' Cole's breath caught. 'With Max. You had to leave London, will you have to leave here?'

'I didn't *have* to leave London,' Leo said. 'I fled London, because I was terrified out of my mind and needed to be somewhere where I knew exactly where all the ghosts are. This is still the only place where I know exactly where all the ghosts are.'

'But will the ghosts be after hunting you now?'

'I don't think so. Most of them retain enough of themselves to not be monstrous. But – yes, I'd rather walk with Max, until I've talked with Polly.'

Braver now, he rolled to face Cole, feeling the brush of naked skin against naked skin as a remote torture. Cole comfortably propped his head on one hand and left the other draped over Leo's waist.

'I hope you don't mind,' he said, with a glance nipplewards. 'You seemed to need direct heat.'

'You must know I don't mind.'

'We've had this discussion before,' Cole reminded him. 'And here I am again, taking advantage of you having a good solid scare. Not to say I didn't get one this time, too. I don't think I've run so fast since racing Walt on Mauritius as a child.'

'You could say,' Leo pointed out, 'that I'm taking advantage of your propensity to comfort me with your, ah, extremely well-formed body.'

'Oh, do you find it so?' Cole glanced down again. 'I like a little more give myself.' He squeezed Leo's hip.

Leo started to scowl, caught the glint in Cole's eye, and ducked his face into Cole's chest. 'I'm sorry I was awful yesterday.'

'I gather *everyone* was awful yesterday.'

'*That* was Fountain Court,' Leo admitted, and felt Cole's chest swell as he took a deep breath. 'It's no excuse. I was angry because you were swooping in to solve my problem with a wave of your over-privileged hand, but that's not an excuse either.'

'I can see how it would be annoying, though,' Cole said amiably.

'I can see how it'd be annoying to *like* to solve people's problems with the means at your disposal, and have a friend who prefers to ignore them until they're too big to be solved.'

Cole traced a finger from Leo's trouser pleats, over the slight dip of his waist and up his ribs, by which Leo was made to understand he was too easily forgiven. He sat up.

'I said horrid things to you, Cole, because I don't trust families. It wasn't my grandfather, he's just a bigoted old man not worth troubling over. My *mother* – my mother loved me, but she disapproved of me, of everything about me, so strongly that it drowned the love out. I couldn't see how your family could be any other way. I assumed you were making the best of where they had decided to hide you and if you stopped hiding, they'd turn on you. It never occurred to me you were exactly where you wanted to be, that you'd had to stand up to Sir Robert to get here, that he could possibly still love you for being yourself when that self hadn't done what he wanted. It's not that I *ever* thought less of you for being a gardener, it's that I decided to righteously resent your family for not allowing you to be anything else. I am sorry: I was wrong, and unfair, and horrid.'

Cole half-sat too, leaning back on his arms so that his chest and shoulders and lean biceps gleamed in the firelight. 'Thank you, Leo,' he said. 'I appreciate hearing that. I would like you to meet Sir Walter and Lady Erica so you can determine for yourself that they're not the small-minded people you think they are. Will you?'

Since it felt like penance, Leo agreed without a murmur of complaint.

'Here,' Cole added with a knowing glance, 'not London. Introduced as no more than my good friend.'

Leo took a breath. Something he told himself was relief washed through him. Humbly, he said, 'Thank you. Your friendship means the world to me, Cole.'

'That's not all you want, though.'

'It is,' Leo insisted. 'I'm very grateful for the chance to put this whole sorry episode behind us and simply be good friends again.'

'I think you misunderstand me. For my turn, I'm sorry I overreacted.'

'Ah, I don't think you *did*.'

'Little touchy on the subject of Walpole,' Cole said. 'I owe you a bigger apology than that, speaking of charging on in to solve your problems. I decided you needed a safe friend to take to bed, you see.' He smiled, because Leo had half-winced and half-scoffed. 'For two weeks, I was mulling it over and you can guess my brilliant solution, can't you?'

'You.' Leo's smile was pained around the edges, but its centre was true. 'Kindly meant, I understand.'

'Not done, *mon chéri*, not done. Because instead of properly considering *why* I decided on myself as the ideal candidate, I approached you with a disingenuous proposal.' In a self-mocking voice, brogue stronger, he said, '*Leo needs a friend. I'm feeling quite curious. It's a passing mood*, pah. And that was wrong and unfair and horrid of *me*.'

'No! I regret not—'

'How long have you been in love with me, Leo?'

Leo stopped. He directed another pained – agonised, now – smile downwards, pulling a blanket over his lap to pick at the wool.

'Oh,' he said, eventually, 'years.'

Cole nodded. 'I hate that I made light of it like I did.'

'No,' Leo said again. 'You weren't to know.'

For some reason, this simple statement, which Leo thought he had delivered with some dignity, made Cole laugh. He rose, and held out his hand. 'Come look at a print Walt sent me, would you?'

Leo took the change of subject gratefully. The print was stiff-backed; Cole had propped it on the mantle. It depicted a stone house, with a regimented cottage garden in flower. Behind, though, the flora was wilder, and hills rose organically, in contrast to the straight, even lines of house and garden. The colours were muted, though not dull, and the greens had a distinctive silvery-grey tinge. Sunshine bathed the scene, making it glow.

'It's by John Glover. Walt sent it over because he thought I'd enjoy the juxtaposition of the very English garden against the very Australian background, which I did. But it's the light that truly struck me.'

'It's Claudian,' Leo said. 'It's similar to the effect I was trying with my watercolour of the Pond Garden, but in oils—' He shook his head, because he recognised the small, fond smile Cole was giving him now. '—and not the point of what you're showing me.'

'I love this light, I love this whole scene, how open it is,' Cole said. 'It makes me feel content in the moment, but also as if endless possibility lies before me. When I said you're not Baroque, I wasn't trying to be dismissive – this painting is what I was thinking of.'

Leo glanced at him in surprise, but he was staring at the print intently. Musingly, he said, 'I love my nephews.'

'I know,' Leo said. 'I would never—'

'But I've never wanted children of my own, not enough to take a wife, anyway,' Cole went on. He turned to Leo. 'And now I know why.'

'Why?' said Leo blankly.

Cole gazed at him as steadfastly as he'd gazed at the landscape. 'I've never experienced the sort of connection that made me want to marry,' he said. 'In fact, I'd given up. You assumed I have a lover somewhere, but I'd resigned myself to being alone because I never found any woman who occupied my thoughts like I thought a lover deserved.' He smiled. 'And now I know why.'

He brushed the backs of his fingers across Leo's cheek and down to his jawline. 'Fridays are my favourite day of the week. I spend the whole morning finding just the right fruit to bring to Chapel Court. Then I bruise it on purpose so you'll feel comfortable eating it. Because I very much like to watch you eat it.' That smile again, glowing. 'And now I know why.'

He touched Leo's lips, slightly parted with astonishment, with his thumb, confiding, 'Sometimes I felt like you wanted to lick it off my fingers, and, believe me, that was a confusing but not unwelcome notion.'

Leo opened his mouth a little wider and took in just the tip of Cole's thumb. Cole's eyes half-shut in languid pleasure as he dragged his thumb across and between Leo's lips. Leo closed his teeth on it.

'I felt such a pit open in my stomach, when I saw you in Walpole's arms.'

Flushing, Leo released him. Cole caught at him, laughing softly. 'And now I *really* know why.'

He took Leo's face in both hands and spoke with the aching tenderness he usually reserved for French.

'I've been in love with you for years, too, Leo. I just didn't realise it.'

Leo stood stock-still, and let himself have this: Cole's fingers against his cheekbones, Cole's open, affectionate regard, Cole's warm breath as he leaned—

He caught Cole's head in his hands and pulled him in faster, harder. Cole made a soft sound of surprise that had a good deal of gratification to it as their mouths met, and dragged both arms down his back to press them chest to chest. They were almost wrestling each other to win more closeness, Leo with his fingers to Cole's nape, Cole sliding both palms over his arse, squeezing until Leo gasped against his mouth and then kissed him again, savage with need.

But a pause to finally catch a breath turned into a pause to consider that he'd been drenched in the rank sweat of terror not very long before. 'I'd like that bath,' he told Cole, panting, 'before we go any further.'

'I'm not sure about going any further today, *mon amour*,' Cole said, notwithstanding he was currently pushing dishevelled hair back from his forehead and looking more than a little flown. 'You need to rest.'

'I do not,' Leo said, before venturing, 'Unless it's in your bed.' He corrected himself, teasing smile fading, because he'd forgotten where they were. 'No, you have a house full of staff.'

'Leo, Mrs Clarke put you in the room adjoining mine,' Cole said. 'I didn't have to ask her, she just did it. *She* told me we would, under no circumstances, be disturbed.'

Alarmed, Leo blurted, 'Oh, no, Cole, I'm sorry.'

'It's *kind*,' Cole said. 'It's a very polite way of indicating she and her staff will not be speculating on the status of my guest.'

'But the rest of the Palace *will* be speculating!' Leo wiped at his face. He could still feel the burn of Cole's mouth across his lips. He wanted to get on his knees. Reluctantly, he said, 'I should go. I need to find Polly, anyway.'

Catching his hand as he tried to slither away, Cole said, 'You do understand why Lady Henry fetched me when you needed help?'

'Yes, but she was reading *Fanny Hill*,' Leo mumbled.

Cole's eyebrows shot up. 'I meant, we're *already* associated in everyone's minds. I've told you before it doesn't bother me.'

'But—'

'I understand you care about my reputation, and your own. And if we got ourselves into legal trouble, it'd be different, I believe you about that. But as it stands, people are more generous, or perhaps less energetic about being bigoted, than you're assuming. Whispers won't sink us.'

Leo must have looked unconvinced, because Cole went on, 'You've been diligently teaching both Fitzhenrys how to take daguerreotypes. You wouldn't do that if you thought they'd fail to obtain a licence or run a studio because of the colour of their skin.'

'No, most people either don't care, or don't care enough to— oh, I see.'

Cole beamed at him. 'We're not even as visible as they are. Men live together all the time; so do women, even more often. Married couples and widows take in lodgers. People might speculate, but that speaks more to their indecent mind than it does to any indecent behaviour that may or may not be occurring.'

Leo said, 'You've argued yourself into letting me share your bed.'

'Ay, did I?' Cole said. 'Daftie me.' He pushed Leo against the wall to kiss him, holding him imprisoned with one hand on his chest and a cocked leg. 'Here's what we're doing, Mr Percival Leander Sweetwater.'

He was close enough that he couldn't miss Leo's definite physical reaction, his intake of breath, his squirm. 'Oh,' he said, sounding charmed. 'Do you like that, Leo?'

There did not seem much point in denying it, though he did quibble. 'It's more that I find it relaxing to have one particular, ah, problem solved for me, in one particular context.'

Cole nodded thoughtfully. He began to speak in an assured and resolute tone that practically reached out and plucked all decisions from Leo's hands. 'Here's what happens now, then. We are going to go upstairs. You are going to strip off the rest of your clothes and get in the bath.'

Leo had so carefully locked away his desire for this man. He was helpless now to do anything other than nod.

'You will come into my bedroom naked.' Leo nodded again, and Cole smiled. 'And then you will crawl under my sheets...'

Weakly, Leo murmured, 'Yes...'

'And get some rest.'

'Oh, you—' Leo dissolved into laughter in the face of Cole's chortling delight. 'Upstairs, then.'

They wrapped up in blankets, carrying their clothes. True to Mrs Clarke's word, they were not observed in their state of dishabille. Leo's room was indeed by Cole's. It was cramped, blessedly free of unexpected spectres, and dominated by a large tin bath, steaming with water anointed with scented oils, still hotter than lukewarm. Leo lowered himself into it gratefully and scrubbed.

Pink-skinned and wrapped in a silken robe he'd found folded by the soap and towel, he cautiously opened the door between his and Cole's rooms. Cole, clean and wrapped in his own robe, was sitting on the bed, a broad expanse of pale linen and dark oak. The book Leo had given him lay on the nightstand, a tattered ribbon marking his place.

Leo made another quick check for ghosts, though the deaths that resulted in ghosts tended not to happen in bedrooms (unless sex was involved in one way or the other).

Cole must have been watching him closely, to see the flicker. 'I don't think anyone's died in here.'

'It has to be a very quick death, to make a ghost.' Again came a strange moment of disorientation, to speak so openly.

'Capability Brown collapsed and died suddenly,' Cole said, 'but it was while visiting one of his daughters. No other Master, Head, or Royal Gardener has held the post lifelong like he did. To my knowledge, no one's died in this house.'

'My thanks.'

Leo's voice sounded husky in his own ears. He was, he realised, as nervous as a blushing bride, if a particularly brazen one, to sneak into a bed instead of waiting trembling beneath the sheets.

To ward off the nerves and further flights of fancy, he dropped the robe and crawled into Cole's lap to kiss him. Cole's silky robe slithered and slipped under his bare body, a cool caress that nonetheless inflamed his already sensitive skin. Leo rocked against him, any whisper of self-consciousness shredding when he felt the rub of Cole's rock-hard erection in return. He moaned as he sucked on Cole's tongue, pressing his hips tighter against his.

'You are so much more intense than I expected,' Cole murmured when Leo let him speak.

'Sorry,' he said, pulling away. It occurred to him Cole might be nervous, too, and had more right to be.

Cole kissed him again. '*Non.* I shouldn't have assumed you'd like the other man in control just because you like a little bossiness.'

'What I like,' Leo said slowly, because here was another thing he didn't often admit aloud, 'is there to be a tussle over who's in control, and for you to win.' Anticipating the cause of Cole's slight frown, he added, 'All pretence, no real force. If I say no, I'll mean it.'

'Ah. Like this, then?' Cole slid his hands under Leo's thighs and flipped him without hesitation off his lap and flat onto his back beside him on the bed.

'Exactly like that,' Leo said, eyes wide, and dragged him down.

'I did say you need to rest,' Cole said, after a time in which he'd ended up atop Leo, palms clasped, legs entwined, robe discarded so there was nothing but heated skin pressed to heated skin, Cole's leanness pressed to Leo's roundness, matching erections rubbing stiff and silky against each other at every shift of their bodies.

Leo managed not to whimper, just. 'Please don't stop.'

Cole wrapped work-rough hands around Leo's wrists and pressed his thumbs into the hollows where his pulse sang. 'I'm not going to,' he agreed. 'Leo, *mon amour, mon beau*. You make me feel greedy for the first time in my life. And now I'm going to have you, yes?'

'Yes,' Leo said fervently.

Cole ran his hands down Leo's arms, his shoulders, his chest, his soft belly, his hips, and then around to his arse to squeeze again, Leo tracking his progress through the torturous ripple of response in the wake of those roughened palms over his skin.

'I want to take it slow, but it's proving a challenge,' Cole murmured.

'I don't,' Leo told him. He'd got his hand around Cole's prick, something he had not let himself even dream about, while working his robe off. He knew what he needed, and it wasn't slow. 'I want your weight on top of me and your prick between my thighs and I want to feel how much you want me.'

'You'll feel how much I want you for less than a minute if you keep that kind of talk up.'

Cole reached between them. Taking both their pricks in his fist, he pumped slowly, rubbing their leaking slits with his thumb and spreading the satiny wetness. Then he slid between Leo's thighs, making a sound in the back of his throat as Leo squeezed him tight.

Rearing up, Cole pushed their hips harder together and locked his hands back around Leo's wrists. Leo twisted them, lifting his elbows, an instinctive struggle that Cole quashed with a hard press of his forearms over Leo's, not without a quick look at Leo's face to be sure he had the right of it. He very much did.

He began to thrust, his prick rubbing lightly against Leo's tight-drawn balls with the motion, the friction of his toned stomach stimulating Leo's prick with every pump of his hips. The sensation was overwhelming and Leo's whole body bowed taut into it, pinioned from wrists to hips to ankles by Cole and his merciless weight. The only part free to move was his head, tossed back against the pillow in ecstasy, and his mouth, effusing gasps and moans in unison with Cole's truncated French syllables, exclamations of pleasure and pleasurable effort.

Leo was going to spend before Cole at this rate, and he wanted, with all of his being, to make this the most perfect experience for him.

Use my mouth,' he gasped.

Cole gave a grunt that might have been enquiry, so Leo elaborated. 'Put your big, thick prick in my—'

Cole spent with a cry and pulsing bucks of his hips, then collapsed fully onto Leo, still panting. His grip slipped from Leo's wrists to tangle their fingers together.

'Oh,' Leo said blandly from under him. '…Next time, then?'

Cole huffed, not moving. His face was turned away, and Leo worried he'd made it all too much for a man having his first encounter with unspeakable vice. After a moment, Cole propped himself up on his elbows and gazed down at him, hair falling in messy locks over his forehead, terracotta-brown eyes serious.

'Next time?' he said, and Leo winced. Cole shifted his hips, rocking against Leo's erection. '*This* time's not finished.'

Leo smiled in sheer relief as Cole kissed him, then dipped his head. He set to his studies, kissing and stroking, licking and tickling, nipping and squeezing, using one hand to firmly press Leo down whenever he tried to squirm.

Which was at increasingly frequent intervals, both because he was immensely aroused and because he was no longer used to this sort of scrutiny, with the comfort of a bed, and the time and safety to be fully, luxuriously undressed, and a man who wanted to *look*.

Still, Cole was not to be deterred, and he was vocally appreciative, if in French, lilting complimentary incomprehensibilities against Leo's skin as he traced his mouth from clavicle to hipbone. His explorations had a promising trajectory.

He encased Leo's prick with a confident grip. 'How do you want it?'

'Your hand's fine,' Leo assured him.

Cole laved Leo's prick from head to root, swirled his tongue over his balls and tasted his own spend from between Leo's sticky thighs, before licking his way back up to plant a firm kiss on the slit.

'How do you want it, Leo?' he repeated.

Leo nodded and said, 'Yes, all the way down your throat.'

'I am *shocked*,' Cole said, deadpan, and opened his lips over Leo's prick, sliding down about halfway before bobbing back up. 'Hmm.'

'Perhaps not, it's an advanced technique.'

This earned him raised brows and an '*Allons!*'

Cole took him in again, slower this time. Lips suctioned tight, he bobbed his head, a little awkward. He shifted, flattened his tongue, and began to take Leo deeper on each downward plunge. Leo moaned and rubbed his hand over and through Cole's hair, hips straining to jerk. He held still as best he could, his fingers curled at Cole's nape, not, through pure self-control, pushing.

He heard Cole make a deep, satisfied grunt as he took the whole length of Leo's prick; it was that satisfied sound more than the sensation that tipped him. He cried out a garbled warning, too late. Cole grunted again, and swallowed around Leo's prick, making him near-sob in pleasure and lift his hips helplessly. Cole took that, too.

Leo went entirely limp as Cole sat back and regarded him, thoughtfully licking his lips. Then he smiled with mischievous glint ascendant.

'It seems I won your favour and *thoroughly* received your grace,' he intoned, and laughed aloud when Leo groaned and threw a pillow at him. He readily caught it. 'That was lovely, Leo. I loved every moment of it.'

They curled up around each other, Leo with his head on Cole's shoulder and a calf draped over his shins, Cole tracing fingers over Leo's back.

He drew circles on Leo's spine. 'I do feel more than a little foolish, not working out my own tastes earlier.'

'I'm not surprised you wouldn't think about it,' Leo said. 'It is unnatural.'

Cole scoffed. 'You don't believe that. If it was truly against natural law, why would we need such punitive man-made laws to prevent it? None of this has felt anything other than as it should be. But no, there was something else.'

'Oh?'

With an unusually self-conscious laugh, Cole said, 'The sheer amount of time I spent staring at Cupid and ignoring Psyche in that Van Dyke painting.'

Leo took a moment to recall it. Oh, yes, *Cupid and Psyche*, on the King's Stairs until Mrs Grundy had spirited it away. 'Talk about an appreciation for the male form. Beautiful legs.'

He ran a palm over Cole's lean, muscular thigh, and delved. 'This line of definition here, on the inner thigh.' He slid his hand higher. 'Lively!' he murmured. 'Is it next time yet?'

Cole laughed softly. 'Not yet,' he said. 'You did get yourself an older man, after all. But it wasn't the legs. It was the *arse. S*o perfectly *round.'*

His hand swept down to Leo's arse, palm spreading over one full cheek. He squeezed.

'I should say,' Leo said, breathless, and quite reluctant to disappoint. 'Your prick won't magically cure me of disliking buggery. In either part.'

He looked up in time to see Cole arch his brows high. 'I wasn't planning on offering. In either part.'

'Ah. Sorry to make assumptions. Men used to promise an awful lot, trying to bed me their way.'

'I'd wager men would promise the very earth for the opportunity,' Cole said, gravely but with that glint in his eye again.

'Gallant!' Leo said, tickled by the blatant flattery. 'You'd do well.'

Cole was promptly pleased with himself, but said, 'Only with you, *mon amour.'*

Leo paused. It was the first time he'd had that. Men did make marriage-like arrangements, but the men he'd made community with in London hadn't, generally. Jack never would have.

He must have looked surprised. Cole shook his head. 'Low standards.'

A touch severely, Leo said, 'It was a different time in my life.'

'All right. I'm struggling to understand why another man hadn't snapped you up, I think.'

Harry had said something similar, but he'd only been talking about sex, not...this. 'Your good luck, I suppose,' he said, since it seemed impolitic to announce that it was because he was *deeply* strange to most people.

'Do you miss it?' Cole's restless hand, gliding up and down, had finally come to rest, fingers spread over Leo's hip. 'That life? London?'

'I did, for the first few months,' Leo said. 'Have I mentioned Friday is also *my* favourite day of the week? I don't wish for any other day of the week, when I've got Friday.'

Cole said, 'So aloof, so independent,' in teasing tones, but followed it up with a heartfelt kiss.

Leo melted against him in gratitude. It wasn't the same sort of gratitude he'd felt for Harry, for the simplicity of their liaison, as badly as it had turned out. It was more a sense of immense contentment, that Cole could so readily gift him the familiar affection of their easy friendship, and then kiss him senseless, and see no contradiction or obstacle in it.

With some rue, he said, 'I do wish you'd seen me ten years ago, though, when I was...'

'I'm glad I didn't meet you ten years ago. I wasn't ready. I still thought I wanted to marry.' He smiled, rue of his own. 'I would have *fled* from you, Leo. As it is, I was spending half my time thinking things like, I like it when Mr Sweetwater smiles at me. Sweetwater's hair is glossy in the sunshine today, I wonder how it would feel to touch it. Leo should wear those trousers more often, they make his arse look spectacular.' He widened his eyes in mock-astonishment. 'What a peculiar thing to think about another man. I should probably not think those things about my friend. I should put those thoughts in a closed box.'

'Oh, the box,' Leo said. 'Yes, I know the box. Lots of padlocks on that box around you.'

'You weren't ready for me ten years ago, either,' Cole added. 'I would have wanted you all to myself, and that wouldn't have been fair. We've found each other at exactly the right time. I don't regret anything, *mon chéri.*'

Leo hummed and said, 'Well, a few weeks earlier wouldn't have gone astray.'

It was his turn to offer an earnest kiss to belie the flippancy, which turned into more kisses. Cole eventually pulled away. He was feeling distinctly more lively under Leo's hand, so Leo half-expected next time had arrived.

'About that,' Cole said. 'Would you like to introduce me to your ghost?'

TWENTY ONE

IT FELT ODD TO BE LOITERING by Banqueting House during the afternoon, and Leo glanced nervously at the two large windows flanking the front entrance. The curtains were firmly closed, and, if Mrs Reynett and her two toddling daughters were within, they were being very quiet.

He'd been surprised, and shouldn't have been, to find it was still daylight outside. They'd walked around the west side of the Palace and past the Great Vine, a path that ensured the lowest chance of encountering a resident at this time of day, besides the Vinekeeper, who, pipe firmly in mouth, merely nodded to his nominal boss and returned to contemplating the huge bare patch of rich soil by the Vinehouse. Under that seemingly-wasted expanse spread the ancient vine's root system, which needed specialised management.

Max was at their heels. There was no gambolling about, begging for pats, when he was on duty. He sat solemnly at Cole's leg and watched Leo pace about the garden wedge. Cole examined some yellowing leaves in the shrubbery, seeking out deficiencies while giving Leo space.

Leo had worked himself up during the walk. It was all very well speaking his secrets aloud in the abstract, but actually introducing them to each other was more confronting than he'd expected.

Cole had squatted to stick his fingers into the soil beneath his afflicted shrub. 'She not here?' he asked, glancing up.

'No,' Leo said. 'This is going to be very odd for you. I know you must already think me irredeemably weird, but this will be a cut above.'

Rising, Cole brushed his hands off. 'Scots retains the old meaning of weird,' he said conversationally. 'Meaning fate. We having a saying, ye maun jist dree your weird. Endure your fate, get on with it.' He took Leo's hand. 'You're who you are, Leo. I love who you are. I know you have things you need to hide. Nothing you choose to keep hidden will change how I feel about you.'

'I wish we weren't in public so I could kiss you,' Leo said softly.

Cole smiled, gave his hand one last squeeze, and let go. 'Shall you give your wee lassie a cooee?'

Leo didn't have to call her. She whisked through the hedge, edges shredding, and flew to his side. 'I only touched you so I could fight the other ghosts. I would never intend you harm, never! I know you can't answer, but at least nod if you forgive me.'

'There's nothing to forgive, unless it's you, of me.' Leo held his hand out to her, conciliatory.

She looked from this offering to Cole to Leo. 'Does he know about me? Did you tell him?'

'Everyone knows, after today,' Leo said. 'They either believe I see ghosts, or consider me mad. He's the former, thankfully.'

He took her hand, feeling her cold palm slide against his, her cold fingers hook around his. It must look to Cole like he was clasping empty air.

'Polly. I am so sorry I shouted at you two days in a row. Please know, I didn't mean any of it. Especially not what I shouted at you yesterday.' He squared his shoulders, because he knew she wouldn't like this next part. 'And for sending you away after you'd risked yourself to help me. That must have felt like a reprise.'

'Nonsense!' she said, pulling free.

He continued, 'I know you've only ever wanted to keep me safe. I thank you for that.'

'Yes, I want you safe,' Polly said, looking at Cole. 'Is this safe?'

'I think,' Leo said carefully, 'I think we need to move beyond safe now, and beyond keeping secrets from the people who matter to us. And so. Miss Mary Lee.' He made an awkward bow. 'Might I introduce you to Mr Solong?'

'Well, I've *met* the man often enough,' Polly said testily, not without fighting off a dawning expression of gratification. She might want Leo to keep his abilities a secret for his own safety; she didn't necessarily like its result any more than he did.

'Pleasure to make your acquaintance, Miss Lee,' Cole said gravely, directing his gaze somewhere in Polly's vicinity. He thought her shorter than she was, apparently, or hadn't yet guessed that she floated.

'He should call me Polly,' she said. She released Leo's hand, and he tucked it under his other arm to warm it again. 'I suppose you've let him take you to bed?'

'Yes, I have.'

Polly drifted closer to Cole, who stood still in the wash of cold air. 'I concede he doesn't seem intent on breaking your heart.'

'If he does, he won't have meant to.'

'I'll have none of that,' Cole said. 'I'm here, so include me. Miss Lee, you can start by telling me why you don't like me.'

'I like you!' Polly cried, which Leo duly relayed, along with the permission to use her nickname.

'Then why'd you warn Leo off me yesterday, lassie?'

'Clever devil, isn't he?' Polly said, grudging.

She flickered, agitation at a well-controlled roil, then said, 'Tell him about Lucy. Tell him I loved her. Tell him she let me into her bed and then barred me from it. Tell him she delivered a lying letter to the king and used me to escape. Tell him I died to keep her secrets safe, and she never thought of me again.'

Cole listened to Leo's somewhat subdued recitation. 'I am sorry, Polly. But you must know – please know that I would *never* treat Leo like that. He is – this is…' Cole trailed off, and then said, '*Je l'aime de tout mon cœur. Je ne peux pas imaginer ma vie sans lui.*'

'She knows,' Leo said, blushing, because Polly, knowing his reticence just as well as Cole did, had not translated the French for him, but her eyes had become very round and glassy as if she wanted to cry, but in a happy way.

They sat in a row on the bench under the tree, Leo in the middle, Polly not quite sitting but floating demurely in a calves-tucked-under position, Max lying across all the feet available to him.

'My next question for Polly,' Cole said. 'Is Leo safe from the other ghosts? Will he have to leave the Palace? He says they're not monsters, but they certainly become monsters if the temptation is too strong.'

'I think they will calm down, as long as the ghosts in Fountain Court go back to sleep.'

Leo couldn't tell if this was blatant reassurance meant for him, or the truth, but he repeated it dutifully.

'Fountain Court,' Cole said, with some satisfaction; he had guessed as much. 'And what's to be done about that?'

'Tell him about the workman,' Polly ordered.

Leo did so, adding, 'But I think – and you must suspect this, too, Polly – I think he's losing control of them. And I think their bodies must be buried there, too, for blood to have stirred the ghosts so. Harry was bleeding,' he added as an aside to Cole.

Cole scrunched up his face, no doubt contemplating he'd been the one to make Harry bleed. Leo gave his hand a brief squeeze.

'All the people walking back and forth over their graves are making them stronger, drop by drop,' Polly said.

Leo repeated Polly's comforting interjection. 'Whatever metaphysical bulwark the workman erected to keep them in place, it's cracking now. And neither of us know what to do about it.'

Cole suggested, 'Dig up the bones and lay them in sanctified ground?'

'The ghosts won't follow their bodies away,' Leo said, if thoughtfully: at least the bodies wouldn't be walked over anymore. 'It might stop them getting stronger, though.'

'Tell him about Lady Bessborough and the spheres of influence!'

'Polly would like me to bring to your attention the Countess of Bessborough, before our time, and her request to use a disused staircase to reach the garden from her apartment,' Leo said. He counted it off on his fingers. 'Permission from the Lord Chamberlain to unlock the stairway doors, permission from the Board of Works to pass into the passageway, permission from the Lord Stewart to exit the passageway at the other end, and permission from the First Commissioner and Board of her Majesty's Office of Woods and Forests to open the garden gate.'

'We don't need anyone's permission if I break a drainage pipe,' Cole said, with remarkable disloyalty to his perpetually beleaguered colleague, Mr Grundy, Superintendent, whose job it was to manage all those competing boards and officials. 'Works would have to send men in to dig up that entire side. They'll uncover the skeletons for sure.'

Polly put her hand over her heart theatrically. 'Not just a pretty face, this one.'

'Polly believes that might help,' Leo translated.

Cole nodded. 'I'll need a few days to get a peek at the old plans and see where I can insert a spot of sabotage without it being too obvious, or too destructive, for that matter.' He rubbed his hands together. 'Next?'

'That awful, awful man,' Polly said promptly. 'Coming about here threatening our Leo!'

'Mr Guy,' Leo said.

'And Walpole,' Cole said. 'Leo, I know you don't like me rushing in to solve your problems, and don't want to drag me into it...' He shrugged. 'But I'm in it now, and I want to solve your problems. Let me call on Sir Walter.'

Leo didn't say he still wasn't convinced the baronet would waste hard-curried patronage on him, nor that he remained reluctant to allow Cole to try it. Instead, he admired his own steadiness as he calmly announced, 'I've already agreed to talk to my ghost for Guy,' and braced for outcry.

Which duly came, his companions chiming in perfect harmony, 'I don't think you should do that.'

'One at a time.' Leo pointed to Cole. Polly pouted and muttered something about unfair advantages involving men and their long plums.

'I don't like you giving Walpole what he wants,' Cole said frankly.

Leo turned to Polly, who said, 'The Palace ghosts are already restless. Messing about with this nonsense might make it worse.'

Once Leo had relayed this, Cole said, 'Ay, that's a *much* better reason.'

'It's not going to be real,' Leo told them, ignoring Polly's preen. 'It'll be me and Polly, pretending. It won't summon spirits from beyond the veil, just as us talking here now doesn't draw other ghosts. *And,*' he added, 'giving Harry what he wants will make him go away, which is the whole intention.'

'Because giving him what he wanted worked so well to make him go away last time, you trollop,' Polly said scathingly. 'Will you at least wait till Cole breaks the pipe and the bodies are exhumed?'

Leo, having repeated her question (but not her scalding pronouncement on his judgement), explained, 'I don't think I can put them off long enough. Harry's moving too fast. He's already had me evicted, he'll go after the daguerreotype licence next.' He finally took a moment to truly appreciate the speed of the retribution. 'In fact, unless Harry's connections are exceedingly keen, I'd wager it's Guy and his gambling house ledger that's yanking on strings.'

He realised he'd lost his audience, both of whom had snagged on an early word in his explanation. '*Evicted?*'

Leo gave a shrug. 'As a prod to action, Harry could have been crueller.'

Polly snorted and Cole's eyes narrowed; Leo went on hastily, 'I can find new lodgings in Hampton, somewhere big enough for the Fitzhenrys, too. We'll manage. Oh, there's a silver lining, Cole: it'll be more discreet than traipsing back and forth across the Palace to visit each other.'

'I do not like that at all,' Polly said.

'I'll be here every day,' Leo said, notwithstanding that his stomach plummeted as he remembered how faded Polly had become when he'd moved to London. He'd been thoughtless, again.

'I'll—' Cole winced. '*Not* leap in to solve it, merely issue an invitation. You are all welcome at Wilderness House. That includes you, Polly.'

'Much better!'

'I can't do that,' Leo said. 'You know I can't.'

'Why do I know that? Even the residents with the most cramped of apartments take lodgers without suspicion, and Wilderness House is meant for a family.'

Cole didn't say this with any undue melancholy, but it struck Leo so. He could almost picture Cole, sitting alone of an evening, the mantle clock ticking out empty hours with monotonous insistence.

This was utterly ridiculous, since Cole, a man of good background, confident stance, easy manners, and warm affect, received far more invitations than Leo ever did.

But still. He returned alone to a large house, meant for a family.

'At least, if you're set on *une vraie séance fantomatique*, do *that* over at Wilderness House, as far from Fountain Court as you can get.'

Leo broke from his cheerless musing. 'Too close to the Tudor ghost.'

'But we are not summoning ghosts, remember?' Polly said, and Leo did not want to admit how much his heart lifted at that blithe *we*. 'You and me, pretending.'

'Why not pretend for real?' Cole asked, upon hearing Polly's point. 'Polly won't even need to be there—'

'I don't like this plan, either,' Polly said indignantly. 'Stop it, the pair of you.'

'—which means she won't need to use your, ah, what is it, *phantasmic pneuma* to demonstrate her existence.'

'I do know you hate that,' she conceded.

Leo said only, 'You *have* been talking to Lady Jane.'

Polly tutted. 'I think we can all agree *she's* been talking to *everyone*.'

Happily left unaware of the commentary, Cole continued, 'Make a show for Guy, let him unmask fakery, he'll feel clever for being too savvy to fall for it, and he'll go back to chasing Walpole for real currency, not a fool's errand.'

Polly whirled up in alarm and a gust of cold air, making Max raise his head to look up at her with a calm, wise gaze. 'He won't feel clever, he'll feel gulled!'

'Polly's right,' Leo said. 'You didn't see how much he wants ghosts to be real, Cole. Any hint he's been tricked, he'll take it out on me and Harry.'

'Not on you,' Cole said. 'I'll be there to make sure of that.' Leo's breath caught, because he hadn't allowed himself to assume *we* included Cole, even with the open invitation to use Wilderness House. 'Walpole was the one who spun him the tale, let Walpole be caught in his own weaving.'

Leo said, 'I don't... I'm sorry, I don't want to leave Harry in his clutches.'

'How often do I have to say that Walpole has options you don't,' Cole said, tone sharpening. 'At any point, he could go to his relations – on his mother's side, if his father really is such an ogre as to have a heavy hand on even his married and independent offspring – and beg the funds. He just doesn't want to humiliate himself. Let him.'

'He can't now,' Leo insisted. 'Guy wants a ghost. He's willing to chance two hundred pounds on it.' He paused. 'I mean, he probably wants the treasure purse, too.'

'I cannot express to you strongly enough that that does not have to be your problem, and I cannot understand why you are bent on making it so.'

'Harry's very young,' Leo said apologetically. 'I'd only just gone to London at his age, and I remember how young and doltish I was.'

Drily, Cole asked, 'And did you sell out your lovers to the magistrate to avoid trouble of your own making?'

'No, but I did abandon my closest and most loyal friend when I was literally the only person she could talk to.'

'Oh,' said Polly. 'Oh, Percy, my dearest darling boy.' She threw her arms around him, but only for the barest moment. 'I don't deny those years were hard on me.' She frowned. 'It did become very thin, as you said, but I do not wish you beholden to me.'

'I didn't mean any of those nasty words,' he said. 'You have been my truest friend, Polly, I cannot resent a moment of the time I spend with you.'

Cole said, 'I suppose your tendency to adopt strays is part of why I love you.'

Leo glowed at how easily, and regularly, Cole expressed his affections, while Polly's earnestness was immediately washed away by umbrage. 'Is he talking about me? How dare he!'

'He means Harry. I don't adopt strays, Cole.'

Cole tilted his head. 'What's your biggest regret about being evicted?'

'I've let down the Fitzhenrys—' He stopped at smiles from both of them. 'I think we can all agree Sally adopted *me*, actually.'

'Don't underrate yourself,' Cole said softly. 'I know you put your head down and *cope* when things go badly, and it's a habit that's saved your life so I'm not quibbling. But once we're done with this, promise me you'll spare a little energy for being justifiably angry at Walpole.'

'I'd write a sternly worded letter,' Leo said, 'except I don't plan to ever see or think of him again.'

'Right.' Cole looked mollified. 'Is your plan that Polly will tell Guy where the purse is? We should dig it up ourselves and pay him off without having to involve ghosts at all.'

'I am not that old!'

'The purse was lost some two hundred and fifty years ago, and Polly's around, oh, two hundred.'

'One hundred and ninety-five!'

'And by the time she'd have accumulated the will to notice other ghosts, the Tudor knight would've already been fading away. They do that over time. You never spoke to him, did you, Polly?'

'No,' she said. 'Why do you think he's a knight?'

'You said he died in the tiltyard?'

She made a thoughtful noise.

'Anyway,' Leo said, frowning at her, 'the point is, Polly can't tell any of us where the purse is. Guy is apparently willing to risk that outcome, for the chance to talk to a ghost.'

'If he's that enamoured with the idea, he'll not be satisfied with a single *séance fantomatique*.'

'We should scare him away so he never comes back,' Polly suggested. From being hesitant about the whole idea, she now became positively enthusiastic, exclaiming, 'I'll make things appear from nowhere, and blow all the candles out, and cause strange noises all about the room. We'll terrify him!'

'Firstly, you can barely move a toothpick,' Leo said. 'Secondly, he *wants* it to be terrifying. He wants to be obviously *not* terrified in the face of phenomena that make lesser men tremble. No, what we're going to do is make it very, very authentic, and very, very *boring*. Here is the one ghost I can talk to, who knows absolutely nothing about anything.'

Polly pouted. 'Must you be so dull?'

'That is the *exact* idea.'

Cole grimaced. 'Leo, everyone in the Palace is now aware you truly see ghosts. Ghosts, plural. There's no way Walpole won't hear of it, and he's vanishingly unlikely to fail to inform Guy, if and when Guy becomes angry that your "one ghost" doesn't know where the purse is, or because he's young and daftie and blurts it out without thinking through the implications. Guy will insist you talk to each and every one, and at a certain point he'll wonder if you can see ghosts elsewhere.'

'That's why I need you to encourage the rumour that I was overtaxed about the eviction,' Leo said. 'Let people think me mad and throwing public fits – again. Let them be contemptuous and smug about it. Mrs Ellice and the other gossips will enjoy helping you with that. I think Colonel Cottin's made a decent start.'

'What was it you said about your reputation?' Cole queried, brows raised.

'Can't be helped,' Leo said. He hoped, at least, that Mrs and Miss Willis would take on the version that best suited their needs. 'But that's all right. If I'm lucky, I'll be in the same basket as Lady Jane. Eccentric, a touch nervy, still worthy of being kind to.' He paused. 'I think I'm already in that basket. An artistic temperament covers very many sins.'

They fell quiet at the sound of piping voices. The two Reynett daughters, Augusta and Georgina, came pelting along the path, the younger barely keeping up with her sister, followed by a bustling nursemaid, and then Lady Reynett, Mrs Vesey and Miss Reynett, the latter still appearing to be on the outers.

'Oh, Mr Sweetwater,' Lady Reynett called, as the trio came to the front door of Banqueting House. 'I do hope you are quite recovered?'

'Poxy harlot,' Polly muttered.

Lady Reynett was one of the few Palace residents Leo had trouble liking, putting her squarely with the likes of Lady George and Colonel Cottin. Like Miss Willis, she had grown up at Hampton Court, on the Green, and remained supercilious and snide towards the former washer-woman's son, a habit that had only increased now she was no longer plain Miss Campbell.

She was fairly well perfect.

After he and Cole had greeted the women, Leo added, very solemnly and formally, 'Yes, I received some ill news that made me disconsolate.'

'Evicted, I hear,' said Mrs Vesey, smugly pleased to *have* the news, but tilting her head to show she was sympathetic *about* the news.

'Indeed. I am fortunate to have Mr Solong's assistance in the matter.'

The ladies exchanged a few more pleasantries, then vanished inside for their tea.

'See?' Leo said. 'I'm still sorry to have to drag you into this, though, Cole.'

'No dragging involved,' Cole said. 'I'd have dived in, even if we were still merely friends.' He flashed his mischievous smile, though it had a touch of shyness to it. 'And now I have the inestimable pleasure of pinning you naked under me while you whisper glorious things in my ear.'

Polly, looking amused, said, 'Does he know I'm still here?'

'I assume Polly's still here,' Cole said. 'But I also gather she's been haunting the palace through the Restoration *and* the Regency. I assume she's heard – and seen – much worse.'

'He should hear what the Hanoverians got up to even *before* the Regency,' Polly said, 'if he's after ideas.'

'I can give him ideas!' Leo protested, and blushed.

'Oh, I have ideas,' Cole said, and Leo blushed harder.

TWENTY-TWO

THE NEXT DAY, IN BETWEEN A steady stream of Palace well-wishers and an inconvenient number of customers, Leo conducted negotiations with three parties.

The first consisted of Harry and Guy. Harry presumed they'd hold the ghost session, Cole's *séance fantomatique,* in the Hoste apartment, and seemed reluctant to leave it, not even to walk across the Palace and look Leo in the eye to make arrangements. Leo couldn't hold it against him too vehemently; he'd have wanted to do the same. Across a series of notes keeping a Palace errand-runner in good cheer and farthings, he eventually had to baldly declare that his ghost friend would not attend a *séance* so close to Fountain Court.

Cole and Polly comprised the second party. It was not so much that Leo was resisting the use of Wilderness House – the Fountain Court ghosts were a far bigger threat than the Tudor remnant, he accepted that – but that he remained reluctant to drag more people into this unsightly affair than necessary. He had Cole promise none of his servants would be there.

That left the third interested, yet unexpected, party, who Leo really *should* have expected.

Sally Fitzhenry was currently helping him prepare the drawing room of Wilderness House for a *séance* on an oppressively dreary December afternoon, the sky outside already darkening.

The room had begun life, around about the same time the workman departed his, as an unusually large yet somewhat extraneous entrance hall, clad with recessed walnut panelling and featuring a big marble fireplace. Capability Brown's tenure had seen various extensions and renovations to accommodate five daughters, including the remodelling of the hall into a spacious drawing room.

Polly informed him of this to explain the room's awkward dimensions and positioning, and the odd dining annex stuck out from one side, while he set out a small fortune in beeswax candles to Sally's specifications: it was more accurate to say *he* was helping *her* prepare the room. Upon winkling out as much of the mess as Leo had felt obliged to share with her, given she and John had to share his eviction and the risk of losing the studio, she'd been adamant about directing what amounted to set dressing.

'I did work at a theatre in London,' he'd protested. 'Behind the scenes. Doing *sets*.'

'Painting,' she'd said, only just short of dismissive. 'I laid out the studio. I sorted the ghost cards. Mr Sweetwater, I know what people are expecting when they want to see ghosts.'

It was inarguable. He'd held firm enough to bar her from the *séance* itself. It would be only him and Cole, Harry and Guy.

And Polly, of course.

'Why does she want so many candles?' she asked. She was as serious and single-minded as she had been when thrashing Colonel Cottin at whist; it was not helping Leo's nerves.

'You intend we dim the lamps?' he asked Sally.

'I think you should have no lamps, sir,' she said firmly. 'And screen the fire. Keep the room dark, and let the flames flicker in the…draught.' Sally waved her hand over an unlit candle demonstratively. 'But make sure it's very warm, so the chill on the back of the neck will be even more apparent than usual.'

Leo gave a shake of his head as he shifted a large mirror at her direction. The most humbling part of this entire misadventure was just how many Palace residents had been politely pretending he wasn't haunted.

Together they pushed a small round walnut-wood table into the middle of the cleared room. It was heavy, with a sturdy pedestal base and a tripod of lion's paws for feet.

As he spread an ivory linen cloth over it, he said, 'What would you say to us all lodging here, Miss Fitzhenry?'

Sally hesitated, hands clasped around a chair back. 'Me and John, up with the other servants?'

She was contemplating demotion. 'Is that where they made you sleep last night?' Leo asked sharply.

He had returned to Wilderness House yesterday evening, he and Cole going by the Athlone apartment to collect Sally. To any resident who expressed sympathy, real or merely an excuse for nosiness, as they passed by on their walk through the Palace courts and grounds, Cole had sombrely intimated that Mr Sweetwater needed to be in company after his nervous attack.

This was in the interests of spreading their chosen story, and that was all, because Leo had collapsed into bed the moment he reached it, and not stirred until the sun was well up. He hadn't had the wherewithal to check on Sally, and regretted it now.

'No, I was by the old nursery,' Sally said, still sounding doubtful. 'The nursemaid's room, I suppose. Or the governess's.'

Polly interjected, 'Brown lodged his assistants and apprentices here, they didn't sleep in the garrets with the lower servants. Once the new kitchen was installed in the old brewhouse, they'd have had the run of the basement rooms. Though, I don't see Cole insisting on shifting her off the first floor in either direction.'

'I would like to officially appoint you as you already are,' Leo said. 'My apprentice. You and John would have quarters here befitting that. I know it seems an unorthodox arrangement, but we already have one of those. I don't mind if you'd find it more respectable to lodge in Hampton.'

Sally set the chair into place. 'I'd be honoured to take on an apprentice-ship with you, Mr Sweetwater.'

'We both know you honour me with your alarming competence, Miss Fitzhenry,' Leo said.

She smiled. 'Do you think people would visit a studio with a woman daguerreotypist?'

'I think they would,' he said. 'But you're not limited to a studio.' She wasn't as constrained as he was, with his need to know where the haunts were. 'You could take scenes, or prepare prints for books. The technology is coming. Change is coming.' He hesitated. 'I hope it will be better for people like you.'

'I hope so, too.' With the air of one making a decision, she said, 'When I first came to work for you, I asked my mother about you. We do that,' she added, 'to make sure an employer is safe.'

'My mother was a washerwoman,' he reminded her gently.

She might have flushed; it was hard to tell in this light. 'She said you were a decent man and would never bother children, and what's more, *I*, in particular, was safe from your sort.'

It was Leo's turn to become flustered. Mrs Fitzhenry had lived for years in East Molesey, where his grandfather had made sure everyone knew exactly what sort he was. He fetched another chair.

'Not that I understood her, then,' she resumed, the moment he dared return to tuck the chair under the little table. 'But I think I understand her now. Any unorthodox arrangement you wish to make with Mr Solong is neither my business nor concern. And I hope that things will be better for people like you, too.'

With the same finality as if she'd literally dusted off her hands, she stepped back to examine her handiwork, candles and mirrors and a thick circle of salt around the table, the dining alcove curtained off by a midnight velvet drape. The dark panelling had taken on menacing shadows in the soft glow of the candlelight, and the marble fireplace gleamed bright, as bright as the salt circle and pale tablecloth.

Onto the table, Leo unrolled the last prop. He'd used his most elaborate hand and his artist's eye to redraw Augustus Paget's rough sketch of a telegraphic alphabet board. He scattered toothpicks.

He was glad his hands weren't shaking. It was almost time.

'Do you think it's eldritch enough?' Sally asked, slightly facetiously.

'Looks it,' Cole said cheerfully from the doorway. 'What's the salt do?'

'Nothing,' she said, with the barest blink of a pause. 'It makes it look more occult.'

Cole nodded in appreciation. 'Are you going to hide with Max in the dining alcove and make unexplained noises to add to the effect?'

'No, she is not,' Leo said firmly. 'She's returning to the Athlone apartment and keeping herself and John well out of this.'

He was refusing to look directly at Cole, who had just come in from overseeing his men during the garden tours, flushed and windswept, hair damp from the start of the evening's rain, a few strands fallen wild over his forehead.

If Leo looked at him, he'd burst into an embarrassingly dizzy smile. He might not have been good for much last night, but he'd woken this morning to find Cole lying beside him with his cheek propped on a fist in an attitude of long-suffering patience and a cheerily accusing, 'I thought you were an early riser, *mon amour*! *Remettre le couvert?*'

Fair to say the ten tolls marking the opening of the State Apartments had them scrabbling from bed (also fair to say Cole's trust in his servants' discretion, or at least Mrs Clarke's shield, was not misplaced).

Polly said, 'Infatuated addle-pates,' very fondly.

'I'm going up to get dressed,' Cole said. 'What do you wear to a *séance*, do you think?'

Sally had opinions, which was why Leo was very well-dressed for a man who'd been dragging furniture about. Cole vanished upstairs to enact them, while Leo ushered Sally to the side door; he was worried she'd run into Harry and Guy, otherwise, and anyway, the side door was more convenient to the Palace and had one of Cole's men waiting with a lantern to walk her home.

She paused on the threshold. 'My father used to tell us stories about a thing called a duppy,' she said. 'Like a bad ghost. Ma hated it, it gave us nightmares, we'd wake screaming that the duppy was riding us. So he told us how to get rid of it, if it came. You'll know it's coming, if you hear it howl. They hate salt, Mr Sweetwater. They hate cursing, and the sign of the cross, and they can't see you if you turn your clothes inside out.'

'Thank you, Miss Fitzhenry,' Leo said solemnly.

'If it chases you, throw the salt,' she said, and slipped out into the drizzle to join her escort just as the bell sounded for the front door.

'You're a regular brick for doing this, darling,' Harry said warmly, when Leo opened the door to him. His smile dropped. 'What's he doing here?'

Leo turned to see Cole coming down the stairs, wearing evening dress in sombre dark colours. Leo had to tear his gaze away to answer Harry.

'This is Wilderness House,' he said. 'The Royal Gardener's residence? He lives here.'

'The bairn's no awfie gleg on the uptak,' Cole murmured. He joined Leo, offering a shallow bow. 'Mr Walpole. Sweetwater would like us to be civil.'

Measuring the tiny gap Cole had left between himself and Leo, Harry folded his arms, gratingly sulky. Leo had forgotten just how young he was, and the strain of Guy's company hadn't helped his petulant streak. Nor, he supposed, would the bruising across his swollen nose and under his eyes.

'Well, Sweetwater,' he said, spiteful, 'I've done a favour for you, too, it seems.'

Cole opened his mouth. Leo, reluctantly playing peacemaker, started to interrupt. Then they both stopped, and looked at each other.

'Whit am A like!' Cole said, smiling at Harry. 'The wee laddie's no wrang. I won't stoop to thanking you, though,' he added, back in English. 'I'll thank my stars you couldn't appreciate the treasure under your nose, Mr Walpole.'

Leo didn't expect Harry to be anything other than contemptuous about this mildly-delivered barb, and was not mistaken. 'I'd rather have the treasure in the stolen purse, all told.'

'Give yourself a few years, lad,' Cole said, breathtakingly condescending. He winked at Leo when Harry turned away in disgust.

'Here's the arsworm,' Polly called. She was keeping well back, so she, and her uncanny chill, could make an appropriate entrance later.

Guy came in behind Harry, drops of rain on his coat, rubbing his hand together. He, too, baulked at the sight of Cole. 'Why's he here?'

'I need a second,' Leo said, 'for safety. Piercing the veil is not for the faint of heart nor the weak of mind, Mr Guy, I need Mr Solong here if our communications with the spirit world go awry. It is particularly dangerous for those of us rare fellows with unique perceptiveness.'

He tried not to overdo it with the accompanying meaningful look. It was a guess, but a safe one. Guy's interest was like enough to Lady Jane's, and he was in a risky line of work: Leo couldn't imagine he hadn't had at least one extremely close brush with death. If he was wrong, it would hopefully come across as flattering regardless.

Guy was too hardened to overtly react, but his sharp eyes measured Leo like he suspected him of giving short weight on a penny loaf. Eventually he nodded and allowed Cole to usher him and Harry through to the drawing room.

Leo latched the front door. He supposed Guy might have a few of his men to hand outside – but so did Cole.

'You are such a good liar when you put your mind to it,' Polly said. 'See you shortly, pet.'

Leo closed the drawing room door behind him. He paused there. The room smelled of the fire, casting flickering shadows on the firescreen, and, more subtly, of sweet beeswax and warm salt and burnt sage, bundles of which Sally had thrown into the flames earlier. The close heat and copious candlelight reminded him again of Lady Augusta's whist party, an effect only strengthened as Harry and Cole took seats opposite each other like a partnership, if partners at whist shot each other such unfriendly glances.

Guy was still admiring the room, nudging at the salt circle with a booted toe, baring his perfect teeth at his mirrored reflection, examining the work of art that was the alphabet board. His eyes were alight with anticipation. It made the contrast with the gravestone teeth and carved lines of his hardened face even more stark.

He flicked at a toothpick. 'What's this for, then?'

One by one, Leo set the five toothpicks into position, precisely vertical in the centre of the eight rows of the diamond. He hadn't thought this part through: the little wooden toothpicks seemed faint and insubstantial against the rich ink of the lettering. Silver or ebony would have been more impressive. Though Polly likely couldn't move anything heavier than a sliver of orangewood.

'It is the means of communicating with my familiar spirit.' He gave a demonstration, angling pairs of toothpicks one after another to show how they triangulated one letter at a time.

'Come now, Sweetwater, you talk to your ghost all the time,' Harry said, scratching his nails against the tablecloth, twitchy and trying not to show it.

Leo turned an aloof look upon him. 'This will allow her to speak directly to Mr Guy, and compel her to tell the truth, for she is a flighty and deceptive spirit who must be properly bridled if you wish for accurate answers tonight.'

He would have appreciated a rejoinder shouted through from Polly – perhaps a 'Hoi, you chatterwick!' or other arcane insult from two centuries ago – but she was too intent on their task.

He took the final chair, opposite Guy, and turned the alphabet board so it was the right way for Guy. Cole gave his knee a pat under the tablecloth.

'Shall we begin?'

'Not yet.' Cole, giving Leo's knee another reassuring pat, eyed Guy and Harry in turn. 'I presume you've honoured your half of this arrangement, Walpole. Paid up your share and got Guy his interview with a ghost. You're on a clean slate now, yes?'

'Yes,' Harry said, not without a nervous glance at Guy as if expecting a denial.

'Right, so you have some sort of written undertaking to that effect? He gave you a receipt, you saw him cross your name from his ledger?'

Harry hesitated, looking at Guy again, who shrugged and leaned back in his chair, watching Cole with a steady, hostile gaze.

Cole nodded. Gruffly, he said, 'Best not be opening uncanny doors with unfinished business hanging over us.'

His plain and practical manner seemed to do far more than Leo's attempt at Lady Jane's more spiritual tones to convince Guy. After a moment, he jerked his chin in assent. Cole fetched pen and ink while Guy retrieved a little notebook from a pocket. He not only scored Harry's name through, but turned to a blank page and wrote a receipt.

'Keep Sweetwater's name off that,' Cole said quietly.

Guy cracked his knuckles. 'I'll still be looking for two hundred pounds' worth from him, hear me?'

He signed his note, and pushed it across to Harry to sign, who then showed some modicum of sense and tore it out himself before sliding the notebook back to Guy. The other three men put away notebook, receipt, pen and inkpot while Leo took a deep breath and steadied himself again.

'We should begin,' he said, once Cole returned to his seat. With a mental apology to him, he went on, 'We must link hands. It completes the summoning circle. We must not break the circle, it will be most hazardous if we do.'

Guy immediately held his hands out to either side, palms up, expectant. Cole took his right hand, Harry, gingerly, his left. Leo took their other hands, Cole's calloused, Harry's soft and damp.

'We must be calm and receptive,' he extemporised. He wished he'd paid more attention to Lady Jane over the years, but it was difficult to seriously take advice on how to ease open a door that was permanently flung wide for him. 'Close your eyes and breathe slowly and deeply. Relax your body and open your mind, and your heart.'

He studied their faces. He was surprised Guy had been willing to shut his eyes, but he'd been the first to obey. He had his head tilted, and he leaned forwards, a man desperately listening out for a call he must not miss. Harry had tipped his face down as if in prayer.

Cole's brow was furrowed. Leo took the opportunity to squeeze his hand, and felt the reassuring squeeze in return.

'We have gathered to seek guidance from the spirit known as Mary Lee.'

This ham-fisted attempt at mysticism would normally be enough to finally break Polly's severe focus, but he didn't receive so much as a snigger from beyond the wall. That was probably for the best. He felt ridiculous and on edge, a combination that might very well have made him break into giveaway titters if Polly had set him off.

Guy was looking more enthralled by the minute, which was worrisome. This part was meant to be tediously melodramatic. He was meant to be grinning and adding his faux-friendly comments; he should have openly sneered at the instruction to open his heart. Instead, his face, eyes tight shut, looked disconcertingly like a little boy about to taste his first plum pudding, certain he'd find the coin.

'O, lost spirit, hear our plea!' Leo continued. 'If you are near, make your presence known. Come into the circle, Mary Lee.' He gave it a beat, then said, hushed, 'I can sense her. She's close. Everyone, you must concentrate! Invite her in, in your hearts.'

The table jiggled, making Harry gasp and Guy's eyelashes flutter. Cole had inserted the tip of his boot under the ankle of the lion's paw closest to him an gien it a wee shoogle. Leo had felt his knee move.

'Are you here, lonely spirit? We welcome you into our circle, *Mary Lee.*'

On the third call of her name, Polly whisked into the room and immediately over to Guy, so that he experienced the full blast of the cold air hitting the back of his neck.

Guy twitched. 'I feel her,' he said, voice rasping.

'I do, too,' Harry whispered.

'Mary Lee, we welcome you into our circle,' Leo repeated, Polly nodding along to the lines like an actress waiting for her cue, Lady Carlisle's trained and determined she-intelligencer. 'Will you speak with us tonight?'

Polly drifted into the centre of the table, which made Leo avert his eyes briefly. Emerging from walls was one thing, cut in half by furniture another.

She laid her hand over his and Cole's clasped ones. They'd agreed Cole's warmth would help offset her chill. With his subtle matter infusing her, she flicked the toothpicks. 'Ready, pet.'

'Open your eyes.'

Guy's eyes sprang open in time to see the toothpicks slowly twitching from letter to letter. *Y*-*§*-*S*.

'She's really here,' he whispered. His bright, hard gaze darted up to Leo, who slightly lifted his hands to show them still safely held by Cole and Harry.

Leo supposed he should draw things out even more, but he was growing more and more alarmed by Guy's disconcertingly honest enthusiasm. He didn't think it was possible to make this boring, after all. It was a matter of getting through it now, and then dealing with whatever came next.

'Ask your question, Mr Guy.'

'Who are you?' Guy breathed.

Polly glanced at Leo in puzzlement. Neither had expected curiosity for its own sake. Leo weighed it up. He already suspected he'd have to perform a few more times for Guy; he might as well set some ground rules now.

'Yes or no questions,' he said. 'And please. The longer I hold the circle open, the more dangerous it becomes. Be quick, for the sake of our souls.'

Harry flinched at that one, but Guy merely shook his head with some frustration. 'Get her to tell us about the purse, then.'

'Harry?' Leo said, pointed.

Very subdued, Harry muttered, 'Sir Frances Bacon wrote about a purse full of gold coins and gems that was stolen from the tiltyard here in 1594. The thieves lost it in the Wilderness.'

'Mary Lee, we seek answers about this stolen and lost purse. Do you know this item?'

O-R-C-H-A-R-D.

By the time she'd got through the seven letters, Polly was flagging, and Leo's fingers, where her hand lingered, were aching with a cold that was beginning to spread up his hand.

'Best keep my answer short,' Polly said, gasping a little as if catching the breath she didn't take.

'She knows where it is!' Harry said.

'She's telling us the Wilderness was an orchard back then,' Cole corrected him.

Harry scrunched his nose. 'I don't think that's right. I think she's telling us she knows where the purse is.'

'Good Lord, this poltroon is *actively* useless,' Polly said.

'Ask her.' Guy leaned in, face-to-face with the invisible Polly.

'Mary Lee, will you tell us where in the orchard the purse was lost?'

Polly frowningly spelled N-O, even as she said, 'Be careful how you're phrasing your questions, pet.'

'She *won't* tell us?' Guy bared his teeth; his manner had notably cooled. 'Why not?'

Leo thought up and discarded several follow-up questions, all of which could be readily misinterpreted with a yes-no answer. The vein of ice had spread up his arm now. He could barely feel Cole's grip, though he knew it was tight. He shouldn't do this for much longer.

'Do you know where the purse is, Mary Lee?' he asked outright.

N-O.

Guy sat back, face suddenly stony again. The question had been too direct, perhaps, and had alerted his honed instinct for deception and subterfuge. Polly was telling the truth, but she was also telling Guy an answer he didn't want but could probably sense Leo was expecting.

He could only interpret what his intuition was telling him one way. 'She's lying.'

'The spirits cannot tell untruths within the circle.'

'And now you're lying.'

The toothpicks flicked rapidly. Ƒ-Ѵ-Ҡ-Ҡ-Ƴ-Ɛ.

'What's she saying?' Guy demanded. 'This is gibberish.'

Leo's lips felt like they were turning blue. Through chattering teeth, he said, 'There's no U or C on the board.'

Guy stared down at the letters for a long moment. Then he yanked his hands free from Cole and Harry, snatched Leo's collar, and jerked him bodily across the table, through Polly. Both she and Leo cried out as their matters swooped through each other.

A howl rose, prickling the hair along Leo's arms and nape. *The duppy*, he had time to think, before Guy planted his meaty hand on the back of his head and whacked his face into the table.

Cole had already been halfway up, and was grappling with Guy on the instant. Harry had leapt backwards, overturning his chair.

'Percy!' Polly flew directly into Guy. 'Poxy churl!'

A white shape shot across the room and slammed into Guy, knocking him away from Cole just as he reached for his pocket, and probably a blade of some sort.

Max, out from behind the curtain to the dining alcove, stood between Cole and Guy, legs braced, head lowered. He wasn't much for growling, normally, but a low rumble sounded deep in his chest as he stared the man down.

'Bite him, Max,' Polly cried.

'Stop it, stop!' Leo struggled to standing, dabbing at the side of his face. He'd instinctively turned his head in time to avoid mashing his nose into the tabletop, and suspected Guy had restrained his full strength.

Thank *God* there was no blood.

'Eneuch!' As Max deigned to sit, Cole reached for Leo. 'This is done. We have to see to your face.'

Guy sneered. 'You walk out of this room, we'll have him before the magistrate by Monday. It's been fascinating, boys, but I haven't had two hundred pounds' worth of entertainment.'

'You were warned it might come to nothing.'

Placing his knuckles on the table, Guy said, 'I don't take gambles I don't expect to win, sunshine.'

He levelled his glare at Harry, who said, quavering, 'I'll make the complaint, Sweetwater, I swear it.'

'Grow a spine, Walpole,' Cole growled. 'You fulfilled your half of the deal, your debt's settled, he can't use you as a lever anymore.'

Harry gave a tiny, frightened shake of his head. In his eyes, Leo saw all the trouble yet to be visited on both of them if they did not placate Guy. It was time to finish this, and he had to do it properly. The only way out was through.

'Cole,' he said softly, lifting an unsteady hand.

It couldn't be said that Cole chose to subside as quickly as Max did, but he eventually reluctantly took a step backwards from Guy, turning his body away to signal his retreat.

Guy leered in triumph. 'That's right, lover boy, take a seat.'

Cole gave Leo a rather reassuring roll of the eyes. Leo took a deep breath in, then said, 'We broke the circle. We are susceptible to bad spirits. Sit down.'

It took a few more moments for hackles and nerves to settle enough for the other men to obey, but eventually Harry picked up his chair and Leo had them all back in their places. Cole sat closer to him now, thigh pressed to his. Max nudged his nose to Leo's hand, the same hand Polly had been touching, before sitting alertly, eyes fixed on Guy.

Leo took a couple more breaths. His temple was throbbing, where he'd struck the table. His hands were trying to tremble. He didn't mind if Cole felt it, but hated that Harry would.

Nonetheless, he held out his hands. 'Make the circle.'

Harry's hand was shaking, too.

'You made her angry, Mr Guy,' Leo said, once they were all linked. 'Spirits are compelled, within this circle, to tell the truth. Mary Lee does you the great favour of entering into it willingly. You must have the grace to accept her words. If she says she does not know where the purse is, she does not know.'

'Give her my apologies,' Guy said, but his manner was idle, his eyes sharp.

The spell of the arcane had broken. He was no longer in awe. He wanted his money.

'Mary Lee,' Leo said anyway, 'are you still there?'

She was floating by the fire, seething. She drifted over and quite deliberately leaned through Guy to reach Leo's hand and the board. A small shiver seemed to run up Guy's spine at the invasion, but he otherwise remained impassive, watchful.

This time, Polly angled a pair of toothpicks only to the Y.

'We beg your forgiveness. Is all well?'

Polly snorted and muttered something dark before she rolled the same two toothpicks, making them shiver in their positions. Y.

'Do you know where the purse is?'

N. N. N.

Struck with inspiration, Leo said, 'Do you know where any other lost treasures are?'

N.

'Do you have any other message for anyone tonight?'

D-O-N-O-T-H-A-R-M-S-W-T-W-T-R.

The toothpicks for the last few letters barely twitched into their positions. She had to be powered by pure outrage, to have managed a message that long.

'What will she do if I do?'

'I think you would rather not be on the wrong side of the spirit world, Mr Guy.'

Guy showed his terribly white teeth, unimpressed and unconvinced.

Leo turned back to addressing Mary Lee. 'Then it only remains to thank you for coming into our presence tonight and sharing your guidance. We bid you farewell.'

Polly eased away, so that the room grew warmer in the vicinity of the table. Leo released his grip and put his hands in his lap, shivering. Cole and Harry tried to pull free of Guy, too, but he held on, digging his nails in.

He smiled, showing his teeth again. 'Just the one ghostie, is it?' he said. 'Harry here heard a fascinating new story about you, buttercup. You could be inviting more than one ghost in here tonight, we hear.'

'I have only a single contact beyond the veil,' Leo said, trying for serenely mystical tones again. 'My familiar spirit.'

'You spoke to plenty of ghosts yesterday. Call one in.'

'I did not,' Leo said. 'I had an attack of the nerves. My sensitive temperament could not tolerate the strain of the eviction you two arranged.'

Guy's craggy face creased further, and Harry said, 'What are you talking about? We didn't evict you.'

Sceptically, Cole said, 'Ay, right, so it was a coincidence he received marching orders in the wake of your threats?'

'Well, yes,' Harry said. 'It would have taken weeks to organise something like that. We were for the magistrate when I got your letter, Sweetwater.'

'I think the dandy pratt's telling the truth,' Polly said, sounding just as surprised as Leo felt.

Leo shook his head. 'Either way,' he said, 'I had a nervous fit which some people misinterpreted. That's all.'

'Seems to me,' Guy said, unmoved, 'that if you can talk to one ghost, you can talk to any ghost. Anywhere.'

Leo swallowed. As evenly as he could, he said, 'The living do not dictate terms to those who dwell on the other side.'

'Do you need another lesson, buttercup?'

'You heard the man,' Cole said, voice flat. 'We're done.'

'I say when we're done,' Guy snapped, and all his menacing joviality had become a snarl that promised blood.

Max stood and gave one sharp bark. Polly said, 'Oh, no.'

And the Tudor miasm came through the wall.

TWENTY-THREE

Leo flinched hard enough that his chair rocked back. He dropped his gaze to the table.

The temperature plummeted. In the corners of Leo's eyes, the dark walnut panelling laced silver with frost and the fire dimmed. Max gave a volley of barks before quietening under Cole's hand laid upon his head.

'There's another one here,' Guy said instantly. Leo could feel his glare burning across the table, as hot as the Tudor was cold.

His heart thudded painfully in his chest. He couldn't bring himself to lift his head, the thought of meeting the Tudor's eyeless stare unbearable. He tried to remind himself that, as overpowering as the cloud of emotion it had devolved into was, it was no more dangerous than any other Palace ghost.

This was, in light of yesterday's fiasco, not comforting.

It had been attracted by the anger and fear swirling about the room, his own included. He had to calm everyone down somehow, and trying to pretend to Guy that another ghost had not entered the room could not achieve that aim – especially not if Guy was even half as sensitive to that roil of dark emotions as Leo was.

'Join hands,' he said. 'There is a second presence.'

Guy grabbed hold of Cole and Harry, intent again. Cole looked at Leo, frowning, and Leo gave him a firm nod, resolute.

'Haud yer wheesht,' Cole told Max. Once the dog had sat, spine taut, body near quivering, he took Leo's hand. Harry reluctantly closed the circle.

'Mary Lee.' He wouldn't look at the miasm directly. 'Is there someone else here?'

It took an age before Polly came back to the table. 'Oh, pet, I hope you know what you're doing.'

She flicked to the Y.

'Does he know where the stolen purse is?'

She started to reach for the toothpicks that would let her signal an N.

Pain spiked through Leo's ears. He tore his hands free, clamping them to the sides of his head. It felt like he'd just bitten down on something icy and it had stabbed up through his teeth and straight through both temples, a killing bolt of cold.

'He's speaking,' Polly said, sounding stunned. 'He says he does.'

The pain drilled in again, ice picks in his ears. Leo cried out and tipped forwards, almost doing Guy's job for him and hitting the table face-first. He caught himself on his elbows, twin shocks of pain nowhere near the equivalent of the sharp stab through his ears.

Cole got his arms around him and hauled him close. 'What is it? This isn't how you said it would be.'

'Mary Lee, stop it from speaking,' he got out.

'No,' Guy said, 'I want to hear what it's saying. Stay where you are, we're not done!' This was to Harry, who had risen with the whites of his eyes showing. Harry sat.

'He can't bear it,' Cole growled.

He was trying to drag Leo to his feet, to help him from the room. Leo's knees were like water. He couldn't stand. There was a heavy fear fogging the room, his own or the Tudor ghost's or everyone's.

'He'll have to, or he can bear the House of Correction.' Guy leaned to catch Leo's eye. 'I want the purse. I'll not leave you be until I get it.'

Leo nodded. Hoarsely, he said, 'Mary Lee. I don't understand what it's saying. Will you offer us your guidance once more tonight?'

Tremulously, Polly said, 'He can't move the toothpicks without coming too close to you, seeing you, touching you. I won't let him. He'll have to speak aloud, and it's hurting you.'

Leo met her worried gaze and looked down at the alphabet board. Slowly, she rolled the two toothpicks already pointing at the Y, so that they quivered.

'Then we may proceed, but quickly now, Mary Lee. My strength is waning.'

He clutched his hands over his ears and huddled under Cole's sheltering arm, bearing through drilling stabs of agony. At least Guy was receiving an object lesson in the hazards of spectral communications; Leo could only hope he had enough sensitivity to be feeling some discomfort, too.

At last, the Tudor miasm stilled, and Polly began to translate. As she murmured the full story, she rapidly flicked toothpicks, stubbornly maintaining the fiction of their necessity. T-H-I-E-F.

'We are in the presence of the man who stole the purse,' Leo whispered through gritted teeth. His body was shuddering in Cole's hold.

C-H-A-S-E.

'A band of thieves roved the tiltyard towers. They broke into a chamber, took the purse. They fled east, through the Great Orchard. Dawn – dawn – dawn breaking through the trees. Men and dogs, closing in.' He put his head down on the table, struggling to breathe. 'No honour among thieves. Stabbed him, took the purse, left him for the dogs to find, distraction. But he'd emptied the purse into his pockets, filled it with stones. Betrayed. Betrayer. He crawled. He crawled.'

Out of the corner of his eye, he watched Polly spell B-O-N-E-S.

'The gold and jewels are mingled with his bones.'

'Where?' Guy demanded. 'Under the apple trees?'

Cole cleared his throat. Rubbing Leo's back, he said, 'The orchard was actually two orchards, which meant a plantation of any trees back then, not just fruit. One was the Great Orchard. The other was the King's Privy Orchard. That's part of the kitchen gardens now, called the melon ground.'

M-O-A-T, Polly telegraphed.

'The two orchards were separated by a moat,' Cole said, nodding at the alphabet board as if to a helpful colleague. 'That's why it's called Old Moat Lane.'

'Crawled into the moat,' Leo moaned.

'Ah,' Cole said. 'Sounds like you're looking to dig up the length of the lane to find a skeleton, then, Mr Guy. A little more public than the depths of the Wilderness. Could be under the foundations of Wilderness House, for that matter.'

Leo peeked through his lashes to see Guy lean back. He looked an unsettling combination of disappointed and satisfied.

'Quite the performance, pet,' Polly said, since the Tudor miasm had already drifted out to the hall once it had finished telling its story, in which the thief had not had time to crawl back to the moat but had died under, in fact, a forever-lost apple tree. She was making sure to hover right by Guy so that he didn't notice the change in temperature.

Now all that remained was to convince Guy that toying with the spirits and breaking the rules was truly dangerous.

'Tell it thank you, Mary Lee.' Leo heaved in a breath and slowly sat up. 'Tell it it may depart.'

At that cue, Polly dashed the toothpicks into Guy's face and Cole stuck his boot under the curve of the tripod leg and flipped the table. It battered Guy and Harry as it flew between them, and landed with a crash. Harry almost fell from his chair.

Polly whirled about the room, running her hands through every candle flame, making them jump and flicker.

'It's angry,' Leo rasped, the words torn from his throat. 'Oh, God, it's so angry.' He thrust his hands out, imploring. 'Make the circle, make the circle, it's not just my soul in danger now.'

Harry grabbed one of his flailing hands in a white-knuckle grip. Cole was quick to grab the other. A glance assured him Guy had joined in.

With no table between them, the four men sat on the edge of their chairs, knees almost touching. Leo hunched as if in agony, clinging to Cole and Harry. Polly brushed over him to collect more subtle matter, and whisked through the candle flames again. They leapt, casting shadows over every face. Harry was almost whimpering, and even Cole looked alarmed. Guy was impassive, but his sharp gaze flicked all about the room, unable to settle on the source of the threat.

'Mary Lee,' Leo cried. 'We beg your help! Banish this restless spirit, send it back beyond the veil, we implore you.' He paused for Polly to make the candlelight flicker again, but she didn't move. She was staring across the room as if frozen. 'Take what strength I have and—'

He missed a beat. Another ghost, bright and cold, had just floated through the far wall into his view, beyond the salt circle.

It was not a ghost he'd ever seen before. The air around it seemed to shimmer and shine, casting the dark walls behind into shadow.

With it came the same heavy psychic fog that had accompanied Polly on the anniversary of her murder.

'Allow no more bad spirits through the door that must now be closed,' he said, almost as a question.

The ghost was a soldier in the red coat of the New Model Army, familiar to Leo from paintings of the Great Rebellion, and wore a lobster-pot helmet. It only needed the short-cropped hair for Leo to be certain of his identification: a Roundhead soldier.

It occurred to him he'd said Polly's real name too many times tonight. She was wearing her lacy nightcap.

'There runs the gulliony wench,' the ghost shouted then, and he flew across the room and locked his gauntlet-clad hands around Polly's neck. 'Thou wilst say whence thy mistress fled. Nay, fellows, bid thy captain not to mercy, we needeth the words of the letter. Speaketh thou, slattern.'

Normally, a ghost would have had to gather subtle matter from a living person like Leo to touch another ghost, but this one's hands seemed effective enough, probably because he and Mary Lee were inside their shared death scene, lit up as if under limelight.

Polly choked and shook, as she had done in the garden by Banqueting House in the moment of her death. She had been alone then, because the two Fountain Court ghosts were imprisoned. No longer. They'd finally cracked wide the workman's defences. Her cap tumbled away.

Leo leapt over the fallen table and grabbed the ghost. His hands sunk in and then their matters merged and he had the Roundhead by the wrists. He wrenched desperately, trying to free his friend.

No part of him remembered she'd been dead for one hundred and ninety-five years.

Distantly, he could hear his name being shouted, and exclamations of alarm. Max was howling. He sounded far away; he must have chased after the Tudor miasm.

Polly's face suddenly lit up. She was looking past her attacker and through Leo. He turned.

The other Fountain Court ghost had arrived, shining like the first.

The Cavaliers in paintings were foppish, all plumes and ringlets and velvet, but the second soldier really only differed from the first one in the colour of his coat and the style of his helmet.

Sword raised, he cried, 'Nay, the wench is ours to question. Take them, men,' and ran at the Roundhead, who had a wicked dagger in hand now, the other hand still about Mary Lee's throat.

Leo looked back in time to see the hope die in Polly's face.

Her words in the garden rang stark. *Their enemies charged in – not to rescue me, mind you ... I was killed because two men didn't notice me while they were busy killing each other.*

She'd been so offhand about it, as was her wont, that he had completely missed how harrowing that moment must have been for her, amid the very worst moments of her life. She had died to keep her loved one safe. She had died knowing that no one, no one at all, had chosen to keep her safe.

Leo shouted, 'No!' and hauled on the Roundhead with all his might, his back turned to that enormous oncoming sword. He could not, he could not, watch his friend be strangled and stabbed, he could not.

He shuddered and his knees collapsed, spilling him to the ground. Two more ghosts had just passed through him. He knew he would not escape the cold this time.

Then he recognised the workman and Sergeant Hamilton. They tore the Roundhead from Polly's throat and threw him and his bared dagger into the Cavalier and his sword. The dagger took the Cavalier in the throat. The sword took the Roundhead in the stomach.

Polly doubled over as if the blade had buried itself in her, too, as it must have done all those years ago, and fell to the ground. Leo crouched over her, while the two Palace ghosts, his ghosts, stood between him and the Caroline captains, who, having finished murdering each other, were now brandishing their blades indiscriminately. They were angry and confused and blasting the room with their foggy turmoil.

At any moment, they might reach for Leo, any of the ghosts surrounding him might touch him. There came a sort of flickering at the corner of his eye, and he cringed.

But it was Max, suddenly arriving panting at his side as if he'd run a great distance, setting his big, shaggy body between Leo and the disturbed spirits.

'Hello, Mr Fluffy Face,' Leo whispered, burying his icy fingers in thick fur. He faced the Fountain Court ghosts. 'The Parliamentarians won.'

They came instantly alert, twin gazes fixed intently on him.

'The letter,' Leo said. 'That letter you wanted to question Mary Lee about. It told the king he would be assassinated. It scared him into escaping the Palace. There were battles...' He was past the edge of his knowledge now. 'He was captured, Cromwell had him executed and ruled as Lord Protector.' He looked directly at the Roundhead. 'Thou didst thy duty, and thy brothers bespoke victory.'

The Roundhead dropped the dagger, sank to his knees, and began to pray. He faded away, as the chorister had done when he'd heard the choir in full voice, with a smile and no fuss at all.

The Cavalier roared and began to swing his sword. Sergeant Hamilton said, 'None of that, sir!' and moved into his way.

It seemed for a horrible moment that he would strike the sergeant down and then come for Polly. Leo scrabbled fingers across the floor, came up with a handful of salt, and threw it. The Cavalier recoiled, hissing, though the grains passed harmlessly through. Probably the sword would have as well. Probably.

Leo raised his voice. 'The crown was restored. Charles the Second came to the throne. His great-great-great, um...'

'She's not *exactly* a direct descendant.' Cole's arms came around him, the solid warmth of his chest against his back, combating the ice burrowing into his bones almost as well as loyal, protective Max. 'They share a mutual ancestor.'

'Queen Victoria rules Britannia,' Leo improvised, 'because the Cavaliers saved Charles. Thou didst thy duty, and thy brothers claimed victory in the fullness of time.'

Again, the soldier knelt. Again, he prayed, words of thanks and pleas for mercy. He vanished.

Sergeant Hamilton said, 'I did my duty, sir.'

He snapped off a salute, and vanished.

'Sergeant?' Leo looked around. He somehow hadn't expected that.

The workman, who must have led Hamilton here, who had stood guard just as bravely as the soldier, smiled down at him. 'The cracks are stopt up,' he said with a tradesman's nod, 'and crampt with iron. Everyone is safe now. Goodbye, Percy.'

He vanished.

'Goodbye,' Leo said slowly, dazedly. The workman had been in the Palace all his life. He hadn't thought—

Polly sat up by inches, wisps of herself curling at her edges. 'I never thought anyone would come to save me.'

Something about her distant tone and the vague look in her eye threw Leo into a panic. He flung his arms about her. 'No, no, you're not vanishing today.'

She said, 'I never thought anyone would keep *me* safe.'

'Polly, Polly, no.'

He was near to sobbing. He felt Cole's hands on his shoulders, steadying him, and Max's head on his leg. He breathed, slow and deep, until he could order his thoughts.

At last, he was able to release his hold. He set his hands on his lap.

'Polly, my friend, if you're ready to go, go,' he said. 'But don't go because of what I said. I didn't mean it, I promise I didn't mean it.'

'Oh, Leo,' Cole whispered, his sympathy wracking Leo.

Polly blinked at him, gaze still hazy and abstracted, body fading at the edges as if a mist was swallowing her.

Leo choked down another sob and closed his eyes, silently releasing his friend to eternal peace.

A few moments later, Leo, leaning on Cole, limped into the hallway, Max snuffling at their heels. Behind them, the drawing room was empty and peaceful, the fire behind its screen burning merrily, the multitude of candles placidly.

Mr Guy was looking determined to remain impassive, but he was also all but tapping his foot while Harry swore at the obstinately stuck latch on the front door.

'We have to try another door,' he called over his shoulder to Guy, just as Leo and Cole emerged. 'Sweetwater! Thank God!'

Leo slumped into Cole's arms and let the nervous reaction he'd been holding back take him. Shaking, voice hoarse, he whispered, 'We broke the circle and the bad spirits came through. They tried to take me.' He patted Cole. 'I am lucky I had a second who is pure of heart to drag me back through the veil and close the way. Without that, we would have been in true strife.'

Harry looked quite convinced, but Guy gave him a slow once-over, rubbing the back of his nape. 'Right,' he said slowly, perhaps assaying the purity of the hearts in his usual vicinity. 'I reckon I almost got my money's worth.'

His look was still speculative, however.

Bitterly, Leo said, 'It'll have to do, Mr Guy. It's not safe, not for any of us, to speak to any of the other Palace ghosts without Mary Lee to shield us, and she's gone. Tonight's mishap cost me my familiar spirit.' His voice broke. He had to swallow hard before he could speak again. 'My lifelong companion. Believe me, I'd have traded two hundred pounds to keep her. As it is, I'm useless to you now.'

Guy examined him, his trembling hands and tear-stained face. He also took a good long look at Cole, who said, coolly, 'A deal's a deal, Guy. And Walpole's got the receipt.'

'That's how it is, then,' Guy said finally. 'I'll dine well on the telling of the tale, at least.'

Leo winced, but there wasn't much to be done about that, and it wasn't like the Palace residents didn't regularly tell ghost stories about him already.

Cole strode past Harry and flicked the latch easily. He opened the door and gestured out into the night. 'I'm sure Mr Guy will walk you back to the Hoste apartment, Mr Walpole, if you're feeling a little uncertain in the dark.'

Guy sneered, though he also eyed the darkness on the other side of the doorway. He set his cuffs and marched out. Cole followed him onto the stoop before coming back in, satisfied. 'My boys are watching him and his leave.'

'You should get along too, Harry,' Leo said, 'if you don't want to walk alone.'

Harry gave him a rather pleading look, which Leo couldn't exactly blame him for. Cole made an irritated noise, but he stepped outside again, summoning one of his men with brisk efficiency. 'Escort Mr Walpole over to the Palace, please.'

Harry hesitated, still looking at Leo, before trailing out with an ungraciously muttered farewell.

Cole put a hand on his arm as he passed him in the doorway. 'If you're not entirely the bampot I assume you are, you'll have learned a lesson,' he said, low and steely. 'Either way, no more threats Sweetwater's way, ye ken? Or you'll find out all about *my* particular friends.'

Harry gave a miserable nod and was gone.

Leo sank to the floor, the usual aftershocks taking him fully. Cole scooped him up and helped him into one of the chairs back in the drawing room.

'You're exhausted, poor fellow,' he said gently. 'Rough night, all round.'

'What did you see?' Leo asked him. It hadn't, evidently, been Leo flinging himself about and raving like a mad thing.

'Hard to describe. It was like a fog came in and you leapt into it, but also, there was no fog. All the candles and the fire winked out, but we could still see. But we couldn't see you.' Cole gestured at Max. 'I followed the dog through the fog, and I also merely stepped out of the salt circle to where the dog had just vanished. It was *profoundly* uncanny. I'm not surprised Guy walked away, no matter the face he tried to put on it.'

'You didn't even know what you were walking *into*.'

'I wasn't going to let Max get all the glory for your heroic rescue,' Cole said with a grin. He took Leo's hand and pressed a kiss to his knuckles. 'I wasn't ever going to leave you to face that alone, *mon chéri*. And so I arrived' – he gave a puzzled sort of shrug – 'and found you giving a half-arsed history lesson to empty air.'

'Fountain Court,' Leo said vaguely.

'I figured.'

Leo gave Max a pat. 'Good dog.'

'Well, excuse me, Mr Percival Leander Sweetwater!'

'Good man,' Leo said, giving Cole a kiss. 'Lovely man.'

He kissed him again, still not as thoroughly as he'd have liked, because they were not alone.

'You both came crashing into my death scene,' Polly said. 'Most impressive. I'm not impressed I'm only worth two hundred pounds to you, though.'

Leo took her hand, smiling, though he was already far too cold, and beginning to feel not just cold, but *thin*. 'I was making it up as I went along,' he said. 'I think I did quite well.'

'You were very convincing,' Cole said loyally.

She patted his hand and loosed herself. 'I always knew you were good at lying, pet.'

'I really thought you were going to leave me.'

He'd had his eyes squeezed closed, trying not to break down in tears because he knew the night wasn't over yet.

Then Polly had announced, 'Go? As if I would! I *told* you I wouldn't give up eternal life for you!' and he'd opened his eyes to find her floating before him, cheery smile at the fore.

'I will be ready, one day,' she said now. 'But not yet, pet. Now make your lovely man sit you by the fire and fetch you tea, you're freezing.'

On the following Friday, which happened to be the anniversary of the day Leo had fallen into the river, Lady Jane basked in vindication of the highest degree.

The Board of Works men, conducting urgent excavations to repair mysteriously broken drainage in Fountain Court, had just uncovered two complete skeletons under the pavement of the west cloister, at her very doorstep.

'Mine as well,' Mrs Otter muttered, but she did not receive even reflected glory, for she had never once complained of eerie knocking on *her* apartment walls.

Leo received the news from three different residents in between locking the door on the Athlone apartment and making his way to the Great Hall. He'd waved Sally and John off early as usual, and spent much of the morning overseeing the last removal of trunks over to Wilderness House.

Mrs Clarke had already added some of the Fitzhenrys' Jamaican recipes to Cook's menus. Who ever could have guessed there were *three* completely different types of spicy heat in the world?

He found Mrs Grundy in the centre of the cavernous Great Hall with hands on hips as she oversaw the cleaning, a duty she took as seriously as the Lord Chamberlain took the bestowal of grace and favour.

'Thank you, Mr Sweetwater,' she said, accepting the surrender of the keys. 'I am glad to hear you've landed on your feet. Lodging at Wilderness House! Such a healthful aspect, and it is so nice that Mr Solong will have the company of a good friend. It doesn't do for men to live alone.' Her gaze lingered on the faded but still colourful bruising down the side of his face before she turned on her heel to cry, 'Oh, Maggie, do watch what you're doing with that cloth!'

Returning out to Clock Court, he almost collided with Colonel Cottin, who gave him a sour look.

It had taken Polly to point out that it had likely been the colonel who'd orchestrated the eviction, in the wake of the humiliating whist game. Since it would have been petty to thank an ailing old man for the nightly pleasure of Cole's good regard, Leo merely greeted him with unruffled politeness. Cottin grunted and stomped on his way.

Leo stopped by Fountain Court, where Lady Jane, amid a warmly-dressed and avid crowd, watched the exhumation with bright eyes.

She declaimed about the Board of Works to a rapt audience. 'These poor wretched men have been worrying at me for years, and that tiresome Board would not lift a finger!'

Spotting him, however, she swiftly took him aside for a much quieter word. 'Thank you, Mr Sweetwater.'

'For what, my lady?'

'The rapping stopped last Saturday night,' she said, giving him a knowing look that encompassed the bruising. 'Not to say I didn't have a terrible evening. I think you did, too?'

'It had its moments,' he said blandly. Dreadful, dreadful moments.

'I am very grateful Mr Hildyard was there to hold my hand, and the atmosphere at the Palace has been much more...*breathable* since then.'

Leo nodded his agreement. The air was coming easier to his lungs these days, too.

He made his way into Chapel Court, glancing up at the rows of windows all around. Mr Willis, Lord Graves, Mr Tickell and Mr Bradshaw all lingered. He thought he might be able to move the former pair on over time, and perhaps Tickell. Mr Bradshaw was likely destined to become a cold spot, like the Tudor ghost and Mr Fitzwilliam and the quiet and nameless echoes of riverbank and bedroom.

Cole and Eliza were chatting, Max at their feet, Polly drifting nearby. Leo paused to smile at her, making sure to catch her eye. She'd worn a terribly hazy look all this week.

Eliza leapt up as he came in. 'Good day, Leo,' she said. 'If you're here already, Matilda will be on her way over to mine for tea.'

Polly brightened. 'Do you think there's something excitingly untoward there?' she asked, sounding enough like her usual vivacious self that Leo felt a low knot in his stomach finally unclench.

I will be ready, eventually ... But not yet. Not yet.

'I doubt it,' he said anyway, adding, 'The Pagets run notoriously late,' to cover it.

'I shall leave you pair to it, regardless,' Eliza said, her smile entirely knowing. 'Have a good afternoon, boys.'

'I'll go see,' Polly decided. 'You two are terribly dull now it's all sex, no pining.'

Leo watched her float away after Eliza, and turned to catch one of Cole's fond looks. 'Sorry,' he said, 'seeing Polly off.'

'I know,' Cole said. 'I was just marvelling at how I could possibly have not recognised that I wanted to kiss your face off every time we met up here.'

Leo blushed as he sat beside him. Max sighed, half-rose, and flopped dramatically, covering Leo's feet. He rubbed behind his ears obligingly.

Cole glanced around, checked to see that Max was showing no signs of anyone in the vicinity, and quickly squeezed Leo's hand, body angled to block the view from the nearest windows. 'Good afternoon, Sweetwater.'

'Good afternoon, Solong,' Leo said softly.

He touched Cole's black armband. Maria's bluff Scottish captain had died; his 'illness' had been a stroke, and a second one had felled him. The brief period of grace between the two attacks meant he'd have left no ghost behind to haunt his Tuscan farmhouse. Sir Walter was even now escorting his mother home from Pisa, where she would spend healing time with her grandsons before coming to visit her stepson. It was the easiest possible beginning to Leo's introduction as Cole's new lodger and *very good friend*, but he could only regret the circumstances.

Cole gave a rueful smile and briefly pressed his forehead to Leo's shoulder. 'Need I ask if you've heard about the skeletons at Fountain Court?'

He nodded. 'Nicely placed spot of flooding, there.'

Cole shrugged, pleased. 'Guid wi ma hands.'

'I've noticed,' Leo said. 'Lady Jane is very pleased to have her case proved, and as a bonus, her vindication comes hand-in-hand with my exposure as nothing more than an oversensitive man with fragile nerves.'

'Only you would announce such a damning reputation in tones of glee.'

'It suits artistic notoriety, justifies my new lodgings, and disproves the ghostly rumours, all in one fell swoop. People might ask Lady Jane for *séances* now, but they won't ask me.'

'I think she'd quite enjoy that.' Cole hesitated. 'Safe, is it?'

'For her, yes.'

Cole nodded, and nudged his shoulder into Leo's. 'Will you join me at home? Mrs Clarke wants to feed you teacakes. You've added an honorary grandmother to your roster of honorary female relatives. I've got something to show you, too.'

'I think I've already seen what you want to show me on *multiple* occasions this week.'

'Awa wi ye.' Then his impish smile appeared. 'Though...there is a certain pleasure, isn't there, in knowing we can't touch each other in public.'

'Is there?' Leo asked, rather fascinated by the look in his eye.

'For example, no one could guess I've got four silk scarves by the bed,' Cole went on conversationally. 'Crimson. I imagine we might put them to good use. I imagine we might make them quite tight. Interested?'

This was rather unfair. Cole was wearing his shapeless gardening coat. Leo took off his hat and set it in his lap. 'Go on.'

'I imagine I might spread you out and draw you taut as a bowstring so I can, ah, play you.'

Leo's artist's eye could picture it perfectly: the bright crimson against snowy linens and his pale skin, limbs firmly secured, Cole kneeling between his spreadeagled legs, Leo helpless, vulnerable, able only to arch his spine as Cole put his hands on him at will, his mouth on him...

'Can we go home now?'

'Ay, we should.' Cole offered Leo a hand up, and held his grip while he looked him right in the eye. 'Because teacakes await.'

'Oh, good *Lord*!'

When they reached Wilderness House, however, Cole aimed for neither drawing room nor bedroom, instead taking Leo through the gate into the walled and well-tended garden on the south side of the main house. While Max sniffed about the espaliered trees in a mini-patrol, Cole led Leo towards a small stone building tucked against the rear wall.

'When Brown had the old brewhouse renovated into the new kitchen, he had a little replacement brewhouse built back here, but it wasn't long before Wilderness House stopped brewing its own,' he explained. 'This has been used for storage ever since.'

He opened the door, onto an almost empty room, the thin daylight streaming into gleamingly clean windows along the northern wall. The walls gleamed, too; they'd been freshly whitewashed. Even on a dully overcast day, they caught and reflected the light in a satisfyingly pure, clear way, making Leo itch for a paintbrush. The stone floor was scrubbed, and a low fire burned behind a small grate in the corner to take the edge off the chilly air.

Leo stood in the doorway, admiring the light and aspect, but also admittedly a little puzzled to be presented with a room that contained only a stool.

'I know you value your time to yourself,' Cole said from behind him. 'I thought you might like to create your own private studio here, for when you want to be alone with your work. Or just alone. Or with Polly. I can't promise Mamam will respect the threshold, however.'

Leo turned and caught Cole by his coat lapel. 'Thank you,' he said, very sincerely. 'This is incredibly thoughtful.'

'You're never especially far from my thoughts, *mon chéri.*'

'It does have a slight problem, though.'

'Oh, what's that?' Cole frowned, only partly serious. 'Does it need blue glass?'

Tugging him inside, Leo closed the door with one last glance to see Max lying nearby, watchful.

'There's no bed in here,' he explained, still very sincerely. 'Not even any cushions. Were you planning on having me against the wall?'

Cole laughed. 'I wasn't planning on—'

Leo put his hands on his chest and nudged an assertive foot into his ankle, and thoroughly pinned him to the wall to take a long, demanding kiss.

Cole said, breathless, 'I damn well wish I'd had curtains installed, though.'

For Leo, hastily making do in secret little rooms for so long, substantial pleasure lay in anticipation of leisurely intimacy later, silken bonds and other luxuries, time and comfort, privacy and safety, love and trust. Cole had recognised that readily enough.

But Cole had not had the reciprocal pleasure of very many experiences that were also worthwhile in the having.

So Leo checked the angles out the windows and said, also breathless,

'We can't be seen from the house and Max will warn us if anyone's coming down the garden,' and slid his hands to Cole's hips.

'On the one hand, I know you're offering because you assume I've missed out on some things,' Cole said. 'On the other hand: *mon Dieu*, that gets my pulse going.'

'Gets something else going, too,' Leo murmured, and Cole made a noise in his throat, tossing back his head as Leo's fingers pressed against the front fall of his trousers and the telltale bulge there.

Then he caught Leo's face in his hands. 'I love you, Leo.'

'Oh,' Leo said, swallowing the sentiment like opium. 'I love you, too, Cole.'

'I'm happy with adventuring within the bounds of our bedroom. I don't need this sort of riskier adventuring, ye ken?'

'Oh,' he said again. 'But would you...*like* it?'

'Like it?' Cole, smiling, tossed his cap aside, followed by Leo's hat. 'I love it. But I want to be sure, first, that you understand, I don't feel like I've missed anything, not at all.' He placed a precise kiss on Leo's parted lips. 'I am content with you, as you are, as *we* are.'

Leo melted into the feel of his mouth on his for a time, but he eventually drew back. 'And yet, open to every possibility?' he queried, fingers working on fastenings. 'Am I being terribly indecent if I draw your attention back to the particular possibility of firmly pushing me to my knees?'

'If the mood's struck you, the mood's struck you.' Cole produced a convincingly philosophical shrug – and his most mischievous look. '*Darling.*'

Leo was laughing as he sank to his knees.

Cole Solong was a *treasure*.

HISTORICAL NOTE

I don't normally add historical notes, but I thought I might this time around, since this setting is particularly historical.

Firstly, though, thanks for reading, with an extra thanks to the readers who've been with me since *Bastard's Grace*. I don't typically seek out reviews or interact with readers very much, but I do know you're out there, and that your word of mouth has been invaluable for an author who is just not very good at self-promotion. So, very sincerely: thank you!

Now. Hampton Court Palace. Special thanks to the *After Dark* podcast episode which inspired the core of this idea by introducing me to both the ghosts and the grace-and-favour apartments.

I'm sure it goes without saying that I did not have the official imprimatur of the Historic Royal Palaces charitable body which manages this and other 'unoccupied' royal palaces; however, *Murder at the Palace* by NR Daws does have that stamp of approval, so if your interest has been whetted, go check that one out (I refrained while writing this, but am looking forward to reading it now).

I consulted a huge array of books, articles, blogs and podcasts for a book covering the Palace, its grace-and-favour residents, and the advent of photography in the form of daguerreotypes, in the era of expanding colonialism (hand-in-hand with the development of modern racism) and the death penalty for consensual adult sexual activity, as well as touching on many other aspects in the long life of the Palace including its role during the English Civil War (or the Great Rebellion as it was generally called then).

Books especially helpful were *The Palace* by Gareth Russell, *Empireland* and *Empireworld* by Sathnam Sanghera, *James and John* by Chris Bryant, and Ernest Law's late nineteenth-century multi-volume magnus opus giving the history of the Palace from its very inception (including so many gossipy asides). Also useful were Wikitree, an immense crowd-sourced font of ancestry information, and the wonderful resources of Gutenberg.org and the Internet Archive for helping preserve the nine-teenth century (and earlier) sources. Long may they survive in these strange times. Several historical bloggers' dogged pursuit of their own special interests came in immensely handy for not having to duplicate their hours of research just to make one line slightly more accurate. I've linked to these on my website.

But I didn't stick entirely to real history, so here I'll try to note all the places I fudged things.

Almost all the named residents – except the entirely fictional Leo and Cole – were in place, as near as I could determine, in late 1842, and we know this thanks to Law's record, the 1841 census, and Sarah Parker's detailed *Grace and Favour: A handbook of who lived where in Hampton Court Palace, 1750 to 1950*s, which I consulted extensively. Every other character, except Yates and Mrs Clarke, had a real-world named equival-ent, including the Fitzhenry family and Mr Guy (the 'principal action man" at famed gambling house, Crockford's).

Leo's apartment (no 26) was occupied by Lady Athlone early on (before 1804), but she didn't die until 1819; I extended her residency. The next known occupant wasn't until 1851, leaving a large question mark over a conveniently timed gap for Leo.

Lord and Lady Henry Gordon, while real, weren't yet at the Palace in 1842; Lady Elizabeth Monck held their eventual apartment's warrant until her death in 1845. They and their large family were the (somewhat oblivious and self-entitled) flood-and-fire troublemakers presented in the book, though the incidents didn't happen till the 1850s in real history.

I also did some fairly dramatic fudging for the cameo from Lady Sale, stalwart soldier's wife. She wasn't rescued from her hostage situation until late August 1842, and even so didn't actually come to London then. She was in residence in 1846, after General 'Fighting Bob" Sale was killed in action, and after her diary kept during her captivity in Afghan

(Affghan, as it was spelled) was published. She only stayed for two years, taking a moment to dine with young Queen Victoria, before returning to India.

I put her in Apartment 26, displacing the Boyles, known to have moved to Surrey in 1840, but she was actually in Apartment 2, Colonel Cottin's. I didn't want to evict the reprehensible Colonel Cottin because, despite being a two-timing polygamist dirtbag, he was one of the very few men with a grace-and-favour warrant in his own right at that time, having managed to inherit it from his wife, who had it as the daughter of George III's architect, Sir William Chambers (not to get all political on you, but maybe widows and orphans wouldn't need to beg for a spot in the 'quality poor house' if you didn't set your society up to enforce utter dependence onto women). He died about a month after the events of this book, by the way, and Marchioness Wellesley took his warrant.

(Another aside: Miss Stapleton, and her crush on Captain Catesby? She got to marry him a decade later.)

Young Augustus Paget really did work as a clerk at the Foreign Office on his path to becoming a diplomatist, which was incredibly convenient for access to an early (just pre-Morse-code) telegraphy system, given it turned out the era of the great Victorian seance (*séance de spiritisme*) as we know it did not get started until the late 1840s, so I had to turn to paranormal superstitions about electromagnetism instead. He needed a friend, so I was thrilled to discover Leopold was the absolute baby of his aunt and uncle's family. Matilda Paget, Maid of Honour, has been immortalised not just with a Ross miniature, but a mention in Queen Victoria's diary – unfortunately unflattering. She's labelled 'wheedling' and 'coaxing'.

To Harry's family. Lieutenant William Hoste went on to become a rear-admiral. Despite him being just about the right age to seduce Leo, and a navy man (cue Jane Austen's joke about rear-admirals), I couldn't bring myself to impugn his reputation, especially because he was the oldest brother of siblings who lost their father young (psychologically speaking, unlikely to be anything other than responsible), and also because he stood by sister Priscilla against his mother when the Black Jack scandal erupted (though that pair of unlikely lovers did not actually meet until the following year, and not at the Palace).

Lady Harriet had one brother and five sisters, and yet hardly any nephews. I thought I was going to have to borrow the too-young Fred, when I finally came across (the still pretty damn young, Leo) Henry

Walpole. Harry married in 1845, and left no known direct descendants to irritate with my portrayal of fictional poor behaviour (as opposed to the very real bad behaviour of which the sons of the titled and wealthy are more than capable).

Miss Smart, Apartment 38, is listed as the daughter of the innkeeper of the Toye Inn, a favoured gathering place for the Duke of Clarence (later King William IV) and his 'Toy Club', but that's all I could find out about her. It's not clear when her occupancy ended, but the next occupant wasn't widowed (often the precipitation for a grant) until 1866, and Miss Smart seemed the more interesting occupant all round, particularly in the role of queer elder to young Leo, so I let her be there in 1842.

Cole, Colley Farquhar Solong, is the fictional natural son of the real Sir Robert Townsend Farquhar, MP, Lieutenant-General of Penang 1804-05 and Baronet of Mauritius. Sir Robert's real natural son, Walter Farquhar Fullerton, was born 1801, and his only legitimate son, Sir Walter Minto in 1810 (yes, he named all his sons Walter, and both his father and younger brother were named Walter, too).

You might assume men abandoned their colonial bastards, but in fact there's a small miniature of (a very English-looking) Walter from 1809, very likely commissioned on the occasion of Sir Robert's marriage to Maria, of the French-Indian Latour colonial family, so we can extrapolate that he took care of his natural children, at least the male ones, and perhaps that Maria was indeed an excellent stepmother. I could find barely a trace of Walter beyond that; you might suppose he died (as it was common custom to give a newborn the name of a dead elder sibling to honour the loss) but he did get two thousand pounds in Sir Robert's will, so presumably was still alive, at least back in 1830. I decided he took his windfall to Australia as part of an assisted migration drive, common between 1830-40 to combat the 'convict stain'.

A few years after Sir Robert died (after years of controversy over his ineffectual management of freeing the slaves on Mauritius), Maria really did remarry a Scottish soldier-poet, who did suffer a stroke and die in December 1842 near Pisa, but it's pure conjecture if Sir Walter went to her aid, leaving his wife and then-four sons to monopolise Cole's attention. His wife Erica was indeed the daughter of an earl, and I found a single mention of her being illegitimate.

The family did have favourable relations with the Wellesleys. The Duke of Wellington is now the more famous of the brothers thanks to Waterloo, but his eldest brother, Richard Colley Wellesley, the Marquess

Wellesley and one-time governor of Bengal, was the one Sir Robert impressed, earning himself the perhaps somewhat inept governship of Penang. The Marquess secured Walter Minto the junior diplomat role in Vienna (with some grumbling about being importuned) and we can suppose he might have supported the natural offspring too, given he had more than a few of his own. There's also no reason to suppose the son of Prinny's physician couldn't have had a passing acquaintance with the then countess, later queen, later Dowager-Queen Adelaide, the Chief Steward and Ranger of Hampton Court, and Keeper of Bushy (or Bushey, as it was spelled then) Park, to wrangle young Cole a position.

The Aiton brothers, Lancelot 'Capability' Brown, and Joseph Paxton were all more-or-less famous late eighteenth and early-to-mid nineteenth century gardeners; Paxton is associated with the Crystal Palace. Brown was the Palace's Master Gardener for nearly twenty years from 1764. I'm not sure Royal Gardener was or remained the official title in the 1840s – depending on the source, the position is variously labelled Master Gardener, Chief Gardener, Head Gardener, Royal Head-Gardener, and King's Gardener – but either way, the real head gardener between 1838-48 was Alexander Turrell (preceded and succeeded by Augustus Turrell, presumably a brother, but I couldn't track much information aside from them being official Keepers of the Vine).

Bloody Stupid Johnson is fictional, but is not mine, of course: the reference is a respectful hat tip to Sir Terry Pratchett's Discworld answer to Capability Brown.

There was a Mrs Grundy who liked to hide the nudes in her, ahem, erotica room (really a locked room she would only deign to unlock if you waved a permit from the Lord Chamberlain at her), but perhaps a later (or earlier) holder of the housekeeper position than our Mrs Grundy, depending which source you consult.

My reference manuals for daguerreotype were from the late 1840s, so our boy Leo might be ahead of his time in his techniques, though there was several substantial advances in technology around 1841 which made the cameras more portable and the exposure time less lengthy. Making prints of daguerreotypes was never really viable; the ghost postcards weren't around until late 1800s/early 1900s.

And there was, of course, no little daguerreotype studio in the Tudor kitchens at Hampton Court Palace in 1842. That said, the guidebooks authors were already spruiking their books on-site so it's not a big stretch to imagine a Sally-equivalent peddling prints and other souvenirs.

I could have moved the book later in the 1840s so I could, without the fudging, have seances and advanced daguerreotype and those refreshing breaks from the stereotypes we hold of Victorian-era women, but then we're butting up against the Great Famine ('great' 'famine') in Ireland and there's really only so much very grim history I can confront in a novel that's meant to be mostly on the lighter side.

Similarly, I know it's a bit of a downer for a romance novel, but it's also a travesty: James Pratt and John Smith really were judicially murdered in 1835 by the courts for no other crime than being spied upon during private and consensual sex between adults. On the one hand, they were horrendously unlucky, to get caught in the first place and then to not have their automatic death sentence commuted (despite *immense* effort from James's wife Elizabeth to produce a petition signed by a huge number of people, the men's accusers included), but on the other hand, plenty of wealthy men engaged in homosexual activities and were not only routinely found not guilty, but often got their accusers charged in return and found guilty of making a felonious accusation.

James and John were the last in Britain to be executed for 'unnatural vice', but given the death penalty remained in place, if unapplied, until 1861 (after a good attempt in 1841 was passed by the House of Commons, but failed in the House of Lords), and the previous Newgate execution for their crime ('crime') had been over a decade before theirs, you can see why the threat might weigh on people's minds a tad. However, I have to thank Graham Robb for his book *Strangers*, which convinced me it wouldn't have been a constant and insupportable strain and source of misery, because despite the risks, people found a way, and found their joy.

No need to head to Hampton with a shovel: the treasure, from either rumoured source, is fictional. Wolsey did have a huge stockpile of gold and silver plate, estimated by Law to be worth one and a half million pounds at the time he was writing. But there's no hint anyone managed to abscond with any portion of it before Henry VIII confiscated it (and the entire palace). Similarly, guests at the tilting yard were indeed robbed, but the culprits were caught and hanged, and I presume their takings were returned or already spent.

But you're really persevering with this overly long historical note to hear about the ghosts.

The 'real' ones are poor Queen Catherine, the second beheaded wife of Henry VIII, screaming along the Haunted Gallery on the implausibly convoluted route between her apartments and the king's chapel cubicle, and sad Queen Jane looking for her baby on the Silver-Stick Stairs, doomed to wander in guilt until forgiven by Anne Boleyn, and Sibell (as Law spells it) Penn, the nursemaid who bravely sat by Elizabeth as she suffered through smallpox. She's said to haunt the place ever since her grave was disturbed in 1829, when the stories of being able to hear her spindle through the walls in the southwest apartments began to spread. Law is a bit of a spoilsport when he points out that her bones were not found in the disturbed tomb; she was buried (or reburied) elsewhere, likely with her husband. In real history, the story of the Grey Lady circulated just after her tomb was disturbed, but then went dormant until the 1880s.

Jowler (or Jewel), the supposed ghost dog, is based off a real legend of Queen Anne accidentally shooting King James's favourite pet, which can still be heard howling. The clock was first said to stop upon Queen Anne's death.

To the on-page ghosts. Yes, Mr Richard Tickell, playwright, fell/jumped from his window and hit the ground headfirst in 1793, opinions divided on suicide or accident, and Lord Graves did cut his own throat in the very same apartment in 1830. The other named suicide was Bradshaw, in 1774, in the Haunted Gallery lodgings, after amassing large debts, though it's also said he died of a fever. Mr Willis did die suddenly on the eve of departure.

Yes, bones were found in the Banqueting House basement during Sir John's renovations, inside the Tudor-era fireplace, according to Law at least, but that's all the information I could find about that. Yes, Mr Fitzwilliam was thrown from his horse while hunting with George and Caroline, but he wasn't killed. Yes, a chorister was killed by a runaway cart and two workmen were killed by a falling wall during the William and Mary renovation years. Yes, the attempt to arrest a drunk and armed Corporal Rickey did result in the fatal injury to poor Sergeant Hamilton.

And yes, two skeletons were unexpectedly dug up in Fountain Court, close by the cloister wall where they would have stayed undisturbed during the big renovations – but not until 1871. They're frequently said to be the bodies of Cavaliers, but were probably the bodies of those two workmen, buried on the cheap by a cheating retainer who pocketed the money entrusted to him to give them a proper respectful burial. Lady Jane Hildyard, who really did hear tap, tap, tapping, no doubt preferred to think she'd been disturbed by Cavaliers. The Tudor at the tilting yard is entirely made up, though participants did die in tilts.

And then, of course, there's Polly. She-intelligencers, both noble and otherwise, were a big part of the English Civil War, operating with extreme effectiveness, and I'll direct you towards *Invisible Agents* by Nadine Akkerman for more about that. Mary maybe-Lee was a she-intelligencer who worked for the lady laundress Elizabeth Wheeler, not Lady Carlisle, who *is* said to have acted for both sides but was not, to my knowledge, involved in the fateful warning prompting Charles's escape, and there was no secret murder in the early hours beforehand (though some she-intelligencers were executed, their sex no protection).

I regret to say that Maremma livestock guardian dogs were not in England in the 1840s, or at least, if they were, they wouldn't have been deployed at the Palace. I just couldn't resist giving real-life good boy Max a role.

Here's a picture of Max as a reward for reading this far.

Wendy Palmer
October 2025

By the Author

Thanks for reading. If you enjoyed this book, find more titles and bonus material at wendypalmer.au.

Standalones
Fair Haven
Grace & Favour

Vaer World
Domesticated Magic
Little Wolf and the Witch

Artisans
The Uses of Illicit Art
The Use of Myriad Arts

Mosaic Virus duology
Bastard's Grace
Six Feet of Ridiculous
Mosaic Garden: Stories from Aspermonde

9 781763 711563